I0823803

EVERYMAN'S LIBRARY

EVERYMAN,

I WILL GO WITH THEE,

AND BE THY GUIDE,

IN THY MOST NEED

TO GO BY THY SIDE

LANGSTON HUGHES

THE WEARY BLUES
NOT WITHOUT LAUGHTER
THE WAYS OF WHITE FOLKS

WITH AN INTRODUCTION
BY JOSHUA BENNETT

EVERYMAN'S LIBRARY
Alfred A. Knopf New York London

426

THIS IS A BORZOI BOOK
PUBLISHED BY ALFRED A. KNOPF

First included in Everyman's Library, 2026
The Weary Blues first published in 1926 by Alfred A. Knopf, Inc., New York
Not Without Laughter first published in 1930 by Alfred A. Knopf, Inc., New York
The Ways of White Folks first published in 1934 by Alfred A. Knopf, Inc., New York.
First published as *Not Without Laughter* (2022) and *The Ways of White Folks* (2022) by Vintage Classics, an imprint of Vintage. Vintage is part of the Penguin Random House group of companies.
This edition published by arrangement with Alfred A. Knopf, an imprint of Knopf Doubleday Publishing Group, a division of Penguin Random House LLC.

Published in the United States by Alfred A. Knopf, a division of Penguin Random House LLC, 1745 Broadway, New York, NY 10019. Published in the United Kingdom by Everyman's Library, 50 Albemarle Street, London W1S 4BD and distributed by Penguin Random House UK, One Embassy Gardens, 8 Viaduct Gardens, London SW11 7BW.

everymanslibrary.com penguinrandomhouse.com
www.penguin.co.uk/about/publishing-houses/everyman

ISBN: 979-8-217-00776-9 (US)
978-1-84159-426-2 (UK)

Typography by Peter B. Willberg and James Sutton
Book design by Barbara de Wilde and Carol Devine Carson
Typeset in the UK by Input Data Services Ltd, Bridgwater, Somerset
Printed and bound in Germany by GGP Media GmbH, Pössneck

The authorized representative in the EU for product safety and compliance is Penguin Random House Ireland, Morrison Chambers, 32 Nassau Street, Dublin D02 YH68, Ireland, https://eu-contact.penguin.ie

CONTENTS

INTRODUCTION

The Blue Hughes

> The only philosophy which can be responsibly practiced in face of despair is the attempt to contemplate all things as they would present themselves from the standpoint of redemption. Knowledge has no light but that shed on the world by redemption: all else is reconstruction, mere technique.
>
> —Theodor Adorno

> If you are burdened, the joy of your brother lightens your burden, if you are crawling on your belly, his joy brings you to your feet. It's true: my soul is a witness. . . . The happiness of someone you love proves that life is possible.
>
> —James Baldwin

What is the relationship between *having the blues* and the practice of the blues as an art form, or form of life? What is the difference, the distance, between blueness as an aesthetic principle and the blues as a state of being? Or blueness and the dreams of those Amiri Baraka once called a *blues people*?

It's late May. With a group of architects, I'm walking across the grounds of Monticello and Montpelier, two Virginia plantations owned by former US presidents, in preparation to construct a memorial to the enslaved. I see blues everywhere. There are the Blue Ridge Mountains to the west, the seemingly endless expanse of azure sky above us, and the blue flora dappling the ground beneath our feet: bluebell, blue false indigo, bachelor button, love-in-a-mist. The periwinkle, at this phase of its blooming, is mostly green. But its name holds the promise of what is to come.

There's a sign at Monticello asking us to "imagine the sounds of 200 years ago." What I hear in my mind is a clash between the unchecked barbarism of chattel slavery and the unkillable inventiveness of black people in the Americas: the stewardship of the land, carpentry and ironwork, communicating in code to keep what's inside alive. This collision is blue. It exists at the nexus of hope and despair, the sense that there is nothing worthwhile left on this mortal plane, and the timeless line my elders used to sing: "I feel like going on." Black optimism is blue. Black pessimism too. The blues are a bridge between. The connective tissue that keeps us honest. A commitment to wrestling with the brutal and beautiful circumstances alike of one's own life.

Ralph Ellison's definition of the blues is perhaps the most famous one we have. He describes them as "personal catastrophe expressed lyrically." Langston Hughes, in his poem "The Weary Blues," offers us another: "I got the Weary Blues / And I can't be satisfied/ I ain't happy no mo'/ And I wish that I had died." While preparing to write this introduction, I read the poem again, and I'm struck by several of its atypical features. First, there's the use of the past perfect tense. The speaker doesn't say, straightforwardly, that he wishes he were dead, or desires in the here and now to die as soon as possible. Rather, he traces this present desire for death to the moment of his wounding. He wishes he had left this world before the blues ever set in. Now he's trapped in limbo, living out a routine—and this is the second element of the line that stops me in my reading—where satisfaction is no longer on offer. This is a blueness born of constant conflict. Weariness produced over time, day after day marked by weathering. From this perspective, the blues poem (the lyric moment as more-than-human company, as uplifting accompaniment) becomes a means of survival. And blueness a world in miniature: a way to describe how it feels to embody such a vexed position.

Blueness, I would argue, is the major theme of Langston Hughes's work, a body of writing that includes more than forty-five collections, published between 1926 and 1967, of poems, novels, plays, works of nonfiction, libretti, and books for children. The titles of these texts bear the trace of this larger, philosophical commitment: *Not Without Laughter*, *Laughing to Keep from Crying*, *Dear Lovely Death*, *The Panther and the Lash*, *The Sweet Flypaper of Life*. All these reflect Langston's blueness. The Blue Hughes. All dance in the space between irony and sincerity, distress and delight. Life is flypaper, a killer of pests; and yet retains its sweetness. The panther's ferocity is positioned as countervailing force: a response to the lash, the metonymic representation of slavery's afterlife.

Alongside poets like Robert Frost, Emily Dickinson, and Edgar Allan Poe, Langston Hughes is one of the most widely taught American poets in grade schools throughout the United States, and has been for well over forty years. His poems are truly ubiquitous: you find them in houses of worship; outdoor markets in New York, Philadelphia, Baltimore, Chicago, and Los Angeles; community programs where teaching artists try to connect with the next generation via poems like "Theme for English B" or "The Negro Speaks of Rivers," which he wrote and published as a teenage boy. His poem "Harlem" gave us a new American idiom, "a dream deferred," which can still be found everywhere from the titles of academic monographs and trade paperbacks, to the speeches of lawmakers and the notes of middle-school orators preparing to speak onstage for the first time. It remains one of the most widely anthologized poems in US history. The literary critic Donald B. Gibson once claimed that Hughes—a populist standout in an age marked by abstraction—had perhaps read his work aloud to more people than any American poet before him.

Far more than individual awards or honors—though he received several, such as a Guggenheim Fellowship and an Anisfield-Wolf Book Award—Langston Hughes's professional life was marked by his work as a teacher, editor, and mentor. It would be difficult to imagine the enterprise of twentieth-century African American poetry without his influence. Everywhere you look, there are poets in conversation with Hughes through lines of verse or else in the flesh. He mentored Gwendolyn Brooks, the first black writer to win a Pulitzer Prize. Hughes read her poems from the time she was a teenager, after an introduction by her mother, Keziah, who, committed to sharing these early reflections of her daughter's genius, walked up to him after a reading at their local church. He would go on to support Brooks throughout her life, nominating her for awards, and singing her praises in print long after the rest of the world became aware of what he had known from the beginning: that she had a voice like no other. Hughes also mentored a range of other black writers, across genre, in the Chicago area, an ensemble that featured luminaries like Richard Wright, and Margaret Walker, the first black writer to win the Yale Series of Younger Poets.

In the late sixties, Hughes was introduced to the writing of Lucille Clifton by another poet, Ishmael Reed, who knew her through a community drama workshop they both attended in Buffalo, New York. Hughes went on to include Clifton's work in the second edition of the anthology, *The Poetry of the Negro*, which was published in 1970. He also helped Reed get his start in the world of fiction by connecting him with Doubleday, the publishing house that would propel his first novel, *The Free-Lance Pallbearers*, out into the world. Not incidentally, Doubleday was also the home of the first two editions of *The Poetry of the Negro*.

Whatever gifts Hughes had available—his time, his network, his talent—he gave away. He introduced Richard Wright to Ralph Ellison, identifying the latter as his protégé. He published Alice Walker's first short story. He collaborated on multiple instances with Zora Neale Hurston (with whom he also had a contentious relationship), not only co-authoring a play, *Mule Bone*, with her, but also working to curate an iconic though short-lived magazine, *Fire!! A Quarterly Devoted to the Younger Negro Artists*, alongside Countee Cullen, Gwendolyn Bennett, and Richard Bruce Nugent among others.

But who was Langston Hughes, exactly? Where, what, and who did he come from? At the turn of the century, he was born James Mercer Langston Hughes in Joplin, Missouri. He was named after both his mother and father, Carrie Langston and James Nathaniel Hughes. James, Sr. left the family shortly after Langston was born, and moved to Mexico. In the wake of his father's departure, Langston was raised mostly by his mother and his grandmother, Mary Sampson Patterson: an abolitionist, and one of the first black women to attend Oberlin College. Mary's first husband, Lewis Sheridan Leary, died fighting alongside John Brown at Harpers Ferry; she would later marry a fellow abolitionist and educator named Charles Langston. During these early years of his life when his mother struggled to find work, Hughes lived primarily with his grandmother in Lawrence, Kansas. He spent his days listening to her stories, honing not only a sense of cultural pride, but also a deeper commitment to the pursuit of justice that he would preserve throughout his life and work. Following his grandmother's death, Langston moved to Lincoln, Illinois to live with his mother.

For middle school, he attended Central School at 100 7th Street. It was there he wrote his first poem: an ode commissioned by his eighth-grade teacher, Ethel Welch, to celebrate the seventy-nine other students in the class of 1916. The poem was printed in that year's commencement program, and dedicated to each of the school's eight teachers. After middle school, Hughes and his mother moved to Cleveland, Ohio, where he attended Central High School and met another teacher, Helen Marie Chesnutt, who encouraged his aspirations as a writer. At Central High, he edited the yearbook, contributed to the student literary magazine, and was even named "class poet." Not long after graduation, Hughes joined his father in Mexico. Almost immediately, they clashed on the subject of Langston's professional future. The young man, unsurprisingly, wanted to keep writing. His father saw a very different pathway forward: the world of engineering. Ultimately they met in the middle. Langston would attend Columbia University, where he would be surrounded by other black writers in Harlem, to study engineering; James would provide financial support.

Hughes's move to Harlem changed everything. Though he experienced profound, racialized hostility on Columbia's campus, the rest of the neighborhood presented itself as a haven and a home, a space in which young Langston could meet with the writers and artists who would become his lifelong collaborators. In between his engineering classes, he continued writing: publishing under a pseudonym in the *Columbia Spectator* and under his given name in the NAACP's flagship publication, *The Crisis*. Langston didn't stay still for long, though. After freshman year, he decided to travel the world: working as a crewman on a transatlantic freighter, and as a doorman in Paris, continuing to write poetry the entire time.

During this period, Hughes further developed the internationalist sensibility that would become a hallmark of his later work: his sense of the interlinked struggle against economic injustice and racial prejudice as one that was always, necessarily, global in its scope. Black experiences in America were always connected, for Hughes, not only to the strivings of black people throughout the diaspora, but oppressed peoples everywhere on Earth. In his poems, the experience of outsiderness was not a source of absolute alienation, but a bridge between strangers. Three years after leaving Columbia, Hughes returned to Harlem. In 1925, he was introduced to the editors at Alfred A. Knopf by the photographer and Harlem Renaissance patron, Carl Van Vechten. A year later, his debut collection of poems, *The Weary Blues*, entered the world.

Which brings us back to the matter of blueness. In a posthumously released work, 1969's *Black Misery*, Hughes wrote the following line: "Misery is when you heard on the radio that the neighborhood you live in is a slum but you always thought it was home." From the outset of his career, he was a writer who set out to reconcile this conflict. To strain against derivative, derogatory perspectives on African American culture via recourse to the abundant life he had known since he was young; the stories of the complex, multifarious people from which he emerged. In "The Negro and the Racial Mountain," an essay published the same year as the release of *The Weary Blues*, he describes this aspect of his broader ethos:

> We younger Negro artists who create now intend to express our individual dark-skinned selves without fear or shame. If white people are pleased we are glad. If they are not, it doesn't matter. We know we are beautiful. And ugly too. The tom-tom cries and the tom-tom laughs. If colored people are pleased we are glad. If they are not, their displeasure doesn't matter either. We build our temples for tomorrow, strong as we know how, and we stand on top of the mountain, free within ourselves.

What can emerge from a rigorous engagement with both ugliness and transcendent beauty? What happens when artists are willing to embrace the polychromatic fullness of black life? For Hughes, the hopeful answer is the arrival of a kind of internal freedom from self-judgement and despair. There is a psychic benefit, he seems to say, in the refusal to render a vision of African American culture that is, as a first principle, entirely recognizable, palatable, unchallenging to a mass audience. One that might be praised by this audience, he imagines, because it does not challenge the way black people appear most frequently at the level of representation in the broader world. Soothing in its familiarity, yet destructive in its consequences.

For Hughes, whiteness and blackness alike are not only epidermal phenomena or social locations. They function, also, as a set of discrete practices. Hence, when he invokes "the ways of white folks," as he does in this volume, he is gesturing toward a theory of racialization where one's place in the cultural matrix is constantly shifting. Here, race is not a permanently fixed set of coordinates. Rather, it is inextricable from one's *comportment.* It is both inheritance and inhabitation, an object on the horizon, an ongoing drama that is not reducible to biology or mere appearance. Even though we inherit these symbols, these traditions of domination and freedom, we nevertheless get to decide who we will be to one another.

How, then, does the work of James Mercer Langston Hughes speak to us in the present day? He believed, to borrow a phrase from Lucille Clifton, that *the future is possible*, and that there is room enough for all of us in it. Against the rising tide of fascism, he extolled the virtues of a more free, pluralistic world. He believed deeply that poems, like music, were for everyone. He exemplified this belief in his life as a writer, reading to auditoriums filled with children, and workers, and ordinary people searching for a respite from the war outside. When asked to define jazz, Thelonious Monk once said "New York, man. You can feel it. It's around in the air." Langston Hughes, I think, would have said much the same about the blues and anywhere in black America. It's around in the air. And in the space where it flies, the entire spectrum of human feeling is made visible. Everything that is loved is alive.

Joshua Bennett

CITED WORKS

Theodor Adorno, *Minima Moralia*, 1951.
James Baldwin, *Just Above My Head*, 1979.
Lucille Clifton, *The Collected Poems of Lucille Clifton*, 2012.
Ralph Ellison, *Shadow and Act*, 1964.

SELECT BIBLIOGRAPHY

HIS OWN WRITINGS

The Panther and the Lash: Poems of Our Times, Alfred A. Knopf, New York, 1967; Vintage, New York, 1992.
Black Misery, Paul S. Eriksson, New York, 1969; Oxford University Press, New York and Oxford, 1994.
The Selected Letters of Langston Hughes, edited by Arnold Rampersad and David Roessel, Alfred A. Knopf, New York, 2015.

BIOGRAPHY

ARNOLD RAMPERSAD, *The Life of Langston Hughes: Volume I: 1902–1941, I, Too, Sing America*, Oxford University Press, New York and Oxford, 1986.
ARNOLD RAMPERSAD, *The Life of Langston Hughes: Volume II: 1941–1967, I Dream a World*, Oxford University Press, New York and Oxford, 1988.

JOSHUA BENNETT is the Distinguished Chair of the Humanities and Professor of Literature at MIT. He is the author of *The Sobbing School*, *Being Property Once Myself*, *Owed*, *The Study of Human Life*, and *Spoken Word: A Cultural History*.

CHRONOLOGY

DATE	AUTHOR'S LIFE	LITERARY CONTEXT
1901	James Mercer Langston Hughes is born on February 1 in Joplin, Missouri to James (Jim) Hughes and Carrie Langston. Parents separate soon after Hughes's birth. While his mother works away from home, he is raised mostly in Kansas by his maternal grandmother, Mary Sampson Patterson Leary Langston, a notable American abolitionist and one of the first black women to attend Oberlin College.	Kipling: *Kim*. Mann: *Buddenbrooks*. Washington: *Up from Slavery*.
1902	(Until recently 1902 was thought to be Hughes's year of birth.)	Dunbar: *The Sport of the Gods*.
1903		Butler: *The Way of All Flesh*. Du Bois: *The Souls of Black Folk*. James: *The Ambassadors*.
1904		Conrad: *Nostromo*. James: *The Golden Bowl*.
1905		Wharton: *The House of Mirth*. *Chicago Defender* founded by Robert S. Abbott.
1906		Sinclair: *The Jungle*. Death of Paul Laurence Dunbar.
1907	Accompanies his mother on a short trip to Mexico to visit his father. Remembers experiencing an earthquake there.	Conrad: *The Secret Agent*. Bell Wright: *The Shepherd of the Hills*.
1908	Lives briefly with his mother near Topeka, Kansas. She takes him to music halls, where his love of the theater is born, and to the public library, where he learns to read and write. Begins education at the Harrison Street	Forster: *A Room with a View*.

HISTORICAL EVENTS

Assassination of US president William McKinley; Theodore Roosevelt sworn in as 26th president. Following the departure of North Carolina Representative George White, no African American will serve in the US Congress until 1928. First transatlantic radio signal. First major oil discovery in Texas. Death of Queen Victoria. First Nobel Prizes awarded.

Cuba gains formal independence from the US. Roosevelt embarks on conservation program.

Wright brothers' first successful flight at Kitty Hawk, North Carolina. Ford Motor Company set up. Marconi demonstrates wireless communication between Great Britain and the US—President Roosevelt sends greetings to King Edward VII.

Roosevelt wins landslide victory in general election. The third Olympic Games take place in America (St. Louis). New York City Subway opens.

Niagara Movement, civil rights organization of black intellectuals, founded by W. E. B. Du Bois and William Monroe Trotter. Industrial Workers of the World founded in Chicago. First Russian Revolution. Beginning of Suffragette militant action in UK. Einstein publishes his Theory of Special Relativity.

Severe anti-black riots in Atlanta. San Francisco earthquake.

Oklahoma and the Indian Territory combine to become a state.

Jack Johnson wins world heavyweight boxing title. Ford Model T marketed.

DATE	AUTHOR'S LIFE	LITERARY CONTEXT
1908 *cont.*	School—at first, he is refused entry, his first remembered experience of segregation.	
1909	Back in Lawrence with his grandmother. Attends the Pinckney School.	Barclay: *The Rosary*. Du Bois: *John Brown: A Biography*. Stein: *Three Lives*. Washington: *The Story of the Negro*.
1910	Watches Theodore Roosevelt give his "New Nationalism Speech" in Osawatomie, Kansas. His grandmother Mary is given a seat of honor on the platform during Roosevelt's dedication of the John Brown Memorial Park, because her first husband died fighting with Brown.	Addams: *Twenty Years of Hull House*. Barclay: *The Mistress of Shenstone*. Forster: *Howards End*. Robinson: *The Town Down the River*. Du Bois founds *Crisis* magazine. Death of Leo Tolstoy and Mark Twain.
1911		Du Bois: *The Quest of the Silver Fleece*. Ferber: *Dawn O'Hara, the Girl Who Laughed*. Pound: *Canzoni*.
1912		Grey: *Riders of the Purple Sage*. Johnson: *The Autobiography of an Ex-Colored Man*. Mann: *Death in Venice*.
1913	Begins work delivering newspapers including the *Saturday Evening Post*, the *Lawrence Democrat* and *Appeal to Reason* (the bestselling socialist weekly).	Cather: *O Pioneers!* Glasgow: *Virginia*. Frost: *A Boy's Will*. Lawrence: *Sons and Lovers*. Proust: *Swann's Way*. Wharton: *The Custom of the Country*.
1914		Joyce: *Dubliners*; *A Portrait of the Artist as a Young Man* (to 1915). Lindsay: *The Congo and Other Poems*.
1915	Death of his grandmother, aged 79. Lives with his mother, his new stepfather Homer Clark, and two-year-old stepbrother, Gwyn, in Lincoln, Illinois. Attends middle school there.	Du Bois: *The Negro*. Gilman: *Herland*. Lawrence: *The Rainbow*. Masters: *Spoon River Anthology*. Death of Booker T. Washington.

CHRONOLOGY

HISTORICAL EVENTS

Rise of "Progressive" movement in US. National Negro Committee formed, reorganized in 1910 as the National Association for the Advancement of Colored People (NAACP).

Mann Act abolishes white-slave trafficking. China abolishes slavery. Mexican Revolution (to 1920) ends the dictatorship of Porfirio Díaz. The "Great Migration" (until 1970)—six million African Americans move from the Southern United States to the Northern, Midwestern, and Western states to escape racial violence and the oppression of the Jim Crow laws, and to pursue economic opportunities.

Roald Amundsen reaches South Pole.

Textile workers strike in Lawrence, Massachusetts. W. C. Handy's revolutionary "Memphis Blues." Sinking of RMS *Titanic*. New Mexico and Arizona become US states. War in the Balkans.

Woodrow Wilson becomes US president. First Women's Suffrage procession in Washington on the eve of his inauguration. Death of Harriet Tubman, abolitionist and social activist. Federal Reserve established. Rockefeller Foundation set up.

Beginning of World War I. President Wilson proclaims US neutrality. Panama Canal opens.

Revival of the Ku Klux Klan in Georgia. World War I rages in Europe. US begins its occupation of Haiti (to 1934).

DATE	AUTHOR'S LIFE	LITERARY CONTEXT
1916	The family moves to Cleveland. Continues schooling at Central High School.	Ibáñez: *The Four Horsemen of the Apocalypse.* Lowell: *Men, Women and Ghosts.* Sandburg: *Chicago Poems.* *Journal of Negro History* founded by Carter G. Woodson.
1917	Homer leaves Carrie. She follows him to Chicago taking Gwyn with her. Hughes takes a room in Cleveland and works in a department store. Teaches young children at a community center.	Williams: *A Book of Poems: Al Que Quiere!*
1918	His verse is published in Central High's *Monthly*. He joins the magazine's editorial staff.	Cather: *My Ántonia.* Douglas Johnson: *The Heart of a Woman and Other Poems.* Ridge: *The Ghetto and Other Poems.* *Negro World* founded by Marcus Garvey.
1919	Hughes reunites with his father and agrees to go with him on a trip to Toluca, Mexico. Jim is cruel and impatient. Hughes collapses before a visit to Mexico City, the first of many episodes of ill health which are mainly psychosomatic. The reason for his illness according to Hughes—"I hated my father."	McKay: "If We Must Die." Reed: *Ten Days that Shook the World.* Jessie Redmon Fauset becomes editor of *Crisis.* Birth of J. D. Salinger.
1920	Writes "The Negro Speaks of Rivers" and "Mother and Son." Graduates from high school with high grades. With eyes set on Columbia University, travels to Toluca to try to persuade his father to pay his fees. Jim refuses, unconvinced by Hughes's hopes of becoming a writer.	Du Bois: *Darkwater: Voices from Within the Veil.* Fitzgerald: *This Side of Paradise.* Joyce: *Ulysses.* Lawrence: *Women in Love.* Sandburg: *Smoke and Steel.* Sinclair Lewis: *Main Street.* Wharton: *The Age of Innocence.*
1921	Jessie Fauset (editor of *Crisis*) publishes "The Negro Speaks of Rivers," Hughes's first published work, beginning a lifelong friendship. W. E. B. Du Bois	Blake: *Shuffle Along.* Dos Passos: *Three Soldiers.* Maran: *Batouala.* Pellicer: *Colors in the Sea.* PEN, international

CHRONOLOGY

HISTORICAL EVENTS

Battles of Verdun, the Somme, Jutland. Marcus Garvey arrives in US. "Organic Act" creates National Park Service.

US declares war on Germany (April 6) and Austria-Hungary (Dec 7). Bolshevik Revolution in Russia. Red Scare in US (to 1920.) Jeannette Rankin first woman in US House of Representatives. New Mexican constitution. First jazz recording.

Wilson's Fourteen Points for world peace. World War I ends (11 November). Collapse of German, Habsburg and Ottoman empires. Worldwide flu epidemic kills millions (to 1920). Leonidas C. Dyer introduces Anti-Lynching Bill. Women over 30 gain the vote in UK. Harlem Renaissance begins.

Paris Peace Conference (to 1920.) US Senate refuses to ratify Treaty of Versailles. Punitive war reparations imposed on Germany. German Workers' Party (later the Nazi Party) founded in Munich. Deadly Anti-black violence across the US, named "Red Summer" by James Weldon Johnson. Wartime strike wave (1916–22) peaks, with over four million US workers on strike. 18th Amendment ratified, prohibiting alcoholic beverages. US Communist Party organized.

League of Nations created, without US participation. 19th Amendment ratified (women's suffrage.) Marcus Garvey speaks in Madison Square Garden. Gandhi launches non-cooperation campaign against British rule in India. President Carranza assassinated in Mexico.

Warren G. Harding US president. Quota laws restrict immigration. Margaret Sanger founds American Birth Control League. Thompson ("Tommy") machine gun goes into production ("the gun that made the Twenties roar"). Oxford Group founded: beginning of "Moral Re-armament" movement in US. Charlie Chaplin's first film (*The Kid*).

DATE	AUTHOR'S LIFE	LITERARY CONTEXT
1921 *cont.*	(founder of *Crisis*) impressed with his work. Father agrees to pay for a year at Columbia University—but only if he studies Engineering.	association of writers founded.
1922	Father falls seriously ill, Hughes refuses to visit him in Mexico. Drops out of Columbia University. Finds a room in Harlem and work at a farm in rural Staten Island. Gets a job for the United States Shipping Board as a crewman; to his frustration his ship is "mothballed" on the Hudson River all winter. Friendship with Countee Cullen.	Cummings: *The Enormous Room.* Eliot: *The Waste Land.* Douglas Johnson: *Bronze: A Book of Verse.* McKay: *Harlem Shadows.* Lewis: *Babbitt.* Van Vechten: *Peter Whiffle.*
1923	Friendship with Alain Leroy Locke. Finds work on a freighter set for the west coast of Africa (June). Returns to Harlem (October). Finds more work on a freighter, *The McKeesport*, this time headed for Rotterdam (December to January). Writes "The Weary Blues."	Toomer: *Cane.* W. C. Williams: *Spring and All.* *Opportunity: A Journal of Negro Life* founded by Charles S. Johnson.
1924	Lives in Paris, after abandoning his job on *The McKeesport* (February to October). Meets René Maran, first black author to win the Prix Goncourt, and Prince Kojo Tovalou Houénou, a prominent critic of the French colonial empire in Africa. Invited by *Les Continents* magazine to submit poems. Attends cabaret benefit for the NAACP and meets Walter White, Mary White Ovington, James Weldon Johnson and Carl Van Vechten. Friendship with Arna Bontemps. Moves to Washington, joining Carrie and Gwyn.	Fauset: *There Is Confusion.* Ferber: *So Big.* Moore: *Observations.* Neruda: *Twenty Love Poems and a Song of Despair.* Pellicer: *Stone of Sacrifice.* White: *The Fire in the Flint.* Birth of James Baldwin.
1925	Meets Georgia Douglas Johnson, Richard Bruce Nugent,	Cullen: *Color.* Fitzgerald: *The Great Gatsby.*

CHRONOLOGY

HISTORICAL EVENTS

Coal mine and railway strikes. Oklahoma under martial law after Ku Klux Klan terrorism. US Senate votes against Anti-Lynching Bill (no anti-lynching legislation is passed by both Houses until 2022). Broadcasting boom in US: 500 stations operating by end of year. Mussolini marches on Rome; fascist government formed in Italy. USSR established.

Calvin Coolidge becomes president after Harding's death. Tri-state conclave of Ku Klux Klan in Indiana, 200,000 members attend. Automatic traffic light developed by Garrett A. Morgan. "The Charleston" song and dance composed, first performed in hit Broadway musical *Runnin' Wild*. German hyperinflation. Hitler's Munich Putsch fails.

US Congress grants indigenous people the right to citizenship. Gershwin's *Rhapsody in Blue*. Death of Lenin; Stalin's rise to power. First Labour government in UK. Louis Armstrong moves to New York and starts recording under his own name. Duke Ellington's first recording.

Scopes "Monkey" trial in Tennessee. Sweet trials in Detroit: Clarence Darrow successfully defends eleven black men charged with murder when

DATE	AUTHOR'S LIFE	LITERARY CONTEXT
1925 *cont.*	and Zora Neale Hurston. Wins first prize in a literary contest run by *Opportunity* for "The Weary Blues." Carl Van Vechten persuades Blanche Knopf to publish the collection *The Weary Blues*, which Van Vechten introduces (May). Hall Johnson, composer, sets "Mother to Son." "The Busboy Poet"—photo in the *Washington Star* of Langston in his work uniform carrying dishes.	Locke: *The New Negro: An Interpretation* (ten of Langston's poems are featured). Lowell: *What's O 'Clock.* Kafka: *The Trial.*
1926	Enrolls for BA degree course at Lincoln College. Publicity tour for *The Weary Blues. The Weary Blues* published in France, Germany, and Belgium. Essay "The Negro Artist and the Racial Mountain" published. "A House of Taos" published in *Palms* magazine and wins Poetry Society of America contest for undergraduate poets. First and last issue of *Fire!!*, magazine launched by Hughes and Richard Nugent.	Hemingway: *The Sun Also Rises.* Van Vechten: *Nigger Heaven.*
1927	Poetry collection *Fine Clothes to the Jew* published by Knopf. Meets with controversy. In response, Langston writes the essay "These Bad New Negroes: A Critique on Critics." Summer in the American South, some of the trip spent with Zora Neale Hurston. Accepts a monthly stipend from Charlotte Osgood Mason, who is known as "Godmother," a wealthy white patron of many black artists and writers of the Harlem Renaissance.	Cather: *Death Comes for the Archbishop.* Cullen: *Caroling Dusk*; *The Ballad of the Brown Girl.* Weldon Johnson: *God's Trombones.* Wilder: *The Bridge of San Luis Rey.* Woolf: *To the Lighthouse.*
1928	In his final year, Hughes writes a report criticizing the university and its students (who, in his survey, vote against a mixed	Du Bois: *Dark Princess: A Romance.* Fauset: *Plum Bun.* Fields and McHugh's *Blackbirds of 1928* opens on Broadway.

HISTORICAL EVENTS

protecting their home and lives against a white mob. Hitler publishes *Mein Kampf*.

Foundation of the Harlem Globetrotters. John Logie Baird demonstrates the television. Fascist youth organizations set up in Germany and Italy. General Strike in UK.

Charles Lindbergh completes the first non-stop, solo transatlantic flight. Sacco and Vanzetti executed. First full-length movie with sound sequences, *The Jazz Singer*. First transatlantic telephone.

Oscar De Priest of Illinois becomes the first African American to serve in Congress since 1901. *The Lights of New York*, first all-talking motion picture. Stalin's first Five-Year Plan.

DATE	AUTHOR'S LIFE	LITERARY CONTEXT
1928 *cont.*	faculty, in favor of an all-white professorate).	Fisher: *Walls of Jericho.* Larsen: *Quicksand.* Lawrence: *Lady Chatterley's Lover.* McKay: *Home to Harlem.* Woolf: *Orlando.*
1929	Graduates from Lincoln College. *Four Lincoln University Poets*, anthology edited by Hughes, including poems by himself, Waring Cuney, William Alyn Hill and Edward Silvera. Moves to New Jersey. Louise Thompson hired by Godmother as a stenographer for Hughes—they become friends for life.	Cullen: *The Black Christ.* Faulkner: *The Sound and the Fury.* Hemingway: *A Farewell to Arms.* Larsen: *Passing.* Thurman: *Harlem: A Melodrama of Negro Life in Harlem* and *The Blacker the Berry.* Wolfe: *Look Homeward, Angel.*
1930	*Not Without Laughter* published. Travels to Cuba. Meets José Antonio Fernández de Castro and Nicolás Guillén. Returns to New Jersey (March). Godmother becomes increasingly possessive. She tries to control what books he reads, what music he listens to and who he writes to. They quarrel and Hughes suggests a financial break—her "patronage" comes to an end.	Dos Passos: *U.S.A. Trilogy* (to 1936.) Faulkner: *As I Lay Dying.* Frost: *Collected Poems.* Hammett: *The Maltese Falcon.*
1931	Wins the Harmon Foundation prize. Legal dispute over the ownership of "The Mule Bone," a play written by Hughes and Hurston. The play is not produced until 1991. Travels around the Caribbean (March to July), visiting Cuba and Haiti. Meets Jacques Roumain. Ideological shift to the left in writing. *The Negro Mother and Other Dramatic Recitations* published. On his return to US meets Mary McLeod Bethune.	Bontemps: *God Sends Sunday.* Hammett: *The Glass Key.* Toomer: *Essentials.*
1932	*The Dream Keeper and Other Poems* published. *Popo and Fifina: Children of Haiti* published, written by Hughes and Arna	Faulkner: *Light in August.* Fisher: *The Conjure-Man Dies.* Huxley: *Brave New World.* Thurman: *Infants of the Spring.*

CHRONOLOGY

HISTORICAL EVENTS

Stock market crash. Herbert Hoover US president. Birth of Martin Luther King, Jr. Museum of Modern Art founded in New York. Charles Hamilton Houston develops outstanding program in law at Howard University (to 1935), training black attorneys who will lead the battle to end segregation. John Hope becomes president of Atlanta University, which establishes the first graduate school for black people.

US tariff raised to levels which damage world trade. Gandhi drafts the Declaration of Indian Independence and embarks on his "Salt March." Nazi Party makes great gains in German elections.

Scottsboro case: nine young Afro-Americans charged with rape of two white women in Alabama, provoking major civil rights controversy. Increasing financial panic and unemployment in US. Empire State Building completed. Second Republic established in Spain.

Landslide victory for Democrat F. D. Roosevelt in US presidential election. Amelia Earhart first woman to fly solo across the Atlantic. Nazis become largest single party in German Reichstag. Mass famine in Ukraine (to 1933). Cockcroft and Walton split the atom.

DATE	AUTHOR'S LIFE	LITERARY CONTEXT
1932 *cont.*	Bontemps. *Scottsboro Limited: Four Poems and a Play in Verse*, published in response to the case. Visits the Scottsboro boys in prison. Visits California (May). Meets Noël Sullivan, a lifelong friend and patron. Extended visit to Soviet Union, China, and Japan with Louise Thompson (to 1933). "Goodbye Christ" published.	
1933	Moves to Carmel-by-the-Sea, California. Joins John Reed Club in support of major strike involving cotton pickers in the San Joaquin Valley. As the only black member, he is at high risk of attack by anti-union groups, which forces him to leave Carmel (1934.)	Fauset: *Comedy: American Style*. Orwell: *Down and Out in Paris and London*. Weldon Johnson: *Along This Way*.
1934	Father dies, Hughes visits Mexico. Short-story collection *The Ways of White Folks* published to great acclaim. Leader of the League of Struggle for Negro Rights.	Fitzgerald: *Tender Is the Night*. Hurston: *Jonah's Gourd Vine*.
1935	Mother diagnosed with breast cancer. *Mulatto* opens on Broadway, the producer, Martin Jones, withholds royalties, attempts to segregate the audience, and does not invite Hughes to the post-production party. Guggenheim fellowship.	Steinbeck: *Tortilla Flat*. Wolfe: *Of Time and the River*.
1936	*Little Ham* performed in Cleveland.	Bontemps: *Black Thunder*. Faulkner: *Absalom! Absalom!* Sandburg: *The People, Yes*.
1937	*Joy To My Soul* performed in Cleveland. Travels to Europe to cover the Spanish Civil War, meets W. H. Auden, Bertolt Brecht, Federico García Lorca, and Ernest Hemingway.	Hemingway: *To Have and Have Not*. Hurston: *Their Eyes Were Watching God*. Steinbeck: *Of Mice and Men*.
1938	Mother dies. *A New Song* published. Back in the US, he founds the Harlem Suitcase	Ward: *Big White Fog*. Wilder: *Our Town*. Wright: *Uncle Tom's Children*.

CHRONOLOGY

HISTORICAL EVENTS

Roosevelt launches "New Deal" recovery program. By this year 11,000 of the 25,000 banks in the US have failed. Unemployment peaks at nearly 13 million (nearly a quarter of the workforce.) 21st Amendment repeals prohibition. Hitler appointed Chancellor of Germany; Albert Einstein and other émigrés flee to US. Nazi book burnings. US recognizes USSR.

US tariff reduced. Mao Zedong's Long March. USSR admitted to League of Nations. Stalin's Great Terror begins (to 1939). Hitler becomes German Führer.

National Labor Relations Act gives workers right to form or join unions. Category 5 Labor Day Hurricane hits Florida Keys. Anti-black riots in Harlem. Nuremberg Laws in Germany, legitimizing persecution of Jews. Italy invades Abyssinia.

Dust Bowl drought, tremendous losses for farmers. Spanish Civil War begins. German troops occupy Rhineland.

Joe Louis wins heavyweight championship bout. Picasso paints *Guernica*. Japanese invasion of China.

Munich Pact: Britain, France and Italy agree to German partition of Czechoslovakia. Fair Labor Standards Act sets first minimum wage in US.

DATE	AUTHOR'S LIFE	LITERARY CONTEXT
1938 *cont.*	Theater with Louise Thompson. *Don't You Want to Be Free?* performed by Harlem Suitcase Theater, Malcolm X speaks at the opening.	
1939	Moves back to California. Founds the New Negro Theater. *Way Down South* film premieres, written by Langston Hughes and Clarence Muse.	Cary: *Mister Johnson.* Césaire: *Notebook of a Return to My Native Land.* Joyce: *Finnegans Wake.* Steinbeck: *The Grapes of Wrath.*
1940	Autobiography *The Big Sea* published, sales are hurt by the re-emergence of the poem "Goodbye Christ" (1932), which denounces the hypocrisy of religion and celebrates communist leaders. A launch party in Pasadena is picketed by evangelical church groups, which brings the poem to national attention. Hughes's apology for writing it, branding it a mistake of his youth, leads to attacks in the communist press.	Cather: *Sapphira and the Slave Girl.* Chandler: *Farewell, My Lovely.* Greene: *The Power and the Glory.* Hemingway: *For Whom the Bell Tolls.* Koestler: *Darkness at Noon.* Lorca: *Poet in New York.* Wright: *Native Son.*
1941	In a period of financial difficulty, agrees to sell rights to his work to Knopf for a lump sum of $400. Awarded fellowship from Rosenwald Fund and moves to Chicago (November).	Somerset Maugham: *Up at the Villa.* Welty: *A Curtain of Green.* Wright: *12 Million Black Voices.* Death of Virginia Woolf and James Joyce.
1942	*Shakespeare in Harlem* published. *Jim Crow's Last Stand* published.	Hurston: *Dust Tracks on a Road.* McCarthy: *The Company She Keeps.*
1943	*Freedom's Plow* published. Fictional character Jesse B. Semple ("Simple") first appears in a column for the *Chicago Defender.* Honorary doctorate from Lincoln University. Writes for Writers War Board.	Ali: *Madonna in a Fur Coat.*
1944	Triumph at the NBC radio debate "Let's Face the Race Question." Regains rights to his works with Knopf. Subjected to surveillance by the FBI for communist	Bellow: *Dangling Man.* Borges: *Ficciones.* Roumain: *Governors of the Dew.*

CHRONOLOGY

HISTORICAL EVENTS

Germany invades Poland; Britain and France declare war on Germany. World War II begins. End of the Spanish Civil War; Britain and France recognize General Franco's Nationalist government in Spain. Ethel Waters becomes the first African American to star in her own television show. Daughters of the American Revolution deny opera singer Marian Anderson from performing at Constitution Hall in Washington DC—the decision is based on a "white performers only" policy.

Franklin D. Roosevelt re-elected for a third term. Winston Churchill becomes British prime minister. Allied retreat on the Western front, with heavy losses; Dunkirk evacuation; fall of France. Hattie McDaniel first African American actor to win an Academy Award.

Japanese Navy launches a surprise attack on the United States at Pearl Harbor (7 December). US enters World War II. Hitler launches German invasion of USSR. British cryptologists break the Enigma code.

American success at the Battle of Midway is a major victory. The Declaration of the United Nations is signed. Manhattan Project begins. Allied forces take back North Africa and invade Italy. Mussolini resigns and Italy surrenders to the Allies. The United States Congress passes the War Labor Disputes Act. Anti-black riots in Harlem.

The Siege of Leningrad ends after 872 days. Allied forces land in Normandy during the D-Day invasion. Paris is liberated from Nazi occupation. Franklin D. Roosevelt becomes the only US president to be elected for a fourth term.

DATE	AUTHOR'S LIFE	LITERARY CONTEXT
1944 *cont.*	activity, attacked by the Special Committee on Un-American Activities of the House of Representatives.	
1945	Tours with the Feakins Inc. speakers' bureau, a breakthrough, as the bureau historically caters to white audiences.	Brooks: *A Street in Bronzeville.* Himes: *If He Hollers Let Him Go.* Orwell: *Animal Farm.* Steinbeck: *Cannery Row.* Waugh: *Brideshead Revisited.* Wright: *Black Boy.*
1946	Charlotte Osgood Mason, "Godmother," dies. Receives medal from the American Academy of Arts and Letters.	Frankl: *Man's Search for Meaning.* Death of Countee Cullen.
1947	*Street Scene* opera debuts, lyrics written by Hughes. Visiting Professor of Creative Writing at Atlanta University.	Greene: *The Heart of the Matter.* Death of Willa Cather.
1948	Purchases first home, in Harlem, where he will live until his death.	Gardner Smith: *Last of the Conquerors.* Paton: *Cry, the Beloved Country.* Death of Claude McKay.
1949	*Poetry of the Negro 1746–1949* edited by Hughes and Bontemps. *One-Way Ticket* published. Teaching position at The Laboratory School (kindergarten to high school age) at the University of Chicago. Première of *Troubled Island.*	Brooks: *Annie Allen.* de Beauvoir: *The Second Sex.* Miller: *Death of a Salesman.* Orwell: *Nineteen Eighty-Four.*
1950	Première of *Barrier* (opera). *Simple Speaks His Mind* published. Translation of various works into Italian, French, Dutch and Czech. First scholarly essay on his work published.	Gwendolyn Brooks wins the Pulitzer Prize, the first African-American writer to do so.
1951	*Montage of a Dream Deferred* published.	Frost: *The Complete Poems.* Salinger: *The Catcher in the Rye.*
1952	*Laughing to Keep from Crying* published.	Baldwin: *Go Tell It on the Mountain.* Beckett: *Waiting for Godot.* Ellison: *Invisible Man.* Guillén: *El son entero.*

HISTORICAL EVENTS

President Roosevelt dies. Vice-President Harry S. Truman assumes the presidency. Allied armies invade Germany; Berlin falls to Red Army. Suicide of Hitler and surrender of Germany (VE Day, May 8). US drops atomic bombs on Hiroshima and Nagasaki. End of World War in the east (VJ Day, August 15).

United Nations' first meeting held in London. Nuremberg Trials of Nazi war criminals.

US Secretary of State George C. Marshall announces the "Marshall Plan" to help rebuild Europe. The Cold War begins. Central Intelligence Agency (CIA) established.

Apartheid introduced in South Africa. Israeli declaration of independence. Soviet blockade of Berlin and Allied airlift (to 1949). President Truman re-elected. Racial segregation in US armed forces is abolished.

Senator Joseph McCarthy's Communist "witch-hunt" begins. Communist leader Mao Zedong establishes the People's Republic of China. NATO founded. The Fourth Geneva Convention is agreed.

President Truman sends US military personnel to assist French forces in Vietnam. Korean War (to 1953.)

US government begins Nevada Nuclear Tests. Development of birth control pill. World's first color network TV broadcast. W. E. B. Du Bois indicted by the US Justice Department for failing to register as an agent of a foreign power, as part of charges against the Peace Information Center.
Polio epidemic in US, with over 57,000 cases reported.

DATE	AUTHOR'S LIFE	LITERARY CONTEXT
1953	*Simple Takes a Wife* published (wins Anisfield-Wolf Book Award in 1954). Testifies twice before Senator McCarthy's Subcommittee on Investigations for his involvement with communism, and is dismissed.	Bellow: *The Adventures of Augie March.* Chandler: *The Long Goodbye.* Wright: *The Outsider.*
1954	*Famous American Negroes* and *The First Book of Rhythms* published.	Amis: *Lucky Jim.* Baldwin: *The Amen Corner.*
1955	*The First Book of Jazz* and *The Sweet Flypaper of Life* published.	Nabokov: *Lolita.* T. Williams: *Cat on a Hot Tin Roof.*
1956	*I Wonder as I Wander* (second autobiography) published. *The First Book of the West Indies* published. *A Pictorial History of the Negro in America* (written with Milton Meltzer) published. Noël Sullivan dies, leaves Hughes $2000 in his will.	Abrahams: *A Wreath for Udomo.* Baldwin: *Giovanni's Room.* Senghor: *Ethiopiques.*
1957	*Simply Heavenly* musical opens in Manhattan. *Simple Stakes a Claim* published. *Famous American Negroes* translated into Hindi, Bengali, Marathi, French, Portuguese, and Arabic. Features in *Life* magazine.	Himes: *Harlem Detective* series (to 1983). Kerouac: *On the Road.* Pasternak: *Doctor Zhivago.*
1958	*The Book of Negro Folklore*, edited by Hughes and Bontemps, and *Tambourines to Glory* (gospel play) published.	Achebe: *Things Fall Apart.* Capote: *Breakfast at Tiffany's.* Genet: *The Blacks.* Lampedusa: *The Leopard.* Soyinka: *The Lion and the Jewel.*
1959	*Selected Poems* published by Knopf. Appears on CBS "Harlem: A Self Portrait." Visits the Caribbean.	Bellow: *Henderson the Rain King.* Hansberry: *A Raisin in the Sun.* Mphahlele: *Down Second Avenue.* Neruda: *100 Love Sonnets.*

CHRONOLOGY

HISTORICAL EVENTS

Dwight D. Eisenhower inaugurated as US president. Death of Stalin.

McCarthy is censured by the Senate. Ellis Island closes as an immigration station. Brown v. Board of Education: US Supreme Court rules that segregation in education is illegal, though this proves difficult to enforce. French defeat in Vietnam at battle of Dien Bien Phu; peace talks in Geneva; withdrawal of French troops; Vietnam divided into North and South.
Rosa Parks arrested after refusing to give up her bus seat to a white passenger.

Suez crisis in Egypt caused by nationalization of the Suez Canal (to 1957). French colonial rule ends in Tunisia and Morocco. USSR invades Hungary. Khrushchev denounces Stalin.

European Economic Community founded (France, Belgium, Italy, Luxembourg, the Netherlands, West Germany.) "Little Rock Nine": Governor of Arkansas calls in National Guard to prevent nine African-American students from entering the Central High School; President Eisenhower calls Federal troops to escort them in. Civil Rights Commission established to safeguard voting rights. Ghana becomes the first African country to gain independence from a colonial power. Beginning of communist insurgency in Vietnam. USSR launches Sputnik 1, beginning the Space Race.
Fourth Republic falls in France as a result of the Algerian crisis. Charles de Gaulle returns to power (Fifth Republic), elected as president. Recession in the US brings large increase in unemployment. NASA created. US launches Explorer 1 satellite, USSR launches Sputnik 3.

Fidel Castro comes to power in Cuba. US vice-president Richard Nixon and USSR premier Nikita Khrushchev engage in the impromptu "Kitchen Debate" arguing the merits of capitalism and communism. Resnais and Truffaut spearhead "New Wave" cinema in France.

DATE	AUTHOR'S LIFE	LITERARY CONTEXT
1960	Lecture tour disrupted by right-wing protesters. Attends Newport Jazz Festival, which ends early due to anti-black riots. Meets Nina Simone. *An African Treasury* and *The First Book of Africa* published. *An African Treasury* banned by white leaders in South Africa. Invited to Nigeria by Nnamdi Azikiwe for his inauguration as Governor General and Commander-in-Chief; other guests include W. E. B. Du Bois and Martin Luther King. Azikiwe recites "Poem" ("We have tomorrow/ Bright before us") from *The Weary Blues* at the ceremony. Receives the Spingarn Medal from the NAACP.	Brooks: *The Bean Eaters.* Lee: *To Kill a Mockingbird.* Salkey: *Escape to an Autumn Pavement.* Updike: *Rabbit, Run.* Death of Richard Wright.
1961	*Ask Your Mama: 12 Moods for Jazz* published. *Black Nativity* premieres. Elected to the National Institute of Arts and Letters. Invited to the White House to a luncheon in honor of President Senghor of Senegal. Visits Nigeria for festival organized by American Society of African Culture.	Heller: *Catch-22.* Naipaul: *A House for Mr. Biswas.* Death of Jessie Fauset and Ernest Hemingway.
1962	*Fight for Freedom: The Story of the NAACP* published. Weekly column for the *New York Post.* Conference in Kampala, Uganda where he is guest of honor, meets Chinua Achebe. European tour of *Black Nativity.*	Baldwin: *Another Country.* Nabokov: *Pale Fire.* Solzhenitsyn: *One Day in the Life of Ivan Denisovich.*
1963	*Something in Common and Other Stories* published. *Poems from Black Africa* published, edited by Langston Hughes. Makes speech defending moderate civil rights approach, promotes non-violence. Celebrates Emancipation Centennial at the White House. Awarded	Baldwin: *The Fire Next Time.* Baraka: *Blues People.* McCarthy: *The Group.* Modisane: *Blame Me on History.* Plath: *The Bell Jar.* Death of W. E. B. Du Bois.

HISTORICAL EVENTS

The US sends its first troops to Vietnam to fight. "Sit In" movement to oppose segregation spreads from North Carolina to colleges throughout the country; the Student Nonviolent Coordinating Committee (SNCC) founded. Sharpeville massacre in South Africa.

John F. Kennedy becomes US president. SNCC organizes "Freedom Rides" in the South. Erection of Berlin Wall. Algerian demonstrators killed by Paris police.

Algeria wins independence from France. Cuban Missile Crisis.

Assassination of President Kennedy. Lyndon B. Johnson becomes US president. Protest march on Washington; Martin Luther King Jr.'s "I have a dream" speech. De Gaulle vetoes British entry into the EEC. Nelson Mandela jailed for life, South Africa.

DATE	AUTHOR'S LIFE	LITERARY CONTEXT
1963 *cont.*	honorary doctorate from Howard University. *Tambourines to Glory* premieres.	
1964	*Jerico-Jim Crow* musical première. *New Negro Poets: USA* edited by Hughes. Honorary degree, Western Reserve University. Hughes helps BBC produce radio series "The Negro in America." Speaks out against black nationalism.	Bellow: *Herzog.* Baraka: *Dutchman and Baptism.* Ellison: *Shadow and Act.* Death of Carl Van Vechten.
1965	Première of *The Prodigal Son.* Teacher in Boston fired for reading Hughes's poetry to black children at a *de facto* segregated school. Final Simple column.	Baldwin: *Going to Meet the Man.* Brown: *Manchild in the Promised Land.* Martin Luther King: *Why We Can't Wait.* Malcolm X: *The Autobiography of Malcolm X.* Soyinka: *The Interpreters.*
1966	*The Panther and the Lash* published. Television production *The Strollin' Twenties* airs, written by Langston Hughes and starring among others: Harry Belafonte, Sidney Poitier, Sammy Davis Jr., Diahann Carroll, and Duke Ellington. *Book of Negro Humor* published. Second book with Milton Meltzer, *Black Magic: A Pictorial History of the Negro in American Entertainment* published. Appointed by President Johnson as official American representative to the First World Festival of Negro Arts in Senegal. President Senghor recites poetry at the event. Weeklong colloquium on "Black Writers in a Troubled World" in Senegal. Travels through other parts of Africa for the State Department. Meets Alice Walker.	Achebe: *A Man of the People.* Capote: *In Cold Blood.* Pynchon: *The Crying of Lot 49.* Tolson: *Harlem Gallery.* Death of Georgia Douglas Johnson, Eric Walrond and Melvin Tolson.
1967	*The Best Short Stories by Negro Writers* edited by Hughes.	J. A. Williams: *The Man Who Cried I Am.*

CHRONOLOGY

HISTORICAL EVENTS

Civil Rights Act prohibits discrimination in US. Brezhnev becomes Communist Party General Secretary in USSR. Muhammad Ali becomes heavyweight boxing champion. Worst riots in Harlem since 1943 after Jimmy Powell, a fifteen-year-old black boy, is shot dead by police.

De Gaulle re-elected. US bombing in Vietnam begins. Martin Luther King Jr. and John Lewis lead march in Montgomery, protesters meet with brutal police action. President Johnson's "We Shall Overcome" speech. Malcolm X assassinated.

Mao's Cultural Revolution begins in China. Anti-black riots across US.

Arab–Israeli Six-Day War. President Johnson commissions a report on racial violence in US. De Gaulle visits Canada. First heart transplant operation.

DATE	AUTHOR'S LIFE	LITERARY CONTEXT
1967 *cont.*	Revision of *Poetry of the Negro* including works by Mari Evans, Sarah Webster Fabio, Audre Lorde, Ishmael Reed, Raymond Patterson and Lucille Clifton. Langston Hughes dies on May 22 from complications after prostate surgery. Funeral is held in Harlem, the service full of jazz and blues music. "The Negro Speaks of Rivers" recited in the final moments before his cremation.	

CHRONOLOGY

HISTORICAL EVENTS

THE WEARY BLUES

To my mother

I wish to thank the editors of *The Crisis*, *Opportunity*, *Survey Graphic*, *Vanity Fair*, *The World Tomorrow*, and *The Amsterdam News* for having first published some of the poems in this book.

CONTENTS

INTRODUCING LANGSTON HUGHES TO THE READER

I

AT THE MOMENT I cannot recall the name of any other person whatever who, at the age of twenty-three, has enjoyed so picturesque and rambling an existence as Langston Hughes. Indeed, a complete account of his disorderly and delightfully fantastic career would make a fascinating picaresque romance which I hope this young Negro will write before so much more befalls him that he may find it difficult to capture all the salient episodes within the limits of a single volume.

Born on February 1, 1902, in Joplin, Missouri, he had lived, before his twelfth year, in the City of Mexico, Topeka, Kansas, Colorado Springs, Charlestown, Indiana, Kansas City, and Buffalo. He attended Central High School, from which he graduated, at Cleveland, Ohio, while in the summer, there and in Chicago, he worked as delivery- and dummy-boy in hat-stores. In his senior year he was elected class poet and editor of the Year Book.

After four years in Cleveland, he once more joined his father in Mexico, only to migrate to New York where he entered Columbia University. There, finding the environment distasteful, or worse, he remained till spring, when he quit, broke with his father and, with thirteen dollars in cash, went on his own. First, he worked for a truck-farmer on Staten Island; next, he delivered flowers for Thorley; at length he partially satisfied an insatiable craving to go to sea by signing up with an old ship anchored in the Hudson for the winter. His first real cruise as a sailor carried him to the Canary Islands, the Azores, and the West Coast of Africa, of which voyage he has written: "Oh, the sun in Dakar! Oh, the little black girls of Burutu! Oh, the blue, blue bay of Loanda! Calabar, the city lost in a forest; the long, shining days at sea, the masts rocking against the stars at night; the black Kru-boy sailors, taken at Freetown, bathing on deck morning and evening; Tom Pey and Haneo, whose dangerous job it was to dive under the seven-ton mahogany logs floating and bobbing at the ship's side and fasten them to the chains of the crane; the vile houses of rotting women at Lagos; the desolation of the Congo; Johnny Walker, and the millions of whisky bottles buried in the sea along the West Coast; the daily fights on board, officers, sailors, everybody drunk; the timorous, frightened missionaries we carried as passengers; and George, the Kentucky colored boy, dancing and singing the Blues on the after-deck under the stars."

Returning to New York with plenty of money and a monkey, he presently shipped again—this time for Holland. Again he came back to New York and again he sailed—on his twenty-second birthday: February 1, 1924. Three weeks later he found himself in Paris with less than seven dollars. However, he was soon provided for: a woman of his own race engaged him as doorman at her *boîte de nuit.* Later he was employed, first as second cook, then as waiter, at the Grand Duc, where the Negro entertainer, Florence, sang at this epoch. Here he made friends with an Italian family who carried him off to their villa at Desenzano on Lago di Garda where he passed a happy month, followed by a night in Verona and a week in Venice. On his way back across Italy his passport was stolen and he became a beach-comber in Genoa. He has described his life there to me: "Wine and figs and *pasta.* And sunlight! And amusing companions, dozens of other beach-combers roving the dockyards and water-front streets, getting their heads whacked by the Fascisti, and breaking one loaf of bread into so many pieces that nobody got more than a crumb. I lived in the public gardens along the water-front and slept in the Albergo Populare for two lire a night amidst the snores of hundreds of other derelicts. . . . I painted my way home as a sailor. It seems that I must have painted the whole ship myself. We made a regular 'grand tour': Livorno, Napoli (we passed so close to Capri I could have cried). Then all around Sicily—Catania, Messina, Palermo—the Lipari Islands, miserable little peaks of pumice stone out in the sea; then across to Spain, divine Spain! My buddy and I went on a spree in Valencia for a night and a day. . . . Oh, the sweet wine of Valencia!"

He arrived in New York on November 10, 1924. That evening I attended a dance given in Harlem by the National Association for the Advancement of Colored People. Some time during the course of the night, Walter White asked me to meet two young Negro poets. He introduced me to Countée Cullen and Langston Hughes. Before that moment I had never heard of either of them.

II

I HAVE MERELY sketched a primitive outline of a career as rich in adventures as a fruit-cake is full of raisins. I have already stated that I hope Langston Hughes may be persuaded to set it down on paper in the minutest detail, for the bull-fights in Mexico, the drunken gaiety of the Grand Duc, the delicately exquisite grace of the little black girls at Burutu, the exotic languor of the Spanish women at Valencia, the barbaric jazz dances of the cabarets in New York's own Harlem, the companionship of sailors of many races and nationalities, all have stamped an indelible impression on the highly sensitized, poetic imagination of this young Negro, an impression which has found its initial expression in the poems assembled in this book.

And also herein may be discerned that nostalgia for color and warmth and beauty which explains this boy's nomadic instincts.

"We should have a land of sun,
Of gorgeous sun,
And a land of fragrant water
Where the twilight

Is a soft bandanna handkerchief
Of rose and gold,
And not this land where life is cold,"

he sings. Again, he tells his dream:

"To fling my arms wide
In the face of the sun,
Dance! whirl! whirl!
Till the quick day is done.
Rest at pale evening. . . .
A tall, slim tree. . . .
Night coming tenderly,
Black like me."

More of this wistful longing may be discovered in the poems entitled *The South* and *As I Grew Older.* His verses, however, are by no means limited to an exclusive mood; he writes caressingly of little black prostitutes in Harlem; his cabaret songs throb with the true jazz rhythm; his sea-pieces ache with a calm, melancholy lyricism; he cries bitterly from the heart of his race in *Cross* and *The Jester*; he sighs, in one of the most successful of his fragile poems, over the loss of a loved friend. Always, however, his stanzas are subjective, personal. They are the (I had almost said informal, for they have a highly deceptive air of spontaneous improvisation) expression of an essentially sensitive and subtly illusive nature, seeking always to break through the veil that obscures for him, at least in some degree, the ultimate needs of that nature.

To the Negro race in America, since the day when Phillis Wheatley indited lines to General George Washington and other aristocratic figures (for Phillis Wheatley never sang "My way's cloudy," or "By an' by, I'm goin' to lay down dis heavy load") there have been born many poets. Paul Laurence Dunbar, James Weldon Johnson, Claude McKay, Jean Toomer, Georgia Douglas Johnson, Countée Cullen, are a few of the more memorable names. Not the least of these names, I think, is that of Langston Hughes, and perhaps his adventures and personality offer the promise of as rich a fulfillment as has been the lot of any of the others.

—CARL VAN VECHTEN
New York
August 3, 1925

PROEM

I am a Negro:
  Black as the night is black,
  Black like the depths of my Africa.

I've been a slave:
  Cæsar told me to keep his door-steps clean.
  I brushed the boots of Washington.

I've been a worker:
  Under my hand the pyramids arose.
  I made mortar for the Woolworth Building.

I've been a singer:
  All the way from Africa to Georgia
  I carried my sorrow songs.
  I made ragtime.

I've been a victim:
  The Belgians cut off my hands in the Congo.
  They lynch me now in Texas.

I am a Negro:
  Black as the night is black,
  Black like the depths of my Africa.

THE WEARY BLUES

THE WEARY BLUES

Droning a drowsy syncopated tune,
Rocking back and forth to a mellow croon,
    I heard a Negro play.
Down on Lenox Avenue the other night
By the pale dull pallor of an old gas light
    He did a lazy sway. . . .
    He did a lazy sway. . . .
To the tune o' those Weary Blues.
With his ebony hands on each ivory key
He made that poor piano moan with melody.
    O Blues!
Swaying to and fro on his rickety stool
He played that sad raggy tune like a musical fool.
    Sweet Blues!
Coming from a black man's soul.
    O Blues!
In a deep song voice with a melancholy tone
I heard that Negro sing, that old piano moan—
    "Ain't got nobody in all this world,
    Ain't got nobody but ma self.
    I's gwine to quit ma frownin'
    And put ma troubles on the shelf."
Thump, thump, thump, went his foot on the floor.
He played a few chords then he sang some more—
    "I got the Weary Blues
    And I can't be satisfied.
    Got the Weary Blues
    And can't be satisfied—
    I ain't happy no mo'
    And I wish that I had died."

And far into the night he crooned that tune.
The stars went out and so did the moon.
The singer stopped playing and went to bed
While the Weary Blues echoed through his head.
He slept like a rock or a man that's dead.

JAZZONIA

Oh, silver tree!
Oh, shining rivers of the soul!

In a Harlem cabaret
Six long-headed jazzers play.
A dancing girl whose eyes are bold
Lifts high a dress of silken gold.

Oh, singing tree!
Oh, shining rivers of the soul!

Were Eve's eyes
In the first garden
Just a bit too bold?
Was Cleopatra gorgeous
In a gown of gold?

Oh, shining tree!
Oh, silver rivers of the soul!

In a whirling cabaret
Six long-headed jazzers play.

NEGRO DANCERS

"Me an' ma baby's
Got two mo' ways,
Two mo' ways to do de Charleston!
    Da, da,
    Da, da, da!
Two mo' ways to do de Charleston!"

Soft light on the tables,
Music gay,
Brown-skin steppers
In a cabaret.

White folks, laugh!
White folks, pray!

"Me an' ma baby's
Got two mo' ways,
Two mo' ways to do de Charleston!"

THE CAT AND THE SAXOPHONE
(2 A.M.)

EVERYBODY
Half-pint,—
Gin?
No, make it
LOVES MY BABY
corn. You like
liquor,
don't you, honey?
BUT MY BABY
Sure. Kiss me,
DON'T LOVE NOBODY
daddy.
BUT ME.
Say!
EVERYBODY
Yes?
WANTS MY BABY
I'm your
BUT MY BABY
sweetie, ain't I?
DON'T WANT NOBODY
Sure.
BUT
Then let's
ME,
do it!
SWEET ME.
Charleston,
mamma!
!

YOUNG SINGER

One who sings "chansons vulgaires"
In a Harlem cellar
Where the jazz-band plays
From dark to dawn
Would not understand
Should you tell her
That she is like a nymph
For some wild faun.

CABARET

Does a jazz-band ever sob?
They say a jazz-band's gay.
Yet as the vulgar dancers whirled
And the wan night wore away,
One said she heard the jazz-band sob
When the little dawn was grey.

TO MIDNIGHT NAN AT LEROY'S

Strut and wiggle,
Shameless gal.
Wouldn't no good fellow
Be your pal.

Hear dat music. . . .
Jungle night.
Hear dat music. . . .
And the moon was white.

Sing your Blues song,
Pretty baby.
You want lovin'
And you don't mean maybe.

Jungle lover. . . .
Night black boy. . . .
Two against the moon
And the moon was joy.

Strut and wiggle,
Shameless Nan.
Wouldn't no good fellow
Be your man.

TO A LITTLE LOVER-LASS, DEAD

She
Who searched for lovers
In the night
Has gone the quiet way
Into the still,
Dark land of death
Beyond the rim of day.

Now like a little lonely waif
She walks
An endless street
And gives her kiss to nothingness.
Would God his lips were sweet!

HARLEM NIGHT CLUB

Sleek black boys in a cabaret.
Jazz-band, jazz-band,—
Play, plAY, PLAY!
Tomorrow. . . . who knows?
Dance today!

White girls' eyes
Call gay black boys.
Black boys' lips
Grin jungle joys.

Dark brown girls
In blond men's arms.
Jazz-band, jazz-band,—
Sing Eve's charms!

White ones, brown ones,
What do you know
About tomorrow
Where all paths go?

Jazz-boys, jazz-boys,—
Play, plAY, PLAY!
Tomorrow. . . . is darkness.
Joy today!

NUDE YOUNG DANCER

What jungle tree have you slept under,
Midnight dancer of the jazzy hour?
What great forest has hung its perfume
Like a sweet veil about your bower?

What jungle tree have you slept under,
Night-dark girl of the swaying hips?
What star-white moon has been your mother?
To what clean boy have you offered your lips?

YOUNG PROSTITUTE

Her dark brown face
Is like a withered flower
On a broken stem.
Those kind come cheap in Harlem
So they say.

TO A BLACK DANCER IN "THE LITTLE SAVOY"

Wine-maiden
Of the jazz-tuned night,
Lips
Sweet as purple dew,
Breasts
Like the pillows of all sweet dreams,
Who crushed
The grapes of joy
And dripped their juice
On you?

SONG FOR A BANJO DANCE

Shake your brown feet, honey,
Shake your brown feet, chile,
Shake your brown feet, honey,
Shake 'em swift and wil'—
    Get way back, honey,
    Do that low-down step.
    Walk on over, darling,
        Now!   Come out
        With your left.
Shake your brown feet, honey,
Shake 'em, honey chile.

Sun's going down this evening—
Might never rise no mo'.
The sun's going down this very night—
Might never rise no mo'—
So dance with swift feet, honey,
    (The banjo's sobbing low)
Dance with swift feet, honey—
    Might never dance no mo'.

Shake your brown feet, Liza,
Shake 'em, Liza, chile,
Shake your brown feet, Liza,
    (The music's soft and wil')
Shake your brown feet, Liza,
    (The banjo's sobbing low)
The sun's going down this very night—
    Might never rise no mo'.

BLUES FANTASY

Hey! Hey!
That's what the
Blues singers say.
Singing minor melodies
They laugh,
Hey! Hey!

My man's done left me,
Chile, he's gone away.
My good man's left me,
Babe, he's gone away.
Now the cryin' blues
Haunts me night and day.

Hey! . . . Hey!

Weary,
Weary,
Trouble, pain.
Sun's gonna shine
Somewhere
Again.

I got a railroad ticket,
Pack my trunk and ride.

Sing 'em, sister!

Got a railroad ticket,
Pack my trunk and ride.

And when I get on the train
I'll cast my blues aside.
Laughing,
Hey! . . . Hey!
Laugh a loud,
Hey!   Hey!

LENOX AVENUE: MIDNIGHT

The rhythm of life
Is a jazz rhythm,
Honey.
The gods are laughing at us.

The broken heart of love,
The weary, weary heart of pain,—
    Overtones,
    Undertones,
To the rumble of street cars,
To the swish of rain.

Lenox Avenue,
Honey.
Midnight,
And the gods are laughing at us.

DREAM VARIATIONS

DREAM VARIATION

To fling my arms wide
In some place of the sun,
To whirl and to dance
Till the white day is done.
Then rest at cool evening
Beneath a tall tree
While night comes on gently,
    Dark like me,—
That is my dream!

To fling my arms wide
In the face of the sun,
Dance!   whirl!   whirl!
Till the quick day is done.
Rest at pale evening. . . .
A tall, slim tree. . . .
Night coming tenderly
    Black like me.

WINTER MOON

How thin and sharp is the moon tonight!
How thin and sharp and ghostly white
Is the slim curved crook of the moon tonight!

POÈME D'AUTOMNE

The autumn leaves
Are too heavy with color.
The slender trees
On the Vulcan Road
Are dressed in scarlet and gold
Like young courtesans
Waiting for their lovers.
But soon
The winter winds
Will strip their bodies bare
And then
The sharp, sleet-stung
Caresses of the cold
Will be their only
Love.

FANTASY IN PURPLE

Beat the drums of tragedy for me.
Beat the drums of tragedy and death.
And let the choir sing a stormy song
To drown the rattle of my dying breath.

Beat the drums of tragedy for me,
And let the white violins whir thin and slow,
But blow one blaring trumpet note of sun
To go with me
to the darkness
where I go.

MARCH MOON

The moon is naked.
The wind has undressed the moon.
The wind has blown all the cloud-garments
Off the body of the moon
And now she's naked,
Stark naked.

But why don't you blush,
O shameless moon?
Don't you know
It isn't nice to be naked?

JOY

I went to look for Joy,
Slim, dancing Joy,
Gay, laughing Joy,
Bright-eyed Joy,—
And I found her
Driving the butcher's cart
In the arms of the butcher boy!
Such company, such company,
As keeps this young nymph, Joy!

THE NEGRO SPEAKS OF RIVERS

THE NEGRO SPEAKS OF RIVERS

(To W. E. B. DuBois)

I've known rivers:
I've known rivers ancient as the world and older than the flow of human blood in human veins.

My soul has grown deep like the rivers.

I bathed in the Euphrates when dawns were young.
I built my hut near the Congo and it lulled me to sleep.
I looked upon the Nile and raised the pyramids above it.
I heard the singing of the Mississippi when Abe Lincoln went down to New Orleans, and I've seen its muddy bosom turn all golden in the sunset.

I've known rivers:
Ancient, dusky rivers.

My soul has grown deep like the rivers.

CROSS

My old man's a white old man
And my old mother's black.
If ever I cursed my white old man
I take my curses back.

If ever I cursed my black old mother
And wished she were in hell,
I'm sorry for that evil wish
And now I wish her well.

My old man died in a fine big house.
My ma died in a shack.
I wonder where I'm gonna die,
Being neither white nor black?

THE JESTER

In one hand
I hold tragedy
And in the other
Comedy,—
Masks for the soul.
Laugh with me.
You would laugh!
Weep with me.
You would weep!
Tears are my laughter.
Laughter is my pain.
Cry at my grinning mouth,
If you will.
Laugh at my sorrow's reign.
I am the Black Jester,
The dumb clown of the world,
The booted, booted fool of silly men.
Once I was wise.
Shall I be wise again?

THE SOUTH

The lazy, laughing South
With blood on its mouth.
The sunny-faced South,
    Beast-strong,
    Idiot-brained.
The child-minded South
Scratching in the dead fire's ashes
For a Negro's bones.
    Cotton and the moon,
    Warmth, earth, warmth,
    The sky, the sun, the stars,
    The magnolia-scented South.
Beautiful, like a woman,
Seductive as a dark-eyed whore,
    Passionate, cruel,
    Honey-lipped, syphilitic—
    That is the South.
And I, who am black, would love her
But she spits in my face.
And I, who am black,
Would give her many rare gifts
But she turns her back upon me.
    So now I seek the North—
    The cold-faced North,
    For she, they say,
    Is a kinder mistress,
And in her house my children
May escape the spell of the South.

AS I GREW OLDER

It was a long time ago.
I have almost forgotten my dream.
But it was there then,
In front of me,
Bright like a sun,—
My dream.

And then the wall rose,
Rose slowly,
Slowly,
Between me and my dream.
Rose slowly, slowly,
Dimming,
Hiding,
The light of my dream.
Rose until it touched the sky,—
The wall.

Shadow.
I am black.

I lie down in the shadow.
No longer the light of my dream before me,
Above me.
Only the thick wall.
Only the shadow.

My hands!
My dark hands!
Break through the wall!

Find my dream!
Help me to shatter this darkness,
To smash this night,
To break this shadow
Into a thousand lights of sun,
Into a thousand whirling dreams
Of sun!

AUNT SUE'S STORIES

Aunt Sue has a head full of stories.
Aunt Sue has a whole heart full of stories.
Summer nights on the front porch
Aunt Sue cuddles a brown-faced child to her bosom
And tells him stories.

Black slaves
Working in the hot sun,
And black slaves
Walking in the dewy night,
And black slaves
Singing sorrow songs on the banks of a mighty river
Mingle themselves softly
In the flow of old Aunt Sue's voice,
Mingle themselves softly
In the dark shadows that cross and recross
Aunt Sue's stories.

And the dark-faced child, listening,
Knows that Aunt Sue's stories are real stories.
He knows that Aunt Sue
Never got her stories out of any book at all,
But that they came
Right out of her own life.

And the dark-faced child is quiet
Of a summer night
Listening to Aunt Sue's stories.

POEM

The night is beautiful,
So the faces of my people.

The stars are beautiful,
So the eyes of my people.

Beautiful, also, is the sun.
Beautiful, also, are the souls of my people.

BLACK PIERROT

A BLACK PIERROT

I am a black Pierrot:
She did not love me,
So I crept away into the night
And the night was black, too.

I am a black Pierrot:
She did not love me,
So I wept until the red dawn
Dripped blood over the eastern hills
And my heart was bleeding, too.

I am a black Pierrot:
She did not love me,
So with my once gay-colored soul
Shrunken like a balloon without air,
I went forth in the morning
To seek a new brown love.

HARLEM NIGHT SONG

Come,
Let us roam the night together
Singing.

I love you.

Across
The Harlem roof-tops
Moon is shining.
Night sky is blue.
Stars are great drops
Of golden dew.
In the cabaret
The jazz-band's playing.

I love you.

Come,
Let us roam the night together
Singing.

SONGS TO THE DARK VIRGIN

I

Would
That I were a jewel,
A shattered jewel,
That all my shining brilliants
Might fall at thy feet,
Thou dark one.

II

Would
That I were a garment,
A shimmering, silken garment,
That all my folds
Might wrap about thy body,
Absorb thy body,
Hold and hide thy body,
Thou dark one.

III

Would
That I were a flame,
But one sharp, leaping flame
To annihilate thy body,
Thou dark one.

ARDELLA

I would liken you
To a night without stars
Were it not for your eyes.
I would liken you
To a sleep without dreams
Were it not for your songs.

POEM

To the Black Beloved

Ah,
My black one,
Thou art not beautiful
Yet thou hast
A loveliness
Surpassing beauty.

Oh,
My black one,
Thou art not good
Yet thou hast
A purity
Surpassing goodness.

Ah,
My black one,
Thou art not luminous
Yet an altar of jewels,
An altar of shimmering jewels,
Would pale in the light
Of thy darkness,
Pale in the light
Of thy nightness.

WHEN SUE WEARS RED

When Susanna Jones wears red
Her face is like an ancient cameo
Turned brown by the ages.

Come with a blast of trumpets,
    Jesus!

When Susanna Jones wears red
A queen from some time-dead Egyptian night
Walks once again.

Blow trumpets, Jesus!

And the beauty of Susanna Jones in red
Burns in my heart a love-fire sharp like pain.

Sweet silver trumpets,
    Jesus!

PIERROT

I work all day,
Said Simple John,
Myself a house to buy.
I work all day,
Said Simple John,
But Pierrot wondered why.

For Pierrot loved the long white road,
And Pierrot loved the moon,
And Pierrot loved a star-filled sky,
And the breath of a rose in June.

I have one wife,
Said Simple John,
And, faith, I love her yet.
I have one wife,
Said Simple John,
But Pierrot left Pierrette.

For Pierrot saw a world of girls,
And Pierrot loved each one,
And Pierrot thought all maidens fair
As flowers in the sun.

Oh, I am good,
Said Simple John,
The Lord will take me in.
Yes, I am good,
Said Simple John,
But Pierrot's steeped in sin.

For Pierrot played on a slim guitar,
And Pierrot loved the moon,
And Pierrot ran down the long white road
With the burgher's wife one June.

WATER-FRONT STREETS

WATER-FRONT STREETS

The spring is not so beautiful there,—
    But dream ships sail away
To where the spring is wondrous rare
    And life is gay.

The spring is not so beautiful there,—
    But lads put out to sea
Who carry beauties in their hearts
    And dreams, like me.

A FAREWELL

With gypsies and sailors,
Wanderers of the hills and seas,
I go to seek my fortune.
With pious folk and fair
I must have a parting.
But you will not miss me,—
You who live between the hills
And have never seen the seas.

LONG TRIP

The sea is a wilderness of waves,
A desert of water.
We dip and dive,
Rise and roll,
Hide and are hidden
On the sea.
    Day, night,
    Night, day,
The sea is a desert of waves,
A wilderness of water.

PORT TOWN

Hello, sailor boy,
In from the sea!
Hello, sailor,
Come with me!

Come on drink cognac.
Rather have wine?
Come here, I love you.
Come and be mine.

Lights, sailor boy,
Warm, white lights.
Solid land, kid.
Wild, white nights.

Come on, sailor,
Out o' the sea.
Let's go, sweetie!
Come with me.

SEA CALM

How still,
How strangely still
The water is today.
It is not good
For water
To be so still that way.

CARIBBEAN SUNSET

God having a hemorrhage,
Blood coughed across the sky,
Staining the dark sea red,
That is sunset in the Caribbean.

YOUNG SAILOR

He carries
His own strength
And his own laughter,
His own today
And his own hereafter,—
This strong young sailor
Of the wide seas.

What is money for?
To spend, he says.
And wine?
To drink.
And women?
To love.
And today?
For joy.
And tomorrow?
For joy.
And the green sea
For strength,
And the brown land
For laughter.
And nothing hereafter.

SEASCAPE

Off the coast of Ireland
    As our ship passed by
We saw a line of fishing ships
    Etched against the sky.

Off the coast of England
    As we rode the foam
We saw an Indian merchantman
    Coming home.

NATCHA

Natcha, offering love.
For ten shillings offering love.
Offering: A night with me, honey.
A long, sweet night with me.
    Come, drink palm wine.
    Come, drink kisses.
A long, dream night with me.

SEA CHARM

Sea charm
The sea's own children
Do not understand.
They know
But that the sea is strong
Like God's hand.
They know
But that sea wind is sweet
Like God's breath,
And that the sea holds
A wide, deep death.

DEATH OF AN OLD SEAMAN

We buried him high on a windy hill,
But his soul went out to sea.
I know, for I heard, when all was still,
His sea-soul say to me:

Put no tombstone at my head,
For here I do not make my bed.
Strew no flowers on my grave,
I've gone back to the wind and wave.
Do not, do not weep for me,
For I am happy with my sea.

SHADOWS IN THE SUN

BEGGAR BOY

What is there within this beggar lad
That I can neither hear nor feel nor see,
That I can neither know nor understand
And still it calls to me?

Is not he but a shadow in the sun—
A bit of clay, brown, ugly, given life?
And yet he plays upon his flute a wild free tune
As if Fate had not bled him with her knife!

TROUBLED WOMAN

She stands
In the quiet darkness,
This troubled woman,
Bowed by
Weariness and pain,
Like an
Autumn flower
In the frozen rain.
Like a
Wind-blown autumn flower
That never lifts its head
Again.

SUICIDE'S NOTE

The calm,
Cool face of the river
Asked me for a kiss.

SICK ROOM

How quiet
It is in this sick room
Where on the bed
A silent woman lies between two lovers—
Life and Death,
And all three covered with a sheet of pain.

SOLEDAD

A Cuban Portrait

The shadows
Of too many nights of love
Have fallen beneath your eyes.
Your eyes,
So full of pain and passion,
So full of lies.
So full of pain and passion,
Soledad,
So deeply scarred,
So still with silent cries.

TO THE DARK MERCEDES OF "EL PALACIO DE AMOR"

Mercedes is a jungle-lily in a death house.
Mercedes is a doomed star.
Mercedes is a charnel rose.
Go where gold
Will fall at the feet of your beauty,
Mercedes.
Go where they will pay you well
For your loveliness.

MEXICAN MARKET WOMAN

This ancient hag
Who sits upon the ground
Selling her scanty wares
Day in, day round,
Has known high wind-swept mountains,
And the sun has made
Her skin so brown.

AFTER MANY SPRINGS

Now,
In June,
When the night is a vast softness
Filled with blue stars,
And broken shafts of moon-glimmer
Fall upon the earth,
Am I too old to see the fairies dance?
I cannot find them any more.

YOUNG BRIDE

They say she died,—
Although I do not know,
They say she died of grief
And in the earth-dark arms of Death
Sought calm relief,
And rest from pain of love
In loveless sleep.

THE DREAM KEEPER

Bring me all of your dreams,
You dreamers.
Bring me all of your
Heart melodies
That I may wrap them
In a blue cloud-cloth
Away from the too rough fingers
Of the world.

POEM

(To F. S.)

I loved my friend.
He went away from me.
There's nothing more to say.
The poem ends,
Soft as it began,—
I loved my friend.

OUR LAND

OUR LAND

Poem for a Decorative Panel

We should have a land of sun,
Of gorgeous sun,
And a land of fragrant water
Where the twilight
Is a soft bandanna handkerchief
Of rose and gold,
And not this land where life is cold.

We should have a land of trees,
Of tall thick trees
Bowed down with chattering parrots
Brilliant as the day,
And not this land where birds are grey.

Ah, we should have a land of joy,
Of love and joy and wine and song,
And not this land where joy is wrong.

Oh, sweet, away!
Ah, my beloved one, away!

LAMENT FOR DARK PEOPLES

I was a red man one time,
But the white men came.
I was a black man, too,
But the white men came.

They drove me out of the forest.
They took me away from the jungles.
I lost my trees.
I lost my silver moons.

Now they've caged me
In the circus of civilization.
Now I herd with the many—
Caged in the circus of civilization.

AFRAID

We cry among the skyscrapers
As our ancestors
Cried among the palms in Africa
Because we are alone,
It is night,
And we're afraid.

POEM

For the portrait of an African boy after
the manner of Gauguin

All the tom-toms of the jungles beat in my blood,
And all the wild hot moons of the jungles shine in my soul.
I am afraid of this civilization—
    So hard,
        So strong,
            So cold.

SUMMER NIGHT

The sounds
Of the Harlem night
Drop one by one into stillness.
The last player-piano is closed.
The last victrola ceases with the
"Jazz Boy Blues."
The last crying baby sleeps
And the night becomes
Still as a whispering heartbeat.
I toss
Without rest in the darkness,
Weary as the tired night,
My soul
Empty as the silence,
Empty with a vague,
Aching emptiness,
Desiring,
Needing someone,
Something.

I toss without rest
In the darkness
Until the new dawn,
Wan and pale,
Descends like a white mist
Into the court-yard.

DISILLUSION

I would be simple again,
Simple and clean
Like the earth,
Like the rain,
Nor ever know,
Dark Harlem,
The wild laughter
Of your mirth
Nor the salt tears
Of your pain.
Be kind to me,
Oh, great dark city.
Let me forget.
I will not come
To you again.

DANSE AFRICAINE

The low beating of the tom-toms,
The slow beating of the tom-toms,
    Low . . . slow
    Slow . . . low—
    Stirs your blood.
        Dance!
A night-veiled girl
    Whirls softly into a
    Circle of light.
    Whirls softly . . . slowly,
Like a wisp of smoke around the fire—
    And the tom-toms beat,
    And the tom-toms beat,
And the low beating of the tom-toms
    Stirs your blood.

THE WHITE ONES

I do not hate you,
For your faces are beautiful, too.
I do not hate you,
Your faces are whirling lights of loveliness and splendor,
    too.
Yet why do you torture me,
O, white strong ones,
Why do you torture me?

MOTHER TO SON

Well, son, I'll tell you:
Life for me ain't been no crystal stair.
It's had tacks in it,
And splinters,
And boards torn up,
And places with no carpet on the floor—
Bare.
But all the time
I'se been a-climbin' on,
And reachin' landin's,
And turnin' corners,
And sometimes goin' in the dark
Where there ain't been no light.
So boy, don't you turn back.
Don't you set down on the steps
'Cause you finds it's kinder hard.
Don't you fall now—
For I'se still goin', honey,
I'se still climbin',
And life for me ain't been no crystal stair.

POEM

We have tomorrow
Bright before us
Like a flame.

Yesterday
A night-gone thing,
A sun-down name.

And dawn-today
Broad arch above the road we came.

EPILOGUE

I, too, sing America.

I am the darker brother.
They send me to eat in the kitchen
When company comes,
But I laugh,
And eat well,
And grow strong.

Tomorrow,
I'll sit at the table
When company comes.
Nobody'll dare
Say to me,
"Eat in the kitchen,"
Then.

Besides,
They'll see how beautiful I am
And be ashamed,—

I, too, am America.

NOT WITHOUT LAUGHTER

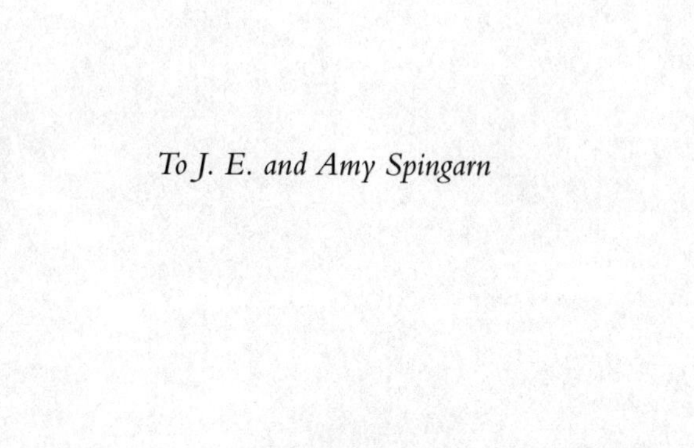

To J. E. and Amy Spingarn

CONTENTS

1
STORM

AUNT HAGER WILLIAMS stood in her doorway and looked out at the sun. The western sky was a sulphurous yellow and the sun a red ball dropping slowly behind the trees and house-tops. Its setting left the rest of the heavens grey with clouds.

"Huh! A storm's comin'," said Aunt Hager aloud.

A pullet ran across the back yard and into a square-cut hole in an unpainted piano-box which served as the roosting-house. An old hen clucked her brood together and, with the tiny chicks, went into a small box beside the large one. The air was very still. Not a leaf stirred on the green apple-tree. Not a single closed flower of the morning-glories trembled on the back fence. The air was very still and yellow. Something sultry and oppressive made a small boy in the doorway stand closer to his grandmother, clutching her apron with his brown hands.

"Sho is a storm comin'," said Aunt Hager.

"I hope mama gets home 'fore it rains," remarked the brown child holding to the old woman's apron. "Hope she gets home."

"I does, too," said Aunt Hager. "But I's skeared she won't."

Just then great drops of water began to fall heavily into the back yard, pounding up little clouds of dust where each drop struck the earth. For a few moments they pattered violently on the roof like a series of hammer-strokes; then suddenly they ceased.

"Come in, chile," said Aunt Hager.

She closed the door as the green apple-tree began to sway in the wind and a small hard apple fell, rolling rapidly down the top of the piano-box that sheltered the chickens. Inside the kitchen it was almost dark. While Aunt Hager lighted an oil-lamp, the child climbed to a chair and peered through the square window into the yard. The leaves and flowers of the morning-glory vines on the back fence were bending with the rising wind. And across the alley at the big house, Mrs. Kennedy's rear screen-door banged to and fro, and Sandy saw her garbage-pail suddenly tip over and roll down into the yard, scattering potato-peelings on the white steps.

"Sho gwine be a terrible storm," said Hager as she turned up the wick of the light and put the chimney on. Then, glancing through the window, she saw a black cloud twisting like a ribbon in the western sky, and the old woman screamed aloud in sudden terror: "It's a cyclone! It's gwine be a cyclone! Sandy, let's get over to Mis' Carter's quick, 'cause we ain't got no cellar here. Come on, chile, let's get! Come on, chile! . . . Come on, chile!"

Hurriedly she blew out the light, grabbed the boy's hand; and together they rushed through the little house towards the front. It was quite dark in the inner rooms, but through the parlor windows came a sort of sooty grey-green light that was rapidly turning to blackness.

"Lawd help us, Jesus!"

Aunt Hager opened the front door, but before she or the child could move, a great roaring sound suddenly shook the world, and, with a deafening division of wood from wood, they saw their front porch rise into the air and go hurtling off into space. Sailing high in the gathering darkness, the porch was soon lost to sight. And the black wind blew with terrific force, numbing the ear-drums.

For a moment the little house trembled and swayed and creaked as though it were about to fall.

"Help me to shut this do'," Aunt Hager screamed; "help me to shut it, Lawd!" as with all her might she struggled against the open door, which the wind held back, but finally it closed and the lock caught. Then she sank to the floor with her back against the wall, while her small grandson trembled like a leaf as she took him in her lap, mumbling: "What a storm! . . . O, Lawdy! . . . O, ma chile, what a storm!"

They could hear the crackling of timbers and the rolling limbs of trees that the wind swept across the roof. Her arms tightened about the boy.

"Dear Jesus!" she said. "I wonder where is yo' mama? S'pose she started out fo' home 'fore this storm come up!" Then in a scream: "Have mercy on ma Annjee! O, Lawd, have mercy on this chile's mama! Have mercy on all ma chillens! Ma Harriett, an' ma Tempy, an' ma Annjee, what's maybe all of 'em out in de storm! O, Lawd!"

A dry crack of lightning split the darkness, and the boy began to wail. Then the rain broke. The old woman could not see the crying child she held, nor could the boy hear the broken voice of his grandmother, who had begun to pray as the rain crashed through the inky blackness. For a long while it roared on the roof of the house and pounded at the windows, until finally the two within became silent, hushing their cries. Then only the lashing noise of the water, coupled with the feeling that something terrible was happening, or had already happened, filled the evening air.

After the rain the moon rose clear and bright and the clouds disappeared from the lately troubled sky. The stars sparkled calmly above the havoc of the storm, and it was still early evening as people emerged from their houses and began to investigate the damage brought by the twisting cyclone that had come with the sunset. Through the rubbish-filled streets men drove slowly with horse and buggy or automobile. The fire-engine was out, banging away, and the soft tang-tang-tang of the motor ambulance could be heard in the distance carrying off the injured.

Black Aunt Hager and her brown grandson put their rubbers on and stood in the water-soaked front yard looking at the porchless house where they lived. Platform, steps, pillars, roof, and all had been blown away. Not a semblance of a porch was left and the front door opened bare into the yard. It was grotesque and funny. Hager laughed.

"Cyclone sho did a good job," she said. "Looks like I ain't never had no porch."

Madam de Carter, from next door, came across the grass, her large mouth full of chattering sympathy for her neighbor.

"But praise God for sparing our lives! It might've been

worse, Sister Williams! It might've been much more calamitouser! As it is, I lost nothin' more'n a chimney and two wash-tubs which was settin' in the back yard. A few trees broke down don't 'mount to nothin'. We's livin', ain't we? And we's more importanter than trees is any day!" Her gold teeth sparkled in the moonlight.

" 'Deed so," agreed Hager emphatically. "Let's move on down de block, Sister, an' see what mo' de Lawd has 'stroyed or spared this evenin'. He's gin us plenty moonlight after de storm so we po' humans can see this lesson o' His'n to a sinful world."

The two elderly colored women picked their way about on the wet walk, littered with twigs and branches of broken foliage. The little brown boy followed, with his eyes wide at the sight of baby-carriages, window-sashes, shingles, and tree-limbs scattered about in the roadway. Large numbers of people were out, some standing on porches, some carrying lanterns, picking up useful articles from the streets, some wringing their hands in a daze.

Near the corner a small crowd had gathered quietly.

"Mis' Gavitt's killed," somebody said.

"Lawd help!" burst from Aunt Hager and Madam de Carter simultaneously.

"Mister and Mis' Gavitt's both dead," added a nervous young white man, bursting with the news. "We live next door to 'em, and their house turned clean over! Came near hitting us and breaking our side-wall in."

"Have mercy!" said the two women, but Sandy slipped away from his grandmother and pushed through the crowd. He ran round the corner to where he could see the overturned house of the unfortunate Gavitts.

Good white folks, the Gavitts, Aunt Hager had often said, and now their large frame dwelling lay on its side like a doll's mansion, with broken furniture strewn carelessly on the wet lawn—and they were dead. Sandy saw a piano flat on its back in the grass. Its ivory keys gleamed in the moonlight like grinning teeth, and the strange sight made his little body shiver, so he hurried back through the crowd looking for his grandmother.

As he passed the corner, he heard a woman sobbing hysterically within the wide house there.

His grandmother was no longer standing where he had left her, but he found Madam de Carter and took hold of her hand. She was in the midst of a group of excited white and colored women. One frail old lady was saying in a high determined voice that she had never seen a cyclone like this in her whole life, and she had lived here in Kansas, if you please, going on seventy-three years. Madam de Carter, chattering nervously, began to tell them how she had recognized its coming and had rushed to the cellar the minute she saw the sky turn green. She had not come up until the rain stopped, so frightened had she been. She was extravagantly enjoying the telling of her fears as Sandy kept tugging at her hand.

"Where's my grandma?" he demanded. Madam de Carter, however, did not cease talking to answer his question.

"What do you want, sonny?" finally one of the white women asked, bending down when he looked as if he were about to cry. "Aunt Hager? . . . Why, she's inside helping them calm poor Mrs. Gavitt's niece. Your grandmother's good to have around when folks are sick or grieving, you know. Run and set on the steps like a nice boy and wait until she comes out." So Sandy left the women and went to sit in the dark on the steps of the big corner house where the niece of the dead Mrs. Gavitt lived. There were some people on the porch, but they soon passed through the screen-door into the house or went away down the street. The moonlight cast weird shadows across the damp steps where Sandy sat, and it was dark there under the trees in spite of the moon, for the old house was built far back from the street in a yard full of oaks and maples, and Sandy could see the light from an upstairs window reflecting on the wet leaves of their nearest boughs. He heard a girl screaming, too, up there where the light was burning, and he knew that Aunt Hager was putting cold cloths on her head, or rubbing her hands, or driving folks out of the room, and talking kind to her so that she would soon be better.

All the neighborhood, white or colored, called his

grandmother when something happened. She was a good nurse, they said, and sick folks liked her around. Aunt Hager always came when they called, too, bringing maybe a little soup that she had made or a jelly. Sometimes they paid her and sometimes they didn't. But Sandy had never had to sit outdoors in the darkness waiting for her before. He leaned his small back against the top step and rested his elbows on the porch behind him. It was growing late and the people in the streets had all disappeared.

There, in the dark, the little fellow began to think about his mother, who worked on the other side of town for a rich white lady named Mrs. J. J. Rice. And suddenly frightful thoughts came into his mind. Suppose she had left for home just as the storm came up! Almost always his mother was home before dark—but she wasn't there tonight when the storm came—and she should have been home! This thought appalled him. She should have been there! But maybe she had been caught by the storm and blown away as she walked down Main Street! Maybe Annjee had been carried off by the great black wind that had overturned the Gavitts' house and taken his grandma's porch flying through the air! Maybe the cyclone had gotten his mother, Sandy thought. He wanted her! Where was she? Had something terrible happened to her? Where was she now?

The big tears began to roll down his cheeks—but the little fellow held back the sobs that wanted to come. He decided he wasn't going to cry and make a racket there by himself on the strange steps of these white folks' house. He wasn't going to cry like a big baby in the dark. So he wiped his eyes, kicked his heels against the cement walk, lay down on the top step, and, by and by, sniffled himself to sleep.

"Wake up, son!" Someone was shaking him. "You'll catch your death o' cold sleeping on the wet steps like this. We're going home now. Don't want me to have to carry a big man like you, do you, boy? . . . Wake up, Sandy!" His mother stooped to lift his long little body from the wide steps. She held him against her soft heavy breasts and let his head rest on one of her shoulders while his feet, in their muddy rubbers, hung down against her dress.

"Where you been, mama?" the boy asked drowsily, tightening his arms about her neck. "I been waiting for you."

"Oh, I been home a long time, worried to death about you and ma till I heard from Madam Carter that you-all was down here nursing the sick. I stopped at your Aunt Tempy's house when I seen the storm coming."

"I was afraid you got blowed away, mama," murmured Sandy sleepily. "Let's go home, mama. I'm glad you ain't got blowed away."

On the porch Aunt Hager was talking to a pale white man and two thin white women standing at the door of the lighted hallway. "Just let Mis' Agnes sleep," she was saying. "She'll be all right now, an' I'll come back in de mawnin' to see 'bout her. . . . Good-night, you-all."

The old colored woman joined her daughter and they started home, walking through the streets filled with debris and puddles of muddy water reflecting the moon.

"You're certainly heavy, boy," remarked Sandy's mother to the child she held, but he didn't answer.

"I'm right glad you come for me, Annjee," Hager said. "I wonder is yo' sister all right out yonder at de country club. . . . An' I was so worried 'bout you I didn't know what to do—skeared you might a got caught in this twister, 'cause it were cert'ly awful!"

"I was at Tempy's!" Annjee replied. "And I was nearly crazy, but I just left everything in the hands o' God. That's all." In silence they walked on, a piece; then hesitantly, to her mother: "There wasn't any mail for me today, was there, ma?"

"Not a speck!" the old woman replied shortly. "Mail-man passed on by."

For a few minutes there was silence again as they walked. Then, "It's goin' on three weeks he's been gone, and he ain't written a line," the younger woman complained, shifting the child to her right arm. "Seems like Jimboy would let a body know where he is, ma, wouldn't it?"

"Huh! That ain't nothin'! He's been gone before this an' he ain't wrote, ain't he? Here you is worryin' 'bout a letter from that good-for-nothing husband o' your'n—an' there's ma house settin' up without a porch to its name! . . . Ain't you seed what de devil's done done on earth this evenin', chile? . . . An' yet de first thing you ask me 'bout is de mail-man! . . . Lawd! Lawd! . . . You an' that Jimboy!"

Aunt Hager lifted her heavy body over fallen tree-trunks and across puddles, but between puffs she managed to voice her indignation, so Annjee said no more concerning letters from her husband. Instead they went back to the subject of the cyclone. "I'm just thankful, ma, it didn't blow the whole house down and you with it, that's all! I was certainly worried! . . . And then you-all was gone when I got home! Gone on out—nursing that white woman. . . . It's too bad 'bout poor Mis' Gavitt, though, and old man Gavitt, ain't it?"

"Yes, indeedy!" said Aunt Hager. "It's sho too bad. They was certainly good old white folks! An' her married niece is takin' it mighty hard, po' little soul. I was nigh two hours, her husband an' me, tryin' to bring her out o' de hysterics. Tremblin' like a lamb all over, she was." They were turning into the yard. "Be careful with that chile, Annjee, you don't trip on none o' them boards nor branches an' fall with him."

"Put me down, 'cause I'm awake," said Sandy.

The old house looked queer without a porch. In the moonlight he could see the long nails that had held the porch roof to the weather-boarding. His grandmother climbed slowly over the door-sill, and his mother lifted him to the floor level as Aunt Hager lit the large oil-lamp on the parlor table. Then they went back to the bedroom, where the youngster took off his clothes, said his prayers, and climbed into the high feather bed where he slept with Annjee. Aunt Hager went to the next room, but for a long time she talked back and forth through the doorway to her daughter about the storm.

"We was just startin' out fo' Mis' Carter's cellar, me an' Sandy," she said several times. "But de Lawd was with us! He held us back! Praise His name! We ain't harmed, none of us—'ceptin' I don't know 'bout ma Harriett at de club. But you's all right. An' you say Tempy's all right, too. An' I prays that Harriett ain't been touched out there in de country where she's workin'. Maybe de storm ain't passed that way."

Then they spoke about the white people where Annjee worked . . . and about the elder sister Tempy's prosperity. Then Sandy heard his grandmother climb into bed, and a few minutes after the springs screaked under her, she had begun to snore. Annjee closed the door between their rooms and slowly began to unlace her wet shoes.

"Sandy," she whispered, "we ain't had no word yet from your father since he left. I know he goes away and stays away like this and don't write, but I'm sure worried. Hope the cyclone ain't passed nowhere near wherever he is, and I hope ain't nothin' hurt him. . . . I'm gonna pray for him, Sandy. I'm gonna ask God right now to take care o' Jimboy. . . . The Lawd knows, I wants him to come back! . . . I loves him. . . . We both loves him, don't we, child? And we want him to come on back!"

She knelt down beside the bed in her night-dress and kept her head bowed for a long time. Before she got up, Sandy had gone to sleep.

2
CONVERSATION

IT WAS BROAD daylight in the town of Stanton and had been for a long time.

"Get out o' that bed, boy!" Aunt Hager yelled. "Here's Buster waitin' out in de yard to play with you, an' you still sleepin'!"

"Aw, tell him to cut off his curls," retorted Sandy, but his grandmother was in no mood for fooling.

"Stop talkin' 'bout that chile's haid and put yo' clothes on. Nine o'clock an' you ain't up yet! Shame on you!" She shouted from the kitchen, where Sandy could hear the fire crackling and smell coffee boiling.

He kicked the sheet off with his bare feet and rolled over and over on the soft feather tick. There was plenty of room to roll now, because his mother had long since got up and gone to Mrs. J. J. Rice's to work.

"Tell Bus I'm coming," Sandy yelled, jumping into his trousers and running with bare feet towards the door. "Is he got his marbles?"

"Come back here, sir, an' put them shoes on," cried Hager, stopping him on his way out. "Yo' feet'll get long as yardsticks and flat as pancakes runnin' round barefooted all de time. An' wash yo' face, sir. Buster ain't got a thing to do but wait. An' eat yo' breakfast."

The air was warm with sunlight, and hundreds of purple and white morning-glories laughed on the back fence. Earth and sky were fresh and clean after the heavy night-rain, and the young corn-shoots stood straight in the garden, and green peavines wound themselves around their crooked sticks. There was the mingled scent of wet soil and golden pollen on the breeze that blew carelessly through the clear air.

Buster sat under the green apple-tree with a pile of black mud from the alley in front of him.

"Hey, Sandy, gonna make marbles and put 'em in the sun to dry," he said.

"All right," agreed Sandy, and they began to roll mud balls in the palms of their hands. But instead of putting them in the sun to dry they threw them against the back of the house, where they flattened and stuck beautifully. Then they began to throw them at each other.

Sandy's playmate was a small ivory-white Negro child with straight golden hair, which his mother made him wear in curls. His eyes were blue and doll-like and he in no way resembled a colored youngster; but he was colored. Sandy himself was the shade of a nicely browned piece of toast, with dark, brown-black eyes and a head of rather kinky, sandy hair that would lie smooth only after a rigorous application of vaseline and water. That was why folks called him Annjee's sandy-headed child, and then just—Sandy.

"He takes after his father," Sister Lowry said, "'cept he's not so light. But he's gonna be a mighty good-lookin' boy when he grows up, that's sho!"

"Well, I hopes he does," Aunt Hager said. "But I'd rather he'd be ugly 'fore he turns out anything like that good-for-nothing Jimboy what comes here an' stays a month, goes away an' stays six, an' don't hit a tap o' work 'cept when he feels like it. If it wasn't for Annjee, don't know how we'd eat, 'cause Sandy's father sho don't do nothin' to support him."

All the colored people in Stanton knew that Hager bore no love for Jimboy Rogers, the tall good-looking yellow fellow whom her second daughter had married.

"First place, I don't like his name," she would say in private. "Who ever heard of a nigger named Jimboy, anyhow? Next place, I ain't never seen a yaller dude yet that meant a dark woman no good—an' Annjee is dark!" Aunt Hager had other objections, too, although she didn't like to talk evil about folks. But what she probably referred to in her mind was the question of his ancestry, for nobody knew who Jimboy's parents were.

*

"Sandy, look out for the house while I run down an' see how is Mis' Gavitt's niece. An' you-all play outdoors. Don't bring no chillen in, litterin' up de place." About eleven o'clock Aunt Hager pulled a dustcap over her head and put on a clean white apron. "Here, tie it for me, chile," she said, turning her broad back. "An' mind you don't hurt yo'self on no rusty nails and rotten boards left from de storm. I'll be back atter while." And she disappeared around the house, walking proudly, her black face shining in the sunlight.

Presently the two boys under the apple-tree were joined by a coal-colored little girl who lived next door, one Willie-Mae Johnson, and the mud balls under her hands became mud pies carefully rounded and patted and placed in the sun on the small box where the little chickens lived. Willie-Mae was the mama, Sandy the papa, and Buster the baby as the old game of "playing house" began anew.

By and by the mail-man's whistle blew and the three children scampered towards the sidewalk to meet him. The carrier handed Sandy a letter. "Take it in the house," he said. But instead the youngsters sat on the front-door-sill, their feet dangling where the porch had been, and began to examine the envelope.

"I bet that's Lincoln's picture," said Buster.

"No, 'taint," declared Willie-Mae. "It's Rossie felt!"

"Aw, it's Washington," said Sandy. "And don't you-all touch my mama's letter with your hands all muddy. It might be from my papa, you can't tell, and she wants it kept clean."

" 'Tis from Jimboy," Aunt Hager declared when she returned, accompanied by her old friend, Sister Whiteside, who peddled on foot fresh garden-truck she raised herself. Aunt Hager had met her at the corner.

"I knows his writin'," went on Hager. "An' it's got a post-mark, K-A-N-, Kansas City! That's what 'tis! Niggers sho do love Kansas City! . . . Huh! . . . So that's where he's at. Well, yo' mama'll be glad to get it. If she knowed it was here, she'd quit work an' come home now. . . . Sit down, Whiteside. We gwine eat in a few minutes. You better have a bite with us an' stay an' rest yo'self awhile, 'cause I knows you been walkin' this mawnin'!"

" 'Deed I is," the old sister declared, dropping her basket of lettuce and peas on the floor and taking a chair next to the table in the kitchen. "An' I ain't sold much neither. Seems like folks ain't got no buyin' appetite after all that storm an' wind last night—but de Lawd will provide! I ain't worried."

"That's right," agreed Hager. "Might o' been me blowed away maself, 'stead o' just ma porch, if Jesus hadn't been with us. . . . You Sandy! Make haste and wash yo' hands, sir. Rest o' you chillens go on home, 'cause I know yo' ma's lookin' for you. . . . Huh! This wood fire's mighty low!"

Hager uncovered a pot that had been simmering on the stove all morning and dished up a great bowlful of black-eyed peas and salt pork. There was biscuit bread left from breakfast. A plate of young onions and a pitcher of lemonade stood on the white oilcloth-covered table. Heads were automatically bowed.

"Lawd, make us thankful for this food. For Christ's sake, amen," said Hager; then the two old women and the child began to eat.

"That's Elvira's boy, ain't it—that yaller-headed young-one was here playin' with Sandy?" Sister Whiteside had her mouth full of onions and beans as she asked the question.

"Shsss! . . . That's her child!" said Hager. "But it ain't Eddie's!" She gave her guest a meaning glance across the table, then lowered her voice, pretending all the while that Sandy's ears were too young to hear. "They say she had that chile 'fore she married Eddie. An' black as Eddie is, you knows an' I knows ain't due to be no golden hair in de family!"

"I knowed there must be something funny," whispered the old sister, screwing up her face. "That's some white man's chile!"

"Sho it is!" agreed Hager. . . . "I knowed it all de time. . . . Have some mo' meat, Whiteside. Help yo'self! We ain't got much, but such as 'tis, you're welcome. . . . Yes, sir, Buster's some white man's chile. . . . Stop reachin' cross de table for bread, Sandy. Where's yo' manners, sir? I declare, chillens do try you sometimes. . . . Pass me de onions."

"Truth, they tries you, yit I gits right lonesome since all ma young-ones is gone." Sister Whiteside worked her few good teeth vigorously, took a long swallow of lemonade, and smacked her lips. "Chillen an' grandchillen all in Chicago an' St. Louis an' Wichita, an' nary chick nor child left with me in de house. . . . Pass me de bread, thank yuh. . . . I feels kinder sad an' sorry at times, po' widder-woman that I is. I has ma garden an' ma hens, but all ma chillens done grown and married. . . . Where's yo' daughter Harriett at now, Hager? Is she married, too? I ain't seen her lately."

Hager pulled a meat skin through her teeth; then she answered: "No, chile, she too young to marry yet! Ain't but sixteen, but she's been workin' out this summer, waitin' table at de Stanton County Country Club. Been in de country three weeks now, since school closed, but she comes in town on Thursdays, though. It's nigh six miles from here, so de women-help sleeps there at night. I's glad she's out there, Sister. Course Harriett's a good girl, but she likes to be frisky—wants to run de streets 'tendin' parties an' dances, an' I can't do much with her no mo', though I hates to say it."

"But she's a songster, Hager! An' I hears she's sho one smart chile, besides. They say she's up with them white folks when it comes to books. An' de high school where she's goin' ain't easy. . . . All ma young ones quit 'fore they got through with it—wouldn't go—ruther have a good time runnin' to Kansas City an' galavantin' round."

"De Lawd knows it's a hard job, keepin' colored chillens in school, Sister Whiteside, a mighty hard job. De niggers don't help 'em, an' de white folks don't care if they stay or not. An' when they gets along sixteen an' seventeen, they wants this, an' they wants that, an' t'other—an' when you ain't got it to give to 'em, they quits school an' goes to work. . . . Harriett say she ain't goin' back next fall. I feels right hurt over it, but she 'clares she ain't goin' back to school. Says there ain't no use in learnin' books fo' nothin' but to work in white folks' kitchens when she's graduated."

"Do she, Hager? I's sho sorry! I's gwine to talk to that gal. Get Reverend Berry to talk to her, too.

". . . You's struggled to bring up yo' chillens, an' all we Christians in de church ought to help you! I gwine see Reverend Berry, see can't he 'suade her to stay in school." The old woman reached for the onions. "But you ain't never raised no boys, though, has you, Hager?"

"No, I ain't. My two boy-chillens both died 'fore they was ten. Just these three girls—Tempy, an' Annjee, an' Harriett—that's all I got. An' this here grandchile, Sandy. . . . Take yo' hands off that meat, sir! You had 'nough!"

"Lawd, you's been lucky! I done raised seven grandchillen 'sides eight o' ma own. An' they don't thank me. No, sir! Go off and kick up they heels an' git married an' don't thank me a bit! Don't even write, some of 'em. . . . Waitin' fo' me to die, I reckon, so's they can squabble over de little house I owns an' ma garden." The old visitor pushed back her chair. "Huh! Yo' dinner was sho good! . . . Waitin' fo' me to die."

"Unhuh! . . . That's de way with 'em, Sister Whiteside. Chillens don't care—but I reckon we old ones can't kick much. They's got to get off fo' themselves. It's natural, that's what 'tis. Now, my Tempy, she's married and doin' well. Got a fine house, an' her husband's a mail-clerk in de civil service makin' good money. They don't 'sociate no mo' with none but de high-toned colored folks, like Dr. Mitchell, an' Mis' Ada Walls, an' Madam C. Frances Smith. Course Tempy don't come to see me much 'cause I still earns ma livin' with ma arms in de tub. But Annjee run in their house out o' the storm last night an' she say Tempy's just bought a new pianer, an' de house looks fine. . . . I's glad fo' de chile."

"Sho, sho you is, Sister Williams, you's a good mother an' I knows you's glad. But I hears from Reverend Berry that Tempy's done withdrawed from our church an' joined de Episcopals!"

"That's right! She is. Last time I seed Tempy, she told me she couldn't stand de Baptist no mo'—too many low niggers belonging, she say, so she's gonna join Father Hill's church, where de best people go. . . . I told her I didn't think much o' joinin' a church so far away from God that they didn't want nothin' but yaller niggers for members, an' so full o' forms an' fashions that a good Christian couldn't shout—but she went on an' joined. It's de stylish temple, that's why, so I ain't said no mo'. Tempy's goin' on thirty-five now, she's ma oldest chile, an' I reckon she knows how she wants to act."

"Yes, I reckon she do. . . . But there ain't no church like de Baptist, praise God! Is there, Sister? If you ain't been dipped in that water an' half drowned, you ain't saved. Tempy don't know like we do. No, sir, she don't know!"

There was no fruit or dessert, and the soiled plates were not removed from the table for a long time, for the two old women, talking about their children, had forgotten the dishes. Young flies crawled over the biscuit bread and hummed above the bowl of peas, while the wood fire died in the stove, and Sandy went out into the sunshine to play.

"Now, ma girl, Maggie," said Sister Whiteside; "de man she married done got to be a big lawyer in St. Louis. He's in de politics there, an' Maggie's got a fine job herself—social servin', they calls it. But I don't hear from her once a year. An' she don't send me a dime. Ma boys looks out for me, though, sometimes, round Christmas. There's Lucius, what runs on de railroad, an' then Andrew, what rides de horses, an' John, in Omaha, sends me a little change now an' then—all but Charlie, an' he never was thoughtful 'bout his mother. He ain't never sent me nothin'."

"Well, you sho is lucky," said Hager, " 'cause they ain't no money comes in this house, Christmas nor no other time, less'n me an' Annjee brings it here. Jimboy ain't no good, an' what Harriett makes goes for clothes and parties an' powderin'-rags. Course, I takes some from her every week, but I gives it right back for her school things. An' I ain't taken nothin' from her these three weeks she's been workin' at de club. She say she's savin' her money herself. She's past sixteen now, so I lets her have it. . . . Po' little thing! . . . She does need to look purty."

Hager's voice softened and her dark old face was half abashed, kind and smiling. "You know, last month I bought her a gold watch—surprise fo' her birthday, de kind you hangs on a little pin on yo' waist. Lawd knows, I couldn't 'ford it—took all de money from three weeks o' washin', but I knowed she'd been wantin' a watch. An' this front room—I moved ma bed out last year an' bought that new rug at de second-hand store an' them lace curtains so's she could have a nice place to entertain her comp'ny. . . . But de chile goes with such a kinder wild crowd o' young folks, Sister Whiteside! It worries me! The boys, they cusses, an' the girls, they paints, an' some of 'em live in de Bottoms. I been tried to get her out of it right along, but seems like I can't. That's why I's glad she's in de country fo' de summer an' comes in but only once a week, an' then she's home with me. It's too far to come in town at night, she say, so she gets her rest now, goin' to bed early an' all, with de country air round her. I hopes she calms down from runnin' round when she comes back here to stay in de fall. . . . She's a good chile. She don't lie to me 'bout where she goes, nor nothin' like that, but she's just wild, that's all, just wild."

"Is she a Christian, Sister Williams?"

"No, she ain't. I's sorry to say it of a chile o' mine, but she ain't. She's been on de moaner's bench time after time, Sunday mawnins' an' prayer-meetin' evenin's, but she never would rise. I prays for her."

"Well, when she takes Jesus, she'll see de light! That's what de matter with her, Sister Williams, she ain't felt Him yit. Make her go to church when she comes back here. . . . I reckon you heard 'bout when de big revival's due to come off this year, ain't you?"

"No, I ain't, not yet."

"Great colored tent-meetin' with de Battle-Ax of de Lawd, Reverend Braswell preachin'! Yes, sir! Gwine start August eighteenth in de Hickory Woods yonder by de edge o' town."

"Good news," cried Hager. "Mo' sinners than enough's in need o' savin'. I's gwine to take Sandy an' get him started right with de Lawd. An' if that onery Jimboy's back here, I gwine make him go, too, an' look Jesus in de face. Annjee an' me's saved, chile! . . . You Sandy, bring us some drinkin'-water from de pump." Aunt Hager rapped on the window with her knuckles to the boy playing outside. "An' stop wrastlin' with that gal."

Sandy rose triumphant from the prone body of black little Willie-Mae, lying squalling on the cinder-path near the back gate. "She started it," he yelled, running towards the pump. The girl began a reply, but at that moment a rickety wagon drawn by a white mule and driven by a grey-haired, leather-colored old man came rattling down the alley.

"Hy, there, Hager!" called the old Negro, tightening his reins on the mule, which immediately began to eat corn-tops over the back fence. "How you been treatin' yo'self?"

"Right tolable," cried Hager, for she and Sister Whiteside had both emerged from the kitchen and were approaching the driver. "How you doin', Brother Logan?"

"Why, if here ain't Sis' Whiteside, too!" said the old beau, sitting up straight on his wagon-seat and showing a row of ivory teeth in a wide grin. "I's doin' purty well for a po' widower what ain't got nobody to bake his bread. Doin' purty well. Hee! Hee! None o' you-all ain't sorry for me, is you? How de storm treat you, Hager? . . . Says it carried off yo' porch? . . . That's certainly too bad! Well, it did some o' these white folks worse'n that. I got 'nough work to do to last me de next fo' weeks, cleanin' up yards an' haulin' off trash, me an' dis mule here. . . . How's yo' chillen, Sis' Williams?"

"Oh, they all right, thank yuh. Annjee's still at Mis' Rice's, an' Harriet's in de country at de club."

"Is she?" said Brother Logan. "I seed her in town night 'fore last down on Pearl Street 'bout ten o'clock."

"You ain't seed Harriett no night 'fore last," disputed Hager vigorously. "She don't come in town 'ceptin' Thursday afternoons, an' that's tomorrow."

"Sister, I ain't blind," said the old man, hurt that his truth should be doubted. "I—seen—Harriett Williams on Pearl Street . . . with Maudel Smothers an' two boys 'bout ten o'clock day before yestidy night! An' they was gwine to de Waiters' Ball, 'cause I asked Maudel where they was gwine, an' she say so. Then I says to Harriett: 'Does yo' mammy know you's out this late?' an' she laughed an' say: 'Oh, that's all right!' . . . Don't tell me I ain't seen Harriett, Hager."

"Well, Lawd help!" Aunt Hager cried, her mouth open. "You done seed my chile in town an' she ain't come anear home! Stayed all night at Maudel's, I reckon. . . . I tells her 'bout runnin' with that gal from de Bottoms. That's what makes her lie to me—tellin' me she don't come in town o' nights. Maudel's folks don't keep no kind o' house, and mens goes there, an' they sells licker, an' they gambles an' fights. . . . Is you sho that's right, Brother Logan, ma chile done been in town an' ain't come home?"

"It ain't wrong!" said old man Logan, cracking his long whip on the white mule's haunches. "Gittiyap! You ole jinny!" and he drove off.

"Um-uh!" said Sister Whiteside to Hager as the two toil-worn old women walked toward the house. "That's de way they does you!" The peddler gathered up her things. "I better be movin', 'cause I got these greens to sell yit, an' it's gittin' 'long towards evenin'. . . . That's de way chillens does you, Sister Williams! I knows! That's de way they does!"

3
JIMBOY'S LETTER

KANSAS CITY, MO.
13 June 1912

Dear Annjelica,

I been laying off to written you ever since I left home but you know how it is. Work has not been so good here. Am with a section gang of coloreds and greeks and somehow strained my back on the Union Pacific laying ties so I will be home on Saturday. Will do my best to try and finish out weak here. Love my darling wife also kiss my son Sandy for me. Am dying to see you,

affectionately as ever
and allways
till the judgment day,
JIMBOY ROGERS

"Strained his back, has he? Unhuh! An' then comes writin' 'bout till de judgment day!" Hager muttered when she heard it. "Always something wrong with that nigger! He'll be back here now, layin' 'round, doin' nothin' fo' de rest o' de summer, turnin' ma house into a theatre with him an' Harriett singin' their rag-time, an' that guitar o' his'n wangin' ever' evenin'! 'Tween him an' Harriett both it's a wonder I ain't plumb crazy. But Harriett do work fo' her livin'. She ain't no loafer. . . . Huh! . . . Annjee, you was sho a fool when you married that boy, an' you still is! . . . I's gwine next do' to Sister Johnson's!" Aunt Hager went out the back and across the yard, where, next door, Tom and Sarah Johnson, Willie-Mae's grandparents, sat on a bench against the side-wall of an unpainted shanty. They were both quietly smoking their corn-cob pipes in the evening dusk.

Sandy, looking at the back of the letter that his mother held, stood at the kitchen-table rapidly devouring a large piece of fresh lemon pie, which she had brought from Mrs. J. J. Rice's. Annjee had said to save the two cold fried lamb chops until tomorrow, or Sandy would have eaten those, too.

"Wish you'd brought home some more pie," the boy declared, his lips white with meringue, but Annjee, who had just got in from work, paid no attention to her son's appreciative remarks on her cookery.

Instead she said: "Ma certainly ain't got no time for Jimboy, has she?" and then sat down with the open letter still in her hand—a single sheet of white paper pencilled in large awkward letters. She put it on the table, rested her dark face in her hands, and began to read it again. . . . She knew how it was, of course, that her husband hadn't written before. That was all right now. Working all day in the hot sun with a gang of Greeks, a man was tired at night, besides living in a box-car, where there was no place to write a letter anyway. He was a great big kid, that's what Jimboy was, cut out for playing. But when he did work, he tried to outdo everybody else. Annjee could see him in her mind, tall and well-built, his legs apart, muscles bulging as he swung the big hammer above his head, driving steel. No wonder he hurt his back, trying to lay more ties a day than anybody else on the railroad. That was just like Jimboy. But she was kind of pleased he had hurt it, since it would bring him home.

"Ain't you glad he's comin', Sandy?"

"Sure," answered the child, swallowing his last mouthful of pie. "I hope he brings me that gun he promised to buy last Easter." The boy wiped his sticky hands on the dish-cloth and ran out into the back yard, calling: "Willie-Mae! Willie-Mae!"

"Stay right over yonder!" answered his grandmother through the dusk. "Willie-Mae's in de bed, sir, an' we old folks settin' out here tryin' to have a little peace." From the tone of Hager's voice he knew he wasn't wanted in the Johnsons' yard, so he went back into the house, looked at his mother reading her letter again, and then lay down on the kitchen-floor.

"Affectionately as ever and allways till the judgment day," she read, "Jimboy Rogers."

He loved her, Annjee was sure of that, and it wasn't another woman that made him go away so often. Eight years they'd been married. No, nine—because Sandy was nine, and he was ready to be born when they had had the wedding. And Jimboy left the week after they were married, to go to Omaha, where he worked all winter. When he came back, Sandy was in the world, sitting up sucking meat skins. It was springtime and they bought a piano for the house—but later the instalment man came and took it back to the store. All that summer her husband stayed home and worked a little, but mostly he fished, played pool, taught Harriett to buck-dance, and quarrelled with Aunt Hager. Then in the winter he went to Jefferson City and got a job at the Capitol.

Jimboy was always going, but Aunt Hager was wrong about his never working. It was just that he couldn't stay in one place all the time. He'd been born running, he said, and had run ever since. Besides, what was there in Stanton anyhow for a young colored fellow to do except dig sewer ditches for a few cents an hour or maybe porter around a store for seven dollars a week. Colored men couldn't get many jobs in Stanton, and foreigners were coming in, taking away what little work they did have. No wonder he didn't stay home. Hadn't Annjee's father been in Stanton forty years and hadn't he died with Aunt Hager still taking in washings to help keep up the house?

There was no well-paid work for Negro men, so Annjee didn't blame Jimboy for going away looking for something better. She'd go with him if it wasn't for her mother. If she went, though, Aunt Hager wouldn't have anybody for company but Harriett, and Harriett was the youngest and wildest of the three children. With Pa Williams dead going on ten years, Hager washing every day, Tempy married, and Annjee herself out working, there had been nobody to take much care of the little sister as she grew up. Harriett had had no raising, even though she was smart and in high school. A female child needed care. But she could sing! Lawdy! And dance, too! That was another reason why Aunt Hager didn't like Jimboy. The devil's musicianer, she called him, straight from hell, teaching Harriett buck-and-winging! But when he took his soft-playing guitar and picked out spirituals and old-time Christian hymns on its sweet strings, Hager forgot she was his enemy, and sang and rocked with the rest of them. When Jimboy was home, you couldn't get lonesome or blue.

"Gee, I'll be glad when he comes!" Annjee said to herself. "But if he goes off again, I'll feel like dying in this dead old town. I ain't never been away from here nohow." She spoke aloud to the dim oil-lamp smoking on the table and the sleeping boy on the floor. "I believe I'll go with him next time. I declare I do!" And then, realizing that Jimboy had never once told her when he was leaving or for what destination, she amended her utterance. "I'll follow him, though, as soon as he writes." Because, almost always after he had been away two or three weeks, he would write. "I'll follow him, sure, if he goes off again. I'll leave Sandy here and send money back to mama. Then Harriett could settle down and take care of ma and stop runnin' the streets so much. . . . Yes, that's what I'll do next time!"

This going away was a new thought, and the dark, strong-bodied young woman at the table suddenly began to dream of the cities she had never seen to which Jimboy would lead her. Why, he had been as far north as Canada and as far south as New Orleans, and it wasn't anything for him to go to Chicago or Denver any time! He was a travelling man—and she, Annjee, was too meek and quiet, that's what she was—too stay-at-homish. Never going nowhere, never saying nothing back to those who scolded her or talked about her, not even sassing white folks when they got beside themselves. And every colored girl in town said that Mrs. J. J. Rice was no easy white woman to work for, yet she had been there now five years, accepting everything without a murmur! Most young folks, girls and boys, left Stanton as soon as they could for the outside world, but here she was, Annjelica Williams, going on twenty-eight, and had never been as far as Kansas City!

"I want to travel," she said to herself. "I want to go places, too."

But that was why Jimboy married her, because she wasn't a runabout. He'd had enough of those kind of women before he struck Stanton, he said. St. Louis was full of them, and Chicago running over. She was the first nice girl he'd ever met who lived at home, so he took her. . . . There were mighty few dark women had a light, strong, good-looking young husband, really a married husband, like Jimboy, and a little brown kid like Sandy.

"I'm mighty lucky," Annjee thought, "even if he ain't here." And two tears of foolish pride fell from the bright eyes in her round black face. They trickled down on the letter, with its blue lines and pencil-scrawled message, and some of the words on the paper began to blur into purple blots because the pencil had been an indelible one. Quickly she fumbled for a handkerchief to wipe the tears away, when a voice made her start.

"You Annjee!" cried Aunt Hager in the open door. "Go to bed, chile! Go on! Settin' up here this late, burnin' de light an' lurin' all sorts o' night-bugs an' creepers into de house!" The old woman came in out of the dark. "Lawd! I might anigh stumbled over this boy in de middle o' de flo'! An' you ain't even took off yo' hat since you got home from work! Is you crazy? Settin' up here at night with yo' hat on, an' lettin' this chile catch his death o' cold sleepin' down on de flo' long after his bedtime!"

Sheepishly Annjee folded her letter and got up. It was true that she still had on her hat and the sweater she had worn to Mrs. Rice's. True, too, the whole room was alive with soft-winged moths fluttering against the hot glass of the light—and on the kitchen-floor a small, brown-skin, infinitely lovable edition of Jimboy lay sprawled contentedly in his grandmother's path, asleep!

"He's my baby!" Annjee said gently, stooping to pick him up. "He's my baby—me and Jimboy's baby!"

4
THURSDAY AFTERNOON

HAGER HAD RISEN at sunrise. On Thursdays she did the Reinharts' washing, on Fridays she ironed it, and on Saturdays she sent it home, clean and beautifully white, and received as pay the sum of seventy-five cents. During the winter Hager usually did half a dozen washings a week, but during the hot season her customers had gone away, and only the Reinharts, on account of an invalid grandmother with whom they could not travel, remained in Stanton.

Wednesday afternoon Sandy, with a boy named Jimmy Lane, called at the back door for their soiled clothes. Each child took a handle and between them carried the large wicker basket seven blocks to Aunt Hager's kitchen. For this service Jimmy Lane received five cents a trip, although Sister Lane had repeatedly said to Hager that he needn't be given anything. She wanted him to learn his Christian duties by being useful to old folks. But Jimmy was not inclined to be Christian. On the contrary, he was a very bad little boy of thirteen, who often led Sandy astray. Sometimes they would run with the basket for no reason at all, then stumble and spill the clothes out on the sidewalk—Mrs. Reinhart's summer dresses, and drawers, and Mr. Reinhart's extra-large B.V.D.'s lying generously exposed to the public. Sometimes, if occasion offered, the youngsters would stop to exchange uncouth epithets with strange little white boys who called them "niggers." Or, again, they might neglect their job for a game of marbles, or a quarter-hour of scrub baseball on a vacant lot; or to tease any little colored girl who might tip timidly by with her hair in tight, well-oiled braids—while the basket of garments would be left forlornly in the street without guardian. But when the clothes were safe in Aunt Hager's kitchen, Jimmy would usually buy candy with his nickel and share it with Sandy before he went home.

After soaking all night, the garments were rubbed through the suds in the morning; and in the afternoon the colored articles were on the line while the white pieces were boiling seriously in a large tin boiler on the kitchen-stove.

"They sho had plenty this week," Hager said to her grandson, who sat on the stoop eating a slice of bread and apple butter. "I's mighty late gettin' 'em hung out to dry, too. Had no business stoppin' this mawnin' to go see sick folks, and me here got all I can do maself! Looks like this warm weather old Mis' Reinhart must change ever' piece from her dress to her shimmy three times a day—sendin' me a washin' like this here!" They heard the screen-door at the front of the house open and slam. "It's a good thing they got me to do it fo' 'em! . . . Sandy, see who's that at de do'."

It was Harriett, home from the country club for the afternoon, cool and slender and pretty in her black uniform with its white collar, her smooth black face and neck powdered pearly, and her crinkly hair shining with pomade. She smelled nice and perfumy as Sandy jumped on her like a dog greeting a favorite friend. Harriett kissed him and let him hang to her arm as they went through the bedroom to the kitchen. She carried a brown cardboard suit-case and a wide straw hat in one hand.

"Hello, mama," she said.

Hager poked the boiling clothes with a vigorous splash of her round stick. The steam rose in clouds of soapy vapor.

"I been waitin' for you, madam!" her mother replied in tones that were not calculated to welcome pleasantly an erring daughter. "I wants to know de truth—was you in town last Monday night or not?"

Harriett dropped her suit-case against the wall. "You seem to have the truth," she said carelessly. "How'd you get it? . . . Here, Sandy, take this out in the yard and eat it, seed and all." She gave her nephew a plum she had brought in her pocket. "I *was* in town, but I didn't have time to come home. I had to go to Maudel's because she's making me a dress."

"To Maudel's! . . . Unhuh! An' to de Waiters' Ball, besides galavantin' up an' down Pearl Street after ten o'clock! I wouldn't cared so much if you'd told me beforehand, but you said you didn't come in town 'ceptin' Thursday afternoon, an' here I was believing yo' lies."

"It's no lies! I haven't been in town before."

"Who brung you here at night anyhow—an' there ain't no trains runnin'?"

"O, I came in with the cook and some of the boys, mama, that's who! They hired an auto for the dance. What would be the use coming home, when you and Annjee go to bed before dark like chickens?"

"That's all right, madam! Annjee's got sense—savin' her health an' strength!"

Harriett was not impressed. "For what? To spend her life in Mrs. Rice's kitchen?" She shrugged her shoulders.

"What you bring yo' suit-case home fo'?"

"I'm quitting the job Saturday," she said. "I've told them already."

"Quitting!" her mother exclaimed. "What fo'? Lawd, if it ain't one thing, it's another!"

"What for?" Harriett retorted angrily. "There's plenty what for! All that work for five dollars a week with what little tips those pikers give you. And white men insulting you besides, asking you to sleep with 'em. Look at my finger-nails, all broke from scrubbing that dining-room floor." She thrust out her dark slim hands. "Waiting table and cleaning silver, washing and ironing table-linen, and then scrubbing the floor besides—that's too much of a good thing! And only three waitresses on the job. That old steward out there's a regular white folks' nigger. He don't care how hard he works us girls. Well, I'm through with the swell new Stanton County Country Club this coming Saturday—I'm telling everybody!" She shrugged her shoulders again.

"What you gonna do then?"

"Maudel says I can get a job with her."

"Maudel? . . . Where?" The old woman had begun to wring the clothes dry and pile them in a large dish-pan.

"At the Banks Hotel, chambermaid, for pretty good pay."

Hager stopped again and turned decisively towards her daughter. "You ain't gonna work in no hotel. You hear me! They's dives o' sin, that's what they is, an' a child o' mine ain't goin' in one. If you was a boy, I wouldn't let you go, much less a girl! They ain't nothin' but strumpets works in hotels."

"Maudel's no strumpet." Harriett's eyes narrowed.

"I don't know if she is or ain't, but I knows I wants you to stop runnin' with her—I done tole you befo'. . . . Her mammy ain't none too straight neither, raisin' them chillen in sin. Look at Sammy in de reform school 'fore he were fifteen for gamblin'. An' de oldest chile, Essie, done gone to Kansas City with that yaller devil she ain't married. An' Maudel runnin' de streets night an' day, with you tryin' to keep up with her! . . . Lawd a mercy! . . . Here, hang up these clothes!"

Her mother pointed to the tin pan on the table filled with damp, twisted, white underwear. Harriett took the pan in both hands. It was heavy and she trembled with anger as she lifted it to her shoulders.

"You can bark at me if you want to, mama, but don't talk about my friends. I don't care what they are! Maudel'd do anything for me. And her brother's a good kid, whether he's been in reform school or not. They oughtn't to put him there just for shooting dice. What's that? I like him, and I like Mrs. Smothers, too. She's not always scolding people for wanting a good time and for being lively and trying to be happy."

Hot tears raced down each cheek, leaving moist lines in the pink powder. Sandy, playing marbles with Buster under the apple-tree, heard her sniffling as she shook out the clothes and hung them on the line in the yard.

"You Sandy," Aunt Hager called loudly from the kitchen-door. "Come in here an' get me some water an' cut mo' firewood." Her black face was wet with perspiration and drawn from fatigue and worry. "I got to get the rest o' these clothes out yet this evenin'. . . . That chile Harriett's aggravatin' me to death! Help me, Sandy, honey."

They ate supper in silence, for Hager's attempts at conversation with her young daughter were futile. Once the old woman said: "That onery Jimboy's comin' home Saturday," and Harriett's face brightened a moment.

"Gee, I'm glad," she replied, and then her mouth went sullen again. Sandy began uncomfortably to kick the table-leg.

"For Christ's sake!" the girl frowned, and the child stopped, hurt that his favorite aunt should yell at him peevishly for so slight an offense.

"Lawd knows, I wish you'd try an' be mo' like yo' sisters, Annjee an' Tempy," Hager began as she washed the dishes, while Harriett stood near the stove, cloth in hand, waiting to dry them. "Here I is, an old woman, an' you tries ma soul! After all I did to raise you, you don't even hear me when I speak." It was the old theme again, without variation. "Now, there's Annjee, ain't a better chile livin'—if she warn't crazy 'bout Jimboy. An' Tempy married an' doin' well, an' respected ever'where. . . . An' you runnin' wild!"

"Tempy?" Harriett sneered suddenly, pricked by this comparison. "So respectable you can't touch her with a ten-foot pole, that's Tempy! . . . Annjee's all right, working herself to death at Mrs. Rice's, but don't tell me about Tempy. Just because she's married a mail-clerk with a little property, she won't even see her own family any more. When niggers get up in the world, they act just like white folks—don't pay you no mind. And Tempy's that kind of a nigger—she's up in the world now!"

"Close yo' mouth, talking that way 'bout yo' own sister! I ain't asked her to be always comin' home, is I, if she's satisfied in her own house?"

"No, you aren't asking her, mama, but you're always talking about her being so respectable. . . . Well, I don't want to be respectable if I have to be stuck up and dicty like Tempy is. . . . She's colored and I'm colored and I haven't seen her since before Easter. . . . It's not being black that matters with her, though, it's being poor, and that's what we are, you and me and Annjee, working for white folks and washing clothes and going in back doors, and taking tips and insults. I'm tired of it, mama! I want to have a good time once in a while."

"That's 'bout all you does have is a good time," Hager said. "An' it ain't right, an' it ain't Christian, that's what it ain't! An' de Lawd is takin' notes on you!" The old woman picked up the heavy iron skillet and began to wash it inside and out.

"Aw, the church has made a lot of you old Negroes act like Salvation Army people," the girl returned, throwing the dried knives and forks on the table. "Afraid to even laugh on Sundays, afraid for a girl and boy to look at one another, or for people to go to dances. Your old Jesus is white, I guess, that's why! He's white and stiff and don't like niggers!"

Hager gasped while Harriett went on excitedly, disregarding her mother's pain: "Look at Tempy, the highest-class Christian in the family—Episcopal, and so holy she can't even visit her own mother. Seems like all the good-time people are bad, and all the old Uncle Toms and mean, dried-up, long-faced niggers fill the churches. I don't never intend to join a church if I can help it."

"Have mercy on this chile! Help her an' save her from hell-fire! Change her heart, Jesus!" the old woman begged, standing in the middle of the kitchen with uplifted arms. "God have mercy on ma daughter."

Harriett, her brow wrinkled in a steady frown, put the dishes away, wiped the table, and emptied the water with a splash through the kitchen-door. Then she went into the bed-room that she shared with her mother, and began to undress. Sandy saw, beneath her thin white underclothes, the soft black skin of her shapely young body.

"Where you goin'?" Hager asked sharply.

"Out," said the girl.

"Out where?"

"O, to a barbecue at Willow Grove, mama! The boys are coming by in an auto at seven o'clock."

"What boys?"

"Maudel's brother and some fellows."

"You ain't goin' a step!"

A pair of curling-irons swung in the chimney of the lighted lamp on the dresser. Harriett continued to get ready. She was making bangs over her forehead, and the scent of scorching hair-oil drifted by Sandy's nose.

"Up half de night in town Monday, an' de Lawd knows how late ever' night in de country, an' then you comes home to run out agin! . . . You ain't goin'!" continued her mother.

Harriett was pulling on a pair of red silk stockings, bright and shimmering to her hips.

"You quit singin' in de church choir. You say you ain't goin' back to school. You won't keep no job! Now what *is* you gonna do? Yo' pappy said years ago, 'fore he died, you was too purty to 'mount to anything, but I ain't believed him. His last dyin' words was: 'Look out fo' ma baby Harriett.' You was his favorite chile. . . . Now look at you! Runnin' de streets an' wearin' red silk stockings!" Hager trembled. " 'Spose yo' pappy was to come back an' see you?"

Harriett powdered her face and neck, pink on ebony, dashed white talcum at each arm-pit, and rubbed her ears with perfume from a thin bottle. Then she slid a light blue dress of many ruffles over her head. The skirt ended midway between the ankle and the knee, and she looked very cute, delicate, and straight, like a black porcelain doll in a Vienna toy shop.

"Some o' Maudel's makin's, that dress—anybody can tell," her mother went on quarrelling. "Short an' shameless as it can be! Regular bad gal's dress, that's what 'tis. . . . What you puttin' it on fo' anyhow, an' I done told you you ain't goin' out? You must think I don't mean ma words. Ain't more'n sixteen last April an' runnin' to barbecues at Willer Grove! De idee! When I was yo' age, wasn't up after eight o'clock, 'ceptin' Sundays in de church house, that's all. . . . Lawd knows where you young ones is headin'. An' me prayin' an' washin' ma fingers to de bone to keep a roof over yo' head."

The sharp honk of an automobile horn sounded from the street. A big red car, full of laughing brown girls gaily dressed, and coatless, slick-headed black boys in green and yellow silk shirts, drew up at the curb. Somebody squeezed the bulb of the horn a second time and another loud and saucy honk! struck the ears.

"You Sandy," Hager commanded. "Run out there an' tell them niggers to leave here, 'cause Harriett ain't goin' no place."

But Sandy did not move, because his young and slender aunt had gripped him firmly by the collar while she searched feverishly in the dresser-drawer for a scarf. She pulled it out, long and flame-colored, with fiery, silky fringe, before she released the little boy.

"You ain't gwine a step this evenin'!" Hager shouted. "Don't you hear me?"

"O, no?" said Harriett coolly in a tone that cut like knives. "You're the one that says I'm not going—*but I am*!"

Then suddenly something happened in the room—the anger fell like a veil from Hager's face, disclosing aged, helpless eyes full of fear and pain.

"Harriett, honey, I wants you to be good," the old woman stammered. The words came pitiful and low—not a command any longer—as she faced her terribly alive young daughter in the ruffled blue dress and the red silk stockings. "I just wants you to grow up decent, chile. I don't want you runnin' to Willer Grove with them boys. It ain't no place fo' you in the night-time—an' you knows it. You's mammy's baby girl. She wants you to be good, honey, and follow Jesus, that's all."

The baritone giggling of the boys in the auto came across the yard as Hager started to put a timid, restraining hand on her daughter's shoulder—but Harriett backed away.

"You old fool!" she cried. "Lemme go! You old Christian fool!"

She ran through the door and across the sidewalk to the waiting car, where the arms of the young men welcomed her eagerly. The big machine sped swiftly down the street and the rapid sput! sput! sput! of its engine grew fainter and fainter. Finally, the auto was only a red tail-light in the summer dusk. Sandy, standing beside his grandmother in the doorway, watched it until it disappeared.

5
GUITAR

Throw yo' arms around me, baby,
Like de circle round de sun!
Baby, throw yo' arms around me
Like de circle round de sun,
An' tell yo' pretty papa
How you want yo' lovin' done!

JIMBOY WAS HOME. All the neighborhood could hear his rich low baritone voice giving birth to the blues. On Saturday night he and Annjee went to bed early. On Sunday night Aunt Hager said: "Put that guitar right up, less'n it's hymns you plans on playin'. An' I don't want too much o' them, 'larmin' de white neighbors."

But this was Monday, and the sun had scarcely fallen below the horizon before the music had begun to float down the alley, over back fences and into kitchen-windows where nice white ladies sedately washed their supper dishes.

Did you ever see peaches
Growin' on a watermelon vine?
Says did you ever see peaches
On a watermelon vine?
Did you ever see a woman
That I couldn't get for mine?

Long, lazy length resting on the kitchen-door-sill, back against the jamb, feet in the yard, fingers picking his sweet guitar, left hand holding against its finger-board the back of an old pocket-knife, sliding the knife upward, downward, getting thus weird croons and sighs from the vibrating strings:

O, I left ma mother
An' I cert'ly can leave you.
Indeed I left ma mother
An' I cert'ly can leave you,
For I'd leave any woman
That mistreats me like you do.

Jimboy, remembering brown-skin mamas in Natchez, Shreveport, Dallas; remembering Creole women in Baton Rouge, Louisiana:

O, yo' windin' an' yo' grindin'
Don't have no effect on me,
Babe, yo' windin' an' yo' grindin'
Don't have no 'fect on me,
'Cause I can wind an' grind
Like a monkey round a coconut-tree!

Then Harriett, standing under the ripening apple-tree, in the back yard, chiming in:

Now I see that you don't want me,
So it's fare thee, fare thee well!
Lawd, I see that you don't want me,
So it's fare—thee—well!
I can still get plenty lovin',
An' you can go to—Kansas City!

"O, play it, sweet daddy Jimboy!" She began to dance.

Then Hager, from her seat on the edge of the platform covering the well, broke out: "Here, madam! Stop that prancin'! Bad enough to have all this singin' without turnin' de yard into a show-house." But Harriett kept on, her hands picking imaginary cherries out of the stars, her hips speaking an earthly language quite their own.

"You got it, kid," said Jimboy, stopping suddenly, then fingering his instrument for another tune. "You do it like the stage women does. You'll be takin' Ada Walker's place if you keep on."

"Wha! Wha! . . . You chillen sho can sing!" Tom Johnson shouted his compliments from across the yard. And Sarah, beside him on the bench behind their shack, added: "Minds me o' de ole plantation times, honey! It sho do!"

"Unhuh! Bound straight fo' de devil, that's what they is," Hager returned calmly from her place beside the pump. "You an' Harriett both—singin' an' dancin' this stuff befo' these chillens here." She pointed to Sandy and Willie-Mae, who sat on the ground with their backs against the chicken-box. "It's a shame!"

"I likes it," said Willie-Mae.

"Me too," the little boy agreed.

"Naturally you would—none o' you-all's converted yet," countered the old woman to the children as she settled back against the pump to listen to some more.

The music rose hoarse and wild:

I wonder where ma easy rider's gone?
He done left me, put ma new gold watch in pawn.

It was Harriett's voice in plaintive moan to the night sky. Jimboy had taught her that song, but a slight, clay-colored brown boy who had hopped bells at the Clinton Hotel for a couple of months, on his way from Houston to Omaha, discovered its meaning to her. Puppy-love, maybe, but it had hurt when he went away, saying nothing. And the guitar in Jimboy's hands echoed that old pain with an even greater throb than the original ache itself possessed.

Approaching footsteps came from the front yard.

"Lord, I can hear you-all two blocks away!" said Annjee, coming around the house, home from work, with a bundle of food under her left arm. "Hello! How are you, daddy? Hello, ma! Gimme a kiss Sandy. . . . Lord, I'm hot and tired and most played out. This late just getting from work! . . . Here, Jimboy, come on in and eat some of these nice things the white folks had for supper." She stepped across her husband's outstretched legs into the kitchen. "I brought a mighty good piece of cold ham for you, hon', from Mis' Rice's."

"All right, sure, I'll be there in a minute," the man said, but he went on playing *Easy Rider*, and Harriett went on singing, while the food was forgotten on the table until long after Annjee had come outdoors again and sat down in the cool, tired of waiting for Jimboy to come in to her.

Off and on for nine years, ever since he had married Annjee, Jimboy and Harriett had been singing together in the evenings. When they started, Harriett was a little girl with braided hair, and each time that her roving brother-in-law stopped in Stanton, he would amuse himself by teaching her the old Southern songs, the popular rag-time ditties, and the hundreds of varying verses of the blues that he would pick up in the big dirty cities of the South. The child, with her strong sweet voice (colored folks called it alto) and her racial sense of rhythm, soon learned to sing the songs as well as Jimboy. He taught her the *parse me la*, too, and a few other movements peculiar to Southern Negro dancing, and sometimes together they went through the buck-and-wing and a few taps. It was all great fun, and innocent fun except when one stopped to think, as white folks did, that some of the blues lines had, not only double, but triple meanings, and some of the dance steps required very definite movements of the hips. But neither Harriett nor Jimboy soiled their minds by thinking. It was music, good exercise—and they loved it.

"Do you know this one, Annjee?" asked Jimboy, calling his wife's name out of sudden politeness because he had forgotten to eat her food, had hardly looked at her, in fact, since she came home. Now he glanced towards her in the darkness where she sat plump on a kitchen-chair in the yard, apart from the others, with her back to the growing corn in the garden. Softly he ran his fingers, light as a breeze, over his guitar strings, imitating the wind rustling through the long leaves of the corn. A rectangle of light from the kitchen-door fell into the yard striking sidewise across the healthy orange-yellow of his skin above the unbuttoned neck of his blue laborer's shirt.

"Come on, sing it with us, Annjee," he said.

"I don't know it," Annjee replied, with a lump in her throat, and her eyes on the silhouette of his long, muscular, animal-hard body. She loved Jimboy too much, that's what was the matter with her! She knew there was nothing between him and her young sister except the love of music, yet he might have dropped the guitar and left Harriett in the yard for a little while to come eat the nice cold slice of ham she had brought him. She hadn't seen him all day long. When she went to work this morning, he was still in bed—and now the blues claimed him.

In the starry blackness the singing notes of the guitar became a plaintive hum, like a breeze in a grove of palmettos; became a low moan, like the wind in a forest of live-oaks strung with long strands of hanging moss. The voice of Annjee's golden, handsome husband on the door-step rang high and far away, lonely-like, crying with only the guitar, not his wife, to understand; crying grotesquely, crying absurdly in the summer night:

I got a mule to ride.
I got a mule to ride.
Down in the South somewhere
I got a mule to ride.

Then asking the question as an anxious, left-lonesome girl-sweetheart would ask it:

You say you goin' North.
You say you goin' North.
How 'bout yo' . . . lovin' gal?
You say you goin' North.

Then sighing in rhythmical despair:

O, don't you leave me here.
Babe, don't you leave me here.
Dog-gone yo' comin' back!
Said don't you leave me here.

On and on the song complained, man-verses and woman-verses, to the evening air in stanzas that Jimboy had heard in the pine-woods of Arkansas from the lumber-camp workers; in other stanzas that were desperate and dirty like the weary roads where they were sung; and in still others that the singer created spontaneously in his own mouth then and there:

O, I done made ma bed,
Says I done made ma bed.
Down in some lonesome grave
I done made ma bed.

It closed with a sad eerie twang.

"That's right decent," said Hager. "Now I wish you-all'd play some o' ma pieces like *When de Saints Come Marchin' In* or *This World Is Not Ma Home*—something Christian from de church."

"Aw, mama, it's not Sunday yet," said Harriett.

"Sing *Casey Jones*," called old man Tom Johnson. "That's ma song."

So the ballad of the immortal engineer with another mama in the Promised Land rang out promptly in the starry darkness, while everybody joined in the choruses.

"Aw, pick it, boy," yelled the old man. "Can't nobody play like you."

And Jimboy remembered when he was a lad in Memphis that W. C. Handy had said: "You ought to make your living out of that, son." But he hadn't followed it up—too many things to see, too many places to go, too many other jobs.

"What song do you like, Annjee?" he asked, remembering her presence again.

"O, I don't care. Any ones you like. All of 'em are pretty." She was pleased and petulant and a little startled that he had asked her.

"All right, then," he said. "Listen to me:"

Here I is in de mean ole jail.
Ain't got nobody to go ma bail.
Lonesome an' sad an' chain gang bound—
Ever' friend I had's done turned me down.

"That's sho it!" shouted Tom Johnson in great sympathy. "Now, when I was in de Turner County Jail . . ."

"Shut up yo' mouth!" squelched Sarah, jabbing her husband in the ribs.

The songs went on, blues, shouts, jingles, old hits: *Bon Bon Buddy, the Chocolate Drop*; *Wrap Me in Your Big Red Shawl*; *Under the Old Apple Tree*; *Turkey in the Straw*—Jimboy and Harriett breaking the silence of the small-town summer night until Aunt Hager interrupted:

"You-all better wind up, chillens, 'cause I wants to go to bed. I ain't used to stayin' 'wake so late, nohow. Play something kinder decent there, son, fo' you stops."

Jimboy, to tease the old woman, began to rock and moan like an elder in the Sanctified Church, patting both feet at the same time as he played a hymn-like, lugubrious tune with a dancing overtone:

Tell me, sister,
Tell me, brother,
Have you heard de latest news?

Then seriously as if he were about to announce the coming of the Judgment:

A woman down in Georgia
Got her two sweet-men confused.

How terrible! How sad! moaned the guitar.

One knocked on de front do',
One knocked on de back—

Sad, sad . . . sad, sad! said the music.

Now that woman down in Georgia's
Door-knob is hung with black.

O, play that funeral march, boy! while the guitar laughed a dirge.

An' de hearse is comin' easy
With two rubber-tired hacks!

Followed by a long-out, churchlike:

Amen . . . !

Then with rapid glides, groans, and shouts the instrument screamed of a sudden in profane frenzy, and Harriett began to ball-the-jack, her arms flopping like the wings of a headless pigeon, the guitar strings whining in ecstasy, the player rocking gaily to the urgent music, his happy mouth crying: "Tack 'em on down, gal! Tack 'em on down, Harrie!"

But Annjee had risen.

"I wish you'd come in and eat the ham I brought you," she said as she picked up her chair and started towards the house. "And you, Sandy! Get up from under that tree and go to bed." She spoke roughly to the little fellow, whom the songs had set a-dreaming. Then to her husband: "Jimboy, I wish you'd come in."

The man stopped playing, with a deep vibration of the strings that seemed to echo through the whole world. Then he leaned his guitar against the side of the house and lifted straight up in his hairy arms Annjee's plump, brown-black little body while he kissed her as she wriggled like a stubborn child, her soft breasts rubbing his hard body through the coarse blue shirt.

"You don't like my old songs, do you, baby? You don't want to hear me sing 'em," he said, laughing. "Well, that's all right. I like you, anyhow, and I like your ham, and I like your kisses, and I like everything you bring me. Let's go in and chow down." And he carried her into the kitchen, where he sat with her on his knees as he ate the food she so faithfully had brought him from Mrs. J. J. Rice's dinner-table.

Outside, Willie-Mae went running home through the dark. And Harriett pumped a cool drink of water for her mother, then helped her to rise from her low seat, Sandy aiding from behind, with both hands pushing firmly in Aunt Hager's fleshy back. Then the three of them came into the house and glanced, as they passed through the kitchen, at Annjee sitting on Jimboy's lap with both dark arms tight around his neck.

"Looks like you're clinging to the Rock of Ages," said Harriett to her sister. "Be sure you don't slip, old evil gal!"

But at midnight, when the owl that nested in a tree near the corner began to hoot, they were all asleep—Annjee and Jimboy in one room, Harriett and Hager in another, with Sandy on the floor at the foot of his grandmother's bed. Far away on the railroad line a whistle blew, lonesome and long.

6

WORK

THE SUNFLOWERS IN Willie-Mae's back yard were taller than Tom Johnson's head, and the hollyhocks in the fence corners were almost as high. The nasturtiums, blood-orange and gold, tumbled over themselves all around Madam de Carter's house. Aunt Hager's sweet-william, her pinks, and her tiger-lilies were abloom and the apples on her single tree would soon be ripe. The adjoining yards of the three neighbors were gay with flowers. "Watch out for them dogs!" his grandmother told Sandy hourly, for the days had come when the bright heat made gentle animals go mad. Bees were heavy with honey, great green flies hummed through the air, yellow-black butterflies suckled at the rambling roses . . . and watermelons were on the market.

The Royal African Knights and Ladies of King Solomon's Scepter were preparing a drill for the September Emancipation celebration, a "Drill of All Nations," in which Annjee was to represent Sweden. It was not to be given for a month or more, but the first rehearsal would take place tonight.

"Sandy," his mother said, shaking him early in the morning as he lay on his pallet at the foot of Aunt Hager's bed, "listen here! I want you to come out to Mis' Rice's this evening and help me get through the dishes so's I can start home early, in time to wash and dress myself to go to the lodge hall. You hears me?"

"Yes'm," said Sandy, keeping his eyes closed to the bright stream of morning sunlight entering the window. But half an hour later, when Jimboy kicked him and said: "Hey, ho! You wanta go fishin'?" he got up at once, slid into his pants; and together they went out in the garden to dig worms. It was seldom that his father took him anywhere, and, of course, he wanted to go. Sandy adored Jimboy, but Jimboy, amiable and indulgent though he was, did not often care to be bothered with his ten-year-old son on his fishing expeditions.

Harriett had gone to her job, and Hager had long been at the tubs under the apple-tree when the two males emerged from the kitchen-door. "Huh! You ain't workin' this mawnin', is you?" the old woman grunted, bending steadily down, then up, over the wash-board.

"Nope," her tall son-in-law answered. "Donahoe laid me off yesterday on account o' the white bricklayers said they couldn't lay bricks with a nigger."

"Always something to keep you from workin'," panted Hager.

"Sure is," agreed Jimboy pleasantly. "But don't worry, me and Sandy's gonna catch you a mess o' fish for supper today. How's that, ma?"

"Don't need no fish," the old woman answered. "An' don't come ma-in' me! Layin' round here fishin' when you ought to be out makin' money to take care o' this house an' that chile o' your'n." The suds rose foamy white about her black arms as the clothes plushed up and down on the zinc wash-board. "Lawd deliver me from a lazy darky!"

But Jimboy and Sandy were already behind the tall corn, digging for bait near the back fence.

"Don't never let no one woman worry you," said the boy's father softly, picking the moist wriggling worms from the up-turned loam. "Treat 'em like chickens, son. Throw 'em a little corn and they'll run after you, but don't give 'em too much. If you do, they'll stop layin' and expect you to wait on 'em."

"Will they?" asked Sandy.

The warm afternoon sun made the river a languid sheet of muddy gold, glittering away towards the bridge and the flour-mills a mile and a half off. Here in the quiet, on the end of a rotting jetty among the reeds, Jimboy and his son sat silently. A long string of small silver fish hung down into the water, keeping fresh, and the fishing-lines were flung far out in the stream, waiting for more bites. Not a breeze on the flat brown-gold river, not a ripple, not a sound. But once the train came by behind them, pouring out a great cloud of smoke and cinders and shaking the jetty.

"That's Number Five," said Jimboy. "Sure is flyin'," as the train disappeared between rows of empty box-cars far down the track, sending back a hollow clatter as it shot past the flour-mills, whose stacks could be dimly seen through the heat haze. Once the engine's whistle moaned shrilly.

"She's gone now," said Jimboy as the last click of the wheels died away. And, except for the drone of a green fly about the can of bait, there was again no sound to disturb the two fishermen.

Jimboy gazed at his lines. Across the river Sandy could make out, in the brilliant sunlight, the gold of wheat-fields and the green of trees on the hills. He wondered if it would be nice to live over there in the country.

"Man alive!" his father cried suddenly, hauling vigorously at one of the lines. "Sure got a real bite now. . . . Look at this catfish." From the water he pulled a large flopping lead-colored creature, with a fierce white mouth bleeding and gaping over the hook.

"He's on my line!" yelled Sandy. "I caught him!"

"Pshaw!" laughed Jimboy. "You was setting there dreaming."

"No, I wasn't!"

But just then, at the mills, the five-o'clock whistles blew. "Oh, gee, dad!" cried the boy, frightened. "I was s'posed to go to Mis' Rice's to help mama, and I come near forgetting it. She wants to get through early this evenin' to go to the lodge meeting. I gotta hurry and go help her."

"Well, you better beat it then, and I'll look out for your line like I been doing and bring the fishes home."

So the little fellow balanced himself across the jetty, scrambled up the bank, and ran down the railroad track towards town. He was quite out of breath when he reached the foot of Penrose Street, with Mrs. Rice's house still ten blocks away, so he walked awhile, then ran again, down the long residential street, with its large houses sitting in green shady lawns far back from the sidewalk. Sometimes a sprinkler attached to a long rubber hose, sprayed fountain-like jets of cold water on the thirsty grass. In one yard three golden-haired little girls were playing under an elm-tree, and in another a man and some children were having a leisurely game of croquet.

Finally Sandy turned into a big yard. The delicious scent of frying beefsteak greeted the sweating youngster as he reached the screen of the white lady's kitchen-door. Inside, Annjee was standing over the hot stove seasoning something in a saucepan, beads of perspiration on her dark face, and large damp spots under the arms of her dress.

"You better get here!" she said. "And me waiting for you for the last hour. Here, take this pick and break some ice for the tea." Sandy climbed up on a stool and raised the ice-box lid while his mother opened the oven and pulled out a pan of golden-brown biscuits. "Made these for your father," she remarked. "The white folks ain't asked for 'em, but they like 'em, too, so they can serve for both. . . . Jimboy's crazy about biscuits. . . . Did he work today?"

"No'm," said Sandy, jabbing at the ice. "We went fishing."

At that moment Mrs. Rice came into the kitchen, tall and blond, in a thin flowered gown. She was a middle-aged white woman with a sharp nasal voice.

"Annjee, I'd like the potatoes served just as they are in the casserole. And make several slices of very thin toast for my father. Now, be sure they *are* thin!"

"Yes, m'am," said Annjee stirring a spoonful of flour into the frying-pan, making a thick brown gravy.

"Old thin toast," muttered Annjee when Mrs. Rice had gone back to the front. "Always bothering round the kitchen! Here 'tis lodge-meeting night—dinner late anyhow—and she coming telling me to stop and make toast for the old man! He ain't too indigestible to eat biscuits like the rest of 'em. . . . White folks sure is a case!" She laid three slices of bread on top of the stove. "So spoiled with colored folks waiting on 'em all their days! Don't know what they'll do in heaven, 'cause I'm gonna sit down up there myself."

Annjee took the biscuits, light and brown, and placed some on a pink plate she had warmed. She carried them, with the butter and jelly, into the dining-room. Then she took the steak from the warmer, dished up the vegetables into gold-rimmed serving-dishes, and poured the gravy, which smelled deliciously onion-flavored.

"Gee, I'm hungry," said the child, with his eyes on the big steak ready to go in to the white people.

"Well, just wait," replied his mother. "You come to work, not to eat. . . . Whee! but it's hot today!" She wiped her wet face and put on a large white bungalow apron that had been hanging behind the door. Then she went with the iced tea and a pitcher of water into the dining-room, struck a Chinese gong, and came back to the kitchen to get the dishes of steaming food, which she carried in to the table.

It was some time before she returned from waiting on the table; so Sandy, to help her, began to scrape out the empty pans and put them to soak in the sink. He ate the stewed corn that had stuck in the bottom of one, and rubbed a piece of bread in the frying-pan where the gravy had been. His mother came out with the water-pitcher, broke some ice for it, and returned to the dining-room where Sandy could hear laughter, and the clinking of spoons in tea-glasses, and women talking. When Annjee came back into the kitchen, she took four custards from the ice-box and placed them on gold-rimmed plates.

"They're about through," she said to her son. "Sit down and I'll fix you up."

Sandy was very hungry and he hoped Mrs. Rice's family hadn't eaten all the steak, which had looked so good with its brown gravy and onions.

Shortly, his mother returned carrying the dishes that had been filled with hot food. She placed them on the kitchen-table in front of Sandy, but they were no longer full and no longer hot. The corn had thickened to a paste, and the potatoes were about gone; but there was still a ragged piece of steak left on the platter.

"Don't eat it all," said Annjee warningly. "I want to take some home to your father."

The bell rang in the dining-room. Annjee went through the swinging door and returned bearing a custard that had been but little touched.

"Here, sonny—the old man says it's too sweet for his stomach, so you can have this." She set the yellow cornstarch before Sandy. "He's seen these ripe peaches out here today and he wants some, that's all. More trouble than he's worth, po' old soul, and me in a hurry!" She began to peel the fruit. "Just like a chile, 'deed he is!" she added, carrying the sliced peaches into the dining-room and leaving Sandy with a plate of food before him, eating slowly. "When you rushing to get out, seems like white folks tries theirselves."

In a moment she returned, ill-tempered, and began to scold Sandy for taking so long with his meal.

"I asked you to help me so's I can get to the lodge on time, and you just set and chew and eat! . . . Here, wipe these dishes, boy!" Annjee began hurriedly to lay plates in a steaming row on the shelf of the sink; so Sandy got up and, between mouthfuls of pudding, wiped them with a large dish-towel.

Soon Mrs. Rice came into the kitchen again, briskly, through the swinging door and glanced about her. Sandy felt ashamed for the white woman to see him eating a left-over pudding from her table, so he put the spoon down.

"Annjee," the mistress said sharply. "I wish you wouldn't put quite so much onion in your sauce for the steak. I've mentioned it to you several times before, and you know very well we don't like it."

"Yes, m'am," said Annjee.

"And do *please* be careful that our drinking water is cold before meals are served. . . . You were certainly careless tonight. You must think more about what you are doing, Annjee."

Mrs. Rice went out again through the swinging door, but Sandy stood near the sink with a burning face and eyes that had suddenly filled with angry tears. He couldn't help it—hearing his sweating mother reprimanded by this tall white woman in the flowered dress. Black, hard-working Annjee answered: "Yes, m'am," and that was all—but Sandy cried.

"Dry up," his mother said crossly when she saw him, thinking he was crying because she had asked him to work. "What's come over you, anyway?—can't even wipe a few plates for me and act nice about it!"

He didn't answer. When the dining-room had been cleared and the kitchen put in order, Annjee told him to empty the garbage while she wrapped in newspapers several little bundles of food to carry to Jimboy. Then they went out the back door, around the big house to the street, and trudged the fourteen blocks to Aunt Hager's, taking short cuts through alleys, passing under arc-lights that sputtered whitely in the deepening twilight, and greeting with an occasional "Howdy" other poor colored folks also coming home from work.

"How are you, Sister Jones?"

"Right smart, I thank yuh!" as they passed.

Once Annjee spoke to her son. "Evening's the only time we niggers have to ourselves!" she said. "Thank God for night . . . 'cause all day you gives to white folks."

7
WHITE FOLKS

WHEN THEY GOT home, Aunt Hager was sitting in the cool of the evening on her new porch, which had been rebuilt for thirty-five dollars added to the mortgage. The old woman was in her rocking-chair, with Jimboy, one foot on the ground and his back against a pillar, lounging at her feet. The two were quarrelling amicably over nothing as Annjee and Sandy approached.

"Good-evenin', you-all," said Annjee. "I brought you a nice piece o' steak, Jimboy-sugar, and some biscuits to go with it. Come on in and eat while I get dressed to go to the drill practice. I got to hurry."

"We don't want no steak now," Jimboy answered without moving. "Aunt Hager and me had fresh fish for supper and egg-corn-bread and we're full. We don't need nothin' more."

"Oh! . . ." said Annjee disappointedly. "Well, come on in anyhow, honey, and talk while I get dressed." So he rose lazily and followed his wife into the house.

Shortly, Sister Johnson, pursued by the ever-present Willie-Mae, came through the blue-grey darkness from next door. "Good-evenin', Sister Williams; how you been today?"

"Tolable," answered Hager, " 'ceptin' I's tired out from washin' an' rinsin'. Have a seat. . . . You Sandy, go in de house an' get Sister Johnson a settin'-chair. . . . Where's Tom?"

"Lawd, chile, he done gone to bed long ago. That there sewer-diggin' job ain't so good fer a man old as Tom. He 'bout played out. . . . I done washed fer Mis' Cohn maself today. . . . Umh! dis cheer feels good! . . . Looked like to me she had near 'bout fifty babies' diddies in de wash. You know she done got twins, 'sides dat young-'un born last year."

The conversation of the two old women rambled on as their

grandchildren ran across the front yard laughing, shrieking, wrestling; catching fire-flies and watching them glow in closed fists, then releasing them to twinkle in the sultry night-air.

Harriett came singing out of the house and sat down on the edge of the porch. "Lord, it's hot! . . . How are you, Mis' Johnson? I didn't see you in the dark."

"Jest tolable, chile," said the old woman, "but I can't kick. Honey, when you gits old as I is, you'll be doin' well if you's livin' a-tall, de way you chillens runs round now days! How come you ain't out to some party dis evenin'?"

"O, there's no party tonight," said Harriett laughing. "Besides, this new job of mine's a heart-breaker, Mis' Johnson. I got to stay home and rest now. I'm kitchen-girl at that New Albert Restaurant, and time you get through wrestling with pots and arguing with white waitresses and colored cooks, you don't feel much like running out at night. But the shifts aren't bad, though, food's good, and—well, you can't expect everything." She shrugged her shoulders against the two-by-four pillar on which her back rested.

"Long's it keeps you off de streets, I's glad," said Hager, rocking contentedly. "Maybe I can git you goin' to church agin now."

"Aw, I don't like church," the girl replied.

"An', chile, I can't blame you much," said Sister Johnson, fumbling in the pocket of her apron. "De way dese churches done got now days. . . . Sandy, run in de house an' ask yo' pappy fo' a match to light ma pipe. . . . It ain't 'Come to Jesus' no mo' a-tall. Ministers dese days an' times don't care nothin' 'bout po' Jesus. 'Stead o' dat it's rally dis an' collection dat, an' de aisle wants a new carpet, an' de pastor needs a 'lectric fan fer his red-hot self." The old sister spat into the yard. "Money! That's all 'tis! An' white folkses' religion—Lawd help! 'Taint no use in mentionin' them."

"True," agreed Hager.

"Cause if de gates o' heaven shuts in white folkses' faces like de do's o' dey church in us niggers' faces, it'll be too bad! Yes, sir! One thing sho, de Lawd ain't prejudiced!"

"No," said Hager; "but He don't love ugly, neither in niggers nor in white folks."

"Now, talking about white folks' religion," said Annjee, emerging from the house with a fresh white dress on, "why, Mis' Rice where I work don't think no more about playing bridge on Sunday than she does about praying—and I ain't never seen her pray yet."

"You're nuts," said Jimboy behind her. "People's due to have a little fun on Sundays. That's what's the matter with colored folks now—work all week and then set up in church all day Sunday, and don't even know what's goin' on in the rest of the world."

"Huh!" grunted Hager.

"Well, we won't argue, daddy," Annjee smiled. "Come on and walk a piece with me, sweetness. Here 'tis nearly nine and I should a been at the hall at eight, but colored folks are always behind the clock. Come on, Jimboy."

"Good-bye, mama," yelled Sandy from the lawn as his parents strolled up the street together.

"Jimboy's right," said Harriett. "Darkies do like the church too much, but white folks don't care nothing about it at all. They're too busy getting theirs out of this world, not from God. And I don't blame 'em, except that they're so mean to niggers. They're right, though, looking out for themselves . . . and yet I hate 'em for it. They don't have to mistreat us besides, do they?"

"Honey, don't talk that way," broke in Hager. "It ain't Christian, chile. If you don't like 'em, pray for 'em, but don't feel evil against 'em. I was in slavery, Harrie, an' I been knowin' white folks all ma life, an' they's good as far as they can see—but when it comes to po' niggers, they just can't see far, that's all."

Harriett opened her mouth to reply, but Jimboy, who left Annjee at the corner and had returned to the porch, beat her to it. "We too dark for 'em, ma," he laughed. "How they gonna see in the dark? You colored folks oughta get lighter, that's what!"

"Shut up yo' mouth, you yaller rooster!" said Sister Johnson. "White folks is white folks, an' dey's mean! I can't help what

Hager say," the old woman disagreed emphatically with her crony. "Ain't I been knowin' crackers sixty-five years, an' ain't dey de cause o' me bein' here in Stanton 'stead o' in ma home right today? De dirty buzzards! Ain't I nussed t'ree of 'em up from babies like ma own chillens, and ain't dem same t'ree boys done turned round an' helped run me an' Tom out o' town?"

The old sister took a long draw on her corn-cob pipe, and a fiery red spot glowed in its bowl, while Willie-Mae and Sandy stopped playing and sat down on the porch as she began a tale they had all heard at least a dozen times.

"I's tole you 'bout it befo', ain't I?" asked Sister Johnson.

"Not me," lied Jimboy, who was anxious to keep her going.

"No, you haven't," Harriett assured her.

"Well, it were like dis," and the story unwound itself, the preliminary details telling how, as a young freed-girl after the Civil War, Sister Johnson had gone into service for a white planter's family in a Mississippi town near Vicksburg. While attached to this family, she married Tom Johnson, then a field-hand, and raised five children of her own during the years that followed, besides caring for three boys belonging to her white mistress, nursing them at her black breasts and sometimes leaving her own young ones in the cabin to come and stay with her white charges when they were ill. These called her mammy, too, and when they were men and married, she still went to see them and occasionally worked for their families.

"Now, we niggers all lived at de edge o' town in what de whites called Crowville, an' most of us owned little houses an' farms, an' we did right well raisin' cotton an' sweet 'taters an' all. Now, dat's where de trouble started! We was doin' too well, an' de white folks said so! But we ain't paid 'em no 'tention, jest thought dey was talkin' fer de pastime of it. . . . Well, we all started fixin' up our houses an' paintin' our fences, an' Crowville looked kinder decent-like when de white folks 'gin to 'mark, so's we servants could hear 'em, 'bout niggers livin' in painted houses an' dressin' fine like we was somebody! . . . Well, dat went on fer some time wid de whites talkin' an' de coloreds doin' better'n better year by year, sellin' mo' cotton ever' day an' gittin' nice furniture an' buyin' pianers, till by an' by a prosp'rous nigger named John Lowdins up an' bought one o' dese here new autimobiles—an' dat settled it! . . . A white man in town one Sat'day night tole John to git out o'dat damn car 'cause a nigger ain't got no business wid a autimobile nohow! An' John say: 'I ain't gonna git out!' Den de white man, what's been drinkin', jump up on de runnin'-bo'ad an' bust John in de mouth fer talkin' back to him—he a white man, an' Lowdins nothin' but a nigger. 'De very idee!' he say, and hit John in de face six or seven times. Den John drawed his gun! One! two! t'ree! he fiah, hit dis old red-neck cracker in de shoulder, but he ain't dead! Ain't nothin' meant to kill a cracker what's drunk. But John think he done kilt this white man, an' so he left him kickin' in de street while he runs that car o' his'n lickety-split out o' town, goes to Vicksburg, an' catches de river boat. . . . Well, sir! Dat night Crowville's plumb full o' white folks wid dogs an' guns an' lanterns, shoutin' an' yellin' an' scarin' de wits out o' us coloreds an' wakin' us up way late in de night-time lookin' fer John, an' dey don't find him. . . . Den dey say dey gwine teach dem Crowville niggers a lesson, all of 'em, paintin' dey houses an' buyin' cars an' livin' like white folks, so dey comes to our do's an' tells us to leave our houses—git de hell out in de fields, 'cause dey don't want to kill nobody there dis evenin'! . . . Well, sir! Niggers in night-gowns an' underwear an' shimmies, half-naked an' barefooted, was runnin' ever' which way in de dark, scratchin' up dey legs in de briah patches, fallin' on dey faces, scared to death! Po' ole Pheeny, what ain't moved from her bed wid de paralytics fo' six years, dey made her daughters carry her out, screamin' an' wall-eyed, an' set her in de middle o' de cotton-patch. An' Brian, what was sleepin' naked, jumps up an' grabs his wife's apron and runs like a rabbit with not another blessed thing on! Chillens squallin' ever'where, an' mens a-pleadin' an' a-cussin', an' womens cryin' 'Lawd 'a' Mercy' wid de whites of dey eyes showin'! . . . Den looked like to me 'bout five hundred white mens took torches an' started burnin' wid fiah ever' last house, an' hen-house, an' shack, an' barn, an' privy, an' shed, an' cow-slant in de place! An' all de niggers, when de fiah blaze up, was moanin' in de fields, callin' on de Lawd fer help! An' de fiah light up de whole country clean back to de woods! You could smell fiah, an' you could see it red, an' taste de smoke, an' feel it stingin' yo' eyes. An' you could hear de bo'ads a-fallin' an' de glass a-poppin', an' po' animals roastin' an' fryin' an' a-tearin' at dey halters. An' one cow run out, fiah all ovah, wid her milk streamin' down. An' de smoke roll up, de cotton-fields were red . . . an' dey ain't been no mo' Crowville after dat night. No, sir! De white folks ain't left nothin' fer de niggers, not nary bo'ad standin' one 'bove another, not even a dog-house. . . . When it were done—nothin' but ashes! . . . De white mens was ever'where wid guns, scarin' de po' blacks an' keepin' 'em off, an' one of 'em say: 'I got good mind to try yo'-all's hide, see is it bullet proof—gittin' so prosp'rous, paintin' yo' houses an' runnin ovah white folks wid yo' damn gasoline buggies! Well, after dis you'll damn sight have to bend yo' backs an' work a little!' . . . Dat's what de white man say. . . . But we didn't—not yit! 'Cause ever' last nigger moved from there dat Sunday mawnin'. It were right funny to see ole folks what ain't never been out o' de backwoods pickin' up dey feet an' goin'. Ma Bailey say: 'De Lawd done let me live eighty years in one place, but ma next eighty'll be spent in St. Louis.' An' she started out walkin' wid neither bag nor baggage. . . . An' me an' Tom took Willie-Mae an' went to Cairo, an' Tom started railroad-workin' wid a gang; then we come on up here, been five summers ago dis August. We ain't had not even a rag o' clothes when we left Crowville—so don't tell me 'bout white folks bein' good, Hager, 'cause I knows 'em. . . . Yes, indeedy, I really knows 'em. . . . Dey done made us leave our home."

The old woman knocked her pipe against the edge of the porch, emptying its dead ashes into the yard, and for a moment no one spoke. Sandy, trembling, watched a falling star drop behind the trees. Then Jimboy's deep voice, like a bitter rumble in the dark, broke the silence.

"I know white folks, too," he said. "I lived in the South."

"And I ain't never been South," added Harriett hoarsely, "but I know 'em right here . . . and I hate 'em!"

"De Lawd hears you," said Hager.

"I don't care if He does hear me, mama! You and Annjee are too easy. You just take whatever white folks give you—*coon* to your face, and *nigger* behind your backs—and don't say nothing. You run to some white person's back door for every job you get, and then they pay you one dollar for five dollars' worth of work, and fire you whenever they get ready."

"They do that all right," said Jimboy. "They don't mind firin' you. Wasn't I layin' brick on the *Daily Leader* building and the white union men started sayin' they couldn't work with me because I wasn't in the union? So the boss come up and paid me off. 'Good man, too,' he says to me, 'but I can't buck the union.' So I said I'd join, but I knew they wouldn't let me before I went to the office. Anyhow, I tried. I told the guys there I was a bricklayer and asked 'em how I was gonna work if I couldn't be in the union. And the fellow who had the cards, secretary I guess he was, says kinder sharp, like he didn't want to be bothered: 'That's your look-out, big boy, not mine.' So you see how much the union cares if a black man works or not."

"Ain't Tom had de same trouble?" affirmed Sister Johnson. "Got put off de job mo'n once on 'count o' de white unions."

"O, they've got us cornered, all right," said Jimboy. "The white folks are like farmers that own all the cows and let the niggers take care of 'em. Then they make you pay a sweet price for skimmed milk and keep the cream for themselves—but I reckon cream's too rich for rusty-kneed niggers anyhow!"

They laughed.

"That's a good one!" said Harriett. "You know old man Wright, what owns the flour-mill and the new hotel—how he made his start off colored women working in his canning factory? Well, when he built that orphan home for colored and gave it to the city last year, he had the whole place made just about the size of the dining-room at his own house. They got the little niggers in that asylum cooped up like chickens. And the reason he built it was to get the colored babies out of the city home, with its nice playgrounds, because he thinks the two races oughtn't to mix! But he don't care how hard he works his colored help in that canning factory of his, does he? Wasn't I there thirteen hours a day in tomato season? Nine cents an hour and five cents overtime after ten hours—and you better work overtime if you want to keep the job! . . . As for the races mixing—ask some of those high yellow women who work there. They know a mighty lot about the races mixing!"

"Most of 'em lives in de Bottoms, where de sportin' houses are," said Hager. "It's a shame de way de white mens keeps them sinful places goin'."

"It ain't Christian, is it?" mocked Harriett . . . . "White folks!" . . . And she shrugged her shoulders scornfully. Many disagreeable things had happened to her through white folks. Her first surprising and unpleasantly lasting impression of the pale world had come when, at the age of five, she had gone alone one day to play in a friendly white family's yard. Some mischievous small boys there, for the fun of it, had taken hold of her short kinky braids and pulled them, dancing round and round her and yelling: "Blackie! Blackie! Blackie!" while she screamed and tried to run away. But they held her and pulled her hair terribly, and her friends laughed because she *was* black and she *did* look funny. So from that time on, Harriett had been uncomfortable in the presence of whiteness, and that early hurt had grown with each new incident into a rancor that she could not hide and a dislike that had become pain.

Now, because she could sing and dance and was always amusing, many of the white girls in high school were her friends. But when the three-thirty bell rang and it was time to go home, Harriett knew their polite "Good-bye" was really a kind way of saying: "We can't be seen on the streets with a colored girl." To loiter with these same young ladies had been all right during their grade-school years, when they were all younger, but now they had begun to feel the eyes of young white boys staring from the windows of pool halls, or from the tennis-courts near the park—so it was not proper to be seen with Harriett.

But a very unexpected stab at the girl's pride had come only a few weeks ago when she had gone with her class-mates, on tickets issued by the school, to see an educational film of the under-sea world at the Palace Theatre, on Main Street. It was a special performance given for the students, and each class had had seats allotted to them beforehand; so Harriett sat with her class and had begun to enjoy immensely the strange wonders of the ocean depths when an usher touched her on the shoulder.

"The last three rows on the left are for colored," the girl in the uniform said.

"I—But—But I'm with my class," Harriett stammered. "We're all supposed to sit here."

"I can't help it," insisted the usher, pointing towards the rear of the theatre, while her voice carried everywhere. "Them's the house rules. No argument now—you'll have to move."

So Harriett rose and stumbled up the dark aisle and out into the sunlight, her slender body hot with embarrassment and rage. The teacher saw her leave the theatre without a word of protest, and none of her white class-mates defended her for being black. They didn't care.

"All white people are alike, in school and out," Harriett concluded bitterly, as she told of her experiences to the folks sitting with her on the porch in the dark.

Once, when she had worked for a Mrs. Leonard Baker on Martin Avenue, she accidentally broke a precious cut-glass pitcher used to serve some out-of-town guests. And when she tried to apologize for the accident, Mrs. Baker screamed in a rage: "Shut up, you impudent little black wench! Talking back to me after breaking up my dishes. All you darkies are alike—careless sluts—and I wouldn't have a one of you in my house if I could get anybody else to work for me without paying a fortune. You're all impossible."

"So that's the way white people feel," Harriett said to Aunt Hager and Sister Johnson and Jimboy, while the two children listened. "They wouldn't have a single one of us around if they could help it. It don't matter to them if we're shut out of a job. It don't matter to them if niggers have only the back row at the movies. It don't matter to them when they hurt our feelings without caring and treat us like slaves down South and like beggars up North. No, it don't matter to them. . . . White folks run the world, and the only thing colored folks are expected to do is work and grin and take off their hats as though it don't matter. . . . O, I hate 'em!" Harriett cried, so fiercely that Sandy was afraid. "I hate white folks!" she said to everybody on the porch in the darkness. "You can pray for 'em if you want to, mama, but I hate 'em! . . . I hate white folks! . . . I hate 'em all!"

8
DANCE

MRS. J. J. RICE and family usually spent ten days during the August heat at Lake Dale, and thither they had gone now, giving Annjee a forced vacation with no pay. Jimboy was not working, and so his wife found ten days of rest without income not especially agreeable. Nevertheless, she decided that she might as well enjoy the time; so she and Jimboy went to the country for a week with Cousin Jessie, who had married one of the colored farmers of the district. Besides, Annjee thought that Jimboy might help on the farm and so make a little money. Anyway, they would get plenty to eat, because Jessie kept a good table. And since Jessie had eight children of her own, they did not take Sandy with them—eight were enough for a woman to be worried with at one time!

Aunt Hager had been ironing all day on the Reinharts' clothes—it was Friday. At seven o'clock Harriett came home, but she had already eaten her supper at the restaurant where she worked.

"Hello, mama! Hy, Sandy!" she said, but that was all, because she and her mother were not on the best of terms. Aunt Hager was attempting to punish her youngest daughter by not allowing her to leave the house after dark, since Harriett, on Tuesday night, had been out until one o'clock in the morning with no better excuse than a party at Maudel's. Aunt Hager had threatened to whip her then and there that night.

"You ain't had a switch on yo' hide fo' three years, but don't think you's gettin' too big fo' me not to fan yo' behind, madam. 'Spare de rod an' spoil de chile,' that's what de Bible say, an' Lawd knows you sho is spoiled! De idee of a young gal yo' age stayin' out till one o'clock in de mawnin', an' me not knowed where you's at. . . . Don't you talk back to me! . . . You rests in this house ever' night this week an' don't put yo' foot out o' this yard after you comes from work, that's what you do. Lawd knows I don't know what I's gonna do with you. I works fo' you an' I prays fo' you, an' if you don't mind, I's sho gonna whip you, even if you is goin' on seventeen years old!"

Tonight as soon as she came from work Harriett went into her mother's room and lay across the bed. It was very warm in the little four-room house, and all the windows and doors were open.

"We's got some watermelon here, daughter," Hager called from the kitchen. "Don't you want a nice cool slice?"

"No," the girl replied. She was fanning herself with a palm-leaf fan, her legs in their cheap silk stockings hanging over the side of the bed, and her heels kicking the floor. Benbow's Band played tonight for the dance at Chaver's Hall, and everybody was going—but her. Gee, it was hard to have a Christian mother! Harriett kicked her slippers off with a bang and rolled over on her stomach, burying her powdery face in the pillows. . . . Somebody knocked at the back door.

A boy's voice was speaking excitedly to Hager: "Hemorrhages . . . and papa can't stop 'em . . . she's coughin' something terrible . . . says can't you please come over and help him"—frightened and out of breath.

"Do, Jesus!" cried Hager. "I'll be with you right away, chile. Don't worry." She rushed into the bedroom to change her apron. "You Harriett, listen; Sister Lane's taken awful sick an' Jimmy says she's bleedin' from de mouth. If I ain't back by nine o'clock, see that that chile Sandy's in de bed. An' you know you ain't to leave this yard under no circumstances. . . . Po' Mis' Lane! She sho do have it hard." In a whisper: "I 'spects she's got de T. B., that what I 'spects!" And the old woman hustled out to join the waiting youngster. Jimmy was leaning against the door, looking at Sandy, and neither of the boys knew what to say. Jimmy Lane wore his mother's cast-off shoes to school, and Sandy used to tease him, but tonight he didn't tease his friend about his shoes.

"You go to bed 'fore it gets late," said his grandmother, starting down the alley with Jimmy.

"Yes'm," Sandy called after her. "So long, Jim!" He stood under the apple-tree and watched them disappear.

Aunt Hager had scarcely gotten out of sight when there was a loud knock at the front door, and Sandy ran around the house to see Harriett's boy friend, Mingo, standing in the dusk outside the screen-door, waiting to be let in.

Mingo was a patent-leather black boy with wide, alive nostrils and a mouth that split into a lighthouse smile on the least provocation. His body was heavy and muscular, resting on bowed legs that curved backward as though the better to brace his chunky torso; and his hands were hard from mixing concrete and digging ditches for the city's new water-mains.

"I know it's tonight, but I can't go," Sandy heard his aunt say at the door. They were speaking of Benbow's dance. "And his band don't come here often, neither. I'm heart-sick having to stay home, dog-gone it all, especially this evening!"

"Aw, come on and go anyway," pleaded Mingo. "After I been savin' up my dough for two weeks to take you, and got my suit cleaned and pressed and all. Heck! If you couldn't go and knew it yesterday, why didn't you tell me? That's a swell way to treat a fellow!"

"Because I wanted to go," said Harriett; "and still want to go. . . . Don't make so much difference about mama, because she's mad anyhow . . . but what could we do with this kid? We can't leave him by himself." She looked at Sandy, who was standing behind Mingo listening to everything.

"You can take me," the child offered anxiously, his eyes dancing at the delightful prospect. "I'll behave, Harrie, if you take me, and I won't tell on you either. . . . Please lemme go, Mingo. I ain't never seen a big dance in my life. I wanta go."

"Should we?" asked Harriett doubtfully, looking at her boy friend standing firmly on his curved legs.

"Sure, if we got to have him . . . damn 'im!" Mingo replied. "Better the kid than no dance. Go git dressed." So Harriett made a dash for the clothes-closet, while Sandy ran to get a clean waist from one of his mother's dresser-drawers, and Mingo helped him put it on, cussing softly to himself all the while. "But it ain't your fault, pal, is it?" he said to the little boy.

"Sure not," Sandy replied. "I didn't tell Aunt Hager to make Harrie stay home. I tried to 'suade grandma to let her go," the child lied, because he liked Mingo. "I guess she won't care about her goin' to just one dance." He wanted to make everything all right so the young man wouldn't be worried. Besides, Sandy very much wanted to go himself.

"Let's beat it," Harriett shrilled excitedly before her dress was fastened, anxious to be gone lest her mother come home. She was powdering her face and neck in the next room, nervous, happy, and afraid all at once. The perfume, the voice, and the pat, pat, pat of the powder-puff came out to the waiting gentleman.

"Yo' car's here, madam," mocked Mingo. "Step right this way and let's be going!"

Wonder where ma easy rider's gone—
He done left me, put ma new gold watch in pawn!

Like a blare from hell the second encore of *Easy Rider* filled every cubic inch of the little hall with hip-rocking notes. Benbow himself was leading and the crowd moved like jellyfish dancing on individual sea-shells, with Mingo and Harriett somewhere among the shakers. But they were not of them, since each couple shook in a world of its own, as, with a weary wail, the music abruptly ceased.

Then, after scarcely a breath of intermission, the band struck up again with a lazy one-step. A tall brown boy in a light tan suit walked his partner straight down the whole length of the floor and, when he reached the corner, turned leisurely in one spot, body riding his hips, eyes on the ceiling, and his girl shaking her full breasts against his pink silk shirt. Then they recrossed the width of the room, turned slowly, repeating themselves, and began again to walk rhythmically down the hall, while the music was like a lazy river flowing between mountains, carving a canyon coolly, calmly, and without insistence. The *Lazy River One-Step* they might have called what the band was playing as the large crowd moved with the greatest ease about the hall. To drum-beats barely audible, the tall boy in the tan suit walked his partner round and round time after time, revolving at each corner with eyes up-lifted, while the piano was the water flowing, and the high, thin chords of the banjo were the mountains floating in the clouds. But in sultry tones, alone and always, the brass cornet spoke harshly about the earth.

Sandy sat against the wall in a hard wooden folding chair. There were other children scattered lonesomely about on chairs, too, watching the dancers, but he didn't seem to know any of them. When the music stopped, all the chairs quickly filled with loud-talking women and girls in brightly colored dresses who fanned themselves with handkerchiefs and wiped their sweating brows. Sandy thought maybe he should give his seat to one of the women when he saw Maudel approaching.

"Here, honey," she said. "Take this dime and buy yourself a bottle of something cold to drink. I know Harriett ain't got you on her mind out there dancin'. This music is certainly righteous, chile!" She laughed as she handed Sandy a coin and closed her pocketbook. He liked Maudel, although he knew his grandmother didn't. She was a large good-natured brown-skinned girl who walked hippishly and used too much rouge on her lips. But she always gave Sandy a dime, and she was always laughing.

He went through the crowd towards the soft-drink stand at the end of the hall. "Gimme a bottle o' cream soda," he said to the fat orange-colored man there, who had his sleeves rolled up and a white butcher's-apron covering his barrel-like belly. The man put his hairy arms down into a zinc tub full of ice and water and began pulling out bottles, looking at their caps, and then dropping them back into the cold liquid.

"Don't seem like we got no cream, sonny. How'd a lemon do you?" he asked above the bedlam of talking voices.

"Naw," said Sandy. "It's too sour."

On the improvised counter of boards the wares displayed consisted of cracker-jacks, salted peanuts, a box of gum, and

Sen Sens, while behind the counter was a lighted oil-stove holding a tin pan full of spare-ribs, sausage, and fish; and near it an ice-cream freezer covered with a brown sack. Some cases of soda were on the floor beside the zinc tub filled with bottles, in which the man was still searching.

"Nope, no cream," said the fat man.

"Well, gimme a fish sandwich then," Sandy replied, feeling very proud because some kids were standing near, looking at him as he made his purchase like a grown man.

"Buy me one, too," suggested a biscuit-colored little girl in a frilly dirty-white dress.

"I only got a dime," Sandy said. "But you can have half of mine." And he gallantly broke in two parts the double square of thick bread, with its hunk of greasy fish between, and gravely handed a portion to the grinning little girl.

"Thanks," she said, running away with the bread and fish in her hands.

"Shame on you!" teased a small boy, rubbing his forefingers at Sandy. "You got a girl! You got a girl!"

"Go chase yourself!" Sandy replied casually, as he picked out the bones and smacked his lips on the sweet fried fish. The orchestra was playing another one-step, with the dancers going like shuttles across the floor. Sandy saw his Aunt Harriett and a slender yellow boy named Billy Sanderlee doing a series of lazy, intricate steps as they wound through the crowd from one end of the hall to the other. Certain less accomplished couples were watching them with admiration.

Sandy, when he had finished eating, decided to look for the wash-room, where he could rinse his hands, because they were greasy and smelled fishy. It was at the far corner of the hall. As he pushed open the door marked GENTS, a thick grey cloud of cigarette-smoke drifted out. The stench of urine and gin and a crowd of men talking, swearing, and drinking licker surrounded the little boy as he elbowed his way towards the wash-bowls. All the fellows were shouting loudly to one another and making fleshy remarks about the women they had danced with.

"Boy, you ought to try Velma," a mahogany-brown boy yelled. "She sure can go."

"Hell," answered a whisky voice somewhere in the smoke. "That nappy-headed black woman? Gimme a high yaller for mine all de time. I can't use no coal!"

"Well, de blacker de berry, de sweeter de juice," protested a slick-haired ebony youth in the center of the place. . . . "Ain't that right, sport?" he demanded of Sandy, grabbing him jokingly by the neck and picking him up.

"I guess it is," said the child, scared, and the men laughed.

"Here, kid, buy yourself a drink," the slick-headed boy said, slipping Sandy a nickel as he set him down gently at the door. "And be sure it's pop—not gin."

Outside, the youngster dried his wet hands on a handkerchief, blinked his smoky eyes, and immediately bought the soda, a red strawberry liquid in a long, thick bottle.

Suddenly and without warning the cornet blared at the other end of the hall in an ear-splitting wail: "Whaw! . . . Whaw! . . . Whaw! . . . Whaw!" and the snare-drum rolled in answer. A pause . . . then the loud brassy notes were repeated and the banjo came in, "Plinka, plink, plink," like timid drops of rain after a terrific crash of thunder. Then quite casually, as though nothing had happened, the piano lazied into a slow drag, with all the other instruments following. And with the utmost nonchalance the drummer struck into time.

"Ever'body shake!" cried Benbow, as a ribbon of laughter swirled round the hall.

Couples began to sway languidly, melting together like candy in the sun as hips rotated effortlessly to the music. Girls snuggled pomaded heads on men's chests, or rested powdered chins on men's shoulders, while wild young boys put both arms tightly around their partners' waists and let their hands hang down carelessly over female haunches. Bodies moved ever so easily together—ever so easily, as Benbow turned towards his musicians and cried through cupped hands: "Aw, screech it, boys!"

A long, tall, gangling gal stepped back from her partner,

adjusted her hips, and did a few easy, gliding steps all her own before her man grabbed her again.

"Eu-o-oo-ooo-oooo!" moaned the cornet titillating with pain, as the banjo cried in stop-time, and the piano sobbed aloud with a rhythmical, secret passion. But the drums kept up their hard steady laughter—like somebody who don't care.

"I see you plowin', Uncle Walt," called a little autumn-leaf brown with switching skirts to a dark-purple man grinding down the center of the floor with a yellow woman. Two short prancing blacks stopped in their tracks to quiver violently. A bushy-headed girl threw out her arms, snapped her fingers, and began to holler: "Hey! . . . Hey!" while her perspiring partner held doggedly to each hip in an effort to keep up with her. All over the hall, people danced their own individual movements to the scream and moan of the music.

"Get low . . . low down . . . down!" cried the drummer, bouncing like a rubber ball in his chair. The banjo scolded in diabolic glee, and the cornet panted as though it were out of breath, and Benbow himself left the band and came out on the floor to dance slowly and ecstatically with a large Indian-brown woman covered with diamonds.

"Aw, do it, Mister Benbow!" one of his admirers shouted frenziedly as the hall itself seemed to tremble.

"High yallers, draw nigh! Brown-skins, come near!" somebody squalled. "But black gals, stay where you are!"

"Whaw! Whaw! Whaw!" mocked the cornet—but the steady tomtom of the drums was no longer laughter now, no longer even pleasant: the drum-beats had become sharp with surly sound, like heavy waves that beat angrily on a granite rock. And under the dissolute spell of its own rhythm the music had got quite beyond itself. The four black men in Benbow's wandering band were exploring depths to which mere sound had no business to go. Cruel, desolate, unadorned was their music now, like the body of a ravished woman on the sun-baked earth; violent and hard, like a giant standing over his bleeding mate in the blazing sun. The odors of bodies, the stings of flesh, and the utter emptiness of soul when all is done—these things the piano and the drums, the cornet and the twanging banjo insisted on hoarsely to a beat that made the dancers move, in that little hall, like pawns on a frenetic checker-board.

"Aw, play it, Mister Benbow!" somebody cried. The earth rolls relentlessly, and the sun blazes for ever on the earth, breeding, breeding. But why do you insist like the earth, music? Rolling and breeding, earth and sun for ever relentlessly. But why do you insist like the sun? Like the lips of women? Like the bodies of men, relentlessly?

"Aw, play it, Mister Benbow!"

But why do you insist, music?

Who understands the earth? Do you, Mingo? Who understands the sun? Do you, Harriett? Does anybody know—among you high yallers, you jelly-beans, you pinks and pretty daddies, among you sealskin browns, smooth blacks, and chocolates-to-the-bone—does anybody know the answer?

"Aw, play it, Benbow!"

"It's midnight. De clock is strikin' twelve, an' . . ."

"Aw, play it, Mister Benbow!"

During intermission, when the members of the band stopped making music to drink gin and talk to women, Harriett and Mingo bought Sandy a box of cracker-jacks and another bottle of soda and left him standing in the middle of the floor holding both. His young aunt had forgotten time, so Sandy decided to go upstairs to the narrow unused balcony that ran the length of one side of the place. It was dusty up there, but a few broken chairs stood near the railing and he sat on one of them. He leaned his arms on the banister, rested his chin in his hands, and when the music started, he looked down on the mass of moving couples crowding the floor. He had a clear view of the energetic little black drummer eagle-rocking with staccato regularity in his chair as his long, thin sticks descended upon the tightly drawn skin of his small drum, while his foot patted the pedal of his big bass-drum, on which was painted in large red letters: "BENBOW'S FAMOUS KANSAS CITY BAND."

As the slow shuffle gained in intensity (and his cracker-jacks gave out), Sandy looked down drowsily on the men and women, the boys and girls, circling and turning beneath him. Dresses and suits of all shades and colors, and a vast confusion of bushy heads on swaying bodies. Faces gleaming like circus balloons—lemon-yellow, coal-black, powder-grey, ebony-black, blue-black faces; chocolate, brown, orange, tan, creamy-gold faces—the room full of floating balloon faces—Sandy's eyes were beginning to blur with sleep—colored balloons with strings, and the music pulling the strings. No! Girls pulling the strings—each boy a balloon by a string. Each face a balloon.

Sandy put his head down on the dusty railing of the gallery. An odor of hair-oil and fish, of women and sweat came up to him as he sat there alone, tired and a little sick. It was very warm and close, and the room was full of chatter during the intervals. Sandy struggled against sleep, but his eyes were just about to close when, with a burst of hopeless sadness, the *St. Louis Blues* spread itself like a bitter syrup over the hall. For a moment the boy opened his eyes to the drowsy flow of sound, long enough to pull two chairs together; then he lay down on them and closed his eyes again. Somebody was singing:

St. Louis woman with her diamond rings . . .

as the band said very weary things in a loud and brassy manner and the dancers moved in a dream that seemed to have forgotten itself:

Got ma man tied to her apron-strings . . .

Wah! Wah! Wah! . . . The cornet laughed with terrible rudeness. Then the drums began to giggle and the banjo whined an insulting leer. The piano said, over and over again: "St. Louis! That big old dirty town where the Mississippi's deep and wide, deep and wide . . ." and the hips of the dancers rolled.

Man's got a heart like a rock cast in de sea . . .

while the cynical banjo covered unplumbable depths with a plinking surface of staccato gaiety, like the sparkling bubbles that rise on deep water over a man who has just drowned himself:

Or else he never would a gone so far from me . . .

then the band stopped with a long-drawn-out wail from the cornet and a flippant little laugh from the drums.

A great burst of applause swept over the room, and the musicians immediately began to play again. This time just blues, not the *St. Louis*, nor the *Memphis*, nor the *Yellow Dog*—but just the plain old familiar blues, heart-breaking and extravagant, ma-baby's-gone-from-me blues.

Nobody thought about anyone else then. Bodies sweatily close, arms locked, cheek to cheek, breast to breast, couples rocked to the pulse-like beat of the rhythm, yet quite oblivious each person of the other. It was true that men and women were dancing together, but their feet had gone down through the floor into the earth, each dancer's alone—down into the center of things—and their minds had gone off to the heart of loneliness, where they didn't even hear the words, the sometimes lying, sometimes laughing words that Benbow, leaning on the piano, was singing against this background of utterly despondent music:

When de blues is got you,
Ain't no use to run away.
When de blue-blues got you,
Ain't no use to run away,
'Cause de blues is like a woman
That can turn yo' good hair grey.

Umn-ump! . . . Umn! . . . Umn-ump!

Well, I tole ma baby,
Says baby, baby, babe, be mine,

But ma baby was deceitful.
She must a thought that I was blind.

De-da! De-da! . . . De da! De da! Dee!

O, Lawdy, Lawdy, Lawdy,
Lawdy, Lawdy, Lawd . . . Lawd . . . Lawd!
She quit me fo' a Texas gambler,
So I had to git another broad.

Whaw-whaw! . . . Whaw-whaw-whaw! As though the laughter of a cornet could reach the heart of loneliness.

These mean old weary blues coming from a little orchestra of four men who needed no written music because they couldn't have read it. Four men and a leader—Rattle Benbow from Galveston; Benbow's buddy, the drummer, from Houston; his banjoist from Birmingham; his cornetist from Atlanta; and the pianist, long-fingered, sissyfied, a coal-black lad from New Orleans who had brought with him an exaggerated rag-time which he called jazz.

"I'm jazzin' it, creepers!" he sometimes yelled as he rolled his eyes towards the dancers and let his fingers beat the keys to a frenzy. . . . But now the piano was cryin' the blues!

Four homeless, plug-ugly niggers, that's all they were, playing mean old loveless blues in a hot, crowded little dance-hall in a Kansas town on Friday night. Playing the heart out of loneliness with a wide-mouthed leader, who sang everybody's troubles until they became his own. The improvising piano, the whanging banjo, the throbbing bass-drum, the hard-hearted little snare-drum, the brassy cornet that laughed, "Whaw-whaw-whaw. . . . Whaw!" were the waves in this lonesome sea of harmony from which Benbow's melancholy voice rose:

You gonna wake up some mawnin'
An' turn yo' smilin' face.
Wake up some early mawnin',
Says turn yo' smilin' face,

Look at yo' sweetie's pillow—
An' find an empty place!

Then the music whipped itself into a slow fury, an awkward, elemental, foot-stamping fury, with the banjo running terrifiedly away in a windy moan and then coming back again, with the cornet wailing like a woman who don't know what it's all about:

Then you gonna call yo' baby,
Call yo' lovin' baby dear—
But you can keep on callin',
'Cause I won't be here!

And for a moment nothing was heard save the shuf-shuf-shuffle of feet and the immense booming of the bass-drum like a living vein pulsing at the heart of loneliness.

"Sandy! . . . Sandy! . . . My stars! Where is that child? . . . Has anybody seen my little nephew?" All over the hall. . . . "Sandy! . . . Oh-o-o, Lord!" Finally, with a sigh of relief: "You little brat, darn you, hiding up here in the balcony where nobody could find you! . . . Sandy, wake up! It's past four o'clock and I'll get killed."

Harriett vigorously shook the sleeping child, who lay stretched on the dusty chairs; then she began to drag him down the narrow steps before he was scarcely awake. The hall was almost empty and the chubby little black drummer was waddling across the floor carrying his drums in canvas cases. Someone was switching off the lights one by one. A mustard-colored man stood near the door quarrelling with a black woman. She began to cry and he slapped her full in the mouth, then turned his back and left with another girl of maple-sugar brown. Harriett jerked Sandy past this linked couple and pulled the boy down the long flight of stairs into the street, where Mingo stood waiting, with a lighted cigarette making a white line against his black skin.

"You better git a move on," he said. "Daylight ain't holdin' itself back for you!" And he told the truth, for the night had already begun to pale.

Sandy felt sick at the stomach. To be awakened precipitately made him cross and ill-humored, but the fresh, cool air soon caused him to feel less sleepy and not quite so ill. He took a deep breath as he trotted rapidly along on the sidewalk beside his striding aunt and her boy friend. He watched the blue-grey dawn blot out the night in the sky; and then pearl-grey blot out the blue, while the stars faded to points of dying fire. And he listened to the birds chirping and trilling in the trees as though they were calling the sun. Then, as he became fully awake, the child began to feel very proud of himself, for this was the first time he had ever been away from home all night.

Harriett was fussing with Mingo. "You shouldn't've kept me out like that," she said. "Why didn't you tell me what time it was? . . . I didn't know."

And Mingo came back: "Hey, didn't I try to drag you away at midnight and you wouldn't come? And ain't I called you at one o'clock and you said: 'Wait a minute'—dancin' with some yaller P. I. from St. Joe, with your arms round his neck like a life-preserver? . . . Don't tell me I didn't want to leave, and me got to go to work at eight o'clock this mornin' with a pick and shovel when the whistle blows! What de hell?"

But Harriett did not care to quarrel now when there would be no time to finish it properly. She was out of breath from hurrying and almost in tears. She was afraid to go home.

"Mingo, I'm scared."

"Well, you know what you can do if your ma puts you out," her escort said quickly, forgetting his anger. "I can take care of you. We could get married."

"Could we, Mingo?"

"Sure!"

She slipped her hand in his. "Aw, daddy!" and the pace became much less hurried.

When they reached the corner near which Harriett lived, she lifted her dark little purple-powdered face for a not very lingering kiss and sent Mingo on his way. Then she frowned anxiously and ran on. The sky was a pale pearly color, waiting for the warm gold of the rising sun.

"I'm scared to death!" said Harriett. "Lord, Sandy, I hope ma ain't up! I hope she didn't come home last night from Mis' Lane's. We shouldn't've gone, Sandy . . . I guess we shouldn't've gone." She was breathing hard and Sandy had to run fast to keep up with her. "Gee, I'm scared!"

The grass was diamond-like with dew, and the red bricks of the sidewalk were damp, as the small boy and his young aunt hurried under the leafy elms along the walk. They passed Madam de Carter's house and cut through the wet grass into their own yard as the first rays of the morning sun sifted through the trees. Quietly they tiptoed towards the porch; quickly and quietly they crossed it; and softly, ever so softly, they opened the parlor door.

In the early dusk the oil-lamp still burned on the front-room table, and in an old arm-chair, with the open Bible on her lap, sat Aunt Hager Williams, a bundle of switches on the floor at her feet.

9
CARNIVAL

BETWEEN THE TENT of Christ and the tents of sin there stretched scarcely a half-mile. Rivalry reigned: the revival and the carnival held sway in Stanton at the same time. Both were at the south edge of town, and both were loud and musical in their activities. In a dirty white tent in the Hickory Woods the Reverend Duke Braswell conducted the services of the Lord for the annual summer tent-meeting of the First Ethiopian Baptist Church. And in Jed Galoway's meadow lots Swank's Combined Shows, the World's Greatest Midway Carnival, had spread canvas for seven days of bunko games and cheap attractions. The old Negroes went to the revival, and the young Negroes went to the carnival, and after sundown these August evenings the mourning songs of the Christians could be heard rising from the Hickory Woods while the profound syncopation of the minstrel band blared from Galoway's Lots, strangely intermingling their notes of praise and joy.

Aunt Hager with Annjee and Sandy went to the revival every night (Sandy unwillingly), while Jimboy, Harriett, and Maudel went to the carnival. Aunt Hager prayed for her youngest daughter at the meetings, but Harriett had not spoken to her mother, if she could avoid it, since the morning after the dance, when she had been whipped. Since their return from the country Annjee and Jimboy were not so loving towards each other, either, as they had been before. Jimboy tired of Jessie's farm, so he came back to town three days before his wife returned. And now the revival and the carnival widened the breach between the Christians and the sinners in Aunt Hager's little household. And Sandy would rather have been with the sinners—Jimboy and Harriett—but he wasn't old enough; so he had to go to meetings until, on Thursday morning, when he and Buster were climbing over the coal-shed in the back yard, Sandy accidentally jumped down on a rusty nail, which penetrated the heel of his bare foot. He set up a wail, cried until noon over the pain, and refused to eat any dinner; so finally Jimboy said that if he would only hush hollering he'd take him to the carnival that evening.

"Yes, take de rascal," said Aunt Hager. "He ain't doin' no good at de services, wiggling and squirming so's we can't hardly hear de sermon. He ain't got religion in his heart, that chile!"

"I hope he ain't," said his father, yawning.

"All you wants him to be is a good-fo'-nothin' rounder like you is," retorted Hager. And she and Jimboy began their daily quarrel, which lasted for hours, each of them enjoying it immensely. But Sandy kept pulling at his father and saying: "Hurry up and let's go," although he knew well that nothing really started at the carnival until sundown. Nevertheless, about four o'clock, Jimboy said: "All right, come on," and they started out in the hot sun towards Galoway's Lots, the man walking tall and easy while the boy hobbled along on his sore foot, a rag tied about his heel.

At the old cross-bar gate on the edge of town, through which Jed Galoway drove his cows to pasture, there had been erected a portable arch strung with electric lights spelling out "SWANK'S SHOWS" in red and yellow letters, but it was not very impressive in the day-time, with the sun blazing on it, and no people about. And from this gate, extending the whole length of the meadow on either side, like a roadway, were the tents and booths of the carnival: the Galatea illusion, the seal and sea-lion circus, the Broadway musical-comedy show, the freaks, the games of chance, the pop-corn- and lemonade-stands, the colored minstrels, the merry-go-round, the fun house, the hoochie-coochie, the Ferris wheel, and, at the far end, a canvas tank under a tiny platform high in the air from which the World's Most Dangerous and Spectacular High Dive took place nightly at ten-thirty.

"We gonna stay to see that, ain't we, papa?" Sandy asked.

"Sure," said Jimboy. "But didn't I tell you there wouldn't be nothin' runnin' this early in the afternoon? See! Not even the band playin', and ain't a thing open but the freak-show and I'll bet all the freaks asleep." But he bought Sandy a bag of peanuts and planked down twenty cents for two tickets into the sultry tent where a perspiring fat woman and a tame-looking wild-man were the only attractions to be found on the platforms. The sword-swallower was not yet at work, nor the electric marvel, nor the human glass-eater. The terrific sun beat fiercely through the canvas on this exhibit of two lone human abnormalities, and the few spectators in the tent kept wiping their faces with their handkerchiefs.

Jimboy struck up a conversation with the Fat Woman, a pink and white creature who said she lived in Columbus, Ohio; and when Jimboy said he'd been there, she was interested. She said she had always lived right next door to colored people at home, and she gave Sandy a postcard picture of herself for nothing, although it had "10¢" marked on the back. She kept saying she didn't see how anybody could stay in Kansas and it a dry state where a soul couldn't even get beer except from a bootlegger.

When Sandy and his father came out, they left the row of tents and went across the meadow to a clump of big shade-trees beneath which several colored men who worked with the show were sitting. A blanket had been spread on the grass, and a crap game was going on to the accompaniment of much arguing and good-natured cussing. But most of the men were just sitting around not playing, and one or two were stretched flat on their faces, asleep. Jimboy seemed to know several of the fellows, so he joined in their talk while Sandy watched the dice roll for a while, but since the boy didn't understand the game, he decided to go back to the tents.

"All right, go ahead," said his father. "I'll pick you up later when the lights are lit and things get started; then we can go in the shows."

Sandy limped off, walking on the toe of his injured foot. In front of the sea-lion circus he found Earl James, a little white boy in his grade at school; the two of them went around together for a while, looking at the large painted canvas pictures in front of the shows or else lying on their stomachs on the ground to peep under the tents. When they reached the minstrel-show tent near the end of the midway, they heard a piano tinkling within and the sound of hands clapping as though someone was dancing.

"Jeezus! Let's see this," Earl cried, so the two boys got down on their bellies, wriggled under the flap of the tent on one side, and looked in.

A battered upright piano stood on the ground in front of the stage, and a fat, bald-headed Negro was beating out a rag. A big white man in a checkered vest was leaning against the piano, derby on head, and a long cigar stuck in his mouth. He was watching a slim black girl, with skirts held high and head thrown back, prancing in a mad circle of crazy steps. Two big colored boys in red uniforms were patting time, while another girl sat on a box, her back towards the peeping youngsters staring up from under the edge of the tent. As the girl who was dancing whirled about, Sandy saw that it was Harriett.

"Pretty good, ain't she, boss?" yelled the wrinkle-necked Negro at the piano as he pounded away.

The white man nodded and kept his eyes on Harriett's legs. The two black boys patting time were grinning from ear to ear.

"Do it, Miss Mama!" one of them shouted as Harriett began to sashay gracefully.

Finally she stopped, panting and perspiring, with her lips smiling and her eyes sparkling gaily. Then she went with the white man and the colored piano-player behind the canvas curtains to the stage. One of the show-boys put his arms around the girl sitting on the box and began tentatively to feel her breasts.

"Don't be so fresh, hot papa," she said. And Sandy recognized Maudel's voice, and saw her brown face as she leaned back to look at the show-man. The boy in the red suit bent over and kissed her several times, while the other fellow kept imitating the steps he had just seen Harriett performing.

"Let's go," Earl said to Sandy, rolling over on the ground. The two small boys went on to the next tent, where one of the carnival men caught them, kicked their behinds soundly, and sent them away.

The sun was setting in a pink haze, and the showgrounds began to take on an air of activity. The steam calliope gave a few trial hoots, and the merry-go-round circled slowly without passengers. The paddle-wheels and the get-'em-hot men, the lemonade-sellers and the souvenir-vendors were opening their booths to the evening trade. A barker began to ballyhoo in front of the freak-show. By and by there would be a crowd. The lights came on along the midway, the Ferris wheel swept languidly up into the air, and when Sandy found his father, the colored band had begun to play in front of the minstrel show.

"I want to ride on the merry-go-round," Sandy insisted. "And go in the Crazy House." So they did both; then they bought hamburger sandwiches with thick slices of white onion and drank strawberry soda and ate pop-corn with butter on it. They went to the sea-lion circus, tried to win a Kewpie doll at the paddle-wheel booth, and watched men losing money on the hidden pea, then trying to win it back at four-card monte behind the Galatea attraction. And all the while Sandy said nothing to his father about having seen Harriett dancing in the minstrel tent that afternoon.

Sandy had lived too long with three women not to have learned to hold his tongue about the private doings of each of them. When Annjee paid two dollars a week on a blue silk shirt for his father at Cohn's cut-rate credit store, and Sandy saw her make the payments, he knew without being told that the matter was never to be mentioned to Aunt Hager. And if his grandmother sometimes threw Harriett's rouge out in the alley, Sandy saw it with his eyes, but not with his mouth. Because he loved all three of them—Harriett and Annjee and Hager—he didn't carry tales on any one of them to the others. Nobody would know he had watched his Aunt Harrie dancing on the carnival lot today in front of a big fat white man in a checkered vest while a Negro in a red suit played the piano.

"We got a half-dollar left for the minstrel show," said Jimboy.

"Come on, let's go." And he pulled his son through the crowd that jammed the long midway between the booths.

All the bright lights of the carnival were on now, and everything was running full blast. The merry-go-round whirled to the ear-splitting hoots of the calliope; bands blared; the canvas paintings of snakes and dancing-girls, human skeletons, fire-eaters, billowed in the evening breeze; pennants flapped, barkers shouted, acrobats twirled in front of a tent; a huge paddle-wheel clicked out numbers. Folks pushed and shoved and women called to their children not to get lost. In the air one smelled the scent of trampled grass, peanuts, and hot dogs, animals and human bodies.

The large white man in the checkered vest was making the ballyhoo in front of the minstrel show, his expansive belly turned towards the crowd that had been attracted by the band. One hand pointed towards a tawdry group of hard-looking Negro performers standing on the platform.

"Here we have, ladies and gents, Madam Caledonia Watson, the Dixie song-bird; Dancing Jenkins, the dark strutter from Jacksonville; little Lizzie Roach, champeen coon-shouter of Georgia; and last, but not least, Sambo and Rastus, the world's funniest comedians. Last performance this evening! . . . Strike her up, perfesser! . . . Come along, now, folks!"

The band burst into sound, Madam Watson and Lizzie Roach opened their brass-lined throats, the men dropped into a momentary clog-dance, and then the whole crowd of performers disappeared into the tent. The ticket-purchasing townspeople followed through the public opening beneath a gaudily painted sign picturing a Mississippi steamboat in the moonlight, and two black bucks shooting gigantic dice on a street-corner.

Jimboy and Sandy followed the band inside and took seats, and soon the frayed curtain rose, showing a plantation scene in the South, where three men, blackened up, and two women in bandannas sang longingly about Dixie. Then Sambo and Rastus came out with long wooden razors and began to argue and shoot dice, but presently the lights went out and a ghost appeared and frightened the two men away, causing them to leave all the money on the stage. (The audience thought it screamingly funny—and just like niggers.) After that one of the women sang a rag-time song and did the eagle-rock. Then a man with a banjo in his hands began to play, but until then the show had been lifeless.

"Listen to him," Jimboy said, punching Sandy. "He's good!"

The piece he was picking was full of intricate runs and trills long drawn out, then suddenly slipping into tantalizing rhythms. It ended with a vibrant whang!—and the audience yelled for more. As an encore he played a blues and sang innumerable verses, always ending:

An' Ah can't be satisfied,
'Cause all Ah love has
Done laid down an' died.

And to Sandy it seemed like the saddest music in the world—but the white people around him laughed.

Then the stage lights went on, the band blared, and all the black actors came trooping back, clapping their hands before the cotton-field curtain as each one in turn danced like fury, vigorously distorting agile limbs into the most amazing positions, while the scene ended with the fattest mammy and the oldest uncle shaking jazzily together.

The booths were all putting out their lights as the people poured through the gate towards town. Sandy hobbled down the road beside his father, his sore heel, which had been forgotten all evening, paining him terribly until Jimboy picked him up and carried him on his shoulder. Automobiles and buggies whirled past them in clouds of gritty dust, and young boys calling vulgar words hurried after tittering girls. When Sandy and his father reached home, Aunt Hager and Annjee had not yet returned from the revival. Jimboy said he thought maybe they had stopped at Mrs. Lane's to sit up all night with the sick woman, so Sandy spread his pallet on the floor at the foot of his grandmother's bed and went to sleep. He did not hear his Aunt Harriett when she came home, but late in the night he woke up with his heel throbbing painfully, his throat dry, and his skin burning, and when he tried to bend his leg, it hurt him so that he began to cry.

Harriett, awakened by his moans, called drowsily: "What's the matter, honey?"

"My foot," said Sandy tearfully.

So his young aunt got out of bed, lit the lamp, and helped him to the kitchen, where she heated a kettle of water, bathed his heel, and covered the nail-wound with vaseline. Then she bound it with a fresh white rag.

"Now that ought to feel better," she said as she led him back to his pallet, and soon they were both asleep again.

The next morning when Hager came from the sickbed of her friend, she sent to the butcher-shop for a bacon rind, cut from it a piece of fat meat, and bound it to Sandy's heel as a cure.

"Don't want you havin' de blood-pisen here," she said. "An' don't you run round an' play on that heel. Set out on de porch an' study yo' reader, 'cause school'll be startin' next month." Then she began Mrs. Reinhart's ironing.

The next day, Saturday, the last day of the carnival, Jimboy carried the Reinharts' clothes home for Hager, since Sandy was crippled and Jimmy Lane's mother was down in bed. But after delivering the clothes Jimboy did not come home for supper. When Annjee and Hager wanted to leave for the revival in the early evening, they asked Harriett if she would stay home with the little boy, for Sandy's heel had swollen purple where the rusty nail had penetrated and he could hardly walk at all.

"You been gone ever' night this week," Hager said to the girl. "An' you ain't been anear de holy tents where de Lawd's word is preached; so you ought to be willin' to stay home one night with a po' little sick boy."

"Yes'm," Harriett muttered in a noncommittal tone. But shortly after her mother and Annjee had gone, she said to her nephew: "You aren't afraid to stay home by yourself, are you?"

And Sandy answered: "Course not, Aunt Harrie."

She gave him a hot bath and put a new piece of fat meat on his festering heel. Then she told him to climb into Annjee's bed and go to sleep, but instead he lay for a long time looking out the window that was beside the bed. He thought about the carnival—the Ferris wheel sweeping up into the air, and the minstrel show. Then he remembered Benbow's dance a few weeks ago and how his Aunt Harriett had stood sullenly the next morning while Hager whipped her—and hadn't cried at all, until the welts came under her silk stockings. . . . Then he wondered what Jimmy Lane would do if his sick mother died from the T. B. and he were left with nobody to take care of him, because Jimmy's step-father was no good. . . . Eu-uuu! His heel hurt! . . . When school began again, he would be in the fifth grade, but he wished he'd hurry up and get to high school, like Harriett was. . . . When he got to be a man, he was going to be a railroad engineer. . . . Gee, he wasn't sleepy—and his heel throbbed painfully.

In the next room Harriett had lighted the oil-lamp and was moving swiftly about taking clothes from the dresser-drawers and spreading them on the bed. She thought Sandy was asleep, he knew—but he couldn't go to sleep the way his foot hurt him. He could see her through the doorway folding her dresses in little piles and he wondered why she was doing that. Then she took an old suit-case from the closet and began to pack it, and when it was full, she pulled a new bag from under the bed, and into it she dumped her toilet-articles, powder, vaseline, nail-polish, straightening comb, and several pairs of old stockings rolled in balls. Then she sat down on the bed between the two closed suit-cases for a long time with her hands in her lap and her eyes staring ahead of her.

Finally she rose and closed the bureau-drawers, tidied up the confusion she had created, and gathered together the discarded things she had thrown on the floor. Then Sandy heard her go out into the back yard towards the trash-pile. When she returned, she put on a tight little hat and went into the kitchen to wash her hands, throwing the water through the back door.

Then she tip-toed into the room where Sandy was lying and kissed him gently on the head. Sandy knew that she thought he was asleep, but in spite of himself he suddenly threw his arms tightly around her neck. He couldn't help it.

"Where you going, Aunt Harriett?" he said, sitting up in bed, clutching the girl.

"Honey, you won't tell on me, will you?" Harriett asked.

"No," he answered, and she knew he wouldn't. "But where are you going, Aunt Harrie?"

"You won't be afraid to stay here until grandma comes?"

"No," burying his face on her breast. "I won't be afraid."

"And you won't forget Aunt Harrie?"

"Course not."

"I'm leaving with the carnival," she told him.

For a moment they sat close together on the bed. Then she kissed him, went into the other room and picked up her suitcases—and the door closed.

10
PUNISHMENT

OLD WHITE DR. McDILLORS, beloved of all the Negroes in Stanton, came on Sunday morning, swabbed Sandy's festering foot with iodine, bound it up, and gave him a bottle of green medicine to take, and by the middle of the week the boy was able to hobble about again without pain; but Hager continued to apply fat meat instead of following the doctor's directions.

When Harriett didn't come back, Sandy no longer slept on a pallet on the floor. He slept in the big bed with his grandma Hager, and the evenings that followed weren't so jolly, with his young aunt off with the carnival, and Jimboy spending most of his time at the pool hall or else loafing on the station platform watching the trains come through—and nobody playing music in the back yard.

They went to bed early these days, and after that eventful week of carnival and revival, a sore heel, and a missing Aunt Harriett, the muscles of Sandy's little body often twitched and jerked in his sleep and he would awaken suddenly from dreaming that he heard sad raggy music playing while a woman shouted for Jesus in the Gospel tent, and a girl in red silk stockings cried because the switches were cutting her legs. Sometimes he would lie staring into the darkness a long time, while Aunt Hager lay snoring at his side. And sometimes in the next room, where Annjee and Jimboy were, he could hear the slow rhythmical creaking of the bedsprings and the low moans of his mother, which he already knew accompanied the grown-up embraces of bodily love. And sometimes through the window he could see the moonlight glinting on the tall, tassel-crowned stalks of corn in the garden. Perhaps he would toss and turn until he had awakened Aunt Hager and she would say drowsily: "What's de matter with you, chile? I'll put you back on de flo' if you can't be still!" Then he would go to sleep again, and before he knew it, the sun would be flooding the room with warm light, and the coffee would be boiling on the stove in the kitchen, and Annjee would have gone to work.

Summer days were long and drowsy for grown-ups, but for Sandy they were full of interest. In the mornings he helped Aunt Hager by feeding the chickens, bringing in the water for her wash-tubs and filling the buckets from which they drank. He chopped wood, too, and piled it behind the kitchen-stove; then he would take the broom and sweep dust-clean the space around the pump and under the apple-tree where he played. Perhaps by that time Willie-Mae would come over or Buster would be there to shoot marbles. Or maybe his grandmother would send him to the store to get a pound of sugar or ten cents' worth of meal for dinner, and on the way there was certain to be an adventure. Yesterday he had seen two bad little boys from the Bottoms, collecting scrap-iron and junk in the alleys, get angry at each other and pretend to start a fight.

The big one said to the smaller one: "I'm a fast-black and you know I sho won't run! Jest you pick up that piece o' iron that belongs to me. Go ahead, jest you try!"

And the short boy replied: "I'm your match, long skinny! Strike me an' see if you don't get burnt up!" And then they started to play the dozens, and Sandy, standing by, learned several new and very vulgar words to use when talking about other people's mothers.

The tall kid said finally: "Aw, go on, you little clay-colored nigger, you looks too much like mustard to me anyhow!" Picking up the disputed piece of scrap-iron, he proceeded on his quest for junk, looking into all the trash-piles and garbage-cans along the alley, but the smaller of the two boys took his gunny-sack and went in the opposite direction alone.

"Be careful, sissy, and don't break your dishes," his late companion called after his retreating buddy, and Sandy carefully memorized the expression to try on Jimmy Lane some time—that is, if Jimmy's mother got well, for Mrs. Lane now was in the last stages of consumption. But if she got better,

Sandy was going to tell her son to be careful and not break his dishes—always wearing his mother's shoes, like a girl.

By that time he had forgotten what Hager sent him to the store to buy, and instead of getting meal he bought washing-powder. When he came home, after nearly an hour's absence, his grandmother threatened to cut an elm switch, but she satisfied herself instead by scolding him for staying so long, and then sending him back to exchange the washing-powder for meal—and she waiting all that time to make corn dumplings to put in the greens!

In the afternoon Sandy played in his back yard or next door at the Johnsons', but Hager never allowed him outside their block. The white children across the street were frequently inclined to say "Nigger," so he was forbidden to play there. Usually Buster, who looked like a white kid, and Willie-Mae, who couldn't have been blacker, were his companions. The three children would run at hide-and-seek, in the tall corn; or they would tag one another in the big yard, or play house under the apple-tree.

Once when they were rummaging in the trash-pile to see what they could find, Sandy came across a pawn ticket which he took into the kitchen to Hager. It was for a watch his Aunt Harriett had pawned the Saturday she ran away.

Sometimes in the late afternoon the children would go next door to Madam de Carter's and she would give them ginger cookies and read to them from the *Bible Story Reader.* Madam de Carter looked very pompous and important in her silk waist as she would put on her *pince-nez* and say: "Now, children, seat yourselves and preserve silence while I read you-all this moralizing history of Samson's treacherous hair. Now, Buster, who were Samson? Willie-Mae, has you ever heard of Delilah?"

Sometimes, if Jimboy was home, he would take down his old guitar and start the children to dancing in the sunlight—but then Hager would always call Sandy to pump water or go to the store as soon as she heard the music.

"Out there dancin' like you ain't got no raisin'!" she would say. "I tells Jimboy 'bout playin' that ole rag-time here! That's what ruint Harriett!"

And on Sundays Sandy went to Sabbath school at the Shiloh Baptist Church, where he was given a colored picture card with a printed text on it. The long, dull lessons were taught by Sister Flora Garden, who had been to Wilberforce College, in Ohio. There were ten little boys in Sandy's class, ranging from nine to fourteen, and they behaved very badly, for Miss Flora Garden, who wore thick-lensed glasses on her roach-colored face, didn't understand little boys.

"Where was Moses when the lights went out?" Gritty Smith asked her every Sunday, and she didn't even know the answer.

Sandy didn't think much of Sunday-school, and frequently instead of putting his nickel in the collection basket he spent it for candy, which he divided with Buster—until one very hot Sunday Hager found it out. He had put a piece of the sticky candy in his shirt-pocket and it melted, stuck, and stained the whole front of his clean clothes. When he came home, with Buster behind him, the first thing Hager said was: "What's all this here stuck up in yo' pocket?" and Buster commenced to giggle and said Sandy had bought candy.

"Where'd you get the money, sir?" demanded Aunt Hager searchingly of her grandson.

"I—we—er—Madam Carter gimme a nickel," Sandy replied haltingly, choosing the first name he could think of, which would have been all right had not Madam de Carter herself stopped by the house, almost immediately afterwards, on her way home from church.

"Is you give Sandy a nickel to buy candy this mawnin'?" Hager asked her as soon as she entered the parlor.

"Why, no, Sister Williams, I isn't. I had no coins about me a-tall at services this morning."

"Umn-huh! I thought so!" said Hager. "You Sandy!"

The little boy, guilt written all over his face, came in from the front porch, where he had been sitting with his father after Buster went home.

"Where'd you tell me you got that nickel this mawnin'?"

And before he could answer, she spat out: "I'm gonna whip you!"

"Jehovah help us! Children sure is bad these days," said Madam de Carter, shaking her head as she left to go next door to her own house. "They sure *are* bad," she added, self-consciously correcting her English.

"I'm gonna whip you," Hager continued, sitting down amazed in her plush chair. "De idee o' with-holdin' yo' Sunday-school money from de Lawd an' buyin' candy."

"I only spent a penny," Sandy lied, wriggling.

"How you gwine get so much candy fo' a penny that you has some left to gum up in yo' pocket? Tell me that, how you gonna do it?"

Sandy, at a loss for an answer, was standing with lowered eyelids, when the screen-door opened and Jimboy came in. Sandy looked up at him for aid, but his father's usually amiable face was stern this time.

"Come here!" he said. The man towered very tall above the little fellow who looked up at him helplessly.

"I's gwine whip him!" interposed Hager.

"Is that right, you spent your Sunday-school nickel for candy?" Jimboy demanded gravely.

Sandy nodded his head. He couldn't lie to his father, and had he spoken now, the sobs would have come.

"Then you told a lie to your grandma—and I'm ashamed of you," his father said.

Sandy wanted to turn his head away and escape the slow gaze of Jimboy's eyes, but he couldn't. If Aunt Hager would only whip him, it would be better; then maybe his father wouldn't say any more. But it was awful to stand still and listen to Jimboy talk to him this way—yet there he stood, stiffly holding back the sobs.

"To take money and use it for what it ain't s'posed to be used is the same as stealing," Jimboy went on gravely to his son. "That's what you done today, and then come home and lie about it. Nobody's ugly as a liar, you know that! . . . I'm not much, maybe. Don't mean to say I am. I won't work a lot, but what I do I do honest. White folks gets rich lyin' and stealin'—and some niggers gets rich that way, too—but I don't need money if I got to get it dishonest, with a lot o' lies trailing behind me, and can't look folks in the face. It makes you feel dirty! It's no good! . . . Don't I give you nickels for candy whenever you want 'em?"

The boy nodded silently, with the tears trickling down his chin.

"And don't I go with you to the store and buy you ice-cream and soda-pop any time you ask me?"

The child nodded again.

"And then you go and take the Sunday-school nickel that your grandma's worked hard for all the week, spend it on candy, and come back home and lie about it. So that's what you do! And then lie!"

Jimboy turned his back and went out on the porch, slamming the screen-door behind him. Aunt Hager did not whip her grandson, but returned to the kitchen and left him standing disgraced in the parlor. Then Sandy began to cry, with one hand in his mouth so no one could hear him, and when Annjee came home from work in the late afternoon, she found him lying across her bed, head under the pillows, still sobbing because Jimboy had called him a liar.

11
SCHOOL

SOME WEEKS LATER the neighbors were treated to an early morning concert:

I got a high yaller
An' a little short black,
But a brown-skin gal
Can bring me right on back!
I'm singin' brown-skin!
Lawdy! . . . Lawd!
Brown-skin! . . . O, ma Lawd!

"It must be Jimboy," said Hager from the kitchen. "A lazy coon, settin' out there in the cool singin', an' me in here sweatin' and washin' maself to dust!"

Kansas City Southern!
I mean de W. & A.!
I'm gonna ride de first train
I catch goin' out ma way.
I'm got de railroad blues—

"I wish to God you'd go on, then!" mumbled Hager over the wash-boilers.

But I ain't got no railroad fare!
I'm gwine to pack ma grip an'
Beat ma way away from here!

"Learn me how to pick a cord, papa," Sandy begged as he sat beside his father under the apple-tree, loaded with ripe fruit.

"All right, look a-here! . . . You put your thumb like this. . . ." Jimboy began to explain. "But, dog-gone, your fingers ain't long enough yet!"

Still they managed to spend a half-day twanging at the old instrument, with Sandy trying to learn a simple tune.

The sunny August mornings had become September mornings, and most of Aunt Hager's "white folks" had returned from their vacations; her kitchen was once more a daily laundry. Great boilers of clothes steamed on the stove and, beside the clothes, pans of apple juice boiled to jelly, and the peelings of peaches simmered to jam.

There was no news from the runaway Harriett. . . . Mrs. Lane died one sultry night, with Hager at the bedside, and was buried by the lodge with three hacks and a fifty-dollar coffin. . . . The following week the Drill of All Nations, after much practising by the women, was given with great success and Annjee, dressed in white and wrapped in a Scandinavian flag, marched proudly as Sweden. . . . Madam de Carter's house was now locked and barred, as she had departed for Oklahoma to organize branches of the lodge there . . . Tempy had stopped to see Hager one afternoon, but she didn't stay long. She told her mother she was out collecting rents and that she and her husband were buying another house. . . . Willie-Mae had a new calico dress. . . . Buster had learned to swear better than Sandy. . . . And next Monday was to be the opening of the new school term.

Sandy hated even to think about going back to school. He was having much fun playing, and Jimboy had been teaching him to box. Then the time to go to classes came.

"Wash yo' face good, sir, put on yo' clean waist, an' polish yo' shoes," Aunt Hager said bright and early, " 'cause I don't want none o' them white teachers sayin' I sends you to school dirty as a 'cuse to put you back in de fourth grade. You hear me, sir!"

"Yes'm," Sandy replied.

This morning he was to enter the "white" fifth grade, having passed last June from the "colored" fourth, for in Stanton the Negro children were kept in separate rooms under colored teachers until they had passed the fourth grade. Then, from the fifth grade on, they went with the other children, and the teachers were white.

When Sandy arrived on the school grounds with his face shining, he found the yard already full of shouting kids. On the girls' side he saw Willie-Mae jumping rope. Sandy found Earl and Buster and some boys whom he knew playing mumble-peg on the boys' side, and he joined them. When the bell rang, they all crowded into the building, as the marching-lines had not yet been formed. Miss Abigail Minter, the principal, stood at the entrance, and there were big signs on all the room doors marking the classes. Sandy found the fifth-grade room upstairs and went in shyly. It was full of whispering youngsters huddled in little groups. He saw two colored children among them, both girls whom he didn't know, but there were no colored boys. Soon the teacher rapped briskly on her desk, and silence ensued.

"Take seats, all of you, please," she rasped out. "Anywhere now until we get order." She rapped again impatiently with the ruler. "Take seats at once." So the children each selected a desk and sat down, most of the girls at the front of the room and most of the boys together at the back, where they could play and look out the windows.

Then the teacher, middle-aged and wearing glasses, passed out tiny slips of paper to each child in the front row, with the command that they be handed backwards, so that every student received one slip.

"Now, write your names on the paper, turning it longways," she said. "Nothing but your names, that's all I want today. You will receive forms to fill out later, but I want to get your seats assigned this morning, however."

Amid much confusion and borrowing of pencils, the slips were finally signed in big awkward letters, and collected by the teacher, who passed up and down the aisles. Then she went to her desk, and there was a delightful period of whispering and wriggling as she sorted the slips and placed them in alphabetical order. Finally she finished.

"Now," she said, "each child rise as I call out your names, so I can see who you are."

The teacher stood up with the papers in her hand.

"Mary Atkins . . . Carl Dietrich . . . Josephine Evans," she called slowly glancing up after each name. "Franklin Rhodes . . . James Rogers." Sandy stood up quickly. "Ethel Shortlidge . . . Roland Thomas." The roll-call continued, each child standing until he had been identified, then sitting down again.

"Now," the teacher said, "everybody rise and make a line around the walls. Quietly! No talking! As I call your names this time, take seats in order, starting with number one in the first row near the window. . . . Mary Atkins . . . Carl Dietrich. . . ." The roll was repeated, each child taking a seat as she had commanded. When all but four of the children were seated, the two colored girls and Sandy still were standing.

"Albert Zwick," she said, and the last white child sat down in his place. "Now," said the teacher, "you three colored children take the seats behind Albert. You girls take the first two, and you," pointing to Sandy, "take the last one. . . . Now I'm going to put on the board the list of books to buy and I want all of you to copy them correctly." And she went on with her details of schoolroom routine.

One of the colored girls turned round to Sandy and whispered: "She just put us in the back cause we're niggers." And Sandy nodded gravely. "My name's Sadie Butler and she's put me behind the Z cause I'm a nigger."

"An old heifer!" said the first little colored girl, whispering loudly. "I'm gonna tell my mama." But Sandy felt like crying. And he was beginning to be ashamed of crying because he was no longer a small boy. But the teacher's putting the colored children in the back of the room made him feel like crying.

At lunch-time he came home with his list of books, and Aunt Hager pulled her wet arms out of the tub, wiped her hands, and held them up in horror.

"Lawdy! Just look! Something else to spend money for. Ever'

year more an' more books, an' chillens learn less an' less! Used to didn't have nothin' but a blue-backed speller, and now look ahere—a list as long as ma arm! Go out there in de yard an' see is yo' pappy got any money to give you for 'em, 'cause I ain't."

Sandy found Jimboy sitting dejectedly on the well-stoop in the sunshine, with his head in his hands. "You got any money, papa?" he asked.

Jimboy looked at the list of books written in Sandy's childish scrawl and slowly handed him a dollar and a half.

"You see what I got left, don't you?" said his father as he turned his pants-pockets inside out, showing the little boy a jack-knife, a half-empty sack of Bull Durham, a key, and a dime. But he smiled, and took Sandy awkwardly in his arms and kissed him. "It's all right, kid."

That afternoon at school they had a long drill on the multiplication table, and then they had a spelling-match, because the teacher said that would be a good way to find out what the children knew. For the spelling-bee they were divided into two sides—the boys and the girls, each side lining up against an opposite wall. Then the teacher gave out words that they should have learned in the lower grades. On the boys' side everyone was spelled down except Sandy, but on the girls' side there were three proud little white girls left standing and Sandy came near spelling them down, too, until he put the *e* before *i* in "chief," and the girls' side won, to the disgust of the boys, and the two colored girls, who wanted Sandy to win.

After school Sandy went uptown with Buster to buy books, but there was so large a crowd of children in the bookstore that it was five o'clock before he was waited on and his list filled. When he reached home, Aunt Hager was at the kitchen-stove frying an eggplant for supper.

"You stayin' out mighty long," she said without taking her attention from the stove.

"Where's papa?" Sandy asked eagerly. He wanted to show Jimboy his new books—a big geography, with pictures of animals in it, and a *Nature Story Reader* that he knew his father would like to see.

"Look in yonder," said Hager, pointing towards Annjee's bedroom.

Sandy rushed in, then stopped, because there was no one there. Suddenly a queer feeling came over him and he put his books down on the bed. Jimboy's clothes were no longer hanging against the wall where his working-shirts and overalls were kept. Then Sandy looked under the bed. His father's old suitcase was not there either, nor his work-shoes, nor his Sunday patent-leathers. And the guitar was missing.

"Where's papa?" he asked again, running back to the kitchen.

"Can't you see he ain't here?" replied his grandmother, busily turning slices of eggplant with great care in the skillet. "Gone—that's where he is—a lazy nigger. Told me to tell Annjee he say goodbye, 'cause his travellin' blues done come on . . .! Huh! Jimboy's yo' pappy, chile, but he sho ain't worth his salt! . . . an' I's right glad he's took his clothes an' left here, maself."

12
HARD WINTER

SEPTEMBER PASSED AND the corn-stalks in the garden were cut. There were no more apples left on the trees, and chilly rains came to beat down the falling leaves from the maples and the elms. Cold and drearily wet October passed, too, with no hint of Indian summer or golden forests. And as yet there was no word from the departed Jimboy. Annjee worried herself sick as usual, hoping every day that a letter would come from this wandering husband whom she loved. And each night she hurried home from Mrs. Rice's, looked on the parlor table for the mail, and found none. Harriett had not written, either, since she went away with the carnival, and Hager never mentioned her youngest daughter's name. Nor did Hager mention Jimboy except when Annjee asked her, after she could hold it no longer: "Are you sure the mail-man ain't left me a letter today?" And then Aunt Hager would reply impatiently: "You think I'd a et it if he did? You know that good-for-nothin', upsettin' scoundrel ain't wrote!"

But in spite of daily disappointments from the postal service Annjee continued to rush from Mrs. Rice's hot kitchen as soon after dinner as she could and to trudge through the chill October rains, anxious to feel in the mail-box outside her door, then hope against hope for a letter inside on the little front-room table—which would always be empty. She caught a terrible cold tramping through the damp streets, forgetting to button her cloak, then sitting down with her wet shoes on when she got home, a look of dumb disappointment in her eyes, too tired and unhappy to remove her clothes.

"You's a fool," said her mother, whose tongue was often much sharper than the meaning behind it. "Mooning after a worthless nigger like Jimboy. I tole you years ago he were no good, when he first come, lookin' like he ought to be wearin' short pants, an' out here courtin' you. Ain't none o' them bell-hoppin', racehoss-followin' kind o' darkies worth havin', an' that's all Jimboy was when you married him an' he ain't much mo'n that now. An' you older'n he is, too!"

"But you know why I married, don't you?"

"You Sandy, go outdoors an' get me some wood fo' this stove. . . . Yes, I knows why, because he were de father o' that chile you was 'bout to bring here, but I don't see why it couldn't just well been some o' these steady, hard-workin' Stanton young men's what was courtin' you at de same time. . . . But, chile or no chile, I couldn't hear nothin' but Jimboy, Jimboy, Jimboy! I told you you better stay in de high school an' get your edication, but no, you had to marry this Jimboy. Now you see what you got, don't you?"

"Well, he ain't been so bad, ma! And I don't care, I love him!"

"Umn-huh! Try an' live on love, daughter! Just try an' live on love. . . . You's made a mistake, that's all, honey. . . . But I guess there ain't no use talkin' 'bout it now. Take off yo' wet shoes 'fore you catch yo' death o' cold!"

On Thanksgiving at Mrs. Rice's, so Annjee reported, they had turkey with chestnut dressing; but at Aunt Hager's she and Sandy had a nice juicy possum, a present from old man Logan, parboiled and baked sweet and brown with yams in the pan. Aunt Hager opened a jar of peach preserves. And she told Sandy to ask Jimmy Lane in to dinner because, since his mother died, he wasn't faring so well and the people he was staying with didn't care much about him. But since Jimmy had quit school, Sandy didn't see him often; and the day before Thanksgiving he couldn't find him at all, so they had no company to help them eat the possum.

The week after Thanksgiving Annjee fell ill and had to go to bed. She had the grippe, Aunt Hager said, and she began to dose her with quinine and to put hot mustard-plasters on her back and gave her onion syrup to drink, but it didn't seem to do much good, and finally she had to send Sandy for Dr. McDillors.

"System's all run down," said the doctor. "Heavy cold on the chest—better be careful. And stay in the bed!" But the warning was unnecessary. Annjee felt too tired and weak ever to rise, and only the mail-man's whistle blowing at somebody else's house would cause her to try to lift her head. Then she would demand weakly: "Did he stop here?"

Hager's home now was like a steam laundry. The kitchen was always hung with lines of clothes to dry, and in the late afternoon and evenings the ironing-board was spread from the table to a chair-back in the middle of the floor. All of the old customers were sending their clothes to Hager again during the winter. And since Annjee was sick, bringing no money into the house on Saturdays, the old woman had even taken an extra washing to do. Being the only wage-earner, Hager kept the suds flying—but with the wet weather she had to dry the clothes in the kitchen most of the time, and when Sandy came home from school for lunch, he would eat under dripping lines of white folks' garments while he listened to his mother coughing in the next room.

In the other rooms of the house there were no stoves, so the doors were kept open in order that the heat might pass through from the kitchen. They couldn't afford to keep more than one fire going; therefore the kitchen was living-room, dining-room, and work-room combined. In the mornings Sandy would jump out of bed and run with his clothes in his hands to the kitchen-stove, where his grandmother would have the fire blazing, the coffee-pot on, and a great tub of water heating for the washings. And in the evenings after supper he would open his geography and read about the strange countries far away, the book spread out on the oilcloth-covered kitchen-table. And Aunt Hager, if her ironing was done, would sit beside the stove and doze, while Annjee tossed and groaned in her chilly bedroom. Only in the kitchen was it really bright and warm.

In the afternoons when Sandy came home from school he would usually find Sister Johnson helping Hager with her ironing, and keeping up a steady conversation.

"Dis gonna be a hard winter. De papers say folks is out o' work ever' where, an', wid all dis sleet an' rain, it's a terror fo' de po' peoples, I tells you! Now, ma Tom, he got a good job tendin' de furnace at de Fair Buildin', so I ain't doin' much washin' long as he's workin'—but so many colored men's out o' work here, wid Christmas comin', it sho is too bad! An' you, Sis Williams, wid yo' daughter sick in bed! Any time yo' clothes git kinder heavy fo' you, I ain't mind helpin' you out. Jest send dis chile atter me or holler 'cross de yard if you kin make me hear! . . . How you press dis dress, wid de collar turn up or down? Which way do Mis' Dunset like it?"

"I always presses it down," returned Hager, who was ironing handkerchiefs and towels on the table. "Better let me iron that, an' you take these here towels."

"All right," agreed Sister Johnson," 'cause you knows how yo' white folks likes dey things, an' I don't. Folks have so many different ways!"

"Sho do," said Hager. "I washed for a woman once what even had her sheets starched."

"But you's sure got a fine repertation as a washer, Sis Williams. One o' de white ladies what I washes fo' say you washes beautiful."

"I reckon white folks does think right smart of me," said Hager proudly. "They always likes you when you tries to do right."

"When you tries to do yo' work right, you means. Dey ain't carin' nothin' 'bout you 'yond workin' fo' 'em. Ain't dey got all de little niggers settin' off in one row at dat school whar Sandy an' Willie-Mae go at? I's like Harriett—ain't got no time fo' white folks maself, 'ceptin' what little money dey pays me. You ain't been run out o' yo' home like I is, Hager. . . . Sandy, make haste go fetch my pipe from over to de house, an' don't stay all day playin' wid Willie-Mae! Tote it here quick! . . . An' you oughter hear de way white folks talks 'bout niggers. Says dey's lazy, an' says dey stinks, an' all. Huh! Dey ought to smell dey-selves! You's smelled white peoples when dey gets to sweatin' ain't you? Smells jest like sour cream, only worser, kinder sickenin' like. And some o' dese foriners what's been eating garlic—phew! Lawdy!"

When Sandy returned with the pipe, the conversation had shifted to the deaths in the colored community. "Hager, folks dyin' right an' left already dis winter. We's had such a bad fall, dat's de reason why. You know dat no-'count Jack Smears passed away last Sunday. Dey had his funeral yesterday an' I went. Good thing he belonged to de lodge, too, else he'd been buried in de po'-field, 'cause he ain't left even de copper cents to put on his eyes. Lodge beared his funeral bill, but I heard more'n one member talkin' 'bout how dey was puttin' a ten-dollar nigger in a hundred-dollar coffin! . . . An' his wife were at de funeral. Yes, sir! A hussy! After she done left him last year wid de little chillens to take care of, an' she runnin' round de streets showin' off. Dere she sot, big as life, in front wid de moaners, long black veil on her face and done dyed her coat black, an' all de time Reverend Butler been preachin' 'bout how holy Jack were, she turn an' twist an' she coughed an' she whiffled an' blowed an' she wiped—tryin' her best to cry an' couldn't, deceitful as she is! Then she jest broke out to screamin', but warn't a tear in her eye; makin' folks look at her, dat's all, 'cause she ain't cared nothin' 'bout Jack. She been livin' in de Bottoms since last Feb'ary wid a young bell-hop ain't much older'n her own son, Bert!"

"Do Jesus!" said Hager. "Some womens is awful."

"Worse'n dat," said Sister Johnson. . . . "Lawdy! Listen at dat sleet beatin' on dese winders! Sho gwine be a real winter! An' how time do pass. Ain't but t'ree mo' weeks till Christmas!"

"Truth!" said Sandy's grandmother. "An' we ain't gwine have no money a-tall. Ain't no mo'n got through payin' ma taxes good, an' de interest on ma mortgage, when Annjee get sick here! Lawd, I tells you, po' colored womens have it hard!"

"Sho do!" said Sister Johnson, sucking at her pipe as she ironed. "How long you been had this house, Sis Williams?"

"Fo' nigh on forty years, ever sence Cudge an' me come here from Montgomery. An' I been washin' fo' white folks ever' week de Lawd sent sence I been here, too. Bought this house washin', and made as many payments myself as Cudge come near; an' raised ma chillens washin'; an' when Cudge taken sick an' laid on his back for mo'n a year, I taken care o' him washin'; an' when he died, paid de funeral bill washin', cause he ain't belonged to no lodge. Sent Tempy through de high school and edicated Annjee till she marry that onery pup of a Jimboy, an' Harriett till she left home. Yes, sir. Washin', an' here I is with me arms still in de tub! . . . But they's one mo' got to go through school yet, an' that's ma little Sandy. If de Lawd lets me live, I's gwine make a edicated man out o' him. He's gwine be another Booker T. Washington." Hager turned a voluminous white petticoat on the ironing-board as she carefully pressed its embroidered hem. "I ain't never raised no boy o' ma own yet, so I wants this one o' Annjee's to 'mount to something. I wants him to know all they is to know, so's he can help this black race o' our'n to come up and see de light and take they places in de world. I wants him to be a Fred Douglass leadin' de people, that's what, an' not followin' in de tracks o' his good-for-nothin' pappy, worthless an' wanderin' like Jimboy is."

"O, don't say that, ma," Annjee cried weakly from her bed in the other room. "Jimboy's all right, but he's just too smart to do this heavy ditch-digging labor, and that's all white folks gives the colored a chance at here in Stanton; so he had to leave."

"There you go excitin' yo'self agin, an' you sick. I thought you was asleep. I ain't meant nothin', honey. Course he's all right," Hager said to quiet her daughter, but she couldn't resist mumbling: "But I ain't seen him doin' you no good."

"Well, he ain't beat her, has he?" asked Sister Johnson, who, for the sake of conversation, often took a contrary view-point. "I's knowed many a man to beat his wife. Tom used to tap me a few times 'fo' I found out a way to stop him, but dat ain't nedder here nor dere!" She folded a towel decisively and gave it a vigorous rub with the hot iron. "Did I ever tell you 'bout de man lived next do' to us in Cairo what cut his wife in de stomach wid a razor an' den stood ovah her when de doctor was sewin' her up moanin': 'I don't see why I cut her in de stomach!

O, Lawd! She always told me she ain't want to be cut in de stomach!' . . . An' it warn't two months atter dat dat he done sliced her in de stomach agin when she was tryin' to git away from him! He were a mean nigger, that man were!"

"Annjee, is you taken yo' medicine yet? It's past fo' o'clock," Hager called. "Sandy, here, take this fifteen cents, chile, and run to de store an' get me a soup bone. I gwine try an' make a little broth for yo' mother. An' don't be gone all day neither, 'cause I got to send these clothes back to Mis' Dunset." Hager was pressing out the stockings as she turned her attention to the conversation again. "They tells me, Sister Johnson, that Seth Jones done beat up his wife something terrible."

"He did, an' he oughter! She was always stayin' way from home an' settin' up in de church, not even cookin' his meals, an' de chillens runnin' ragged in de street."

"She's a religious frantic, ain't she?" asked Hager. . . . "You Sandy, hurry up, sir! an' go get that soup bone!"

"No, chile, 'tain't that," said Sister Johnson. "She ain't carin' so much 'bout religion. It's Reverend Butler she's runnin' atter. Ever' time de church do' opens, there she sets in de preacher's mouth, tryin' to 'tract de shepherd from his sheep. She de one what taken her husband's money an' bought Reverend Butler dat gold-headed walkin'-cane he's got. I ain't blame Seth fer hittin' her bap on de head, an' she takin' his money an' buyin' canes fer ministers!"

"Sadie Butler's in my school," said Sandy, putting on his stocking cap. "Reverend Butler's her step-father."

"Shut up! You hears too much," said Hager. "Ain't I told you to go on an' get that soup bone?"

"Yes'm. I'm going."

"An' I reckon I'll be movin' too," said Sister Johnson, placing the iron on the stove. "It's near 'bout time to be startin' Tom's supper. I done told Willie-Mae to peel de taters 'fo' I come ovah here, but I spects she ain't done it. Dat's de worse black gal to get to work! Soon as she eat, she run outdo's to de privy to keep from washin' de dishes!"

Sandy started to the store, and Sister Johnson, with an old

coat over her head, scooted across the back yard to her door. It was a chill December afternoon and the steady sleet stung Sandy in the face as he ran along, but the air smelled good after the muggy kitchen and the stale scent of Annjee's sick-room. Near the corner Sandy met the mail-man, his face red with cold.

"Got anything for us?" asked the little boy.

"No," said the man as he went on without stopping.

Sandy wished his mother would get well soon. She looked so sad lying there in bed. And Aunt Hager was always busy washing and ironing. His grandmother didn't even have time to mend his stockings any more and there were great holes in the heels when he went to school. His shoes were worn out under the bottoms, too. Yesterday his mother had said: "Honey, you better take them high brown shoes of mine from underneath the bed and put 'em on to keep your feet dry this wet weather. I can't afford to buy you none now, and you ain't got no rubbers."

"You want me to wear old women's shoes like Jimmy Lane?" Sandy objected. "I won't catch cold with my feet wet."

But Hager from the kitchen overruled his objections. "Put on them shoes, sir, an' don't argue with yo' mother, an' she sick in de bed! Put 'em on an' hush yo' mouth, till you get something better."

So this morning at recess Sandy had to fight a boy for calling him "sissy" on account of his mother's shoes he was wearing.

But only a week and a half more and the Christmas vacation would come! Uptown the windows were already full of toys, dolls, skates, and sleds. Sandy wanted a Golden Flyer sled for Christmas. That's all he wanted—a Golden Flyer with flexible rudders, so you could guide it easy. Boy! Wouldn't he come shooting down that hill by the Hickory Woods where the fellows coasted every year! They cost only four dollars and ninety-five cents and surely his grandma could afford that for him, even if his mother was sick and she had just paid her taxes. Four ninety-five—but he wouldn't want anything else if Aunt Hager would buy that sled for Santa Claus to bring him! Every day, after school, he passed by the store, where many sleds were displayed, and stood for a long time looking at this Golden Flyer of narrow hard-wood timbers varnished a shiny yellow. It had bright red runners and a beautiful bar with which to steer.

When he told Aunt Hager about it, all she said was: "Boy, is you crazy?" But Annjee smiled from her bed and answered: "Wait and see." Maybe they would get it for him—but Santa Claus was mean to poor kids sometimes, Sandy knew, when their parents had no money.

"Fifteen cents' worth of hamburger," he said absent-mindedly to the butcher when he reached the market. . . . And when Sandy came home, his grandmother whipped him for bringing ground meat instead of the soup bone for which she had sent him.

So the cold days passed, heavy and cloudy, with Annjee still in bed, and the kitchen full of garments hanging on lines to dry because, out of doors, the frozen rain kept falling. Always in Hager's room a great pile of rough-dried clothes eternally waited to be ironed. Sandy helped his grandmother as much as he could, running errands, bringing in coal and wood, pumping water in the mornings before school, and sitting by his mother in the evenings, reading to her from his *Nature Story Reader* when it wasn't too cold in her bedroom.

Annjee was able to sit up now and she said she felt better, but she looked ashen and tired. She wanted to get back to work, so she would have a little money for Christmas and be able to help Hager with the doctor's bill, but she guessed she couldn't. And she was still worrying about Jimboy. Three months had passed since he went away—a longer time than usual that he hadn't written. Maybe something *had* happened to him. Maybe he was out of work and hungry, because this was a hard winter. *Maybe he was dead!*

"O, my God, no!" Annjee cried as the thought struck her.

But one Sunday morning, ten days before Christmas, the door-bell rang violently and a special-delivery boy stood on the front porch. Annjee's heart jumped as she sat up in bed. She had seen the youngster approaching from the window. Word from Jimboy surely—or word about him!

"Ma! Sandy! Go quick and see what it is!"

"Letter for Mrs. Annjelica Rogers," said the boy, stamping the snow from his feet. "Sign here."

While Sandy held the door open, letting the cold wind blow through the house, Hager haltingly scrawled something on the boy's pink pad. Then, with the child behind her, the old woman hurried to her daughter's bed with the white envelope.

"It's from him!" Annjee cried; "I know it's from Jimboy," as she tore open the letter with trembling fingers.

A scrap of dirty tablet-paper fell on the quilt, and Annjee quickly picked it up. It was written in pencil in a feminine hand.

DEAR SISTER,

I am stranded in Memphis, Tenn. and the show has gone on to New Orleans. I can't buy anything to eat because I am broke and don't know anybody in this town. Annjee, please send me my fare to come home and mail it to the Beale Street Colored Hotel. I'm sending my love to you and mama.

Your baby sister,

HARRIETT

13
CHRISTMAS

"PO' LITTLE THING," said Hager. "Po' little thing. An' here we ain't got no money." The night before, on Saturday, Hager had bought a sack of flour, a chunk of salt pork, and some groceries. Old Dr. McDillors had called in the afternoon, and she had paid him, too.

"I reckon it would take mo'n thirty dollars to send fo' Harriett, an' Lawd knows we ain't got three dollars in de house."

Annjee lay limply back on her pillows staring out of the window at the falling snow. She had been crying.

"But never mind," her mother went on, "I's gwine see Mr. John Frank tomorrow an' see can't I borry a little mo' money on this mortgage we's got with him."

So on Monday morning the old lady left her washing and went uptown to the office of the money-lender, but the clerk there said Mr. Frank had gone to Chicago and would not be back for two weeks. There was nothing the clerk could do about it, since he himself could not lend money.

That afternoon Annjee sat up in bed and wrote a long letter to Harriett, telling her of their troubles, and before she sealed it, Sandy saw his mother slip into the envelope the three one-dollar bills that she had been guarding under her pillow.

"There goes your Santa Claus," she said to her son, "but maybe Harriett's hungry. And you don't want Aunt Harrie to be hungry, do you?"

"No'm," Sandy said.

The grey days passed and Annjee was able to get up and sit beside the kitchen-stove while her mother ironed. Every afternoon Sandy went downtown to look at the shop windows, gay with Christmas things. And he would stand and stare at the Golden Flyer sleds in Edmondson's hardware-shop. He could feel himself coasting down a long hill on one of those light, swift, red and yellow coasters, the envy of all the other boys, white and colored, who looked on.

When he went home, he described the sled minutely to Annjee and Aunt Hager and wondered aloud if that might be what he would get for Christmas. But Hager would say: "Santa Claus are just like other folks. He don't work for nothin'!" And his mother would add weakly from her chair: "This is gonna be a slim Christmas, honey, but mama'll see what she can do." She knew his heart was set on a sled, and he could tell that she knew; so maybe he would get it.

One day Annjee gathered her strength together, put a woollen dress over her kimono, wrapped a heavy cloak about herself, and went out into the back yard. Sandy, from the window, watched her picking her way slowly across the frozen ground towards the outhouse. At the trash-pile near the alley fence she stopped and, stooping down, began to pull short pieces of boards and wood from the little pile of lumber that had been left there since last summer by the carpenters who had built the porch. Several times in her labor she rose and leaned weakly against the back fence for support, and once Sandy ran out to see if he could help her, but she told him irritably to get back in the house out of the weather or she would put him to bed without any supper. Then, after placing the boards that she had succeeded in unearthing in a pile by the path, she came wearily back to the kitchen, trembling with cold.

"I'm mighty weak yet," she said to Hager, "but I'm sure much better than I was. I don't want to have the grippe no more. . . . Sandy, look in the mail-box and see has the mailman come by yet."

As the little boy returned empty-handed, he heard his mother talking about old man Logan, who used to be a carpenter.

"Maybe he can make it," she was saying, but stopped when she heard Sandy behind her. "I guess I'll lay back down now."

Aunt Hager wrung out the last piece of clothes that she had been rinsing. "Yes, chile," she said, "you go on and lay down. I's gwine make you some tea after while." And the old woman went outdoors to take from the line the frozen garments blowing in the sharp north wind.

After supper that night Aunt Hager said casually: "Well, I reckon I'll run down an' see Brother Logan a minute whilst I got nothin' else to do. Sandy, don't you let de fire go out, and take care o' yo' mama."

"Yes'm," said the little boy, drawing pictures on the oilcloth-covered table with a pin. His grandmother went out the back door and he looked through the frosty window to see which way she was going. The old woman picked up the boards that his mother had piled near the alley fence, and with them in her arms she disappeared down the alley in the dark.

After a little, Aunt Hager returned puffing and blowing.

"Can he do it?" Annjee demanded anxiously from the bedroom when she heard her mother enter.

"Yes, chile," Hager answered. "Lawd, it sho is cold out yonder! Whee! Lemme git here to this stove!"

That night it began to snow again. The great heavy flakes fell with languid gentility over the town and silently the whiteness covered everything. The next morning the snow froze to a hard sparkling crust on roofs and ground, and in the late afternoon when Sandy went to return the Reinharts' clothes, you could walk on top of the snow without sinking.

At the back door of the Reinharts' house a warm smell of plum-pudding and mince pies drifted out as he waited for the cook to bring the money. When she returned with seventy-five cents, she had a nickel for Sandy, too. As he slid along the street, he saw in many windows gay holly wreaths with red berries and big bows of ribbon tied to them. Sandy wished he could buy a holly wreath for their house. It might make his mother's room look cheerful. At home it didn't seem like Christmas with the kitchen full of drying clothes, and no Christmas-tree.

Sandy wondered if, after all, Santa Claus might, by some good fortune, bring him that Golden Flyer sled on Christmas morning. How fine this hard snow would be to coast on, down the long hill past the Hickory Woods! How light and swift he would fly with his new sled! Certainly he had been a good boy, carrying Aunt Hager's clothes for her, waiting on his mother when she was in bed, emptying the slops and cutting wood every day. And at night when he said his prayers:

Now I lay me down to sleep.
Pray the Lord my soul to keep.
If I should die before I wake,
Pray the Lord my soul to take. . . .

he had added with great earnestness: "And let Santa bring me a Golden Flyer sled, please, Lord. Amen."

But Sandy knew very well that there wasn't really any Santa Claus! He knew in his heart that Hager and his mother were Santa Claus—and that they didn't have any money. They were poor people. He was wearing his mama's shoes, as Jimmy Lane had once done. And his father and Harriett, who used to make the house gay, laughing and singing, were far away somewhere. . . . There wasn't any Santa Claus.

"I don't care," he said, tramping over the snow in the twilight on his way from the Reinharts'.

Christmas Eve. Candles and poinsettia flowers. Wreaths of evergreen. Baby trees hung with long strands of tinsel and fragile ornaments of colored glass. Sandy passed the windows of many white folks' houses where the curtains were up and warm floods of electric light made bright the cozy rooms. In Negro shacks, too, there was the dim warmth of oil-lamps and Christmas candles glowing. But at home there wasn't even a holly wreath. And the snow was whiter and harder than ever on the ground.

Tonight, though, there were no clothes drying in the kitchen when he went in. The ironing-board had been put away behind the door, and the whole place was made tidy and clean. The fire blazed and crackled in the little range; but nothing else said Christmas—no laughter, no tinsel, no tree.

Annjee had been about all day, still weak, but this afternoon she had made a trip to the store for a quarter's worth of mixed candies and nuts and a single orange, which she had hidden away until morning. Hager had baked a little cake, but there was no frosting on it such as there had been in other years, and there were no strange tissue-wrapped packages stuck away in the corners of trunks and drawers days ahead of time.

Although the little kitchen was warm enough, the two bedrooms were chilly, and the front room was freezing-cold because they kept the door there closed all the time. It was hard to afford a fire in one stove, let alone two, Aunt Hager kept saying, with nobody working but herself.

"I's thinking about Harriett," she remarked after their Christmas Eve supper as she rocked before the fire, "and how I's always tried to raise her right."

"And I'm thinking about—well, there ain't no use mentionin' him," Annjee said.

A sleigh slid by with jingling bells and shouts of laughter from the occupants, and a band of young people passed on their way to church, singing carols. After a while another sleigh came along with a jolly sound.

"Santa Claus!" said Annjee, smiling at her serious little son. "You better hurry and go to bed, because he'll be coming soon. And be sure to hang up your stocking."

But Sandy was afraid that she was fooling, and, as he pulled off his clothes, he left his stockings on the floor, stuck into the women's shoes he had been wearing. Then, leaving the bedroom door half open so that the heat and a little light from the kitchen would come in, he climbed into his mother's bed. But he wasn't going to close his eyes yet. Sandy had discovered long ago that you could hear and see many things by not going to sleep when the family expected you to; therefore he remained awake tonight.

His mother was talking to Aunt Hager now: "I don't think he'll charge us anything, do you, ma?" And the old woman answered: "No, chile, Brother Logan's been tryin' to be ma beau for twenty years, an' he ain't gonna charge us nothin'."

Annjee came into the half-dark bedroom and looked at Sandy, lying still on the side of the bed towards the window. Then she took down her heavy coat from the wall and, sitting on the edge of a chair, began to pull on her rubbers. In a few moments he heard the front door close softly. His mother had gone out.

Where could she be going, he wondered, this time of night? He heard her footsteps crunching the hard snow and, rolling over close to the window, he pulled aside the shade a little and looked out. In the moonlight he saw Annjee moving slowly down the street past Sister Johnson's house, walking carefully over the snow like a very weak woman.

"Mama's still sick," the child thought, with his nose pressed against the cold window-pane. "I wish I could a bought her a present today."

Soon an occasional snore from the kitchen told Sandy that Hager dozed peacefully in her rocker beside the stove. He sat up in bed, wrapped a quilt about his shoulders, and remained looking out the window, with the shade hanging behind his back.

The white snow sparkled in the moonlight, and the trees made striking black shadows across the yard. Next door at the Johnsons' all was dark and quiet, but across the street, where white folks lived, the lights were burning brightly and a big Christmas-tree with all its candles aglow stood in the large bay window while a woman loaded it with toys. Sandy knew that four children lived there, three boys and a girl, whom he had often watched playing on the lawn. Sometimes he wished he had a brother or sister to play with him, too, because it was very quiet in a house with only grown-ups about. And right now it was dismal and lonely to be by himself looking out the window of a cold bedroom on Christmas Eve.

Then a woman's cloaked figure came slowly back past Sister Johnson's house in the moonlight, and Sandy saw that it was his mother returning, her head down and her shadow moving blackly on the snow. You could hear the dry grate of her heels on the frozen whiteness as she walked, leaning forward, dragging something heavy behind her. Sandy prepared to lie down quickly in bed again, but he kept his eyes against the window-pane to see what Annjee was pulling, and, as she came closer to the house, he could distinguish quite clearly behind her a solid, home-made sled bumping rudely over the snow.

Before Annjee's feet touched the porch, he was lying still as though he had been asleep a long time.

The morning sunlight was tumbling brightly into the windows when Sandy opened his eyes and blinked at the white world outside.

"Aren't you ever going to get up?" asked Annjee, smiling timidly above him. "It's Christmas morning, honey. Come see what Santa Claus brought you. Get up quick."

But he didn't want to get up. He knew what Santa Claus had brought him and he wanted to stay in bed with his face to the wall. It wasn't a Golden Flyer sled—and now he couldn't even hope for one any longer. He wanted to pull the covers over his head and cry, but, "Boy! You ain't up yet?" called Aunt Hager cheerily from the kitchen. "De little Lawd Jesus is in His manger fillin' all de world with light. An' old Santa done been here an' gone! Get out from there, chile, an' see!"

"I'm coming, grandma," said Sandy slowly, wiping his tear-filled eyes and rolling out of bed as he forced his mouth to smile wide and steady at the few little presents he saw on the floor—for the child knew he was expected to smile.

"O! A sled!" he cried in a voice of mock surprise that wasn't his own at all; for there it stood, heavy and awkward, against the wall and beside it on the floor lay two picture-books from the ten-cent store and a pair of white cotton gloves. Above the sled his stocking, tacked to the wall, was partly filled with candy, and the single orange peeped out from the top.

But the sled! Home-made by some rough carpenter, with strips of rusty tin nailed along the wooden runners, and a piece of clothes-line to pull it with!

"It's fine," Sandy lied, as he tried to lift it and place it on the floor as you would in coasting; but it was very heavy, and too wide for a boy to run with in his hands. You could never get a swift start. And a board was warped in the middle.

"It's a nice sled, grandma," he lied. "I like it, mama."

"Mr. Logan made it for you," his mother answered proudly, happy that he was pleased. "I knew you wanted a sled all the time."

"It's a nice sled," Sandy repeated, grinning steadily as he held the heavy object in his hands. "It's an awful nice sled."

"Well, make haste and look at de gloves, and de candy, and them pretty books, too," called Hager from the kitchen, where she was frying strips of salt pork. "My, you sho is a slow chile on Christmas mawnin'! Come 'ere and lemme kiss you." She came to the bedroom and picked him up in her arms. "Christmas gift to Hager's baby chile! Come on, Annjee, bring his clothes out here behind de stove an' bring his books, too. . . . This here's Little Red Riding Hood and the Wolf, and this here's Hansee and Gretsle on de cover—but I reckon you can read 'em better'n I can. . . . Daughter, set de table. Breakfast's 'bout ready now. Look in de oven an' see 'bout that cornbread. . . . Lawd, this here Sandy's just like a baby lettin' ole Hager hold him and dress him. . . . Put yo' foot in that stocking, boy!" And Sandy began to feel happier, sitting on his grandmother's lap behind the stove.

Before noon Buster had come and gone, showing off his new shoes and telling his friend about the train he had gotten that ran on a real track when you wound it up. After dinner Willie-Mae appeared bringing a naked rag doll and a set of china dishes in a blue box. And Sister Johnson sent them a mince pie as a Christmas gift.

Almost all Aunt Hager's callers knocked at the back door, but in the late afternoon the front bell rang and Annjee sent Sandy through the cold parlor to answer it. There on the porch stood his Aunt Tempy, with several gaily wrapped packages in her arms. She was almost a stranger to Sandy, yet she kissed him peremptorily on the forehead as he stood in the doorway. Then she came through the house into the kitchen, with much the air of a mistress of the manor descending to the servants' quarters.

"Land sakes alive!" said Hager, rising to kiss her.

Tempy hugged Annjee, too, before she sat down, stiffly, as

though the house she was in had never been her home. To little black Willie-Mae she said nothing.

"I'm sorry I couldn't invite you for Christmas dinner today, but you know how Mr. Siles is," Tempy began to explain to her mother and sister. "My husband is home so infrequently, and he doesn't like a house full of company, but of course Dr. and Mrs. Glenn Mitchell will be in later in the evening. They drop around any time. . . . But I had to run down and bring you a few presents. . . . You haven't seen my new piano yet, have you, mother? I must come and take you home with me some nice afternoon." She smiled appropriately, but her voice was hard.

"How is you an' yo' new church makin' it?" asked Hager, slightly embarrassed in the presence of her finely dressed society daughter.

"Wonderful!" Tempy replied. "Wonderful! Father Hill is so dignified, and the services are absolutely refined! There's never anything niggerish about them—so you know, mother, they suit me."

"I's glad you likes it," said Hager.

There was an awkward silence; then Tempy distributed her gifts, kissed them all as though it were her Christian duty, and went her way, saying that she had calls to make at Lawyer and Mrs. Moore's, and Professor Booth's, and Madam Temple's before she returned home. When she had gone, everybody felt relieved—as though a white person had left the house. Willie-Mae began to play again, and Hager pushed her feet out of her shoes once more, while Annjee went into the bedroom and lay down.

Sandy sat on the floor and untied his present, wrapped in several thicknesses of pink tissue paper, and found, in a bright Christmas box, a big illustrated volume of *Andersen's Fairy Tales* decorated in letters of gold. With its heavy pages and fine pictures, it made the ten-cent-store books that Hager had bought him appear cheap and thin. It made his mother's sled look cheap, too, and shamed all the other gifts the ones he loved had given him.

"I don't want it," he said suddenly, as loud as he could. "I don't want Tempy's old book!" And from where he was sitting, he threw it with all his might underneath the stove.

Hager gasped in astonishment. "Pick that up, sir," she cried amazed. "Yo' Aunt Tempy done bought you a fine purty book an' here you throwin' it un'neath de stove in de ashes! Lawd have mercy! Pick it up, I say, this minute!"

"I won't!" cried Sandy stubbornly. "I won't! I like my sled what you-all gave me, but I don't want no old book from Tempy! I won't pick it up!"

Then the astonished Hager grabbed him by the scruff of the neck and jerked him to his feet.

"Do I have to whip you yet this holy day? . . . Pick up that book, sir!"

"No!" he yelled.

She gave him a startled rap on the head with the back of her hand. "Talkin' sassy to yo' old grandma an' tellin' her no!"

"What is it?" Annjee called from the bedroom, as Sandy began to wail.

"Nothin'," Hager replied, "'ceptin' this chile's done got beside hisself an' I has to hit him—that's all!"

But Sandy was not hurt by his grandmother's easy rap. He was used to being struck on the back of the head for misdemeanors, and this time he welcomed the blow because it gave him, at last, what he had been looking for all day—a sufficient excuse to cry. Now his pent-up tears flowed without ceasing while Willie-Mae sat in a corner clutching her rag doll to her breast, and Tempy's expensive gift lay in the ashes beneath the stove.

14
RETURN

AFTER CHRISTMAS THERE followed a period of cold weather, made bright by the winter sun shining on the hard crusty snow, where children slid and rolled, and over which hay-wagons made into sleighs on great heavy runners drove jingling into town from the country. There was skating on the frozen river and fine sledding on the hills beyond the woods, but Sandy never went out where the crowds were with his sled, because he was ashamed of it.

After New Year's Annjee went back to work at Mrs. Rice's, still coughing a little and still weak. But with bills to pay and Sandy in need of shoes and stockings and clothes to wear to school, she couldn't remain idle any longer. Even with her mother washing and ironing every day except the Sabbath, expenses were difficult to meet, and Aunt Hager was getting pretty old to work so hard. Annjee thought that Tempy ought to help them a little, but she was too proud to ask her. Besides, Tempy had never been very affectionate towards her sisters even when they were all girls together—but she ought to help look out for their mother. Hager, however, when Annjee brought up the subject of Tempy's help, said that she was still able to wash, thank God, and wasn't depending on any of her children for anything—not so long as white folks wore clothes.

At school Sandy passed all of his mid-year tests and, along with Sadie Butler, was advanced to the fifth A, but the other colored child in the class, a little fat girl named Mary Jones, failed and had to stay behind. Mary's mother, a large sulphur-yellow woman who cooked at the Drummer's Hotel, came to the school and told the teacher, before all the children, just what she thought of her for letting Mary fail—and her thoughts were not very complimentary to the stiff, middle-aged white lady who taught the class. The question of color came up, too, during the discussion.

"Look at ma chile settin' back there behind all de white ones," screamed the sulphur-yellow woman. "An' me payin' as much taxes as anybody! You treats us colored folks like we ain't citizerzens—that's what you does!" The argument had to be settled in the principal's office, where the teacher went with the enraged mother, while the white children giggled that a fat, yellow colored lady should come to school to quarrel about her daughter's not being promoted. But the colored children in the class couldn't laugh.

St. Valentine's day came and Sadie Butler sent Sandy a big red heart. But for Annjee, "the mail-man passed and didn't leave no news," because Jimboy hadn't written yet, nor had Harriett thanked her for the three dollars she had mailed to Memphis before Christmas. There were no letters from anybody.

The work at Mrs. Rice's was very heavy, because Mrs. Rice's sister, with two children, had come from Indiana to spend the winter, and Annjee had to cook for them and clean their rooms, too. But she was managing to save a little money every week. She bought Sandy a new blue serge suit with a Norfolk coat and knickerbocker pants. And then he sat up very stiffly in Sterner's studio and had his picture taken.

The freckled-faced white boy, Paul Biggers, who sat across from Sandy in school, delivered the *Daily Leader* to several streets in Sandy's neighborhood, and Sandy sometimes went with him, helping to fold and throw the papers in the various doorways. One night it was almost seven o'clock when he got home.

"I had a great mind not to wait for you," said Aunt Hager, who had long had the table set for supper. "Wash yo' face an' hands, sir! An' brush that snow off yo' coat 'fo' you hang it up."

His grandmother took a pan of hot spoon-bread from the oven and put it on the table, where the little oil-lamp glowed warmly and the plain white dishes looked clean and inviting. On the stove there was a skillet full of fried apples and bacon, and Hager was making a pot of tea.

"Umn-nn! Smells good!" said Sandy, speaking of everything at once as he slid into his chair. "Gimme a lot o' apples, grandma."

"Is that de way you ask fo' 'em, sir? Can't you say please no mo'?"

"Please, ma'am," said the boy, grinning, for Hager's sharpness wasn't serious, and her old eyes were twinkling.

While they were eating, Annjee came in from work with a small bucket of oyster soup in her hands. They heated this and added it to their supper, and Sandy's mother sat down in front of the stove, with her feet propped up on the grate to dry quickly. It was very comfortable in the little kitchen.

"Seems like the snow's melting," said Annjee. "It's kinder sloppy and nasty underfoot. . . . Ain't been no mail today, has they?"

"No, honey," said Hager. "Leastwise, I been washin' so hard ain't had no time to look in de box. Sandy, run there to de front do' an' see. But I knows there ain't nothin', nohow."

"Might be," said Annjee as Sandy took a match and went through the dark bedroom and parlor to the front porch. There was no mail. But Sandy saw, coming across the slushy dirty-white snow towards the house, a slender figure approaching in the gloom. He waited, shivering in the doorway a moment to see who it was; then all at once he yelled at the top of his lungs: "Aunt Harrie's here!"

Pulling her by the hand, after having kissed and hugged and almost choked her, he ran back to the kitchen. "Look, here's Aunt Harrie!" he cried. "Aunt Harrie's home!" And Hager turned from the table, upsetting her tea, and opened wide her arms to take her to her bosom.

"Ma chile!" she shouted. "Done come home again! Ma baby chile come home!"

Annjee hugged and kissed Harriett, too, as her sister sat on Hager's knees—and the kitchen was filled with sound, warm and free and loving, for the prodigal returned.

"Ma chile's come back!" her mother repeated over and over. "Thank de Lawd! Ma chile's back!"

"You want some fried apples, Harrie?" asked Sandy, offering her his plate. "You want some tea?"

"No, thank you, honey," she replied when the excitement had subsided and Aunt Hager had released her, with her little black hat askew and the powder kissed off one side of her face.

She got up, shook herself, and removed her hat to brush down her hair, but she kept her faded coat on as she laid her little purse of metal mesh on the table. Then she sat down on the chair that Annjee offered her near the fire. She was thinner and her hair had been bobbed, giving her a boyish appearance, like the black pages in old Venetian paintings. But her lips were red and there were two little spots of rouge burning on each cheek, although her eyes were dark with heavy shadows as though she had been ill.

Hager was worried. "Has you been sick, chile?" she asked.

"No, mama," Harriett said. "I've been all right—just had a hard time, that's all. I got mad, and quit the show in Memphis, and they wouldn't pay me—so that was that! The minstrels left the carnival for the winter and started playing the theatres, and the new manager was a cheap skate. I couldn't get along with him."

"Did you get my letter and the money?" Annjee asked. "We didn't have no more to send you, and afterwards, when you didn't write, I didn't know if you got it."

"I got it and meant to thank you, sis, but I don't know—just didn't get round to it. But, anyway, I'm out of the South now. It's a hell—I mean it's an awful place if you don't know anybody! And more hungry niggers down there! I wonder who made up that song about *Dear Old Southland*. There's nothing dear about it that I can see. Good God! It's awful! . . . But I'm back." She smiled. "Where's Jimboy? . . . O, that's right, Annjee—you told me in the letter. But I sort-a miss him around here. Lord, I hope he didn't go to Memphis!"

"Did you find a job down there?" Annjee asked, looking at her sister's delicate hands.

"Sure, I found a *job* all right," Harriett replied in a tone that made Annjee ask no more questions. "Jobs are like hen's teeth—try and find 'em." And she shrugged her shoulders as Sandy had so often seen her do, but she no longer seemed to him like a little girl. She was grown-up and hard and strange now, but he still loved her.

"Aunt Harrie, I passed to the fifth A," he announced proudly.

"That's wonderful," she answered. "My, but you're smart! You'll be a great man some day, sure, Sandy."

"Where's yo' suit-case, honey?" Hager interrupted, too happy to touch her food on the table or to take her eyes away from the face of her returned child. "Didn't you bring it back with you? Where is it?"

"Sure, I got it. . . . But I'm gonna live at Maudel's this time, mama. . . . I left it at the station. I didn't think you-all'd want me here." She tried to make the words careless-like, but they were pitifully forced.

"Aw, honey!" Annjee cried, the tears coming.

The shadow of inner pain passed over Hager's black face, but the only reply she made was: "You's growed up now, chile. I reckon you knows what you's doin'. You's been ten thousand miles away from yo' mammy, an' I reckon you knows. . . . Come on, Sandy, let's we eat." Slowly the old woman returned to the cold food on her plate. "Won't you eat something with us, daughter?"

Harriett's eyes lowered and her shoulders drooped. "No, mama, thank you. I'm—not hungry."

Then a long, embarrassing silence followed while Hager gulped at her tea, Sandy tried to swallow a mouthful of bread that seemed to choke him, and Annjee stared stupidly at the stove.

Finally Harriett said: "I got to go now." She stood up to button her coat and put on her hat. Then she took her metal purse from the table.

"Maudel'll be waiting for me, but I'll be seeing you-all again soon, I guess. Good-bye, Sandy honey! I got to go. . . . Annjee, I got to go now. . . . Good-bye, mama!" She was trembling. As she bent down to kiss Hager, her purse slipped out of her hands and fell in a little metal heap on the floor. She stooped to pick it up.

"I got to go now."

A tiny perfume-bottle in the bag had broken from the fall, and as she went through the cold front room towards the door, the odor of cheap and poignant drugstore violets dripped across the house.

15
ONE BY ONE

YOU COULD SMELL the spring.

" 'Tain't gwine be warm fo' weeks yet!" Hager said.

Nevertheless, you could smell the spring. Little boys were already running in the streets without their overcoats, and the ground-hog had seen its shadow. Snow remained in the fence corners, but it had melted on the roofs. The yards were wet and muddy, but no longer white.

It was a sunny afternoon in late March that a letter came. On his last delivery the mail-man stopped, dropped it in the box—and Sandy saw him. It was addressed to his mother and he knew it must be from Jimboy.

"Go on an' take it to her," his grandma said, as soon as she saw the boy coming with it in his hand. "I knows that's what you want to do. Go on an' take it." And she bent over her ironing again.

Sandy ran almost all the way to Mrs. Rice's, dropping the letter more than once on the muddy sidewalk, so excited he did not think to put it in his pocket. Into the big yard and around to the white lady's back door he sped—and it was locked! He knocked loudly for a long time, and finally an upper window opened and Annjee, a dust-rag around her head, looked down, squinting in the sunlight.

"Who's there?" she called stridently, thinking of some peddler or belated tradesman for whom she did not wish to stop her cleaning.

Sandy pantingly held up the letter and was about to say something when the window closed with a bang. He could hear his mother almost falling down the back stairs, she was coming so fast. Then the key turned swiftly in the lock, the door opened, and, without closing it, Annjee took the letter from him and tore it open where she stood.

"It's from Jimboy!"

Sandy stood on the steps looking at his mother, her bosom heaving, her sleeves rolled up, and the white cloth tied about her head, doubly white against her dark-brown face.

"He's in Detroit, it says. . . . Umn! I ain't never seen him write such a long letter. 'I had a hard time this winter till I landed here,' it says, 'but things look pretty good now, and there is lots of building going on and plenty of work opening up in the automobile plants . . . a mighty lot of colored folks here . . . hope you and Sandy been well. Sorry couldn't send you nothing Xmas, but I was in St. Paul broke. . . . Kiss my son for me. . . . Tell ma hello even if she don't want to hear it. Your loving husband, Jimboy Rogers.' "

Annjee did her best to hold the letter with one hand and pick up Sandy with the other, but he had grown considerably during the winter and she was still a little weak from her illness; so she bent down to his level and kissed him several times before she re-read the letter.

"From your daddy!" she said. "Umn-mn. . . . Come on in here and warm yourself. Lemme see what he says again!" . . . She lighted the gas oven in the white kitchen and sat down in front of it with her letter, forgetting the clock and the approaching time for Mrs. Rice's dinner, forgetting everything. "A letter from my daddy! From my far-off sugar-daddy!"

"From *my* daddy," corrected Sandy. . . . "Say, gimme a nickel to buy some marbles, mama. I wanta go play."

Without taking her eyes from the precious note Annjee fumbled in her apron and found a coin. "Take it and go on!" she said.

It was a dime. Sandy skipped around the house and down the street in the chilly sunshine. He decided to stop at Buster's for a while before going home, since he had to pass there anyway, and he found his friend in the house trying to carve boats from clothes-pins with a rusty jack-knife.

Buster's mother was a seamstress, and, after opening the front door and greeting Sandy with a cheery "Hello," she returned to her machine and a friend who was calling on her. She was a tall young light-mulatto woman, with skin like old ivory. Maybe that was why Buster was so white. But her husband was a black man who worked on the city's garbage-trucks and was active politically when election time came, getting colored men to vote Republican. Everybody said he made lots of money, but that he wasn't really Buster's father.

The golden-haired child gave Sandy a butcher-knife and together they whacked at the clothes-pins. You could hear the two women talking plainly in the little sewing-room, where the machine ran between snatches of conversation.

"Yes," Buster's mother was saying, "I have the hardest time keeping that boy colored! He goes on just like he was white. Do you know what he did last week? Cut all the blossoms off my geranium plants here in the house, took them to school, and gave them to Dorothy Marlow, in his grade. And you know who Dorothy is, don't you? Senator Marlow's daughter! . . . I said: 'Buster, if you ever cut my flowers to carry to any little girl again, I'll punish you severely, but if you cut them to carry to little white girls, I don't know what I'll do with you. . . . Don't you know they hang colored boys for things like that?' I wanted to scare him—because you know there might be trouble even among kids in school over such things. . . . But I had to laugh."

Her friend laughed too. "He's a hot one, taking flowers to the women already, and a white girl at that! You've got a fast-working son, Elvira, I must say. . . . But, do you know, when you first moved here and I saw you and the boy going in and out, I thought sure you were both white folks. I didn't know you was colored till my husband said: 'That's Eddie's wife!' You-all sure looked white to me."

The machine started to whir, making the conversation inaudible for a few minutes, and when Sandy caught their words again, they were talking about the Elks' club-house that the colored people were planning to build.

"Can you go out?" Sandy demanded of Buster, since they were making no headway with the tough clothes-pins and dull knives.

"Maybe," said Buster. "I'll go see." And he went into the other room and asked his mother.

"Put on your overcoat," she commanded. "It's not summer yet. And be back in here before dark."

"All right, Vira," the child said.

The two children went to Mrs. Rumford's shop on the corner and bought three cents' worth of candy and seven cents' worth of peewees with which to play marbles when it got warm. Then Sandy walked back past Buster's house with him and they played for a while in the street before Sandy turned to run home.

Aunt Hager was making mush for supper. She sent him to the store for a pint bottle of milk as soon as he arrived, but he forgot to take the bottle and had to come back for it.

"You'd forget yo' head if it wasn't tied to you!" the old woman reminded him.

They were just finishing supper when Annjee got home with two chocolate éclairs in her coat-pocket, mashed together against Jimboy's letter.

"Huh! I'm crazy!" she said, running her hand down into the sticky mess. "But listen, ma! He's got a job and is doing well in Detroit, Jimboy says. . . . And I'm going to him!"

"You what?" Hager gasped, dropping her spoon in her mush-bowl. "What you sayin'?"

"I said I'm going to him, ma! I got to!" Annjee stood with her coat and hat still on, holding the sticky letter. "I'm going where my heart is, ma! . . . Oh, not today." She put her arms around her mother's neck. "I don't mean today, mama, nor next week. I got to save some money first. I only got a little now. But I mean I'm going to him soon's I can. I can't help it, ma—I love him!"

"Lawd, is you foolish!" cried Hager. "What's you gwine do with this chile, trapesin' round after Jimboy? What you gwine do if he leaves you in Detroiter or wherever he are? What you gwine do then? You loves him! Huh!"

"But he ain't gonna leave me in Detroit, 'cause I'm going with him everywhere he goes," she said, her eyes shining. "He ain't gonna leave me no more!"

"An' Sandy?"

"Couldn't he stay with you, mama? And then maybe we'd come back here and live, Jimboy and me, some time, when we get a little money ahead, and could pay off the mortgage on the house. . . . But there ain't no use arguing, mama, I got to go!"

Hager had never seen Annjee so positive before; she sat speechless, looking at the bowl of mush.

"I got to go where it ain't lonesome and where I ain't unhappy—and that's where Jimboy is! I got to go soon as I can."

Hager rose to put some water on the stove to heat for the dishes.

"One by one you leaves me—Tempy, then Harriett, then you," she said. "But Sandy's gonna stick by me, ain't you, son? He ain't gwine leave his grandma."

The youngster looked at Hager, moving slowly about the kitchen putting away the supper things.

"And I's gwine to make a fine man out o' you, Sandy. I's gwine raise one chile right yet, if de Lawd lets me live—just one chile right!" she murmured.

That night the March wind began to blow and the window-panes rattled. Sandy woke up in the dark, lying close and warm beside his mother. When he went back to sleep again, he dreamed that his Aunt Tempy's Christmas book had been turned into a chariot, and that he was riding through the sky with Tempy standing very dignifiedly beside him as he drove. And he couldn't see anybody down on earth, not even Hager.

When his mother rolled out at six o'clock to go to work, he woke up again, and while she dressed, he lay watching his breath curl mistily upwards in the cold room. Outside the window it was bleak and grey and the March wind, humming through the leafless branches of the trees, blew terrifically. He heard Aunt Hager in the kitchen poking at the stove, making up a blaze to start the coffee boiling. Then the front door closed when his mother went out and, as the door slammed, the wind howled fiercely. It was nice and warm in bed, so he lay under the heavy quilts half dreaming, half thinking, until his grandmother shook him to get up. And many were the queer, dream-drowsy thoughts that floated through his mind—not only that morning, but almost every morning while he lay beneath the warm quilts until Hager had called him three or four times to get ready for school.

He wondered sometimes whether if he washed and washed his face and hands, he would ever be white. Someone had told him once that blackness was only skin-deep. . . . And would he ever have a big house with electric lights in it, like his Aunt Tempy—but it was mostly white people who had such fine things, and they were mean to colored. . . . Some white folks were nice, though. Earl was nice at school, but not the little boys across the street, who called him "nigger" every day . . . and not Mrs. Rice, who scolded his mother. . . . Aunt Harrie didn't like any white folks at all. . . . But Jesus was white and wore a long, white robe, like a woman's, on the Sunday-school cards. . . . Once Jimmy Lane said: "God damn Jesus" when the teacher scolded him for not knowing his Bible lesson. He said it out loud in church, too, and the church didn't fall down on him, as Sandy thought it might. . . . Grandma said it was a sin to cuss and swear, but all the fellows at school swore—and Jimboy did, too. But every time Sandy said "God damn," he felt bad, because Aunt Hager said God was mighty good and it was wrong to take His name in vain. But he would like to learn to say "God damn" without feeling anything like most boys said it—just "God damn! . . . God damn! . . . God damn!" without being ashamed of himself. . . . The Lord never seemed to notice, anyhow. . . . And when he got big, he wanted to travel like Jimboy. He wanted to be a railroad engineer, but Harriett had said there weren't any colored engineers on trains. . . . What would he be, then? Maybe a doctor; but it was more fun being an engineer and travelling far away.

Sandy wished Annjee would take him with her when she went to join Jimboy—but then Aunt Hager would be all by herself, and grandma was so nice to him he would hate to leave her alone. Who would cut wood for her then? . . . But when he got big, he would go to Detroit. And maybe New York, too, where his geography said they had the tallest buildings in the world, and trains that ran under the river. . . . He wondered if there were any colored people in New York. . . . How ugly African colored folks looked in the geography—with bushy heads and wild eyes! Aunt Hager said her mother was an African, but she wasn't ugly and wild; neither was Aunt Hager; neither was little dark Willie-Mae, and they were all black like Africans. . . . And Reverend Braswell was as black as ink, but he knew God. . . . God didn't care if people were black, did He? . . . What was God? Was He a man or a lamb or what? Buster's mother said God was a light, but Aunt Hager said He was a King and had a throne and wore a crown—she intended to sit down by His side by and by. . . . Was Buster's father white? Buster was white and colored both. But he didn't look like he was colored. What made Buster not colored? . . . And what made girls different from boys? . . . Once when they were playing house, Willie-Mae told him how girls were different from boys, but they didn't know why. Now Willie-Mae was in the seventh grade and had hard little breasts that stuck out sharp-like, and Jimmy Lane said dirty things about Willie-Mae. . . . Once he asked his mother what his navel was for and she said, "Layovers to catch meddlers." What did that mean? . . . And how come ladies got sick and stayed in bed when they had babies? Where did babies come from, anyhow? Not from storks—a fairy-story like Santa Claus. . . . Did God love people who told fairy-stories and lied to kids about storks and Santa Claus? . . . Santa Claus was no good, anyhow! God damn Santa Claus for not bringing him the sled he wanted at Christmas! It was all a lie about Santa Claus!

The sound of Hager pouring coal on the fire and dragging her wash-tubs across the kitchen-floor to get ready for work broke in on Sandy's drowsy half-dreams, and as he rolled over in bed, his grandmother, hearing the springs creak, called loudly: "You Sandy! Get up from there! It's seven and past! You want to be late gettin' to yo' school?"

"Yes'm, I'm coming, grandma!" he said under the quilts. "But it's cold in here."

"You knows you don't dress in yonder! Bring them clothes on out behind this stove, sir."

"Yes'm." So with a kick of the feet his covers went flying back and Sandy ran to the warmth of the little kitchen, where he dressed, washed, and ate. Then he yelled for Willie-Mae—when he felt like it—or else went on to school without her, joining some of the boys on the way.

So spring was coming and Annjee worked diligently at Mrs. Rice's day after day. Often she did something extra for Mrs. Rice's sister and her children—pressed a shirtwaist or ironed some stockings—and so added a few quarters or maybe even a dollar to her weekly wages, all of which she saved to help carry her to Jimboy in Detroit.

For ten years she had been cooking, washing, ironing, scrubbing—and for what? For only the few weeks in a year, or a half-year, when Jimboy would come home from some strange place and take her in his strong arms and kiss her and murmur: "Annjee, baby!" That's what she had been working for—then the dreary months were as nothing, and the hard years faded away. But now he had been gone all winter, and, from his letter, he might not come back soon, because he said Detroit was a fine place for colored folks. . . . But Stanton—well, Annjee thought there must surely be better towns, where a woman wouldn't have to work so hard to live. . . . And where Jimboy was.

So before the first buds opened on the apple-tree in the back yard, Annjee had gone to Detroit, leaving Sandy behind with his grandmother. And when the apple blossoms came in full bloom, there was no one living in the little house but a grey-headed old woman and her grandchild.

"One by one they leaves you," Hager said slowly. "One by one yo' chillen goes."

16
NOTHING BUT LOVE

"A YEAR AGO tonight was de storm what blowed ma porch away! You 'members, honey? . . . Done seem like this year took more'n ma porch, too. My baby chile's left home an' gone to stay down yonder in de Bottoms with them triflin' Smothers family, where de piano's goin' night an' day. An' yo' mammy's done gone a-trapesin' after Jimboy. . . . Well, I thanks de Lawd you ain't gone too. You's mighty little an' knee-high to a duck, but you's ma stand-by. You's all I got, an' you ain't gwine leave yo' old grandma, is you?"

Hager had turned to Sandy in these lonely days for comfort and companionship. Through the long summer evenings they sat together on the front porch and she told her grandchild stories. Sometimes Sister Johnson came over and sat with them for a while smoking. Sometimes Madam de Carter, full of chatter and big words about the lodge and the race, would be there. But more often the two were alone—the black wash-woman with the grey hair and the little brown boy. Slavery-time stories, myths, folk-tales like the Rabbit and the Tar Baby; the war, Abe Lincoln, freedom; visions of the Lord; years of faith and labor, love and struggle filled Aunt Hager's talk of a summer night, while the lightning-bugs glowed and glimmered and the katydids chirruped, and the stars sparkled in the far-off heavens.

Sandy was getting to be too big a boy to sit in his grandmother's lap and be rocked to sleep as in summers gone by; now he sat on a little stool beside her, leaning his head on her legs when he was tired. Or else he lay flat on the floor of the porch listening, and looking up at the stars. Tonight Hager talked about love.

"These young ones what's comin' up now, they calls us ole fogies, an' handkerchief heads, an' white folks' niggers 'cause we don't get mad an' rar' up in arms like they does 'cause things is kinder hard, but, honey, when you gets old, you knows they ain't no sense in gettin' mad an' sourin' yo' soul with hatin' peoples. White folks is white folks, an' colored folks is colored, an' neither one of 'em is bad as t'other make out. For mighty nigh seventy years I been knowin' both of 'em, an' I ain't never had no room in ma heart to hate neither white nor colored. When you starts hatin' people, you gets uglier than they is—an' I ain't never had no time for ugliness, 'cause that's where de devil comes in—in ugliness!

"They talks 'bout slavery time an' they makes out now like it were de most awfullest time what ever was, but don't you believe it, chile, 'cause it weren't all that bad. Some o' de white folks was just as nice to their niggers as they could be, nicer than many of 'em is now, what makes 'em work for less than they needs to eat. An' in those days they had to feed 'em. An' they ain't every white man beat his slaves neither! Course I ain't sayin' 'twas no paradise, but I ain't going to say it were no hell either. An' maybe I's kinder seein' it on de bestest side 'cause I worked in de big house an' ain't never went to de fields like most o' de niggers did. Ma mammy were de big-house cook an' I grewed up right with her in de kitchen an' played with little Miss Jeanne. An' Miss Jeanne taught me to read what little I knowed. An' when she growed up an' I growed up, she kept me with her like her friend all de time. I loved her an' she loved me. Miss Jeanne were de mistress' daughter, but warn't no difference 'tween us 'ceptin' she called me Hager an' I called her Miss Jeanne. But what difference do one word like 'Miss' make in yo' heart? None, chile, none. De words don't make no difference if de love's there.

"I disremembers what year it were de war broke out, but white folks was scared, an' niggers, too. Didn't know what might happen. An' we heard talk o' Abraham Lincoln 'way down yonder in de South. An' de ole marster, ole man Winfield, took his gun an' went to war, an' de young son, too, an' de superintender and de overseer—all of 'em gone to follow Lee. Ain't left nothin' but womens an' niggers on de plantation.

De womens was a-cryin' an' de niggers was, too, 'cause they was sorry for de po' grievin' white folks.

"Is I ever told you how Miss Jeanne an' Marster Robert was married in de springtime o' de war, with de magnolias all a-bloomin' like candles for they weddin'? Is I ever told you, Sandy? . . . Well, I must some time. An' then Marster Robert had to go right off with his mens, 'cause he's a high officer in de army an' they heard Sherman were comin'. An' he left her a-standin' with her weddin'-clothes on, leanin' 'gainst a pillar o' de big white porch, with nobody but me to dry her eyes—ole Missis done dead an' de men-folks all gone to war. An' nobody in that big whole mansion but black ole deaf Aunt Granny Jones, what kept de house straight, an' me, what was stayin' with ma mistress.

"O, de white folks needed niggers then mo'n they ever did befo', an' they ain't a colored person what didn't stick by 'em when all they men-folks were gone an' de white womens was a-cryin' an' a-faintin' like they did in them days.

"But lemme tell you 'bout Miss Jeanne. She just set in her room an' cry. A-holdin' Marster Bob's pitcher, she set an' cry, an' she ain't come out o' her room to see 'bout nothin'—house, horses, cotton—nothin'. But de niggers, they ain't cheat her nor steal from her. An' come de news dat her brother done got wounded an' died in Virginia, an' her cousins got de yaller fever. Then come de news that Marster Robert, Miss Jeanne's husband, ain't no mo'! Killed in de battle! An' I thought Miss Jeanne would like to go crazy. De news say he died like a soldier, brave an' fightin'. But when she heard it, she went to de drawer an' got out her weddin'-veil an' took her flowers in her hands like she were goin' to de altar to meet de groom. Then she just sink in de flo' an' cry till I pick her up an' hold her like a chile.

"Well, de freedom come, an' all de niggers scatter like buckshot, goin' to live in town. An' de yard niggers say I's a ole fool! I's free now—why don't I come with them? But I say no, I's gwine stay with Miss Jeanne—an' I stayed. I 'lowed ain't nary one o' them colored folks needed me like Miss Jeanne did, so I ain't went with 'em.

"An' de time pass; it pass an' it pass, an' de ole house get rusty for lack o' paint, an' de things, they 'gin to fall to pieces. An' Miss Jeanne say: 'Hager, I ain't got nobody in de world but you.' An' I say: 'Miss Jeanne, I ain't got nobody in de world but you neither.'

"And then she'd start talkin' 'bout her young husband what died so handsome an' brave, what ain't even had time that last day fo' to 'scort her to de church for de weddin', nor to hold her in his arms 'fore de orders come to leave. An' we would set on de big high ole porch, with its tall stone pillars, in de evenin's twilight till de bats start flyin' overhead an' de sunset glow done gone, she in her wide white skirts a-billowin' round her slender waist, an' me in ma apron an' cap an' this here chain she gimme you see on ma neck all de time an' what's done wore so thin.

"They was a ole stump of a blasted tree in de yard front o' de porch 'bout tall as a man, with two black pieces o' branches raised up like arms in de air. We used to set an' look at it, an' Miss Jeanne could see it from her bedroom winder upstairs, an' sometimes this stump, it look like it were movin' right up de path like a man.

"After she done gone to bed, late one springtime night when de moon were shinin', I hear Miss Jeanne a-cryin': 'He's come! . . . Hager, ma Robert's come back to me!' An' I jumped out o' ma bed in de next room where I were sleepin' an' run in to her, an' there she was in her long, white night-clothes standin' out in de moonlight on de little balcony, high up in de middle o' that big stone porch. She was lookin' down into de yard at this stump of a tree a-holdin' up its arms. An' she thinks it's Marster Robert a-callin' her. She thinks he's standin' there in his uniform, come back from de war, a-callin' her. An' she say: 'I'm comin', Bob, dear;' . . . An' 'fore I think what she's doin', Miss Jeanne done stepped over de little rail o' de balcony like she were walkin' on moonlight. An' she say: 'I'm comin', Bob!'

"She ain't left no will, so de house an' all went to de State, an' I been left with nothin'. But I ain't care 'bout that. I followed her to de grave, an' I been with her all de time, 'cause she's ma friend. An' I were sorry for her, 'cause I knowed that love were painin' her soul, an' warn't nobody left to help her but me.

"An' since then I's met many a white lady an' many a white gentleman, an' some of 'em's been kind to me an' some of 'em ain't; some of 'em's cussed me an' wouldn't pay me fo' ma work; an' some of 'em's hurted me awful. But I's been sorry fo' white folks, fo' I knows something inside must be aggravatin' de po' souls. An' I's kept a room in ma heart fo' 'em, 'cause white folks needs us, honey, even if they don't know it. They's like spoilt chillens what's got too much o' ever'thing—an' they needs us niggers, what ain't got nothin'.

"I's been livin' a long time in yesterday, Sandy chile, an' I knows there ain't no room in de world fo' nothin' mo'n love. I knows, chile! Ever'thing there is but lovin' leaves a rust on yo' soul. An' to love sho 'nough, you got to have a spot in yo' heart fo' ever'body—great an' small, white an' black, an' them what's good an' them what's evil—'cause love ain't got no crowded-out places where de good ones stays an' de bad ones can't come in. When it gets that way, then it ain't love.

"White peoples maybe mistreats you an' hates you, but when you hates 'em back, you's de one what's hurted, 'cause hate makes yo' heart ugly—that's all it does. It closes up de sweet door to life an' makes ever'thing small an' mean an' dirty. Honey, there ain't no room in de world fo' hate, white folks hatin' niggers, an' niggers hatin' white folks. There ain't no room in this world fo' nothin' but love, Sandy chile. That's all they's room fo'—nothin' but love."

17
BARBER-SHOP

MR. LOGAN, HEARING that Aunt Hager had an empty room since all her daughters were gone, sent her one evening a newcomer in town looking for a place to stay. His name was Wim Dogberry and he was a brickmason and hod-carrier, a tall, quiet, stoop-shouldered black man, neither old nor young. He took, for two dollars and a half a week, the room that had been Annjee's, and Hager gave him a key to the front door.

Wim Dogberry was carrying hod then on a new moving-picture theatre that was being built. He rose early and came in late, face, hands, and overalls covered with mortar dust. He washed in a tin basin by the pump and went to bed, and about all he ever said to Aunt Hager and Sandy was "Good-mornin'" and "Good-evenin'," and maybe a stumbling "How is you?" But on Sunday mornings Hager usually asked him to breakfast if he got up on time—for on Saturday nights Wim drank licker and came home mumbling to himself a little later than on week-day evenings, so sometimes he would sleep until noon Sundays.

One Saturday night he wet the bed, and when Hager went to make it up on the Sabbath morning, she found a damp yellow spot in the middle. Of this act Dogberry was so ashamed that he did not even say "Good-mornin'" for several days, and if, from the corner, he saw Aunt Hager and her grandson sitting on the porch in the twilight when he came towards home, he would pass his street and walk until he thought they had gone inside to bed. But he was a quiet roomer, he didn't give anyone any trouble, and he paid regularly. And since Hager was in no position to despise two dollars and a half every week, she rather liked Dogberry.

Now Hager kept the growing Sandy close by her all the time to help her while she washed and ironed and to talk to her while she sat on the porch in the evenings. Of course, he played sometimes in his own yard whenever Willie-Mae or Buster or, on Sundays, Jimmy Lane came to the house. But Jimmy Lane was running wild since his mother died, and Hager didn't like him to visit her grandson any more. He was bad.

When Sandy wanted to go to the vacant lot to play baseball with the neighbor boys, his grandmother would usually not allow him to leave her. "Stay here, sir, with Hager. I needs you to pump ma water fo' me an' fill up these tubs," she would say. Or else she would yell: "Ain't I told you you might get hurt down there with them old rough white boys? Stay here in yo' own yard, where you can keep out o' mischief."

So he grew accustomed to remaining near his grandmother, and at night, when the other children would be playing duck-on-the-rock under the arc-light at the corner, he would be sitting on the front porch listening to Aunt Hager telling her tales of slavery and talking of her own far-off youth. When school opened in the fall, the old woman said: "I don't know what I's gwine do all day without you, Sandy. You sho been company to me, with all my own chillens gone." But Sandy was glad to get back to a roomful of boys and girls again.

One Indian-summer afternoon when Aunt Hager was hanging up clothes in the back yard while the boy held the basket of clothes-pins, old man Logan drove past on his rickety trash-wagon and bowed elaborately to Hager. She went to the back fence to joke and gossip with him as usual, while his white mule switched off persistent flies with her tail.

Before the old beau drove away, he said: "Say, Hager, does you want that there young one o' your'n to work? I knows a little job he can have if you does," pointing to Sandy.

"What'll he got to do?" demanded Hager.

"Well, Pete Scott say he need a boy down yonder at de barber-shop on Saturdays to kinder clean up where de kinks fall, an' shine shoes fo' de customers. Ain't nothin' hard 'bout it, an' I was thinkin' it would just 'bout be Sandy's size. He could make a few pennies ever' week to kinder help things 'long."

"True, he sho could," said Hager. "I'll have him go see Pete."

So Sandy went to see Mr. Peter Scott at the colored barber-shop on Pearl Street that evening and was given his first regular job. Every Saturday, which was the barber-shop's only busy day, when the working-men got paid off, Sandy went on the job at noon and worked until eight or nine in the evening. His duties were to keep the place swept clean of the hair that the three barbers sheared and to shine the shoes of any customer who might ask for a shine. Only a few customers permitted themselves that last luxury, for many of them came to the shop in their working-shoes, covered with mud or lime, and most of them shined their own boots at home on Sunday mornings before church. But occasionally Cudge Windsor, who owned a pool hall, or some of the dressed-up bootleggers, might climb on the stand and permit their shoes to be cleaned by the brown youngster, who asked shyly: "Shine, mister?"

The barber-shop was a new world to Sandy, who had lived thus far tied to Aunt Hager's apron-strings. He was a dreamy-eyed boy who had grown to his present age largely under the dominant influence of women—Annjee, Harriett, his grandmother—because Jimboy had been so seldom home. But the barber-shop then was a man's world, and, on Saturdays, while a dozen or more big laborers awaited their turns, the place was filled with loud man-talk and smoke and laughter. Baseball, Jack Johnson, racehorses, white folks, Teddy Roosevelt, local gossip, Booker Washington, women, labor prospects in Topeka, Kansas City, Omaha, religion, politics, women, God—discussions and arguments all afternoon and far up into the night, while crisp kinks rolled to the floor, cigarette and cigar-butts were thrown on the hearth of the monkey-stove, and Sandy called out: "Shine, mister?"

Sometimes the boy earned one or two dollars from shines, but on damp or snowy days he might not make anything except the fifty cents Pete Scott paid him for sweeping up. Or perhaps one of the barbers, too busy to go out for supper, would send Sandy for a sandwich and a bottle of milk, and thus he would make an extra nickel or dime.

The patrons liked him and often kidded him about his sandy

hair. "Boy, you's too dark to have hair like that. Ain't nobody but white folks s'posed to have sandy-colored hair. An' your'n's nappy at that!" Then Sandy would blush with embarrassment—if the change from a dry chocolate to a damp chocolate can be called a blush, as he grew warm and perspired—because he didn't like to be kidded about his hair. And he hadn't been around uncouth fellows long enough to learn the protective art of turning back a joke. He had discovered already, though, that so-called jokes are often not really jokes at all, but rather unpleasant realities that hurt unless you can think of something equally funny and unpleasant to say in return. But the men who patronized Pete Scott's barber-shop seldom grew angry at the hard pleasantries that passed for humor, and they could play the dozens for hours without anger, unless the parties concerned became serious, when they were invited to take it on the outside. And even at that a fight was fun, too.

After a winter of Saturday nights at Pete's shop Sandy himself became pretty adept at "kidding"; but at first he was timid about it and afraid to joke with grown-up people, or to give smart answers to strangers when they teased him about his crinkly, sand-colored head. One day, however, one of the barbers gave him a tin of Madam Walker's and told him: "Lay that hair down an' stop these niggers from laughin' at you." Sandy took his advice.

Madam Walker's—a thick yellow pomade—and a good wetting with water proved most efficacious to the boy's hair, when aided with a stocking cap—the top of a woman's stocking cut off and tied in a knot at one end so as to fit tightly over one's head, pressing the hair smooth. Thereafter Sandy appeared with his hair slick and shiny. And the salve and water together made it seem a dark brown, just the color of his skin, instead of the peculiar sandy tint it possessed in its natural state. Besides he soon advanced far enough in the art of "kidding" to say: "So's your pa's," to people who informed him that his head was nappy.

During the autumn Harriett had been home once to see her mother and had said that she was working as chambermaid with Maudel at the hotel. But in the barber-shop that winter Sandy often heard his aunt's name mentioned in less proper connections. Sometimes the boy pretended not to hear, and if Pete Scott was there, he always stopped the men from talking.

"Tired o' all this nasty talk 'bout women in ma shop," he said one Saturday night. "Some o' you men better look after your own womenfolks if you got any."

"Aw, all de womens in de world ain't worth two cents to me," said a waiter sitting in the middle chair, his face covered with lather. "I don't respect no woman but my mother."

"An' neither do I," answered Greensbury Jones. "All of 'em's evil, specially if they's black an' got blue gums."

"I's done told you to hush," said Pete Scott behind the first chair, where he was clipping Jap Logan's hair. "Ma wife's black herself, so don't start talkin' 'bout no blue gums! I's tired o' this here female talk anyhow. This is ma shop, an' ma razors sho can cut somethin' else 'sides hair—so now just keep on talkin' 'bout blue gums!"

"I see where Bryant's runnin' for president agin," said Greensbury Jones.

But one Saturday, while the proprietor was out to snatch a bite to eat, a discussion came up as to who was the prettiest colored girl in town. Was she yellow, high-brown, chocolate, or black? Of course, there was no agreement, but names were mentioned and qualities were described. One girl had eyes like Eve herself; another had hips like Miss Cleopatra; one smooth brown-skin had legs like—like—like—

"Aw, man! De Statue of Liberty!" somebody suggested when the name of a famous beauty failed the speaker's memory.

"But, feller, there ain't nothin' in all them rainbow shades," a young teamster argued against Uncle Dan Givens, who preferred high yellows. "Gimme a cool black gal ever' time! They's too dark to fade—and when they are good-looking, I mean they *are* good-looking! I'm talkin' 'bout Harrietta Williams, too! That's who I mean! Now, find a better-looking gal than she is!"

"I admits Harrietta's all right," said the old man; "all right to look at but—sput-t-tsss!" He spat contemptuously at the stove.

"O, I know that!" said the teamster; "but I ain't talkin' 'bout what she is! I'm talkin' 'bout how she looks. An' a songster out o' this world don't care if she is a—!"

"S-s-s-sh! Soft-pedal it brother." One of the men nudged the speaker. "There's one o' the Williamses right here—that kid over yonder shinin' shoes's Harriett's nephew or somethin' 'nother."

"You niggers talks too free, anyhow," one of the barbers added. "Somebody gwine cut your lips off some o' these days. De idee o' ole Uncle Dan Givens' arguin' 'bout women and he done got whiskers all round his head like a wore-out cheese."

"That's all right, you young whip-snapper," squeaked Uncle Dan heatedly. "Might have whiskers round ma head, but I ain't wore out!"

Laughter and smoke filled the little shop, while the winter wind blew sleet against the big plate-glass window and whistled through the cracks in the doorway, making the gas lights flicker overhead. Sandy smacked his polishing cloth on the toes of a gleaming pair of brown button shoes belonging to a stranger in town, then looked up with a grin and said: "Yes, sir!" as the man handed him a quarter.

"Keep the change," said the new-comer grandly.

"That guy's an actor," one of the barbers said when the man went out. "He's playin' with the *Smart Set* at the Opery House tonight. I bet the top gallery'll be full o' niggers sence it's a jig show, but I ain't goin' anear there myself to be Jim-Crowed, 'cause I don't believe in goin' nowhere I ain't allowed to set with the rest of the folks. If I can't be the table-cloth, I won't be the dish-rag—that's my motto. And if I can't buy the seats I want at a show, I sure God can keep my change!"

"Yes, and miss all the good shows," countered a little red-eyed porter. "Just as well say if you can't eat in a restaurant where white folks eat, you ain't gonna eat."

"Anybody want a shine?" yelled Sandy above the racket. "And if you don't want a shine, stay out of my chair and do your arguing on the floor!"

A brown-skin chorus girl, on her way to the theatre, stepped into the shop and asked if she could buy a *Chicago Defender* there. The barber directed her to the colored restaurant, while all the men immediately stopped talking to stare at her until she went out.

"Whew! . . . Some legs!" the teamster cried as the door closed on a vision of silk stockings. "How'd you like to shine that long, sweet brown-skin mama's shoes, boy?"

"She wouldn't have to pay me!" said Sandy.

"Whoopee! Gallery or no gallery," shouted Jap Logan, "I'm gonna see that show! Don't care if they do Jim-Crow niggers in the white folks' Opery House!"

"Yes," muttered one of the barbers, "that's just what's the matter now—you ain't got no race-pride! You niggers ain't got no shame!"

18
CHILDREN'S DAY

WHEN EASTER CAME that spring, Sandy had saved enough money to buy himself a suit and a new cap from his earnings at the barber-shop. He was very proud of this accomplishment and so was Aunt Hager.

"You's a 'dustrious chile, sho is! Gwine make a smart man even if yo' daddy warn't nothin'. Gwine get ahead an' do good fo' yo'self an' de race, yes, sir!"

The spring came early and the clear balmy days found Hager's back yard billowing with clean white clothes on lines in the sun. Her roomer had left her when the theatre was built and had gone to work on a dam somewhere up the river, so Annjee's room was empty again. Sandy had slept with his grandmother during the cold weather, but in summer he slept on a pallet.

The boy did not miss his mother. When she had been home, Annjee had worked out all day, and she was quiet at night because she was always tired. Harriett had been the one to keep the fun and laughter going—Harriett and Jimboy, whenever he was in town. Sandy wished Harrie would live at home instead of staying at Maudel's house, but he never said anything about it to his grandmother. He went to school regularly, went to work at the barber-shop on Saturdays and to Sunday-school on Sundays, and remained with Aunt Hager the rest of his time. She was always worried if she didn't know where he was.

"Colored boys, when they gets round twelve an' thirteen, they gets so bad, Sandy," she would say. "I wants you to stay nice an' make something out o' yo'self. If Hager lives, she ain't gonna see you go down. She's gonna make a fine man out o' you fo' de glory o' God an' de black race. You gwine to 'mount to something in this world. You hear me?"

Sandy did hear her, and he knew what she meant. She meant

a man like Booker T. Washington, or Frederick Douglass, or like Paul Lawrence Dunbar, who did poetry-writing. Or maybe Jack Johnson. But Hager said Jack Johnson was the devil's kind of greatness, not God's.

"That's what you get from workin' round that old barbershop where all they talks 'bout is prize-fightin' an' hossracin'. Jack Johnson done married a white woman, anyhow! What he care 'bout de race?"

The little boy wondered if Jack Johnson's kids looked like Buster. But maybe he didn't have any kids. He must ask Pete Scott about that when he went back to work on Saturday.

In the summer a new amusement park opened in Stanton, the first of its kind in the city, with a merry-go-round, a shoot-the-shoots, a Ferris wheel, a dance-hall, and a bandstand for week-end concerts. In order to help popularize the park, which was far on the north edge of town, the *Daily Leader* announced, under its auspices, what was called a Free Children's Day Party open to all the readers of that paper who clipped the coupons published in each issue. On July 26 these coupons, presented at the gate, would entitle every child in Stanton to free admittance to the park, free pop-corn, free lemonade, and one ride on each of the amusement attractions—the merry-go-round, the shoot-the-shoots, and the Ferris wheel. All you had to do was to be a reader of the *Daily Leader* and present the coupons cut from that paper.

Aunt Hager and Sister Johnson both took the *Leader* regularly, as did almost everybody else in Stanton, so Sandy and Willie-Mae started to clip coupons. All the children in the neighborhood were doing the same thing. The Children's Day would be a big event for all the little people in town. None of them had ever seen a shoot-the-shoots before, a contrivance that pulled little cars full of folks high into the air and then let them come whizzing down an incline into an artificial pond, where the cars would float like boats. Sandy and Willie-Mae looked forward to thrill after thrill.

When the afternoon of the great day came at last, Willie-Mae stopped for Sandy, dressed in her whitest white dress and her new patent-leather shoes, which hurt her feet awfully. Sandy's grandmother was making him wash his ears when she came in.

"You gwine out yonder 'mongst all them white chillens, I wants you to at least look clean!" said Hager.

They started out.

"Here!" called Aunt Hager. "Ain't you gwine to take yo' coupons?" In his rush to get away, Sandy had forgotten them.

It was a long walk to the park, and Willie-Mae stopped and took off her shoes and stockings and carried them in her hands until she got near the gate; then she put them on again and limped bravely along, clutching her precious bits of newspaper. They could hear the band playing and children shouting and squealing as the cars on the shoot-the-shoots shot downward with a splash into the pond. They could see the giant Ferris wheel, larger than the one the carnival had had, circling high in the air.

"I'm gonna ride on that first," said Sandy.

There were crowds of children under the bright red and white wooden shelter at the park entrance. They were lining up at the gate—laughing, merry, clean little white children, pushing and yelling and giggling amiably. Sandy let Willie-Mae go first and he got in line behind her. The band was playing gaily inside. . . . They were almost to the entrance now. . . . There were just two boys in front of them. . . . Willie-Mae held out her black little hand clutching the coupons. They moved forward. The man looked down.

"Sorry," he said. "This party's for white kids."

Willie-Mae did not understand. She stood holding out the coupons, waiting for the tall white man to take them.

"Stand back, you two," he said, looking at Sandy as well. "I told you little darkies this wasn't your party. . . . Come on—next little girl." And the line of white children pushed past Willie-Mae and Sandy, going into the park. Stunned, the two dark ones drew aside. Then they noticed a group of a dozen or more other colored youngsters standing apart in the sun, just without the bright entrance pavilion, and among them was

Sadie Butler, Sandy's class-mate. Three or four of the colored children were crying, but most of them looked sullen and angry, and some of them had turned to go home.

"My papa takes the *Leader*," Sadie Butler was saying. "And you see what it says here on the coupons, too—'Free Admittance to Every Child in Stanton.' Can't you read it, Sandy?"

"Sure, I can read it, but I guess they didn't mean colored," he answered, as the boy watched the white children going in the gate. "They wouldn't let us in."

Willie-Mae, between the painful shoes and the hurt of her disappointment, was on the verge of tears. One of the small boys in the crowd, a hard-looking little fellow from Pearl Street, was cursing childishly.

"God damn old sons of biscuit-eaters, that what they are! I wish I was a big man, dog-gone, I'd shoot 'em all, that's what I'd do!"

"I suppose they didn't mean colored kids," said Sandy again.

"Buster went in all right," said Sadie. "I seen him. But they didn't know he was colored, I guess. When I went up to the gate, the man said: 'Whoa! Where you goin'?' just like I was a horse. . . . I'm going home now and tell my papa."

She walked away, followed by five or six other little girls in their Sunday dresses. Willie-Mae was sitting on the ground taking off her shoes again, sweat and tears running down her black cheeks. Sandy saw his white schoolmate, Earl, approaching.

"What's matter, Sandy? Ain't you goin' in?" Earl demanded, looking at his friend's worried face. "Did the little girl hurt her foot?"

"No," said Sandy. "We just ain't going in. . . . Here, Earl, you can have my coupons. If you have extra ones, the papers says you get more lemonade . . . so you take 'em."

The white boy, puzzled, accepted the proffered coupons, stood dumbly for a moment wondering what to say to his brown friend, then went on into the park.

"It's yo' party, white chile!" a little tan-skin girl called after him, mimicking the way the man at the gate had talked. "Whoa! Stay out! You's a nigger!" she said to Sandy.

The other children, in spite of themselves, laughed at the accuracy of her burlesque imitation. Then, with the music of the merry-go-round from beyond the high fence and the laughter of happy children following them, the group of dark-skinned ones started down the dusty road together—and to all the colored boys and girls they met on the way they called out, "Ain't no use, jigaboos! That party's for white folks!"

When Willie-Mae and Sandy got home and told their story, Sister Johnson was angry as a wet hen.

"Crackers is devils," she cried. "I 'spected as much! Dey ain't nary hell hot 'nough to burn ole white folks, 'cause dey's devils deyselves! De dirty hounds!"

But all Hager said was: "They's po' trash owns that park what don't know no better, hurtin' chillens' feelin's, but we'll forgive 'em! Don't fret yo'self, Sister Johnson. What good can frettin' do? Come on here, let's we have a party of our own." She went out in the yard and took a watermelon from a tub of well-water where it had been cooling and cut it into four juicy slices; then they sat down on the grass at the shady side of the house and ate, trying to forget about white folks.

"Don't you mind, Willie-Mae," Hager said to the little black girl, who was still crying. "You's colored, honey, an' you's liable to have a hard time in this life—but don't cry. . . . You, Sandy, run round de house an' see didn't I heard de mail-man blowin'."

"Yes'm," said Sandy when he came back. "Was the mail-man, and I got a letter from mama." The boy sat on the grass to read it, anxious to see what Annjee said. And later, when the company had gone, he read it aloud to Hager.

DEAR LITTLE SON:

How have you all been? how is grandma? I get worried about you when I do not hear. You know Aunt Hager is old and can't write much so you must do it for her because she is not used to adress letters and the last one was two weeks getting here and had went all around everywhere. Your father says tell you hello. I got a job in a boarding house for old white folks what are cranky about how they beds is made. There are white and colored here in the auto business and women to. Tell Madam de Carter I will send my Lodge dues back because I do not want to be transfer as I might come home sometime. I ain't seen you all now for more'n a year. Jimboy he keeps changing jobs from one thing to another but he likes this town pretty well. You know he broke his guitar carrying it in a crowded street car. Ma says you are growing and have bought yourself a new suit last Easter. Mama certainly does right well to keep on washing and ironing at her age and worrying with you besides. Tempy ought to help ma but seem like she don't think so. Do you ever see your Aunt Harrie? I hope she is settling down in her ways. If ma wasn't all by herself maybe I could send for you to come live with us in Detroit but maybe I will be home to see you if I ever get any money ahead. Rent is so high here I never wittnessed so many folks in one house, rooming five and six together, and nobody can save a dime. Are you still working at the barber shop. I heard Sister Johnson was under the weather but I couldn't make out from ma's scribbling what was the matter with her. Did she have a physicianer? You behave yourself with Willie-Mae because you are getting to be a big boy now and she is a girl older then you are. I am going to send you some pants next time I go down town but I get off from work so late I don't have a chance to do nothing and your father eats in the restaurant count of me not home to fix for him and I don't care where you go colored folks has a hard time. I want you to mind your grandma and help her work. She is too old to be straining at the pump drawing water to wash clothes with. Now write to me. Love to you all both and seven kisses XXXXXXX right here on the paper,

Your loving mother,
ANNJELICA ROGERS

Sandy laughed at the clumsy cross-mark kisses. He was glad to get a letter from his mother, and word in it about Jimboy. And he was sorry his father had broken his guitar. But not even watermelon and the long letter could drive away his sick feeling about the park.

"I guess Kansas is getting like the South, isn't it, ma?" Sandy said to his grandmother as they came out on the porch that evening after supper. "They don't like us here either, do they?"

But Aunt Hager gave him no answer. In silence they watched the sunset fade from the sky. Slowly the evening star grew bright, and, looking at the stars, Hager began to sing, very softly at first:

From this world o' trouble free,
Stars beyond!
Stars beyond!

And Sandy, as he stood beside his grandmother on the porch, heard a great chorus out of the black past—singing generations of toil-worn Negroes, echoing Hager's voice as it deepened and grew in volume:

There's a star fo' you an' me,
Stars beyond!

19

TEN DOLLARS AND COSTS

IN THE FALL Sandy found a job that occupied him after school hours, as well as on Saturday and Sunday. One afternoon at the barber-shop, Charlie Nutter, a bell-hop who had come to have his hair cut, asked Sandy to step outside a minute. Once out of earshot of the barbers and loafers within, Charlie went on: "Say, kid, I got some dope to buzz to yuh 'bout a job. Joe Willis, the white guy what keeps the hotel where I work, is lookin' for a boy to kinder sweep up around the lobby every day, dust off, and sort o' help the bell-boys out sometimes. Ain't nothin' hard attached to it, and yuh can bring 'long your shine-box and rub up shoes in the lobby, too, if yuh wants to. I though' maybe yuh might like to have the job. Yuh'd make more'n yuh do here. And more'n that, too, when yuh got on to the ropes. Course yuh'd have to fix me up with a couple o' bucks o' so for gettin' yuh the job, but if yuh want it, just lemme know and I'll fix it with the boss. He tole me to start lookin' for somebody and that's what I'm doin'." Charlie Nutter went on talking, without stopping to wait for an answer. "Course a boy like you don't know nothin' 'bout hotel work, but yuh ain't never too young to learn, and that's a nice easy way to start. Yuh might work up to me some time, yuh never can tell—head bell-hop! 'Cause I ain't gonna stay in this burg all my life; I figger if I can hop bells here, I can hop bells in Chicago or some place worth livin' at. But the tips ain't bad down there at the Drummer's though—lots o' sportin' women and folks like that what don't mind givin' yuh a quarter any time. . . . And yuh can get well yourself once in a while. What yuh say? Do yuh want it?"

Sandy thought quick. With Christmas not far off, his shoes about worn out, and the desire to help Aunt Hager, too—"I guess I better take it," he said. "But do I have to pay you now?"

"Hell, naw, not now! I'll keep my eye on yuh, and yuh can

just slip me a little change now and then down to the hotel when you start workin'. Other boy ain't quittin' nohow till next week. S'pose yuh come round there Sunday morning and I'll kinder show yuh what to do. And don't pay no mind to Willis when he hollers at yuh. He's all right—just got a hard way about him with the help, that's all—but he ain't a bad boss. I'll see yuh, then! Drop by Sunday and lemme know for sure. So long!"

But Aunt Hager was not much pleased when Sandy came home that night and she heard the news. "I ain't never wanted none o' my chillens to work in no ole hotels," she said. "They's evil, full o' nastiness, an' you don't learn nothin' good in 'em. I don't want you to go there, chile."

"But grandma," Sandy argued, "I want to send mama a Christmas present. And just look at my shoes, all worn out! I don't make much money any more since that new colored barber-shop opened up. It's all white inside and folks don't have to wait so long 'cause there's five barbers. Jimmy Lane's got the porter's job down there . . . and I have to start working regular some time, don't I?"

"I reckons you does, but I hates to see you workin' in hotels, chile, with all them low-down Bottoms niggers, and bad womens comin' an' goin'. But I reckon you does need de job. Yo' mammy ain't sent no money here fo' de Lawd knows when, an' I ain't able to buy you nice clothes an' all like you needs to go to school in. . . . But don't forget, honey, no matter where you works—you be good an' do right. . . . I reckon you'll get along."

So Sandy found Charlie Nutter on Sunday and told him for sure he would take the job. Then he told Pete Scott he was no longer coming to work at his barber-shop, and Pete got mad and told him to go to hell, quitting when business was bad after all he had done for Sandy, besides letting him shine shoes and keep all his earnings. At other shops he couldn't have done that; besides he had intended to teach Sandy to be a barber when he got big enough.

"But go on!" said Pete Scott. "Go on! I don't need you.

Plenty other boys I can find to work for me. But I bet you won't stay at that Drummer's Hotel no time, though—I can tell you that!"

The long Indian summer lingered until almost Thanksgiving, and the weather was sunny and warm. The day before Sandy went to work on his new job, he came home from school, brought in the wood for the stove, and delivered a basket of newly ironed clothes to the white folks. When he returned, he found his grandmother standing on the front porch in the sunset, reading the evening paper, which the boy had recently delivered. Sandy stopped in the twilight beside Hager, breathing in the crisp cool air and wondering what they were going to have for supper.

Suddenly his grandmother gave a deep cry and leaned heavily against the door-jamb, letting the paper fall from her hands. "O, ma Lawd!" she moaned. "O, ma Lawd!" and an expression of the uttermost pain made the old woman's eyes widen in horror. "Is I read de name right?"

Sandy, frightened, picked up the paper from the porch and found on the front page the little four-line item that his grandmother had just read:

NEGRESSES ARRESTED

> Harrietta Williams and Maudel Smothers, two young negresses, were arrested last night on Pearl Street for street-walking. They were brought before Judge Brinton and fined ten dollars and costs.

"What does that mean, ma—street-walking?" the child asked, but his grandmother raised her apron to her eyes and stumbled into the house. Sandy stopped, perplexed at the meaning of the article, at his aunt's arrest, at his grandmother's horror. Then he followed Hager, the open newspaper still in his hands, and found her standing at the window in the kitchen, crying. Racking sobs were shaking her body and the boy, who had never seen an old person weep like that before, was terribly afraid. He didn't know that grown-up people cried, except at funerals, where it was the proper thing to do. He didn't know they ever cried alone, by themselves in their own houses.

"I'm gonna get Sister Johnson," he said, dropping the paper on the floor. "I'm gonna get Sister Johnson quick!"

"No, honey, don't get her," stammered the old woman. "She can't help us none, chile. Can't nobody help us . . . but de Lawd."

In the dusk Sandy saw that his grandmother was trying hard to make her lips speak plainly and to control her sobs.

"Let's we pray, son, fo' yo' po' lost Aunt Harriett—fo' ma own baby chile, what's done turned from de light an' is walkin' in darkness."

She dropped on her knees near the kitchen-stove with her arms on the seat of a chair and her head bowed. Sandy got on his knees, too, and while his grandmother prayed aloud for the body and soul of her daughter, the boy repeated over and over in his mind: "I wish you'd come home, Aunt Harrie. It's lonesome around here! Gee, I wish you'd come home."

20
HEY, BOY!

IN THE LOBBY of the Drummer's Hotel there were six large brass spittoons—one in the center of the place, one in each corner, and one near the clerk's desk. It was Sandy's duty to clean these spittoons. Every evening that winter after school he came in the back door of the hotel, put his books in the closet where he kept his brooms and cleaning rags, swept the two short upper halls and the two flights of stairs, swept the lobby and dusted, then took the spittoons, emptied their slimy contents into the alley, rinsed them out, and polished them until they shone as brightly as if they were made of gold. Except for the stench of emptying them, Sandy rather liked this job. He always felt very proud of himself when, about six o'clock, he could look around the dingy old lobby and see the six gleaming brass bowls catching the glow of the electric lamps on their shining surfaces before they were again covered with spit. The thought that he himself had created this brightness with his own hands, aided by a can of brass-polish, never failed to make Sandy happy.

He liked to clean things, to make them beautiful, to make them shine. Aunt Hager did, too. When she wasn't washing clothes, she was always cleaning something about the house, dusting, polishing the range, or scrubbing the kitchen-floor until it was white enough to eat from. To Hager a clean thing was beautiful—also to Sandy, proud every evening of his six unblemished brass spittoons. Yet each day when he came to work, they were covered anew with tobacco juice, cigarette-butts, wads of chewing-gum, and phlegm. But to make them clean was Sandy's job—and they were beautiful when they were clean.

Charlie Nutter was right—there was nothing very hard about the work and he liked it for a while. The new kinds of life which he saw in the hotel interested and puzzled him, but, being naturally a silent child, he asked no questions, and, beyond the directions for his work, nobody told him anything. Sandy did his cleaning well and the boss had not yet had occasion to bellow at him, as he often bellowed at the two bell-boys.

The Drummer's Hotel was not a large hotel, nor a nice one. A three-story frame structure, dilapidated and run down, it had not been painted for years. In the lobby two large panes of plate glass looked on the street, and in front of these were rows of hard wooden chairs. At the rear of the lobby was the clerk's desk, a case of cigars and cigarettes, a cooler for water, and the door to the men's room. It was Sandy's duty to clean this toilet, too.

Upstairs on the second and third floors were the bedrooms. Only the poorest of travelling salesmen, transient railroad workers, occasionally a few show-people, and the ladies of the streets with their clients rented them. The night trade was always the most brisk at the Drummer's Hotel, but it was only on Saturdays that Sandy worked after six o'clock. That night he would not get home until ten or eleven, but Aunt Hager would always be waiting for him, keeping the fire warm, with the wash-tub full of water for his weekly bath.

There was no dining-room attached to the hotel, and, aside from Sandy, there were only five employees. The boss himself, Joe Willis, was usually at the desk. There were two chambermaids who worked in the mornings, an old man who did the heavy cleaning and scrubbing once or twice a week, and two bell-boys—one night boy and one day boy supposedly, but both bellmen had been there so long that they arranged the hours to suit themselves. Charlie Nutter had started small, like Sandy, and had grown up there. The other bell-boy, really no boy at all, but an old man, had been in the hotel ever since it opened, and Sandy was as much afraid of him as he was of the boss.

This bellman's name was Mr. George Clark. His uniform was frayed and greasy, but he wore it with the air of a major, and he acted as though all the burdens of running the hotel were on his shoulders. He knew how everything was to be done, where everything was kept, what every old guest liked. And he could divine the tastes of each new guest before he had been there a day. Subservient and grinning to white folks, evil and tyrannical to the colored help, George was the chief authority, next to Joe Willis, in the Drummer's Hotel. He it was who found some fault with Sandy's work every day until he learned to like the child because Sandy never answered back or tried to be fly, as George said most young niggers were. After a time the old fellow seldom bothered to inspect Sandy's spittoons or to look in the corners for dust, but, nevertheless, he remained a person to be humored and obeyed if one wished to work at the Drummer's Hotel.

Besides being the boss's right-hand man, George Clark was the official bootlegger for the house, too. In fact, he kept his liquor-supply in the hotel cellar. When he was off duty, Charlie, the other bell-hop, sold it for him if there were any calls from the rooms above. They made no sales other than to guests of the house, but such sales were frequent. Some of the white women who used the rooms collected a commission from George for the sales they helped make to their men visitors.

Sandy was a long time learning the tricks of hotel work. "Yuh sure a dumb little joker," Charlie was constantly informing him. "But just stay around awhile and yuh'll get on to it."

Christmas came and Sandy sent his mother in Detroit a big box of drugstore candy. For Aunt Hager he started to buy a long pair of green earrings for fifty cents, but he was afraid she might not like them, so he bought her white handkerchiefs instead. And he sent a pretty card to Harriett, for one snowy December day his aunt had seen him through the windows sweeping out the lobby of the hotel and she had called him to the door to talk to her. She thrust a little piece of paper into his hand with her new address on it.

"Maudel's moved to Kansas City," she said, "so I don't live there any more. You better keep this address yourself and if mama ever needs me, you can know where I am."

Then she went on through the snow, looking very pretty in a cheap fur coat and black, high-heeled slippers, with grey silk stockings. Sandy saw her pass the hotel often with different men. Sometimes she went by with Cudge Windsor, the owner of the pool hall, or Billy Sanderlee. Almost always she was with sporty-looking fellows who wore derbies and had gold teeth. Sandy noticed that she didn't urge him to come to see her at this new house-number she had given him, so he put the paper in his pocket and went back to his sweeping, glad, anyway, to have seen his Aunt Harriett.

One Saturday afternoon several white men were sitting in the lobby smoking and reading the papers. Sandy swept around their chairs, dusted, and then took the spittoons out to clean. This work did not require his attention; while he applied the polish with a handful of soft rags, he could let his mind wander to other things. He thought about Harriett. Then he thought about school and what he would do when he was a man; about Willie-Mae, who had a job washing dinner dishes for a white family; about Jimmy Lane, who had no mama; and Sandy wondered what his own mother and father were doing in another town, and if they wanted him with them. He thought how old and tired and grey-headed Aunt Hager had become; how she puffed and blowed over the wash-tubs now, but never complained; how she waited for him on Saturday nights with the kitchen-stove blazing, so he would be warm after walking so far in the cold; and how she prayed he would be a great man some day. . . . Sitting there in the back room of the hotel, Sandy wondered how people got to be great, as, one by one, he made the spittoons bright and beautiful. He wondered how people made themselves great.

That night he would have to work late picking up papers in the lobby, running errands for the boss, and shining shoes. After he had put the spittoons around, he would go out and get a hamburger sandwich and a cup of coffee for supper; then he would come back and help Charlie if he could. . . . Charlie was a good old boy. He had taken only a dollar for getting Sandy his job and he often helped him make tips by allowing Sandy to run to the telegraph office or do some other little odd job for a guest upstairs. . . . Sure, Charlie was a nice guy.

Things were pretty busy tonight. Several men had their shoes shined as they sat tipped back in the lobby chairs while Sandy with his boot-black box let them put up a foot at a time to be polished. One tall farmer gave him a quarter tip and a pat on the head.

"Bright little feller, that," he remarked to the boss.

About ten o'clock the blond Miss Marcia McKay's bell rang, and, Charlie being engaged, Joe Willis sent Sandy up to see what she wanted. Miss McKay had just come in out of the snow a short time before with a heavy-set man. Both of them were drunk. Sandy knocked timidly outside her room.

"Come in," growled the man's voice.

Sandy opened the door and saw Miss McKay standing naked in the middle of the floor combing her hair. He stopped on the threshold.

"Aw, come in," said the man. "She won't bite you! Where's that other bell-boy? We want some licker! . . . Damn it! Say, send Charlie up here! He knows what I want!"

Sandy scampered away, and when he found Charlie, he told him about Miss McKay. The child was scared because he had often heard of colored boys' being lynched for looking at white women, even with their clothes on—but the bell-boy only laughed.

"Yuh're a dumb little joker!" he said. "Just stay around here awhile and yuh'll see lots more'n that!" He winked and gave Sandy a nudge in the ribs. "Boy, I done sold ten quarts o' licker tonight," he whispered jubilantly. "And some a it was mine, too!"

Sandy went back to the lobby and the shining of shoes. A big, red-necked stranger smoking and drinking with a crowd of drummers in one corner of the room called to him "Hey, boy! Shine me up here!" So he edged into the center of the group of men with his blacking-box, got down on his knees before the big fellow, took out his cans and his cloths, and went to work.

The white men were telling dirty stories, uglier than any Sandy had heard at the colored barber-shop and not very funny—and some of them made him sick at the stomach.

The big man whose shoes he was shining said: "Now I'm gonna tell one." He talked with a Southern drawl and a soft slurring of word-endings like some old colored folks. He had been drinking, too. "This is 'bout a nigger went to see Aunt Hanner one night. . . .'

A roar of laughter greeted his first effort and he was encouraged to tell another.

"Old darky caught a gal on the levee . . ." he commenced.

Sandy finished polishing the shoes and put the cloths inside his wooden box and stood up waiting for his pay, but the speaker did not notice the colored boy until he had finished his tale and laughed heartily with the other men. Then he looked at Sandy. Suddenly he grinned.

"Say, little coon, let's see you hit a step for the boys! . . . Down where I live, folks, all our niggers can dance! . . . Come on, boy, snap it up!"

"I can't," Sandy said, frowning instead of smiling, and growing warm as he stood there in the smoky circle of grinning white men. "I don't know how to dance."

"O, you're one of them stubborn Kansas coons, heh?" said the red-necked fellow disgustedly, the thickness of whisky on his tongue. "You Northern darkies are dumb as hell, anyhow!" Then, turning to the crowd of amused lobby loungers, he announced: "Now down in Mississippi, whar I come from, if you offer a nigger a dime, he'll dance his can off . . . an' they better dance, what I mean!"

He turned to the men around him for approbation, while Sandy still waited uncomfortably to be paid for the shine. But the man kept him standing there, looking at him drunkenly, then at the amused crowd of Saturday-night loungers.

"Now, a nigger his size down South would no more think o' not dancin' if a white man asked him than he would think o' flyin'. This boy's jest tryin' to be smart, that's all. Up here you-all've got darkies spoilt, believin' they're somebody. Now, in my home we keep 'em in their places." He again turned his attention to Sandy. "Boy! I want to see you dance!" he commanded.

But Sandy picked up his blacking-box and had begun to push through the circle of chairs, not caring any longer about his pay, when the Southerner rose and grabbed him roughly by the arm, exhaling alcoholic breath in the boy's face as he jokingly pulled him back.

"Com'ere, you little—" but he got no further, for Sandy, strengthened by the anger that suddenly possessed him at the touch of this white man's hand, uttered a yell that could be heard for blocks.

Everyone in the lobby turned to see what had happened, but before Joe Willis got out from behind the clerk's desk, the boy, wriggling free, had reached the street-door. There Sandy turned, raised his boot-black box furiously above his head, and flung it with all his strength at the group of laughing white men in which the drunken Southerner was standing. From one end of the whizzing box a stream of polish-bottles, brushes, and cans fell clattering across the lobby while Sandy disappeared through the door, running as fast as his legs could carry him in the falling snow.

"Hey! You black bastard!" Joe Willis yelled from the hotel entrance, but his voice was blown away in the darkness. As Sandy ran, he felt the snow-flakes falling in his face.

21
NOTE TO HARRIETT

SEVERAL DAYS LATER, when Sandy took out of his pocket the piece of paper that his Aunt Harriett had given him that day in front of the hotel, he noticed that the address written on it was somewhere in the Bottoms. He felt vaguely worried, so he did not show it to his grandmother, because he had often heard her say that the Bottoms was a bad place. And when he was working at the barber-shop, he had heard the men talking about what went on there—and in a sense he knew what they meant.

It was a gay place—people did what they wanted to, or what they had to do, and didn't care—for in the Bottoms folks ceased to struggle against the boundaries between good and bad, or white and black, and surrendered amiably to immorality. Beyond Pearl Street, across the tracks, people of all colors came together for the sake of joy, the curtains being drawn only between themselves and the opposite side of the railroad, where the churches were and the big white Y.M.C.A.

At night in the Bottoms victrolas moaned and banjos cried ecstatically in the darkness. Summer evenings little yellow and brown and black girls in pink or blue bungalow aprons laughed invitingly in doorways, and dice rattled with the staccato gaiety of jazz music on long tables in rear rooms. Pimps played pool; bootleggers lounged in big red cars; children ran in the streets until midnight, with no voice of parental authority forcing them to an early sleep; young blacks fought like cocks and enjoyed it; white boys walked through the streets winking at colored girls; men came in autos; old women ate pigs' feet and watermelon and drank beer; whisky flowed; gin was like water; soft indolent laughter didn't care about anything; and deep nigger-throated voices that had long ago stopped rebelling against the ways of this world rose in song.

To those who lived on the other side of the railroad and never realized the utter stupidity of the word "sin," the Bottoms was vile and wicked. But to the girls who lived there, and the boys who pimped and fought and sold licker there, "sin" was a silly word that did not enter their heads. They had never looked at life through the spectacles of the Sunday-school. The glasses good people wore wouldn't have fitted their eyes, for they hung no curtain of words between themselves and reality. To them, things were—what they were.

"Ma bed is hard, but I'm layin' in it jest de same!"

sang the raucous-throated blues-singer in her song;

"Hey! . . . Hey! Who wants to lay with me?"

It was to one of these streets in the Bottoms that Sandy came breathlessly one bright morning with a note in his hand. He knocked at the door of a big grey house.

"Is this where Harriett Williams lives?" he panted.

"You means Harrietta?" said a large, sleek yellow woman in a blue silk kimono who opened the door. "Come in, baby, and sit down. I'll see if she's up yet." Then the woman left Sandy in the parlor while she went up the stairs calling his aunt in a clear, lazy voice.

There were heavy velvet draperies at the windows and doors in this front room where Sandy sat, and a thick, well-worn rug on the floor. There was a divan, a davenport covered with pillows, a center table, and several chairs. Through the curtains at the double door leading into the next room, Sandy saw a piano, more sofas and chairs, and a cleared oiled floor that might be used for dancing. Both rooms were in great disorder, and the air in the house smelled stale and beerish. Licker-bottles and ginger-ale bottles were underneath the center table, underneath the sofas, and on top of the piano. Ash-trays were everywhere, overflowing with cigar-butts and cigarette-ends—on the floor, under chairs, overturned among the sofa-pillows. A small brass tray under one of the sofas held a half-dozen small glasses, some of them still partly full of whisky or gin.

Sandy sat down to wait for his aunt. It was very quiet in the house, although it was almost ten o'clock. A man came down the stairs with his coat on his arm, blinking sleepily. He passed through the hall and out into the street. Bedroom-slippered feet shuffled to the head of the steps on the second floor, and the lazy woman's voice called: "She'll be down in a minute, darling. Just wait there."

Sandy waited. He heard the splash of water above and the hoarse gurgling of a bath-tub being emptied. Presently Harriett appeared in a little pink wash dress such as a child wears, the skirt striking her just above the knees. She smelled like cashmere-bouquet soap, and her face was not yet powdered, nor her hair done up, but she was smiling broadly, happy to see her nephew, as her arms went round his neck.

"My! I'm glad to see you, honey! How'd you happen to come? How'd you find me?"

"Grandma's sick," said Sandy. "She's awful sick and Aunt Tempy sent you this note."

The girl opened the letter. It read:

> Your mother is not expected to live. You better come to see her since she has asked for you. Tempy.

"O! . . . Wait a minute," said Harriett softly. "I'll hurry."

Sandy sat down again in the room full of ash-trays and licker-bottles. Many feet pattered upstairs, and, as doors opened and closed, women's voices were heard: "Can I help you, girlie? Can I lend you anything? Does you need a veil?"

When Harriett came down, she was wearing a tan coat-suit and a white turban, pulled tight on her head. Her face was powdered and her lips rouged ever so slightly. The bag she carried was beaded, blue and gold.

"Come on, Sandy," she said. "I guess I'm ready."

As they went out, they heard a man's voice in a shabby

house across the street singing softly to a two-finger piano accompaniment:

Sugar babe, I'm leavin'
An' it won't be long. . . .

While outside, on his front door-step, two nappy-headed little yellow kids were solemnly balling-the-jack.

Two days before, Sandy had come home from school and found his grandmother lying across the bed, the full tubs still standing in the kitchen, her clothes not yet hung out to dry.

"What's the matter?" he asked.

"I's washed down, chile," said the old woman, panting. "I feels kinder tired-like, that's all."

But Sandy knew that there must be something else wrong with Aunt Hager, because he had never seen her lying on the bed in broad daylight, with her clothes still in the tubs.

"Does your back ache?" asked the child.

"I does feel a little misery," sighed Aunt Hager. "But seems to be mo' ma side an' not ma back this time. But 'tain't nothin'. I's just tired."

But Sandy was scared. "You want some soda and water, grandma?"

"No, honey." Then, in her usual tones of assumed anger: "Go on away from here an' let a body rest. Ain't I told you they ain't nothin' the matter 'ceptin' I's all washed out an' just got to lay down a minute? Go on an' fetch in yo' wood . . . an' spin yo' top out yonder with Buster and them. Go on!"

It was nearly five o'clock when the boy came in again. Aunt Hager was sitting in the rocker near the stove then, her face drawn and ashy. She had been trying to finish her washing.

"Chile, go get Sister Johnson an' ask her if she can't wring out ma clothes fo' me—Mis' Dunset ain't sent much washin' this week, an' you can help her hang 'em up. I reckon it ain't gonna rain tonight, so's they can dry befo' mawnin'."

Sandy ran towards the door.

"Now, don't butt your brains out!" said the old lady. "Ain't no need o' runnin'."

Not only did Sister Johnson come at once and hang out the washing, but she made Hager get in bed, with a hot-water bottle on her paining side. And she gave her a big dose of peppermint and water.

"I 'spects it's from yo' stomick," she said. "I knows you et cabbage fo' dinner!"

"Maybe 'tis," said Hager.

Sister Johnson took Sandy to her house for supper that evening and he and Willie-Mae ate five sweet potatoes each.

"You-all gwine bust!" said Tom Johnson.

About nine o'clock the boy went to bed with his grandmother, and all that night Hager tossed and groaned, in spite of her efforts to lie quiet and not keep Sandy awake. In the morning she said: "Son, I reckon you better stay home from school, 'cause I's feelin' mighty po'ly. Seems like that cabbage ain't digested yet. Feels like I done et a stone. . . . Go see if you can't make de fire up an' heat me a cup o' hot water."

About eleven o'clock Madam de Carter came over. "I thought I didn't perceive you nowhere in the yard this morning and the sun 'luminating so bright and cheerful. You ain't indispensed, are you? Sandy said you was kinder ill." She chattered away. "You know it don't look natural not to see you hanging out clothes long before the noon comes."

"I ain't well a-tall this mawnin'," said Hager when she got a chance to speak. "I's feelin' right bad. I suffers with a pain in ma side; seems like it ain't gettin' no better. Sister Johnson just left here from rubbin' it, but I still suffers terrible an' can't eat nothin'. . . . You can use de phone, can't you, Sister Carter?"

"Why, yes! Yes indeedy! I oftens phones from over to Mis' Petit's. You think you needs a physicianer?"

In spite of herself a groan came from the old woman's lips as she tried to turn towards her friend. Aunt Hager, who had never moaned for lesser hurts, did not intend to complain over this one—but the pain!

"It's cuttin' me in two." She gasped. "Send fo' old Doc McDillors an' he'll come."

Madam de Carter, proud and important at the prospect of using her white neighbor's phone, rushed away.

"I didn't know you were so sick, grandma!" Sandy's eyes were wide with fright and sympathy. "I'm gonna get Mis' Johnson to come rub you again."

"O! . . . O, ma Lawd, help!" Alone for a moment with no one to hear her, she couldn't hold back the moans any longer. A cold sweat stood on her forehead.

The doctor came—the kind old white man who had known Hager for years and in whom she had faith.

"Well," he said, "it's quite a surprise to see you in bed, Aunty." Then, looking very serious and professional, he took her pulse.

"Go out and close the door," he said gently to Madam de Carter and Sister Johnson, Willie-Mae and Sandy, all of whom had gathered around the bed in the little room. "Somebody heat some water." He turned back the quilts from the woman's body and unbuttoned her gown.

Ten minutes later he said frankly, but with great kindness in his tones: "You're a sick woman, Hager, a very sick woman."

That afternoon Tempy came, like a stranger to the house, and took charge of things. Sandy felt uncomfortable and shy in her presence. This aunt of his had a hard, cold, correct way of talking that resembled Mrs. Rice's manner of speaking to his mother when Annjee used to work there. But Tempy quickly put the house in order, bathed her mother, and spread the bed with clean sheets and a white counterpane. Before evening, members of Hager's Lodge began to drop in bringing soups and custards. White people of the neighborhood stopped, too, to inquire if there was anything they could do for the old woman who had so often waited on them in their illnesses. About six o'clock old man Logan drove up the alley and tied his white mule to the back fence.

The sun was setting when Tempy called Sandy in from the back yard, where he was chopping wood for the stove. She said:

"James"—how queerly his correct name struck his ears as it fell from the lips of this cold aunt!—"James, you had better send this telegram to your mother. Now, here is a dollar bill and you can bring back the change. Look on her last letter and get the correct address."

Sandy took the written sheet of paper and the money that his aunt gave him. Then he looked through the various drawers in the house for his mother's last letter. It had been nearly a month since they had heard from her, but finally the boy found the letter in the cupboard, under a jelly-glass full of small coins that his grandmother kept there. He carried the envelope with him to the telegraph office, and there he paid for a message to Annjee in Detroit:

Mother very sick, come at once. Tempy.

As the boy walked home in the gathering dusk, he felt strangely alone in the world, as though Aunt Hager had already gone away, and when he reached the house, it was full of lodge members who had come to keep watch. Tempy went home, but Sister Johnson remained in the sick-room, changing the hot-water bottles and administering, every three hours, the medicine the doctor had left.

There were so many people in the house that Sandy came out into the back yard and sat down on the edge of the well. It was cool and clear, and a slit of moon rode in a light-blue sky spangled with stars. Soon the apple-trees would bud and the grass would be growing. Sandy was a big boy. When his next birthday came, he would be fourteen, and he had begun to grow tall and heavy. Aunt Hager said she was going to buy him a pair of long pants this coming summer. And his mother would hardly know him when she saw him again, if she ever came home.

Tonight, inside, there were so many old sisters from the lodge that Sandy couldn't even talk to his grandmother while she lay in bed. They were constantly going in and out of the sick-room, drinking coffee in the kitchen, or gossiping in the parlor. He wished they would all go away. He could take care of his grandmother himself until she got well—he and Sister Johnson. They didn't even need Tempy, who, he felt, shouldn't be there, because he didn't like her.

"They callin' you inside," Willie-Mae came out to tell him as he sat by himself in the cold on the edge of the well. She was taller than Sandy now and had a regular job taking care of a white lady's baby. She no longer wore her hair in braids. She did it up, and she had a big leather pocketbook that she carried on her arm like a woman. Boys came to take her to the movies on Saturday nights. "They want you inside."

Sandy got up, his legs stiff and numb, and went into the kitchen. An elderly brown woman, dressed in black silk that swished as she moved, opened the door to Hager's bedroom and whispered to him loudly: "Be quiet, chile."

Sandy entered between a lane of old women. Hager looked up at him and smiled—so grave and solemn he appeared.

"Is they takin' care o' you?" she asked weakly. "Ain't it bedtime, honey? Is you had something to eat? Come on an' kiss yo' old grandma befo' you go to sleep. She'll be better in de mawnin'."

She couldn't seem to lift her head, so Sandy sat down on the bed and kissed her. All he said was: "I'm all right, grandma," because there were so many old women in there that he couldn't talk. Then he went out into the other room.

The air in the house was close and stuffy and the boy soon became groggy with sleep. He fell across the bed that had been Annjee's, and later Dogberry's, with all his clothes on. One of the lodge women in the room said: "You better take off yo' things, chile, an' go to sleep right." Then she said to the other sisters: "Come on in de kitchen, you-all, an' let this chile go to bed."

In the morning Tempy woke him. "Are you sure you had Annjee's address correct last night?" she demanded. "The telegraph office says she couldn't be found, so the message was not delivered. Let me see the letter."

Sandy found the letter again, and the address was verified.

"Well, that's strange," said Tempy. "I suppose, as careless and irresponsible as Jimboy is, they've got it wrong, or else moved. . . . Do you know where Harriett can be? I don't suppose you do, but mother has been calling for her all night. I suppose we'll have to try to get her, wherever she is."

"I got her address," said Sandy. "She wrote it down for me when I was working at the hotel this winter. I can find her."

"Then I'll give you a note," said Tempy. "Take it to her."

So Sandy went to the big grey house in the Bottoms that morning to deliver Tempy's message, before the girls there had risen from their beds.

22
BEYOND THE JORDAN

DURING THE DAY the lodge members went to their work in the various kitchens and restaurants and laundries of the town. And Madam de Carter was ordered to Tulsa, Oklahoma, where a split in her organization was threatened because of the elections of the grand officers. Hager was resting easy, no pain now, but very weak.

"It's only a matter of time," said the doctor. "Give her the medicine so she won't worry, but it does no good. There's nothing we can do."

"She's going to die!" Sandy thought.

Harriett sat by the bedside holding her mother's hand as the afternoon sunlight fell on the white spread. Hager had been glad to see the girl again, and the old woman held nothing against her daughter for no longer living at home.

"Is you happy, chile?" Hager asked. "You looks so nice. Yo' clothes is right purty. I hopes you's findin' what you wants in life. You's young, honey, an' you needs to be happy. . . . Sandy!" She called so weakly that he could hardly hear her, though he was standing at the head of the bed. "Sandy, look in that drawer, chile, under ma night-gowns an' things, an' hand me that there little box you sees down in de corner."

The child found it and gave it to her, a small, white box from a cheap jeweller's. It was wrapped carefully in a soft handkerchief. The old woman took it eagerly and tried to hold it out towards her daughter. Harriett unwound the handkerchief and opened the lid of the box. Then she saw that it contained the tiny gold watch that her mother had given her on her sixteenth birthday, which she had pawned months ago in order to run away with the carnival. Quick tears came to the girl's eyes.

"I got it out o' pawn fo' you," Hager said, " 'cause I wanted you to have it fo' yo'self, chile. You know yo' mammy bought it fo' you."

It was such a little watch! Old-timy, with a breastpin on it. Harriett quickly put her handkerchief over her wrist to hide the flashy new timepiece she was wearing on a gold bracelet.

That night Hager died. The undertakers came at dawn with their wagon and carried the body away to embalm it. Sandy stood on the front porch looking at the morning star as the clatter of the horses' hoofs echoed in the street. A sleepy young white boy was driving the undertaker's wagon, and the horse that pulled it was white.

The women who had been sitting up all night began to go home now to get their husbands' breakfasts and to prepare to go to work themselves.

"It's Wednesday," Sandy thought. "Today I'm supposed to go get Mrs. Reinhart's clothes, but grandma's dead. I guess I won't get them now. There's nobody to wash them."

Sister Johnson called him to the kitchen to drink a cup of coffee. Harriett was there weeping softly. Tempy was inside busily cleaning the room from which they had removed the body. She had opened all the windows and was airing the house.

Out in the yard a rooster flapped his wings and crowed shrilly at the rising sun. The fire crackled, and the coffee boiling sent up a fragrant aroma. Sister Johnson opened a can of condensed milk by punching it with the butcher-knife. She put some cups and saucers on the table.

"Tempy, won't you have some?"

"No, thank you, Mrs. Johnson," she called from the dead woman's bedroom.

When Aunt Hager was brought back to her house, she was in a long box covered with black plush. They placed it on a folding stand by the window in the front room. There was a crepe on the door, and the shades were kept lowered, and people whispered in the house as though someone were asleep. Flowers began to be delivered by boys on bicycles, and the lodge members came to sit up again that night. The time was set for burial, and the *Daily Leader* carried this paragraph in small type on its back page:

> Hager Williams, aged colored laundress of 419 Cypress Street, passed away at her home last night. She was known and respected by many white families in the community. Three daughters and a grandson survive.

They tried again to reach Annjee in Detroit by telegram, but without success. On the afternoon of the funeral it was cold and rainy. The little Baptist Church was packed with people. The sisters of the lodge came in full regalia, with banners and insignia, and the brothers turned out with them. Hager's coffin was banked with flowers. There were many fine pieces from the families for whom she had washed and from the white neighbors she had nursed in sickness. There were offerings, too, from Tempy's high-toned friends and from Harriett's girl companions in the house in the Bottoms. Many of the bell-boys, porters, and bootleggers sent wreaths and crosses with golden letters on them: "At Rest in Jesus," "Beyond the Jordan," or simply: "Gone Home." There was a bouquet of violets from Buster's mother and a blanket of roses from Tempy herself. They were all pretty, but, to Sandy, the perfume was sickening in the close little church.

The Baptist minister preached, but Tempy had Father Hill from her church to say a few words, too. The choir sang *Shall We Meet Beyond the River?* People wept and fainted. The services seemed interminable. Then came the long drive to the cemetery in horse-drawn hacks, with a few automobiles in line behind. In at the wide gates and through a vast expanse of tombstones the procession passed, across the graveyard, towards the far, lonesome corner where most of the Negroes rested. There Sandy saw the open grave. Then he saw the casket going down . . . down . . . down, into the earth.

The boy stood quietly between his Aunt Tempy and his Aunt Harriett at the edge of the grave while Tempy stared straight ahead into the drizzling rain, and Harriett cried, streaking the powder on her cheeks.

"That's all right, mama," Harriett sobbed to the body in the long, black box. "You won't get lonesome out here. Harrie'll come back tomorrow. Harrie'll come back every day and bring you flowers. You won't get lonesome, mama."

They were throwing wet dirt on the coffin as the mourners walked away through the sticky clay towards their carriages. Some old sister at the grave began to sing:

Dark was the night,
Cold was the ground . . .

in a high weird monotone. Others took it up, and, as the mourners drove away, the air was filled with the minor wailing of the old women. Harriett was wearing Hager's gift, the little gold watch, pinned beneath her coat.

When they got back to the house where Aunt Hager had lived for so long, Sister Johnson said the mail-man had left a letter under the door that afternoon addressed to the dead woman. Harriett was about to open it when Tempy took it from her. It was from Annjee.

"Dear mama," it began.

> We have moved to Toledo because Jimboy thought he would do better here and the reason I haven't written, we have been so long getting settled. I have been out of work but we both got jobs now and maybe I will be able to send you some money soon. I hope you are well, ma, and all right. Kiss Sandy for me and take care of yourself. With love and God's blessings from your daughter,
>
> ANNJEE

Tempy immediately turned the letter over and wrote on the back:

> We buried your mother today. I tried to reach you in Detroit, but could not get you, since you were no longer there and neglected to send us your new address. It is too bad you weren't here for the funeral. Your child is going to stay with me until I hear from you.
>
> TEMPY

Then she turned to the boy, who stood dazed beside Sister Johnson in the silent, familiar old house. "You will come home with me, James," she said. "We'll see that this place is locked first. You try all the windows and I'll fasten the doors; then we'll go out the front. . . . Mrs. Johnson, it's been good of you to help us in our troubles. Thank you."

Sister Johnson went home, leaving Harriett in the parlor. When Sandy and Tempy returned from locking the back windows and doors, they found the girl still standing there, and for a moment the two sisters looked at one another in silence. Then Tempy said coldly: "We're going."

Harriett went out alone into the drizzling rain. Tempy tried the parlor windows to be sure they were well fastened; then, stepping outside on the porch, she locked the door and put the key in her bag.

"Come on," she said.

Sandy looked up and down the street, but in the thick twilight of fog and rain Harriett had disappeared, so he followed his aunt into the waiting cab. As the hack clattered off, the boy gave an involuntary shiver.

"Do you want to hold my hand?" Tempy asked, unbending a little.

"No," Sandy said. So they rode in silence.

23
TEMPY'S HOUSE

"JAMES, YOU MUST get up on time in this house. Breakfast has been ready twenty minutes. I can't come upstairs every morning to call you. You are old enough now to wake yourself and you must learn to do so—you've too far to walk to school to lie abed."

Sandy tumbled out. Tempy left the room so that he would be free to dress, and soon he came downstairs to breakfast.

He had never had a room of his own before. He had never even slept in a room alone, but here his aunt had given him a small chamber on the second floor which had a window that looked out into a tidy back yard where there was a brick walk running to the back gate. The room, which was very clean, contained only the bed, one chair, and a dresser. There was, too, a little closet in which to hang clothes, but Sandy did not have many to put in it.

The thing that impressed him most about the second floor was the bathroom. He had never lived where there was running water indoors. And in this room, too, everything was so spotlessly clean that Sandy was afraid to move lest he disturb something or splash water on the wall.

When he came downstairs for breakfast, he found the table set for two. Mr. Siles, being in the railway postal service, was out on a trip. The grapefruit was waiting as Sandy slid shyly into his place opposite the ash-brown woman who had become his guardian since his grandma's death. She bowed her head to say a short grace; then they ate.

"Have you been accustomed to drinking milk in the mornings?" Tempy asked as they were finishing the meal. "If you have, the milkman can leave another bottle. Young people should have plenty of milk."

"Yes'm, I'd like it, but we only had coffee at home."

"You needn't say 'yes'm' in this house. We are not used to slavery talk here. If you like milk, I'll get it for you. . . . Now, how are your clothes? I see your stocking has a hole in it, and one pants-leg is hanging."

"It don't stay fastened."

"It *doesn't*, James! I'll buy you some more pants tomorrow. What else do you need?"

Sandy told her, and in a few days she took him to Wertheimer's, the city's largest store, and outfitted him completely. And, as they shopped, she informed him that she was the only colored woman in town who ran a bill there.

"I want white people to know that Negroes have a little taste; that's why I always trade at good shops. . . . And if you're going to live with me, you'll have to learn to do things right, too."

The tearful letter that came from Annjee when she heard of her mother's death said that Toledo was a very difficult place to get work in, and that she had no money to send railroad fare for Sandy, but that she would try to send for him as soon as she could. Jimboy was working on a lake steamer and was seldom home, and she couldn't have Sandy with her anyway until they got a nicer place to stay; so would Tempy please keep him a little while?

By return post Tempy replied that if Annjee had any sense, she would let Sandy remain in Stanton, where he could get a good education, and not be following after his worthless father all over the country. Mr. Siles and she had no children, and Sandy seemed like a quiet, decent child, smart in his classes. Colored people needed to encourage talent so that the white race would realize Negroes weren't all mere guitar-players and house-maids. And Sandy could be a credit if he were raised right. Of course, Tempy knew he hadn't had the correct environment to begin with—living with Jimboy and Harriett and going to a Baptist church, but undoubtedly he could be trained. He was young. "And I think it would be only fair to the boy that you let him stay with us, because, Annjee, you are certainly not the person to bring him up as he should be reared." The letter was signed: "Your sister, Tempy," and written properly with pen and ink.

So it happened that Sandy came to live with Mr. and Mrs. Arkins Siles, for that was the name by which his aunt and uncle were known in the Negro society of the town. Mr. Siles was a mail-clerk on the railroad—a position that colored people considered a high one because you were working for "Uncle Sam." He was a paste-colored man of forty-eight who had inherited three houses from his father.

Tempy, when she married, had owned houses too, one of which had been willed her by Mrs. Barr-Grant, for whom she had worked for years as personal maid. She had acquired her job while yet in high school, and Mrs. Barr-Grant, who travelled a great deal in the interest of woman suffrage and prohibition, had taken Tempy east with her. On their return to Stanton she allowed the colored maid to take charge of her home, where she also employed a cook and a parlor girl. Thus was the mistress left free to write pamphlets and prepare lectures on the various evils of the world standing in need of correction.

Tempy pleased Mrs. Barr-Grant by being prompt and exact in obeying orders and by appearing to worship her Puritan intelligence. In truth Tempy did worship her mistress, for the colored girl found that by following Mrs. Barr-Grant's early directions she had become an expert housekeeper; by imitating her manner of speech she had acquired a precise flow of language; and by reading her books she had become interested in things that most Negro girls never thought about. Several times the mistress had remarked to her maid: "You're so smart and such a good, clean, quick little worker, Tempy, that it's too bad you aren't white." And Tempy had taken this to heart, not as an insult, but as a compliment.

When the white lady died, she left one of her small houses to her maid as a token of appreciation for faithful services. By dint of saving, and of having resided with her mistress where there had been no living expenses, Tempy had managed to buy another house, too. When Mr. Siles asked her to be his wife, everybody said it was a fine match, for both owned property, both were old enough to know what they wanted, and both were eminently respectable. . . . Now they prospered together.

Tempy no longer worked out, but stayed home, keeping house, except that she went each month to collect her rents and those of her husband. She had a woman to do the laundry and help with the cleaning, but Tempy herself did the cooking, and all her meals were models of economical preparation. Just enough food was prepared each time for three people. Sandy never had a third helping of dessert in her house. No big pots of black-eyed peas and pigtails scented her front hall, either. She got her recipes from *The Ladies' Home Journal*—and she never bought a watermelon.

White people were for ever picturing colored folks with huge slices of watermelon in their hands. Well, she was one colored woman who did not like them! Her favorite fruits were tangerines and grapefruit, for Mrs. Barr-Grant had always eaten those, and Tempy had admired Mrs. Barr-Grant more than anybody else—more, of course, than she had admired Aunt Hager, who spent her days at the wash-tub, and had loved watermelon.

Colored people certainly needed to come up in the world, Tempy thought, up to the level of white people—dress like white people, talk like white people, think like white people—and then they would no longer be called "niggers."

In Tempy this feeling was an emotional reaction, born of white admiration, but in Mr. Siles, who shared his wife's views, the same attitude was born of practical thought. The whites had the money, and if Negroes wanted any, the quicker they learned to be like the whites, the better. Stop being lazy, stop singing all the time, stop attending revivals, and learn to get the dollar—because money buys everything, even the respect of white people.

Blues and spirituals Tempy and her husband hated because they were too Negro. In their house Sandy dared not sing a word of *Swing Low, Sweet Chariot*, for what had darky slave songs to do with respectable people? And rag-time belonged in the Bottoms with the sinners. (It was ironically strange that the Bottoms should be the only section of Stanton where Negroes and whites mingled freely on equal terms.) That part of town, according to Tempy, was lost to God, and the fact that she had a sister living there burned like a hidden cancer in her breast. She never mentioned Harriett to anyone.

Tempy's friends were all people of standing in the darker world—doctors, school-teachers, a dentist, a lawyer, a hair-dresser. And she moved among these friends as importantly as Mrs. Barr-Grant had moved among a similar group in the white race. Many of them had had wash-women for mothers and day-laborers for fathers; but none ever spoke of that. And while Aunt Hager lived, Tempy, after getting her position with Mrs. Barr-Grant, was seldom seen with the old woman. After her marriage she was even more ashamed of her family connections—a little sister running wild, and another sister married for the sake of love—Tempy could never abide Jimboy, or understand why Annjee had taken up with a rounder from the South. One's family as a topic of conversation, however, was not popular in high circles, for too many of Stanton's dark society folks had sprung from humble family trees and low black bottoms.

"But back in Washington, where I was born," said Mrs. Doctor Mitchell once, "we really have blood! All the best people at the capital come from noted ancestry—Senator Bruce, John M. Langston, Governor Pinchback, Frederick Douglass. Why, one of our colored families on their white side can even trace its lineage back to George Washington! . . . O, yes, we have a background! But, of course, we are too refined to boast about it."

Tempy thought of her mother then and wished that black Aunt Hager had not always worn her apron in the streets, uptown and everywhere! Of course, it was clean and white and seemed to suit the old lady, but aprons weren't worn by the best people. When Tempy was in the hospital for an operation shortly after her marriage, they wouldn't let Hager enter by the front door—and Tempy never knew whether it was on account of her color or the apron! The Presbyterian Hospital was prejudiced against Negroes and didn't like them to use the elevator, but certainly her mother should not have come there in an apron!

Well, Aunt Hager had meant well, Tempy thought, even if she didn't dress right. And now this child, Sandy—James was his correct name! At that first breakfast they ate together, she asked him if he had a comb and brush of his own.

"No'm, I ain't," said Sandy.

"I haven't," she corrected him. "I certainly don't want my white neighbors to hear you saying 'ain't' . . . You've come to live with me now and you must talk like a gentleman."

24
A SHELF OF BOOKS

THAT SPRING, SHORTLY after Sandy went to stay with Tempy, there was an epidemic of mumps among the schoolchildren in Stanton, and, old as he was, he was among its early victims. With jaws swollen to twice their normal size and a red sign, MUMPS, on the house, he was forced to remain at home for three weeks. It was then that the boy began to read books other than the ones he had had to study for his lessons. At Aunt Hager's house there had been no books, anyway, except the Bible and the few fairytales that he had been given at Christmas; but Tempy had a case full of dusty volumes that were used to give dignity to her sitting-room: a row of English classics bound in red, an *Encyclopedia of World Knowledge* in twelve volumes, a book on household medicine full of queer drawings, and some modern novels—*The Rosary*, *The Little Shepherd of Kingdom Come*, the newest Harold Bell Wright, and all that had ever been written by Gene Stratton Porter, Tempy's favorite author. The Negro was represented by Chestnut's *House Behind the Cedars*, and the *Complete Poems* of Paul Lawrence Dunbar, whom Tempy tolerated on account of his fame, but condemned because he had written so much in dialect and so often of the lower classes of colored people. Tempy subscribed to *Harper's Magazine*, too, because Mrs. Barr-Grant had taken it. And in her sewing-room closet there was also a pile of *The Crisis*, the thin Negro monthly that she had been taking from the beginning of its publication.

Sandy had heard of that magazine, but he had never seen a copy; so he went through them all, looking at the pictures of prominent Negroes and reading about racial activities all over the country, and about racial wrongs in the South. In every issue he found, too, stirring and beautifully written editorials about the frustrated longings of the black race, and the hidden beauties in the Negro soul. A man named DuBois wrote them.

"Dr. William Edward Burghardt DuBois," said Tempy, "and he is a great man."

"Great like Booker T. Washington?" asked Sandy.

"Teaching Negroes to be servants, that's all Washington did!" Tempy snorted in so acid a tone that Sandy was silent. "DuBois wants our rights. He wants us to be real men and women. He believes in social equality. But Washington—huh!" The fact that he had established an industrial school damned Washington in Tempy's eyes, for there were enough colored workers already. But DuBois was a doctor of philosophy and had studied in Europe! . . . That's what Negroes needed to do, get smart, study books, go to Europe! "Don't talk to me about Washington," Tempy fumed. "Take DuBois for your model, not some white folks' nigger."

"Well, Aunt Hager said—" then Sandy stopped. His grandmother had thought that Booker T. was the greatest of men, but maybe she had been wrong. Anyway, this DuBois could write! Gee, it made you burn all over to read what he said about a lynching. But Sandy did not mention Booker Washington again to Tempy, although, months later, at the library he read his book called *Up from Slavery*, and he was sure that Aunt Hager hadn't been wrong. "I guess they are both great men," he thought.

Sandy's range of reading increased, too, when his aunt found a job for him that winter in Mr. Prentiss's gift-card- and printing-shop, where he kept the place clean and acted as delivery boy. This shop kept a shelf of current novels and some volumes of the new poetry—Sandburg, Lindsay, Masters—which the Young Women's Club of Stanton was then studying, to the shocked horror of the older white ladies of the town. Sandy knew of this because Mr. Prentiss's daughter, a student at Goucher College, used to keep shop and she pointed out volumes for the boy to read and told him who their authors were and what the books meant. She said that none of the colored boys they had employed before had ever been interested in reading; so she often lent him, by way of encouragement, shopworn copies to be taken home at night and returned the next day. Thus Sandy spent much of his first year with Tempy deep in novels too mature for a fourteen-year-old boy. But Tempy was very proud of her studious young nephew. She began to decide that she had made no mistake in keeping him with her, and when he entered the high school, she bought him his first long-trouser suit as a spur towards further application.

Sandy became taller week by week, and it seemed to Tempy as if his shirt-sleeves became too short for him overnight. His voice was changing, too, and he had acquired a liking for football, but his after-school job at Prentiss's kept him from playing much. At night he read, or sometimes went to the movies with Buster—but Tempy kept him home as much as she could. Occasionally he saw Willie-Mae, who was keeping company with the second cook at Wright's Hotel. And sometimes he saw Jimmy Lane, who was a bell-hop now and hung out with a sporty crowd in the rear room of Cudge Windsor's pool hall. But whenever Sandy went into his old neighborhood, he felt sad, remembering Aunt Hager and his mother, and Jimboy, and Harriett—for his young aunt had gone away from Stanton, too, and the last he heard about her rumored that she was on the stage in Kansas City. Now the little house where Sandy had lived with his grandmother belonged to Tempy, who kept it rented to a family of strangers.

In high school Sandy was taking, at his aunt's request, the classical course, which included Latin, ancient history, and English, and which required a great deal of reading. His teacher of English was a large, masculine woman named Martha Fry, who had once been to Europe and who loved to talk about the splendors of old England and to read aloud in a deep, mannish kind of voice, dramatizing the printed words. It was from her that Sandy received an introduction to Shakespeare, for in the spring term they studied *The Merchant of Venice*. In the spring also, under Miss Fry's direction, the first-year students were required to write an essay for the freshman essay prizes of both money and medals. And in this contest Sandy won the second prize. It was the first time in the history of the school that a colored pupil had ever done anything of the sort, and Tempy was greatly elated. There was a note in the papers about it, and Sandy brought his five dollars home for his aunt to put away. But he gave his bronze medal to a girl named Pansetta Young, who was his class-mate and a new-found friend.

From the first moment in school that he saw Pansetta, he knew that he liked her, and he would sit looking at her for hours in every class that they had together—for she was a little baby-doll kind of girl, with big black eyes and a smooth pinkish-brown skin, and her hair was curly on top of her head. Her widowed mother was a cook at the Goucher College dining-hall; and she was an all-alone little girl, for Pansetta had no brothers or sisters. After Thanksgiving Sandy began to walk part of the way home with her every day. He could not accompany her all the way because he had to go to work at Mr. Prentiss's shop. But on Christmas he bought her a box of candy—and sent it to her by mail. And at Easter-time she gave him a chocolate egg.

"Unh-huh! You got a girl now, ain't you?" teased Buster one April afternoon when he caught Sandy standing in front of the high school waiting for Pansetta to come out.

"Aw, go chase yourself!" said Sandy, for Buster had a way of talking dirty about girls, and Sandy was afraid he would begin that with Pansetta; but today his friend changed the subject instead.

"Say come on round to the pool hall tonight and I'll teach you to play billiards."

"Don't think I'd better, Bus. Aunt Tempy might get sore," Sandy replied, shaking his head. "Besides, I have to study."

"Are you gonna read yourself to death?" Buster demanded indignantly. "You've got to come out some time, man! Tell her you're going to the movies and we'll go down to Cudge's instead."

Sandy thought for a moment.

"All the boys come round there at night."

"Well, I might."

"Little apron-string boy!" teased Buster.

"If I hit you a couple of times, you'll find out I'm not!" Sandy doubled up his fists in pretended anger. "I'll black your blue eyes for you!"

"Ya-a-a-a?" yelled his friend, running up the street. "See you tonight at Cudge's—apron-string boy!"

And that evening Sandy didn't finish reading, as he had planned, *Moby-Dick*, which Mr. Prentiss's daughter had lent him. Instead he practised handling a cue-stick under the tutelage of Buster.

25
POOL HALL

THERE WERE NO community houses in Stanton and no recreation centers for young men except the Y.M.C.A., which was closed to you if you were not a white boy; so, for the Negro youths of the town, Cudge Windsor's pool hall was the evening meeting-place. There one could play billiards, shoot dice in a back room, or sit in summer on the two long benches outside, talking and looking at the girls as they passed. In good weather these benches were crowded all the time.

Next door to the pool hall was Cudge Windsor's lunchroom. Of course, the best colored people did not patronize Cudge's, even though his business was not in the Bottoms. It was located on Pearl Street, some three or four blocks before that thoroughfare plunged across the tracks into the low terrain of tinkling pianos and ladies who loved for cash. But since Cudge catered to what Mr. Siles called "the common element," the best people stayed away.

After months of bookishness and subjection to Tempy's prim plans for his improvement, Sandy found the pool hall an easy and amusing place in which to pass time. It was better than the movies, where people on the screen were only shadows. And it was much better than the Episcopal Church, with its stoop-shouldered rector, for here at Cudge's everybody was alive, and the girls who passed in front swinging their arms and grinning at the men were warm-bodied and gay, while the boys rolling dice in the rear room or playing pool at the tables were loud-mouthed and careless. Life sat easily on their muscular shoulders.

Adventurers and vagabonds who passed through Stanton on the main line would often drop in at Cudge's to play a game or get a bite to eat, and many times on summer nights reckless black boys, a long way from home, kept the natives entertained with tales of the road, or trips on side-door Pullmans, and of far-off cities where things were easy and women generous. They had a song that went:

O, the gals in Texas,
They never be's unkind.
They feeds their men an'
Buys 'em gin an' wine.
But these women in Stanton,
Their hearts is hard an' cold.
When you's out of a job, they
Denies you jelly roll.

Then, often, arguments would begin—boastings, proving and fending; or telling of exploits with guns, knives, and razors, with cops and detectives, with evil women and wicked men; out-bragging and out-lying one another, all talking at once. Sometimes they would create a racket that could be heard for blocks. To the uninitiated it would seem that a fight was imminent. But underneath, all was good-natured and friendly—and through and above everything went laughter. No matter how belligerent or lewd their talk was, or how sordid the tales they told—of dangerous pleasures and strange perversities—these black men laughed. That must be the reason, thought Sandy, why poverty-stricken old Negroes like Uncle Dan Givens lived so long—because to them, no matter how hard life might be, it was not without laughter.

Uncle Dan was the world's champion liar, Cudge Windsor said, and the jolly old man's unending flow of fabulous reminiscences were entertaining enough to earn him a frequent meal in Cudge's lunch-room or a drink of licker from the patrons of the pool hall, who liked to start the old fellow talking.

One August evening when Tempy was away attending a convention of the Midwest Colored Women's Clubs, Sandy and Buster, Uncle Dan, Jimmy Lane, and Jap Logan sat until late with a big group of youngsters in front of the pool hall watching the girls go by. A particularly pretty high yellow damsel passed in a thin cool dress of flowered voile, trailing the sweetness of powder and perfume behind her.

"Dog-gone my soul!" yelled Jimmy Lane. "Just gimme a bone and lemme be your dog—I mean your salty dog!" But the girl, pretending not to hear, strolled leisurely on, followed by a train of compliments from the pool-hall benches.

"Sweet mama Venus!" cried a tall raw-bony boy, gazing after her longingly.

"If angels come like that, lemme go to heaven—and if they don't, lemme be lost to glory!" Jap exclaimed.

"Shut up, Jap! What you know 'bout women?" asked Uncle Dan, leaning forward on his cane to interrupt the comments. "Here you-all is, ain't knee-high to ducks yit, an' talkin' 'bout womens! Shut up, all o' you! Nary one o' you's past seben-teen, but when I were yo' age—Hee! Hee! You-all want to know what dey called me when I were yo' age?" The old man warmed to his tale. "Dey called me de 'stud nigger'! Yes, dey did! On 'count o' de kind o' slavery-time work I was doin'—I were breedin' babies fo' to sell!"

"Another lie!" said Jap.

"No, 'tain't, boy! You listen here to what I's gwine tell you. I were de onliest real healthy nigger buck ma white folks had on de plantation, an' dese was ole po' white folks what can't 'ford to buy many slaves, so dey figures to raise a heap o' darky babies an' sell 'em later on—dat's why dey made me de breeder. . . . Hee! Hee! . . . An' I sho breeded a gang o' pickaninnies, too! But I were young then, jest like you-all is, an' I ain't had a pint o' sense—laying wid de womens all night, ever' night."

"Yes, we believe you," drawled Jimmy.

"An' it warn't no time befo' little yaller chillens an' black chillens an' red chillens an' all kinds o' chillens was runnin' round de yard eatin' out o' de hog-pen an' a-callin' me pappy. . . . An' here I is today gwine on ninety-three year ole an' I done outlived 'em all. Dat is, I done outlived all I ever were able to keep track on after de war, 'cause we darkies sho scat-tered once we was free! Yes, sah! But befo' de fightin' ended

I done been pappy to forty-nine chillens—an' thirty-three of 'em were boys!"

"Aw, I know you're lying now, Uncle Dan," Jimmy laughed.

"No, I ain't, sah! . . . Hee! Hee! . . . I were a great one when I were young! Yes, sah!" The old man went on undaunted. "I went an' snuck off to a dance one night, me an' nudder boy, went 'way ovah in Macon County at ole man Laird's plantation, who been a bitter enemy to our white folks. Did I ever tell you 'bout it? We took one o' ole massa's best hosses out de barn to ride, after he done gone to his bed. . . . Well, sah! It were late when we got started, an' we rid dat hoss lickety-split uphill an' down holler, ovah de crick an' past de mill, me an' ma buddy both on his back, through de cane-brake an' up an' nudder hill, till he wobble an' foam at de mouth like he's 'bout to drap. When we git to de dance, long 'bout midnight, we jump off dis hoss an' ties him to a post an' goes in de cabin whar de music were—an' de function were gwine on big. Man! We grabs ourselves a gal an' dance till de moon riz, kickin' up our heels an' callin' figgers, an' jest havin' a scrumptious time. Ay, Lawd! We sho did dance! . . . Well, come 'long 'bout two o'clock in de mawnin', niggers all leavin', an' we goes out in de yard to git on dis hoss what we had left standin' at de post. . . . An' Lawd have mercy—de hoss were dead! Yes, sah! He done fell down right whar he were tied, eyeballs rolled back, mouth a-foamin', an' were stone-dead! . . . Well, we ain't knowed how we gwine git home ner what we gwine do 'bout massa's hoss—an' we was skeered, Lawdy! 'Cause we know he beat us to death if he find out we done rid his best hoss anyhow—let lone ridin' de crittur to death. . . . An' all de low-down Macon niggers what was at de party was whaw-whawin' fit to kill, laughin' 'cause it were so funny to see us gittin' ready to git on our hoss an' de hoss were dead! . . . Well, sah, me an' ma buddy ain't wasted no time. We took dat animule up by de hind legs an' we drug him all de way home to massa's plantation befo' day! We sho did! Uphill an' down holler, sixteen miles! Yes, sah! An' put dat damn hoss back in massa's barn like he war befo' we left. An' when de sun riz, me an' ma buddy were in de slavery quarters sleepin' sweet an' lowly-like as if we ain't been nowhar. . . . De next day old massa 'maze how dat hoss die all tied up in his stall wid his halter on! An' we niggers 'maze, too, when we heard dat massa's hoss been dead, 'cause we ain't knowed a thing 'bout it. No, sah! Ain't none o' us niggers knowed a thing! Hee! Hee! Not a thing!"

"Weren't you scared?" asked Sandy.

"Sho, we was scared," said Uncle Dan, "but we ain't act like it. Niggers was smart in them days."

"They're still smart," said Jap Logan, "if they can lie like you."

"I mean!" said Buster.

"Uncle Dan's the world's champeen liar," drawled a tall lanky boy. "Come on, let's chip in and buy him a sandwich, 'cause he's lied enough fo' one evening."

They soon crowded into the lunch-room and sat on stools at the counter ordering soda or ice-cream from the fat good-natured waitress. While they were eating, a gambler bolted in from the back room of the pool hall with a handful of coins he had just won.

"Gonna feed ma belly while I got it in ma hand," he shouted. "Can't tell when I might lose, 'cause de dice is runnin' they own way tonight. Say, Mattie," he yelled, "tell chef to gimme a beef-steak all beat up like Jim Jeffries, cup o' coffee strong as Jack Johnson, an' come flyin' like a airship so I can get back in the game. Tell that kitchen buggar sweet-papa Stingaree's out here!"

"All right, keep yo' collar on," said Mattie. "De steak's got to be cooked."

"What you want, Uncle Dan?" yelled the gambler to the old man. "While I's winnin', might as well feed you, too. Take some ham and cabbage or something. That sandwich ain't 'nough to fill you up."

Uncle Dan accepted a plate of spare-ribs, and Stingaree threw down a pile of nickels on the counter.

"Injuns an' buffaloes," he said loudly. "Two things de white folks done killed, so they puts 'em on de backs o' nickels. . . . Rush up that steak there, gal, I's hongry!"

Sandy finished his drink and bought a copy of the *Chicago Defender*, the World's Greatest Negro Weekly, which was sold at the counter. Across the front in big red letters there was a headline: *Negro Boy Lynched.* There was also an account of a race riot in a Northern industrial city. On the theatrical page a picture of pretty Baby Alice Whitman, the tap-dancer, attracted his attention, and he read a few of the items there concerning colored shows; but as he was about to turn the page, a little article in the bottom corner made him pause and put the paper down on the counter.

ACTRESS MAKES HIT

St. Louis, Mo., Aug. 3: Harrietta Williams, sensational young blues-singer, has been packing the Booker Washington Theatre to the doors here this week. Jones and Jones are the headliners for the all-colored vaudeville bill, but the singing of Miss Williams has been the outstanding drawing card. She is being held over for a continued engagement, with Billy Sanderlee at the piano.

"Billy Sanderlee," said Buster, who was looking over Sandy's shoulder. "That's that freckled-faced yellow guy who used to play for dances around here, isn't it? He could really beat a piano to death, all right!"

"Sure could," replied Sandy. "Gee, they must make a great team together, 'cause my Aunt Harrie can certainly sing and dance!"

"Ain't the only thing she can do!" bellowed the gambler, swallowing a huge chunk of steak. "Yo' Aunt Harrie's a whang, son!"

"Shut yo' mouth!" said Uncle Dan.

26
THE DOORS OF LIFE

DURING SANDY'S SECOND year at high school Tempy was busy sewing for the local Red Cross and organizing Liberty Bond clubs among the colored population of Stanton. She earnestly believed that the world would really become safe for democracy, even in America, when the war ended, and that colored folks would no longer be snubbed in private and discriminated against in public.

"Colored boys are over there fighting," she said. "Our men are buying hundreds of dollars' worth of bonds, colored women are aiding the Red Cross, our clubs are sending boxes to the camps and to the front. White folks will see that the Negro can be trusted in war as well as peace. Times will be better after this for all of us."

One day a letter came from Annjee, who had moved to Chicago. She said that Sandy's father had not long remained in camp, but had been sent to France almost immediately after he enlisted, and she didn't know what she was going to do, she was so worried and alone! There had been but one letter from Jimboy since he left. And now she needed Sandy with her, but she wasn't able to send for him yet. She said she hoped and prayed that nothing would happen to his father at the front, but every day there were colored soldiers' names on the casualty list.

"Good thing he's gone," grunted Tempy when she read the letter as they were seated at the supper-table. Then, suddenly changing the subject, she asked Sandy: "Did you see Dr. Frank Crane's beautiful article this morning?"

"No, I didn't," said the boy.

"You certainly don't read as much as you did last winter," complained his aunt. "And you're staying out entirely too late to suit me. I'm quite sure you're not at the movies all that time, either. I want these late hours stopped, young man. Every night in the week out somewhere until ten and eleven o'clock!"

"Well, boys do have to get around a little, Tempy," Mr. Siles objected. "It's not like when you and I were coming up."

"I'm raising this boy, Mr. Siles," Tempy snapped. "When do you study, James? That's what I want to know."

"When I come in," said Sandy, which was true. His light was on until after twelve almost every night. And when he did not study late, his old habit of lying awake clung to him and he could not go to sleep early.

"You think too much," Buster once said. "Stop being so smart; then you'll sleep better."

"Yep," added Jimmy Lane. "Better be healthy and dumb than smart and sick like some o' these college darkies I see with goggles on their eyes and breath smellin' bad."

"O, I'm not sick," objected Sandy, "but I just get to thinking about things at night—the war, and white folks, and God, and girls, and—O, I don't know—everything in general."

"Sure, keep on thinking," jeered Buster, "and turn right ashy after while and be all stoop-shouldered like Father Hill." (The Episcopalian rector was said to be the smartest colored man in town.) "But I'm not gonna worry about being smart myself. A few more years, boy, and I'll be in some big town passing for white, making money, and getting along swell. And I won't need to be smart, either—I'll be ofay! So if you see me some time in St. Louis or Chi with a little blond on my arm—don't recognize me, hear! I want my kids to be so yellow-headed they won't have to think about a color line."

And Sandy knew that Buster meant what he said, for his light-skinned friend was one of those people who always go directly towards the things they want, as though the road is straight before them and they can see clearly all the way. But to Sandy himself nothing ever seemed quite that clear. Why was his country going stupidly to war? . . . Why were white people and colored people so far apart? Why was it wrong to desire the bodies of women? . . . With his mind a maelstrom of thoughts as he lay in bed night after night unable to go to sleep quickly, Sandy wondered many things and asked himself many questions.

Sometimes he would think about Pansetta Young, his classmate with the soft brown skin, and the pointed and delicate breasts of her doll-like body. He had never been alone with Pansetta, never even kissed her, yet she was "his girl" and he liked her a great deal. Maybe he loved her! . . . But what did it mean to love a girl? Were you supposed to marry her then and live with her for ever? . . . His father had married his mother—good-natured, guitar-playing Jimboy—but they weren't always together, and Sandy knew that Jimboy was enjoying the war now, just as he had always enjoyed everything else.

"Gee, he must of married early to be my father and still look so young!" he thought. "Suppose I marry Pansetta now!" But what did he really know about marriage other than the dirty fragments he had picked up from Jimmy and Buster and the fellows at the pool hall?

On his fifteenth birthday Tempy had given him a book written for young men on the subject of love and living, called *The Doors of Life*, addressed to all Christian youths in their teens—but it had been written by a white New England minister of the Presbyterian faith who stood aghast before the flesh; so its advice consisted almost entirely in how to pray in the orthodox manner, and in how *not* to love.

"Avoid evil companions lest they be your undoing (see Psalms cxix, 115-20); and beware of lewd women, for their footsteps lead down to hell (see Proverbs vii, 25-7)," said the book, and that was the extent of its instructions on sex, except that it urged everyone to marry early and settle down to a healthy, moral, Christian life. . . . But how could you marry early when you had no money and no home to which to take a wife, Sandy wondered. And who were evil companions. Neither Aunt Hager nor Annjee had ever said anything to Sandy about love in its bodily sense; Jimboy had gone away too soon to talk with him; and Tempy and her husband were too proper to discuss such subjects; so the boy's sex knowledge consisted only in the distorted ideas that youngsters whisper; the dirty stories heard in the hotel lobby where he had worked; and the fact that they sold in drugstores articles that weren't mentioned in the company of nice people.

But who were nice people anyway? Sandy hated the word "nice." His Aunt Tempy was always using it. All of her friends were nice, she said, respectable and refined. They went around with their noses in the air and they didn't speak to porters and wash-women—though they weren't nearly so much fun as the folks they tried to scorn. Sandy liked Cudge Windsor or Jap Logan better than he did Dr. Mitchell, who had been to college—and never forgotten it.

Sandy wondered if Booker T. Washington had been like Tempy's friends? Or if Dr. DuBois was a snob just because he was a college man? He wondered if those two men had a good time being great. Booker T. was dead, but he had left a living school in the South. Maybe he could teach in the South, too, Sandy thought, if he ever learned enough. Did colored folks need to know the things he was studying in books now? Did French and Latin and Shakespeare make people wise and happy? Jap Logan never went beyond the seventh grade and he was happy. And Jimboy never attended school much either. Maybe school didn't matter. Yet to get a good job you had to be smart––and white, too. That was the trouble, you had to be white!

"But I want to learn!" thought Sandy as he lay awake in the dark after he had gone to bed at night. "I want to go to college. I want to go to Europe and study. 'Work and make ready and maybe your chance will come,' it said under the picture of Lincoln on the calendar given away by the First National Bank, where Earl, his white friend, already had a job promised him when he came out of school. . . . It was not nearly so difficult for white boys. They could work at anything—in stores, on newspapers, in offices. They could become president of the United States if they were clever enough. But a colored boy. . . . No wonder Buster was going to pass for white when he left Stanton.

"I don't blame him," thought Sandy. "Sometimes I hate

white people, too, like Aunt Harrie used to say she did. Still, some of them are pretty decent—my English-teacher, and Mr. Prentiss where I work. Yet even Mr. Prentiss wouldn't give me a job clerking in his shop. All I can do there is run errands and scrub the floor when everybody else is gone. There's no advancement for colored fellows. If they start as porters, they stay porters for ever and they can't come up. Being colored is like being born in the basement of life, with the door to the light locked and barred—and the white folks live upstairs. They don't want us up there with them, even when we're respectable like Dr. Mitchell, or smart like Dr. DuBois. . . . And guys like Jap Logan—well, Jap don't care anyway! Maybe it's best not to care, and stay poor and meek waiting for heaven like Aunt Hager did. . . . But I don't want heaven! I want to live first!" Sandy thought. "I want to live!"

He understood then why many old Negroes said: "Take all this world and give me Jesus!" It was because they couldn't get this world anyway—it belonged to the white folks. They alone had the power to give or withhold at their back doors. Always back doors—even for Tempy and Dr. Mitchell if they chose to go into Wright's Hotel or the New Albert Restaurant. And no door at all for Negroes if they wanted to attend the Rialto Theatre, or join the Stanton Y.M.C.A., or work behind the grilling at the National Bank.

The Doors of Life. . . . God damn that simple-minded book that Tempy had given him! What did an old white minister know about the doors of life for him and Pansetta and Jimmy Lane, for Willie-Mae and Buster and Jap Logan and all the black and brown and yellow youngsters standing on the threshold of the great beginning in a Western town called Stanton? What did an old white minister know about the doors of life anywhere? And, least of all, the doors to a Negro's life? . . . Black youth. . . . Dark hands knocking, knocking! Pansetta's little brown hands knocking on the doors of life! Baby-doll hands, tiny autumn-leaf girl-hands! . . . Gee, Pansetta! . . . The Doors of Life . . . the great big doors. . . . Sandy was asleep . . . of life.

27
BEWARE OF WOMEN

"I WON'T PERMIT IT," said Tempy. "I won't stand for it. You'll have to mend your ways, young man! Spending your evenings in Windsor's pool parlor and running the streets with a gang of common boys that have had no raising, that Jimmy Lane among them. I won't stand for it while you stay in my house. . . . But that's not the worst of it. Mr. Prentiss tells me you've been getting to work late after school three times this week. And what have you been doing? O, don't think I don't know! I saw you with my own eyes yesterday walking home with that girl Pansetta Young! . . . Well, I want you to understand that I won't have it!"

"I didn't walk home with her," said Sandy. "I only go part way with her every day. She's in my class in high school and we have to talk over our lessons. She's the only colored kid in my class I have to talk to."

"Lessons! Yes, I know it's lessons," said Tempy sarcastically. "If she were a girl of our own kind, it would be all right. I don't see why you don't associate more with the young people of the church. Marie Steward or Grace Mitchell are both nice girls and you don't notice them. No, you have to take up with this Pansetta, whose mother works out all day, leaving her daughter to do as she chooses. Well, she's not going to ruin you, after all I've done to try to make something out of you."

"Beware of women, son," said Mr. Siles pontifically from his deep morris-chair. It was one of his few evenings home and Tempy had asked him to talk to her nephew, who had gotten beyond her control, for Sandy no longer remained in at night even when she expressly commanded it; and he no longer attended church regularly, but slept on Sunday mornings instead. He kept up his school-work, it was true, but he seemed to have lost all interest in acquiring the respectable bearing and attitude towards life that Tempy thought he should have. She bought him fine clothes and he went about with ruffians.

"In other words, he has been acting just like a nigger, Mr. Siles!" she told her husband. "And he's taken up with a girl who's not of the best, to say the least, even if she does go to the high school. Mrs. Francis Cannon, who lives near her, tells me that this Pansetta has boys at her house all the time, and her mother is never at home until after dark. She's a cook or something somewhere. . . . A fine person for a nephew of ours to associate with, this Pansy daughter of hers!"

"Pansetta's a nice girl," said Sandy. "And she's smart in school, too. She helps me get my Latin every day, and I might fail if she didn't."

"Huh! It's little help you need with your Latin, young man! Bring it here and I'll help you. I had Latin when I was in school. And certainly you don't need to walk on the streets with her in order to study Latin, do you? First thing you know you'll be getting in trouble with her and she'll be having a baby—I see I have to be plain—and whether it's yours or not, she'll say it is. Common girls like that always want to marry a boy they think is going to amount to something—going to college and be somebody in the world. Besides, you're from the Williams family and you're good-looking! But I'm going to stop this affair right now. . . . From now on you are to leave that girl alone, do you understand me? She's dangerous!"

"Yes," grunted Mr. Siles. "She's dangerous."

Angry and confused, Sandy left the room and went upstairs to bed, but he could not sleep. What right had they to talk that way about his friends? Besides, what did they mean about her being dangerous? About his getting in trouble with her? About her wanting to marry him because her mother was a cook and he was going to college?

A white boy in Sandy's high-school class had "got in trouble" with an Italian girl and they had had to go to the juvenile court to fix it up, but it had been kept quiet. Even now Sandy couldn't quite give an exact explanation of what getting in trouble with a girl meant. Did a girl have to have a baby just because a fellow walked home with her when he didn't even go in? Pansetta had asked him into her house often, but he always had to go back uptown to work. He was due at work at four o'clock—besides he knew it wasn't quite correct to call on a young lady if her mother was not at home. But it wasn't necessarily bad, was it? And how could a girl have a baby and say it was his if it wasn't his? Why couldn't he talk to his Aunt Tempy about such things and get a clear and simple answer instead of being given an old book like *The Doors of Life* that didn't explain anything at all?

Pansetta hadn't said a word to him about babies, or anything like that, but she let him kiss her once and hold her on his lap at Sadie Butler's Christmas party. Gee, but she could kiss—and such a long time! He wouldn't care if she did make him marry her, only he wanted to travel first. If his mother would send for him now, he would like to go to Chicago. His Aunt Tempy was too cranky, and too proper. She didn't like any of his friends, and she hated the pool hall. But where else was there for a fellow to play? Who wanted to go to those high-toned people's houses, like the Mitchells', and look bored all the time while they put Caruso's Italian records on their new victrola? Even if it was the finest victrola owned by a Negro in Stanton, as they always informed you, Sandy got tired of listening to records in a language that none of them understood.

"But this is opera!" they said. Well, maybe it was, but he thought that his father and Harriett used to sing better. And they sang nicer songs. One of them was:

Love, O love, O careless love—
Goes to your head like wine!

"And maybe I really am in love with Pansetta. . . . But if she thinks she can fool me into marrying her before I've travelled all around the world, like my father, she's wrong," Sandy thought. "She can't trick me, not this kid!" Then he was immediately sorry that he had allowed Tempy's insinuations to influence his thoughts.

"Pretty, baby-faced Pansetta! Why, she wouldn't try to trick anybody into anything. If she wanted me to love her, she'd let me, but she wouldn't try to trick a fellow. She wouldn't let me love her that way anyhow—like Tempy meant. Gee, that was ugly of Aunt Tempy to say that! . . . But Buster said she would. . . . Aw, he always talked that way about girls! He said no women were any good—as if he knew! And Jimmy Lane said white women were worse than colored—but all the boys who worked at hotels said that."

Let 'em talk! Sandy liked Pansetta anyhow. . . . But maybe his Aunt Tempy was right! Maybe he had better stop walking home with her. He didn't want to "get in trouble" and not be able to travel to Chicago some time, where his mother was. Maybe he could go to Chicago next summer if he began to save his money now. He wanted to see the big city, where the buildings were like towers, the trains ran overhead, and the lake was like a sea. He didn't want to "get in trouble" with Pansetta even if he did like her. Besides, he had to live with Tempy for awhile yet and he hated to be quarrelling with his aunt all the time. He'd stop going to the pool hall so much and stay home at night and study. . . . But, heck! it was too beautiful out of doors to stay in the house—especially since spring had come!

Through his open window, as he lay in bed after Tempy's tirade about the girl, he could see the stars and the tops of the budding maple-trees. A cool earth-smelling breeze lifted the white curtains, scattering the geometry papers that he had left lying on his study table. He got out of bed to pick up the papers and put them away, and stood for a moment in his pyjamas looking out of the window at the roofs of the houses and the tops of the trees under the night sky.

"I wish I had a brother," Sandy thought as he stood there. "Maybe I could talk to him about things and I wouldn't have to think so much. It's no fun being the only kid in the family, and your father never home either. . . . When I get married, I'm gonna have a lot of children; then they won't have to grow up by themselves."

The next day after school he walked nearly home with Pansetta as usual, although he was still thinking of what Tempy had said, but he hadn't decided to obey his aunt yet. At the corner of the block in which the girl lived, he gave her her books.

"I got to beat it back to the shop now. Old man Prentiss'll have a dozen deliveries waiting for me just because I'm late."

"All right," said Pansetta in her sweet little voice. "I'm sorry you can't come on down to my house awhile. Say, why don't you work at the hotel, anyway? Wouldn't you make more money there?"

"Guess I would," replied the boy. "But my aunt thinks it's better where I am."

"Oh," said Pansetta. "Well, I saw Jimmy Lane last night and he's making lots of money at the hotel. He wanted to meet me around to school this afternoon, but I told him no. I said you took me home."

"I do," said Sandy.

"Yes," laughed Pansetta; "but I didn't tell him you wouldn't ever come in."

During the sunny spring weeks that followed, Sandy did not walk home with her any more after school. Having to go to work earlier was the excuse he gave, but at first Pansetta seemed worried and puzzled. She asked him if he was mad at her, or something, but he said he wasn't. Then in a short time other boys were meeting her on the corner near the school, buying her cones when the ice-cream wagon passed and taking her home in the afternoons. To see other fellows buying her ice-cream and walking home with her made Sandy angry, but it was his own fault, he thought. And he felt lonesome having no one to walk with after classes.

Pansetta, in school, was just as pleasant as before, but in a kind of impersonal way, as though she hadn't been his girl once. And now Sandy was worried, because it had been easy to drop her, but would it be easy to get her back again if he should want her? The hotel boys had money, and once or twice he saw her talking with Jimmy Lane. Gee, but she looked pretty in her thin spring dresses and her wide straw hat.

Why had he listened to Tempy at all? She didn't know Pansetta, and just because her mother worked out in service she wanted him to snub the girl. What was that to be afraid of—her mother not being home after school? Even if Pansetta would let him go in the house with her and put his arms around her and love her, why shouldn't he? Didn't he have a right to have a girl like that, as well as the other fellows? Didn't he have a right to be free with women, too, like all the rest of the young men? . . . But Pansetta wasn't that kind of girl! . . . What made his mind run away with him? Because of what Tempy had said? . . . To hell with Tempy!

"She's just an old-fashioned darky Episcopalian, that's what Tempy is! And she wanted me to drop Pansetta because her mother doesn't belong to the Dunbar Whist Club. Gee, but I'm ashamed of myself. I'm a cad and a snob, that's all I am, and I'm going to apologize." Subconsciously he was living over a scene from an English novel he had read at the printing-shop, in which the Lord dropped the Squire's daughter for a great Lady, but later returned to his first love. Sandy retained the words "cad" and "snob" in his vocabulary, but he wasn't thinking of the novel now. He really believed, after three weeks of seeing Pansetta walking with other boys, that he had done wrong, and that Tempy was the villainess in the situation. It was worrying him a great deal; he decided to make up with Pansetta if he could.

One Friday afternoon she left school with a great armful of books. They had to write an English composition for Monday and she had taken some volumes from the school library for reference. He might have offered to carry them for her, but he hadn't. Instead he went to work—and there had been no other colored boys on the corner waiting for her as she went out. Now he could have kicked himself for his neglect, he thought, as he cleaned the rear room of Mr. Prentiss's gift-card shop. Suddenly he dropped the broom with which he was sweeping, grabbed his cap, and left the place, for the desire to make friends with Pansetta possessed him more fiercely than ever, and he no longer cared about his work.

"I'm going to see her right now," he thought, "before I go home to supper. Gee, but I'm ashamed of the way I've treated her."

On the way to Pansetta's house the lawns looked fresh and green and on some of them tulips were blooming. The late afternoon sky was aglow with sunset. Little boys were out in the streets with marbles and tops, and little girls were jumping rope on the sidewalks. Workmen were coming home, empty dinner-pails in their hands, and a band of Negro laborers passed Sandy, singing softly together.

"I must hurry," the boy thought. "It will soon be our supper-time." He ran until he was at Pansetta's house—then came the indecision: Should he go in? Or not go in? He was ashamed of his treatment of her and embarrassed. Should he go on by as if he had not meant to call? Suppose she shut the door in his face! Or, worse, suppose she asked him to stay awhile! Should he stay? What Tempy had said didn't matter any more. He wanted to be friends with Pansetta again. He wanted her to know he still liked her and wanted to walk home with her. But how could he say it? Had she seen him from the window? Maybe he could turn around and go back, and see her Monday at school.

"No! I'm not a coward," he declared. "Afraid of a girl! I'll walk right up on the front porch and knock!" But the small house looked very quiet and the lace curtains were tightly drawn together at the windows. . . . He knocked again. Maybe there was no one home. . . . Yes, he heard somebody.

Finally Pansetta peeped through the curtains of the glass in the front door. Then she opened the door and smiled surprisingly, her hair mussed and her creamy-brown skin pink from the warm blood pulsing just under the surface. Her eyes were dark and luminous, and her lips were moist and red.

"It's Sandy!" she said, turning to address someone inside the front room.

"O, come in, old man," a boy's voice called in a tone of

forced welcome, and Sandy saw Jimmy Lane sitting on the couch adjusting his collar self-consciously. "How's everything, old scout?"

"All right," Sandy stammered. "Say, Pansy, I—I—Do you know—I mean, what is the subject we're supposed to write on for English Monday? I must of forgotten to take it down."

"Why, 'A Trip to Shakespeare's England.' That's easy to remember, silly. You must have been asleep. . . . Won't you sit down?"

"No, thanks, I've—I guess I got to get back to supper."

"Jesus!" cried Jimmy jumping up from the sofa. "Is it that late? I'm due on bells at six o'clock. Wait a minute, Sandy, and I'll walk up with you as far as the hotel. Boy, I'm behind time!" He picked up his coat from the floor, and Pansetta held it for him while he thrust his arms into the sleeves, glancing around meanwhile for his cap, which lay among the sofa-pillows. Then he kissed the girl carelessly on the lips as he slid one arm familiarly around her waist.

"So long, baby," he said, and the two boys went out. On the porch Jimmy lit a cigarette and passed the pack to Sandy.

Jimmy Lane looked and acted as if he were much older than his companion, but Jimmy had been out of school several years, and hopping bells taught a fellow a great deal more about life than books did—and also about women. Besides, he was supporting himself now, which gave him an air of independence that boys who still lived at home didn't have.

When they had walked about a block, the bell-boy said carelessly: "Pansetta can go! Can't she, man?"

"I don't know," said Sandy.

"Aw, boy, you're lying," Jimmy Lane returned. "Don't try to hand me that kid stuff! You had her for a year, didn't you?"

"Yes," replied Sandy slowly, "but not like you mean."

"Stop kidding," Jimmy insisted.

"No, honest, I never touched her that way," the boy said. "I never was at her house before."

Jimmy opened his mouth astonished. "What!" he exclaimed.

"And her old lady out working till eight and nine every night! Say, Sandy, we're friends, but you're either just a big liar—or else a God-damn fool!" He threw his cigarette away and put both hands in his pockets. "Pansetta's easy as hell, man!"

28
CHICAGO

CHICAGO, ILL.
May 16, 1918

DEAR SANDY:

Have just come home from work and am very tired but thought I would write you this letter right now while I had time and wasn't sleepy. You are a big boy and I think you can be of some help to me. I don't want you to stay in Stanton any longer as a burden on your Aunt Tempy. She says in her letters you have begun to stay out late nights and not pay her any mind. You ought to be with your mother now because you are all she has since I do not know what has happened to your father in France. The war is awful and so many mens are getting killed. Have not had no word from Jimboy for 7 months from Over There and am worried till I'm sick. Will try and send you how much money you need for your fare before the end of the month so when school is out in June you can come. Let me know how much you saved and I will send you the rest to come to Chicago because Mr. Harris where I stay is head elevator man at a big hotel in the Loop and he says he can put you on there in July. That will be a good job for you and maybe by saving your money you can go back to school in Sept. I will help you if I can but you will have to help me too because I have not been doing so well. Am working for a colored lady in her hair dressing parlor and am learning hairdressing myself, shampoo and straighten and give massauges on the face and all. But colored folks are hard people to work for. Madam King is from down south somewhere and these southern Negroes are not like us in their ways, but she seems to like me. Mr. Harris is from the south too in a place called

Baton Rouge. They eat rice all the time. Well I must close hoping to see you soon once more because it has been five years since I have looked at my child. With love to you and Tempy, be a good boy,

Your mother,
ANNJELICA ROGERS.

A week later another letter came to Sandy from his mother. This time it was a registered special-delivery, which said: "If you'll come right away you can get your job at once. Mr. Harris says he will have a vacancy Saturday because one of the elevator boys are quitting." And sufficient bills to cover Sandy's fare tumbled out.

With a tremendous creaking and grinding and steady clacking of wheels the long train went roaring through the night towards Chicago as Sandy, in a day coach, took from his pocket Annjee's two letters and re-read them for the tenth time since leaving Stanton. He could hardly believe himself actually at that moment on the way to Chicago!

In the stuffy coach papers littered the floor and the scent of bananas and human feet filled the car. The lights were dim and most of the passengers slumbered in the straight-backed green-plush seats, but Sandy was still awake. The thrill of his first all-night rail journey and his dream-expectations of the great city were too much to allow a sixteen-year-old boy to go calmly to sleep, although the man next to him had long been snoring.

Annjee's special-delivery letter had come that morning. Sandy had discovered it when he came home for lunch, and upon his return to the high school for the afternoon classes he went at once to the principal to inquire if he might be excused from the remaining days of the spring term.

"Let me see! Your record's pretty good, isn't it, Rogers?" said Professor Perkins looking over his glasses at the young colored fellow standing before him. "Going to Chicago, heh? Well, I guess we can let you transfer and give you full credit for this year's work without your waiting here for the examinations—there are only ten days or so of the term remaining. You are an honor student and would get through your exams all right. Now, if you'll just send us your address when you get to Chicago, we'll see that you get your report. . . . Intending to go to school there, are you? . . . That's right! I like to see your people get ahead. . . . Well, good luck to you, James." The old gentleman rose and held out his hand.

"Good old scout," thought Sandy. "Miss Fry was a good teacher, too! Some white folks *are* nice all right! Not all of them are mean. . . . Gee, old man Prentiss hated to see me quit his place. Said I was the best boy he ever had working there, even if I was late once in awhile. But I don't mind leaving Stanton. Gee, Chicago ought to be great! And I'm sure glad to get away from Tempy's house. She's too tight!"

But Tempy had not been glad to see her nephew leave. She had grown fond of the boy in spite of her almost nightly lectures to him recently on his behavior and in spite of his never having become her model youth. Not that he was bad, but he might have been so much better! She wanted to show her white neighbors a perfect colored boy—and such a boy certainly wouldn't be a user of slang, a lover of pool halls and non-Episcopalian ways. Tempy had given Sandy every opportunity to move in the best colored society and he had not taken advantage of it. Nevertheless, she cried a little as she packed a lunch for him to eat on the train. She had done all she could. He was a good-looking boy, and quite smart. Now, if he wanted to go to his mother, well—"I can only hope Chicago won't ruin you," she said. "It's a wicked city! Good-bye, James. Remember what I've tried to teach you. Stand up straight and look like you're somebody!"

Stanton, Sandy's Kansas home, was back in the darkness, and the train sped towards the great center where all the small-town boys in the whole Middle West wanted to go.

"I'm going now!" thought Sandy. "Chicago now!"

A few weeks past he had gone to see Sister Johnson, who was quite feeble with the rheumatism. As she sat in the corner of her kitchen smoking a corn-cob pipe, no longer able to wash clothes, but still able to keep up a rapid flow of conversation, she told him all the news.

"Tom, he's still at de bank keepin' de furnace goin' an' sort o' handy man. . . . Willie-Mae, I 'spects you knows, is figurin' on gettin' married next month to Mose Jenkins, an' I tells her she better stay single, young as she is, but she ain't payin' me no mind. Umn-unh! Jest let her go on! . . . Did you heerd Sister Whiteside's daughter done brought her third husband home to stay wid her ma—an' five o' her first husband's chillens there too? Gals ain't got no regard for de old folks. Sister Whiteside say if she warn't a Christian in her heart, she don't believe she could stand it! . . . I tells Willie-Mae she better not bring no husbands here to stay wid me—do an' I'll run him out! These mens ought be shame o' demselves comin' livin' on de womenfolks."

As the old woman talked, Sandy, thinking of his grandmother, gazed out of the window towards the house next door, where he had lived with Aunt Hager. Some small children were playing in the back yard, running and yelling. They belonged to the Southern family to whom Tempy had rented the place. . . . Madam de Carter, who still owned the second house, had been made a national grand officer in the women's division of the lodge and many of the members of the order now had on the walls of their homes a large picture of her dressed in full regalia, inscribed: "Yours in His Grace," and signed: "Madam Fannie Rosalie de Carter."

"Used to be just plain old Rose Carter befo' she got so important," said Sister Johnson, explaining her neighbor's lengthy name. "All these womens dey mammy named Jane an' Mary an' Cora, soon's dey gets a little somethin', dey changes dey names to Janette or Mariana or Corina or somethin' mo' flowery then what dey had. Willie-Mae say she gwine change her'n to Willetta-Mayola, an' I tole her if she do, I'll beat her—don't care how old she is!"

Sandy liked to listen to the rambling talk of old colored folks. "I guess there won't be many like that in Chicago," he thought, as he doubled back his long legs under the green-plush seat of the day coach. "I better try to get to sleep—there's a long ways to go until morning."

Although it was not yet June, the heat was terrific when, with the old bags that Tempy had given him, Sandy got out of the dusty train in Chicago and walked the length of the sheds into the station. He caught sight of his mother waiting in the crowd, a fatter and much older woman than he had remembered her to be; and at first she didn't know him among the stream of people coming from the train. Perhaps, unconsciously, she was looking for the little boy she left in Stanton; but Sandy was taller than Annjee now and he looked quite a young man in his blue serge suit with long trousers. His mother threw both plump arms around him and hugged and kissed him for a long time.

They went uptown in the street-cars, Annjee a trifle out of breath from helping with the bags, and both of them perspiring freely from the heat. And they were not very talkative either. A strange and unexpected silence seemed to come between them. Annjee had been away from her son for five growing years and he was no longer her baby boy, small and eager for a kiss. She could see from the little cuts on his face that he had even begun to shave on the chin. And his voice was like a man's, deep and musical as Jimboy's, but not so sure of itself.

But Sandy was not thinking of his mother as they rode uptown on the street-car. He was looking out of the windows at the blocks of dirty grey warehouses lining the streets through which they were passing. He hadn't expected the great city to be monotonous and ugly like this and he was vaguely disappointed. No towers, no dreams come true! Where were the thrilling visions of grandeur he had held? Hidden in the dusty streets? Hidden in the long, hot alleys through which he could see at a distance the tracks of the elevated trains?

"Street-cars are slower, but I ain't got used to them air lines yet," said Annjee, searching her mind for something to say. "I always think maybe them elevated cars'll fall off o' there sometimes. They go so fast!"

"I believe I'd rather ride on them, though," said Sandy, as

he looked at the monotonous box-like tenements and dismal alleys on the ground level. No trees, no yards, no grass such as he had known at home, and yet, on the other hand, no bigness or beauty about the bleak warehouses and sorry shops that hugged the sidewalk. Soon, however, the street began to take on a racial aspect and to become more darkly alive. Negroes leaned from windows with heads uncombed, or sat fanning in doorways with legs apart, talking in kimonos and lounging in overalls, and more and more they became a part of the passing panorama.

"This is State Street," said Annjee. "They call it the Black Belt. We have to get off in a minute. You got your suit-case?"

She rang the bell and at Thirty-seventh Street they walked over to Wabash Avenue. The cool shade of the tiny porch that Annjee mounted was more than welcome, and as she took out her key to unlock the front door, Sandy sat on the steps and mopped his forehead with a grimy handkerchief. Inside, there was a dusky gloom in the hallway, that smelled of hair-oil and cabbage steaming,

"Guess Mis' Harris is in the kitchen," said Annjee. "Come on—we'll go upstairs and I'll show you our room. I guess we can both stay together till we can do better. You're still little enough to sleep with your mother, ain't you?"

They went down the completely dark hall on the second floor, and his mother opened a door that led into a rear room with two windows looking out into the alley, giving an extremely near view of the elevated structure on which a downtown train suddenly rushed past with an ear-splitting roar that made the entire house tremble and the window-sashes rattle. There was a wash-stand with a white bowl and pitcher in the room, Annjee's trunk, a chair, and a brass bed, covered with a fresh spread and starched pillow-covers in honor of Sandy's arrival.

"See," said Annjee. "There's room enough for us both, and we'll be saving rent. There's no closet, but we can drive a few extra nails behind the door. And with the two windows we can get plenty of air these hot nights."

"It's nice, mama," Sandy said, but he had to repeat his

statement twice, because another L train thundered past so that he couldn't hear his own words as he uttered them. "It's awful nice, mama!"

He took off his coat and sat down on the trunk between the two windows. Annjee came over and kissed him, rubbing her hand across his crinkly brown hair.

"Well, you're a great big boy now. . . . Mama's baby—in long pants. And you're handsome, just like your father!" She had Jimboy's picture stuck in a corner of the wash-stand—a postcard photo in his army uniform, in which he looked very boyish and proud, sent from the training-camp before his company went to France. "But I got no time to be setting here petting you, Sandy, even if you have just come. I got to get on back to the hairdressing-parlor to make some money."

So Annjee went to work again—as she had been off only long enough to meet the train—and Sandy lay down on the bed and slept the hot afternoon away. That evening as a treat they had supper at a restaurant, where Annjee picked carefully from the cheap menu so that their bill wouldn't be high.

"But don't think this is regular. We can't afford it," she said. "I bring things home and fix them on an oil-stove in the room and spread papers on the trunk for a table. A restaurant supper's just in honor of you."

When they came back to the house that evening, Sandy was introduced to Mrs. Harris, their landlady, and to her husband, the elevator-starter, who was to give him the job at the hotel.

"That's a fine-looking boy you got there, Mis' Rogers," he said, appraising Sandy. "He'll do pretty well for one of them main lobby cars, since we don't use nothing but first-class intelligent help down where I am, like I told you. And we has only the best class o' white folks stoppin' there, too. . . . Be up at six in the mornin', buddy, and I'll take you downtown with me."

Annjee was tired, so they went upstairs to the back room and lit the gas over the bed, but the frequent roar of the L trains prevented steady conversation and made Sandy jump each time that the long chain of cars thundered by. He hadn't yet become accustomed to them, or to the vast humming of the city, which was strange to his small-town ears. And he wanted to go out and look around a bit, to walk up and down the streets at night and see what they were like.

"Well, go on if you want to," said his mother, "but don't forget this house number. I'm gonna lie down, but I guess I'll be awake when you come back. Or somebody'll be setting on the porch and the door'll be open."

At the corner Sandy stopped and looked around to be sure of his bearings when he returned. He marked in his mind the signboard advertising CHESTERFIELDS and the frame-house with the tumbledown stairs on the outside. In the street some kids were playing hopscotch under the arc-light. Somebody stopped beside him.

"Nice evening?" said a small yellow man with a womanish kind of voice, smiling at Sandy.

"Yes," said the boy, starting across the street, but the stranger followed him, offering Pall Malls. He smelled of perfume, and his face looked as though it had been powdered with white talcum as he lit a tiny pocket-lighter.

"Stranger?" murmured the soft voice, lighting Sandy's cigarette.

"I'm from Stanton," he replied, wishing the man had not chosen to walk with him.

"Ah, Kentucky," exclaimed the perfumed fellow. "I been down there. Nice women in that town, heh?"

"But it's not Kentucky," Sandy objected. "It's Kansas."

"Oh, out west where the girls are raring to go! I know! Just like wild horses out there—so passionate, aren't they?"

"I guess so," Sandy ventured. The powdered voice was softly persistent.

"Say, kid," it whispered smoothly, touching the boy's arm, "listen, I got some swell French pictures up in my room—naked women and everything! Want to come up and see them?"

"No," said Sandy quickening his pace. "I got to go somewhere."

"But I room right around the corner," the voice insisted.

"Come on by. You're a nice kid, you know it? Listen, don't walk so fast. Stop, let me talk to you."

But Sandy was beginning to understand. A warm sweat broke out on his neck and forehead. Sometimes, at the pool hall in Stanton, he had heard the men talk about queer fellows who stopped boys in the streets and tried to coax them to their rooms.

"He thinks I'm dumb," thought Sandy, "but I'm wise to him!" Yet he wondered what such men did with the boys who accompanied them. Curious, he'd like to find out—but he was afraid; so at the next corner he turned and started rapidly towards State Street, but the queer fellow kept close beside him, begging.

". . . and we'll have a nice time. . . . I got wine in the room, if you want some, and a vic, too."

"Get away, will you!"

They had reached State Street where the lights were bright and people were passing all the time. Sandy could see the fellow's anxious face quite clearly now.

"Listen, kid . . . you . . ."

But suddenly the man was no longer beside him—for Sandy commenced to run. On the brightly lighted avenue panic seized him. He had to escape this powdered face at his shoulder. The whining voice made him sick inside—and, almost without knowing it, his legs began swerving swiftly between the crowds along the curb. When he stopped in front of the Monogram Theatre, two blocks away, he was freed of his companion.

"Gee, that's nice," panted Sandy, grinning as he stood looking at the pictures in front of the vaudeville house, while hundreds of dark people passed up and down on the sidewalk behind him. Lots of folks were going into the theatre, laughing and pushing, for one of the great blues-singing Smiths was appearing there. Sandy walked towards the ticket-booth to see what the prices were.

"Buy me a ticket, will you?" said a feminine voice beside him. This time it was a girl—a very ugly, skinny girl, whose smile revealed a row of dirty teeth. She sidled up to the startled boy whom she had accosted and took his hand.

"I'm not going in," Sandy said shortly, as he backed away, wiping the palm of his hand on his coat-sleeve.

"All right then, stingy!" hissed the girl, flouncing her hips and digging into her own purse for the coins to buy a ticket. "I got money."

Some men standing on the edge of the sidewalk laughed as Sandy went up the street. A little black child in front of him toddled along in the crowd, seemingly by itself, licking a big chocolate ice-cream cone that dripped down the front of its dress.

So this was Chicago where the buildings were like towers and the lake was like a sea . . . State Street, the greatest Negro street in the world, where people were always happy, lights for ever bright; and where the prettiest brown-skin women on earth could be found—so the men in Stanton said.

"I guess I didn't walk the right way. But maybe tomorrow I'll see other things," Sandy thought, "the Loop and the lake and the museum and the library. Maybe they'll be better."

He turned into a side street going back towards Wabash Avenue. It was darker there, and near the alley a painted woman called him, stepping out from among the shadows.

"Say, baby, com'ere!" But the boy went on.

Crossing overhead an L train thundered by, flashing its flow of yellow light on the pavement beneath.

Sandy turned into Wabash Avenue and cut across the street. As he approached the colored Y.M.C.A., three boys came out with swimming suits on their arms, and one of them said: "Damn, but it's hot!" They went up the street laughing and talking with friendly voices, and at the corner they turned off.

"I must be nearly home," Sandy thought, as he made out a group of kids still playing under the street-light. Then he distinguished, among the other shabby buildings, the brick house where he lived. The front porch was still crowded with roomers trying to keep cool, and as the boy came up to the foot of the steps, some of the fellows seated there moved to let him pass.

"Good-evenin', Mr. Rogers," Mrs. Harris called, and as Sandy had never been called Mr. Rogers before, it made him feel very manly and a little embarrassed as he threaded his way through the group on the porch.

Upstairs he found his mother sleeping deeply on one side of the bed. He undressed, keeping on his underwear, and crawled in on the other side, but he lay awake a long while because it was suffocatingly hot, and very close in their room. The bed-bugs bit him on the legs. Every time he got half asleep, an L train roared by, shrieking outside their open windows, lighting up the room, and shaking the whole house. Each time the train came, he started and trembled as though a sudden dragon were rushing at the bed. But then, after midnight, when the elevated cars passed less frequently, and he became more used to their passing, he went to sleep.

29
ELEVATOR

THE FOLLOWING DAY Sandy went to work as elevator-boy at the hotel in the Loop where Mr. Harris was head bellman, and during the hot summer months that followed, his life in Chicago gradually settled into a groove of work and home—work, and home to Annjee's stuffy little room against the elevated tracks, where at night his mother read the war news and cried because there had been no letter from Jimboy. Whether Sandy's father was in Brest or Saint-Lazare with the labor battalions, or at the front, she did not know. The *Chicago Defender* said that colored troops were fighting in the Champagne sector with great distinction, but Annjee cried anew when she read that.

"No news is good news," Sandy repeated every night to comfort his mother, for he couldn't imagine Jimboy dead. "Papa's all right!" But Annjee worried and wept, half sick all the time, for ever reading the death lists fearfully for her husband's name.

That summer the heat was unbearable. Uptown in the Black Belt the air was like a steaming blanket around your head. In the Loop the sky was white-hot metal. Even on the lake front there was no relief unless you hurried into the crowded water. And there were long stretches of beach where the whites did not want Negroes to swim; so it was often dangerous to bathe if you were colored.

Sandy sweltered as he stood at the door of his boxlike, mirrored car in the big hotel lobby. He wore a red uniform with brass buttons and a tight coat that had to be kept fastened no matter how warm it was. But he felt very proud of himself holding his first full-time job, helping his mother with the room rent, and trying to save a little money out of each pay in order to return to high school in the fall.

The prospects of returning to school, however, were not

bright. Some weeks it was impossible for Sandy to save even a half-dollar. And Annjee said now that she believed he should stay out of school and work to take care of himself, since he was as large as a man and had more education already than she'd had at his age. Aunt Hager would not have felt that way, though, Sandy thought, remembering his grandmother's great ambition for him. But Annjee was different, less far-seeing than her mother had been, less full of hopes for her son, not ambitious about him—caring only for the war and Jimboy.

At the hotel Sandy's hours on duty were long, and his legs and back ached with weariness from standing straight in one spot all the time, opening and closing the bronze door of the elevator. He had been assigned the last car in a row of six, each manned by a colored youth standing inside his metal box in a red uniform, operating the lever that sent the car up from the basement grill to the roof-garden restaurant on the fifteenth floor and then back down again all day. Repeating up-down—up-down—up-down interminably, carrying white guests.

After two months of this there were times when Sandy felt as though he could stand it no longer. The same flow of people week after week—fashionable women, officers, business men; the fetid air of the elevator-shaft, heavy with breath and the perfume of bodies; the same doors opening at the same unchanging levels hundreds of times each innumerable, monotonous day. The L in the morning; the L again at night. The street or the porch for a few minutes of air. Then bed. And the same thing tomorrow.

"I've got to get out of this," Sandy thought. "It's an awful job." Yet some of the fellows had been there for years. Three of the elevator-men on Sandy's shift were more than forty years old—and had never gotten ahead in life. Mr. Harris had been a bell-hop since his boyhood, doing the same thing day after day—and now he was very proud of being head bell-boy in Chicago.

"I've got to get out of this," Sandy kept repeating. "Or maybe I'll get stuck here, too, like they are, and never get away. I've got to go back to school."

Yet he knew that his mother was making very little money—serving more or less as an apprentice in the hairdressing-shop, trying to learn the trade. And if he quit work, how would he live? Annjee did not favor his returning to school. And could he study if he were hungry? Could he study if he were worried about having no money? Worried about Annjee's displeasure?

"Yes! I can!" he said. "I'm going to study!" He thought about Booker Washington sleeping under the wooden pavements at Richmond—because he had had no place to stay on his way to Hampton in search of an education. He thought about Frederick Douglass—a fugitive slave, owning not even himself, and yet a student. "If they could study, I can, too! When school opens, I'm going to quit this job. Maybe I can get another one at night or in the late afternoon—but it doesn't matter—I'm going back to my classes in September. . . . I'm through with elevators."

Jimboy! Jimboy! Like Jimboy! something inside him warned, quitting work with no money, uncaring.

"Not like Jimboy," Sandy countered against himself. "Not like my father, always wanting to go somewhere. I'd get as tired of travelling all the time, as I do of running this elevator up and down day after day. . . . I'm more like Harriett—not wanting to be a servant at the mercies of white people for ever. . . . I want to do something for myself, by myself. . . . Free. . . . I want a house to live in, too, when I'm older—like Tempy's and Mr. Siles's. . . . But I wouldn't want to be like Tempy's friends—or her husband, dull and colorless, putting all his money away in a white bank, ashamed of colored people."

"A lot of minstrels—that's all niggers are!" Mr. Siles had said once. "Clowns, jazzers, just a band of dancers—that's why they never have anything. Never be anything but servants to the white people."

Clowns! Jazzers! Band of dancers! . . . Harriett! Jimboy! Aunt Hager! . . . A band of dancers! . . . Sandy remembered his grandmother whirling around in front of the altar at revival meetings in the midst of the other sisters, her face shining with light, arms outstretched as though all the cares of the world had been cast away; Harriett in the back yard under the apple-tree, eagle-rocking in the summer evenings to the tunes of the guitar; Jimboy singing. . . . But was that why Negroes were poor, because they were dancers, jazzers, clowns? . . . The other way round would be better: dancers because of their poverty; singers because they suffered; laughing all the time because they must forget. . . . It's more like that, thought Sandy.

A band of dancers. . . . Black dancers—captured in a white world. . . . Dancers of the spirit, too. Each black dreamer a captured dancer of the spirit. . . . Aunt Hager's dreams for Sandy dancing far beyond the limitations of their poverty, of their humble station in life, of their dark skins.

"I wants you to be a great man, son," she often told him, sitting on the porch in the darkness, singing, dreaming, calling up the deep past, creating dreams within the child. "I wants you to be a great man."

"And I won't disappoint you!" Sandy said that hot Chicago summer, just as though Hager were still there, planning for him. "I won't disappoint you!" he said, standing straight in his sweltering red suit in the cage of the hotel elevator. "I won't disappoint you, Aunt Hager," dreaming at night in the stuffy little room in the great Black Belt of Chicago. "I won't disappoint you now," opening his eyes at dawn when Annjee shook him to get up and go to work again.

30
PRINCESS OF THE BLUES

ONE HOT MONDAY in August Harrietta Williams, billed as "The Princess of the Blues," opened at the Monogram Theatre on State Street. The screen had carried a slide of her act the week previous, so Sandy knew she would be there, and he and his mother were waiting anxiously for her appearance. They were unable to find out before the performance where she would be living, or if she had arrived in town, but early that Monday evening Sandy hurried home from work, and he and Annjee managed to get seats in the theatre, although it was soon crowded to capacity and people stood in the aisles.

It was a typical Black Belt audience, laughing uproariously, stamping its feet to the music, kidding the actors, and joining in the performance, too. Rows of shiny black faces, gay white teeth, bobbing heads. Everybody having a grand time with the vaudeville, swift and amusing. A young tap-dancer rhymed his feet across the stage, grinning from ear to ear, stepping to the tantalizing music, ending with a series of intricate and amazing contortions that brought down the house. Then a sister act came on, with a stock of sentimental ballads offered in a wholly jazzy manner. They sang even a very melancholy mammy song with their hips moving gaily at every beat.

O, what would I do
Without dear you,
Sweet mammy?

they moaned reverently, with their thighs shaking.

"Aw, step it, sweet gals!" the men and boys in the audience called approvingly. "We'll be yo' mammy and yo' pappy, too! Do it, pretty mamas!"

A pair of black-faced comedians tumbled on the stage as the

girls went off, and began the usual line of old jokes and razor comedy.

"Gee, I wish Aunt Harriett's act would come on," Sandy said as he and Annjee laughed nervously at the comedians.

Finally the two blacked-up fellows broke into a song called *Walking the Dog*, flopping their long-toed shoes, twirling their middles like egg-beaters, and made their exit to a roar of laughter and applause. Then the canvas street-scene rose, disclosing a gorgeous background of blue velvet, with a piano and a floor-lamp in the center of the stage.

"This is Harriett's part now," Sandy whispered excitedly as a tall, yellow, slick-headed young man came in and immediately began playing the piano. "And, mama, that's Billy Sanderlee!"

"Sure is!" said Annjee.

Suddenly the footlights were lowered and the spotlight flared, steadied itself at the right of the stage, and waited. Then, stepping out from among the blue curtains, Harriett entered in a dress of glowing orange, flame-like against the ebony of her skin, barbaric, yet beautiful as a jungle princess. She swayed towards the footlights, while Billy teased the keys of the piano into a hesitating delicate jazz. Then she began to croon a new song—a popular version of an old Negro melody, refashioned with words from Broadway.

"Gee, Aunt Harrie's prettier than ever!" Sandy exclaimed to his mother.

"Same old Harriett," said Annjee. "But kinder hoarse."

"Sings good, though," Sandy cried when Harriett began to snap her fingers, putting a slow, rocking pep into the chorus, rolling her bright eyes to the tune of the melody as the piano rippled and cried under Billy Sanderlee's swift fingers.

"She's the same Harrie," murmured Annjee.

When she appeared again, in an apron of blue calico, with a bandanna handkerchief knotted about her head, she walked very slowly. The man at the piano had begun to play blues—the old familiar folk-blues—and the audience settled into a receptive silence broken only by a "Lawdy! . . . Good Lawdy! Lawd!"

from some southern lips at the back of the house, as Harriett sang:

Red sun, red sun, why don't you rise today?
Red sun, O sun! Why don't you rise today?
Ma heart is breakin'—ma baby's gone away.

A few rows ahead of Annjee a woman cried out: "True, Lawd!" and swayed her body.

Little birds, little birds, ain't you gonna sing this morn?
Says, little chirpin' birds, ain't you gonna sing this morn?
I cannot sleep—ma lovin' man is gone.

"Whee-ee-e! . . . Hab mercy! . . . Moan it, gal!" exclamations and shouts broke loose in the understanding audience.

"Just like when papa used to play for her," said Sandy. But Annjee was crying, remembering Jimboy, and fumbling in her bag for a handkerchief. On the stage the singer went on—as though singing to herself—her voice sinking to a bitter moan as the listeners rocked and swayed.

It's a mighty blue mornin' when yo' daddy leaves yo' bed.
I says a blue, blue mornin' when yo' daddy leaves yo' bed—
'Cause if you lose yo' man, you'd just as well be dead!

Her final number was a dance-song which she sang in a sparkling dress of white sequins, ending the act with a mad collection of steps and a swift sudden whirl across the whole stage as the orchestra joined Billy's piano in a triumphant arch of jazz.

The audience yelled and clapped and whistled for more, stamping their feet and turning to one another with shouted comments of enjoyment.

"Gee! She's great," said Sandy. When another act finally had the stage after Harriett's encores, he was anxious to get back to the dressing-room to see her.

"Maybe they won't let us in," Annjee objected timidly.

"Let's try," Sandy insisted, pulling his mother up. "We don't want to hear this fat woman with the flag singing *Over There*. You'll start crying, anyhow. Come on, mama."

When they got backstage, they found Harriett standing in the dressing-room door laughing with one of the black-face comedians, a summer fur over her shoulders, ready for the street. Billy Sanderlee and the tap-dancing boy were drinking gin from a bottle that Billy held, and Harriett was holding her glass, when she saw Sandy coming.

Her furs slipped to the floor. "My Lord!" she cried, enveloping them in kisses. "What are you doing in Chicago, Annjee? My, I'm mighty glad to see you, Sandy! . . . I'm certainly surprised—and so happy I could cry. . . . Did you catch our act tonight? Can't Billy play the piano, though? . . . Great heavens! Sandy, you're twice as tall as me! When did you leave home? How's that long-faced sister o' mine, Tempy?"

After repeated huggings the new-comers were introduced to everybody around. Sandy noticed a certain harshness in his aunt's voice. "Smoking so much," she explained later. "Drinking, too, I guess. But a blues-singer's supposed to sing deep and hoarse, so it's all right."

Beyond the drop curtain Sandy could hear the audience laughing in the theatre, and occasionally somebody shouting at the performers.

"Come on! Let's go and get a bite to eat," Harriett suggested when they had finally calmed down enough to decide to move on. "Billy and me are always hungry. . . . Where's Jimboy, Annjee? In the war, I suppose! It'd be just like that big jigaboo to go and enlist first thing, whether he had to or not. Billy here was due to go, too, but licker kept him out. This white folk's war for democracy ain't so hot, nohow! . . . Say, how'd you like to have some chop suey instead of going to a regular restaurant?"

In a Chinese café they found a quiet booth, where the two sisters talked until past midnight—with Sandy and Billy silent for the most part. Harriett told Annjee about Aunt Hager's death and the funeral that chill rainy day, and how Tempy had behaved so coldly when it was all over.

"I left Stanton the week after," Harriett said, "and haven't been back since. Had hard times, too, but we're kinder lucky now, Billy and me—got some dates booked over the Orpheum circuit soon. Liable to get wind of us at the Palace on Broadway one o' these days. Can't tell! Things are breakin' pretty good for spade acts—since Jews are not like the rest of the white folks. They will give you a break if you've got some hot numbers to show 'em, whether you're colored or not. And Jews control the theatres."

But the conversation went back to Stanton, when Hager and Jimboy and all of them had lived together, laughing and quarrelling and playing the guitar—while the tea got cold and the chop suey hardened to a sticky mess as the sisters wept. Billy marked busily on the table-cloth meanwhile with a stubby pencil, explaining to Sandy a new and intricate system he had found for betting on the numbers.

"Harrie and me plays every day. Won a hundred forty dollars last week in Cleveland," he said.

"Gee! I ought to start playing," Sandy exclaimed. "How much do you put on each number?"

"Well, for a nickel you can win . . ."

"No, you oughtn't," checked Harriett, suddenly conscious of Billy's conversation, turning towards Sandy with a handkerchief to her eyes. "Don't you fool with those numbers, honey! . . . What are you trying to do, Billy, start the boy off on your track? . . . You've got to get your education, Sandy, and amount to something. . . . Guess you're in high school now, aren't you, kid?"

"Third year," said Sandy slowly, dreading a new argument with his mother.

"And determined to keep on going here this fall, in spite o' my telling him I don't see how," put in Annjee. "Jimboy's over yonder, Lord knows where, and I certainly can't take care of Sandy and send him to school, too. No need of my trying—since he's big enough and old enough to hold a job and make his own living. He ought to be wanting to help me, anyway. Instead of that, he's determined to go back to school."

"Make his own living!" Harriett exclaimed, looking at Annjee in astonishment. "You mean you want Sandy to stay out of school to help you? What good is his little money to you?"

"Well, he helps with the room rent," his mother said. "And gets his meals where he works. That's better'n we'd be doing with him studying and depending on me to keep things up."

"What do you mean better?" Harriett cried, glaring at her sister excitedly, forgetting they had been weeping together five minutes before. "For crying out loud—better? Why, Aunt Hager'd turn over in her grave if she heard you talking so calmly about Sandy leaving school—the way she wanted to make something out of this kid. . . . How much do you earn a week?" Harriett asked suddenly, looking at her nephew across the table.

"Fourteen dollars."

"Pshaw! Is that all? I can give you that much myself," Harriett said. "We've got straight bookings until Christmas—then cabaret work's good around here. Bill and I can always make the dough—and you go to school."

"I want to, Aunt Harrie," Sandy said, suddenly content.

"Yea, old man," put in Billy. "And I'll shoot you a little change myself—to play the numbers," he added, winking.

"Well," Annjee began, "what about . . ."

But Harriett ignored Billy's interjection as well as her sister's open mouth. "Running an elevator for fourteen dollars a week and losing your education!" she cried. "Good Lord! Annjee, you ought to be ashamed, wanting him to keep that up. This boy's gotta get ahead—all of us niggers are too far back in this white man's country to let any brains go to waste! Don't you realize that? . . . You and me was foolish all right, breaking mama's heart, leaving school, but Sandy can't do like us. He's gotta be what his grandma Hager wanted him to be—able to help the black race, Annjee! You hear me? Help the whole race!"

"I want to," Sandy said.

"Then you'll stay in school!" Harriett affirmed, still looking at Annjee. "You surely wouldn't want him stuck in an elevator for ever—just to help you, would you, sister?"

"I reckon I wouldn't," Annjee murmured, shaking her head.

"You know damn well you wouldn't," Harriett concluded. And, before they parted, she slipped a ten-dollar bill into her nephew's hand.

"For your books," she said.

When Sandy and his mother started home, it was very late, but in a little Southern church in a side street, some old black worshippers were still holding their nightly meeting. High and fervently they were singing:

By an' by when de mawnin' comes,
Saints an' sinners all are gathered home. . . .

As the deep volume of sound rolled through the open door, Annjee and her son stopped to listen.

"It's like Stanton," Sandy said, "and the tent in the Hickory Woods."

"Sure is!" his mother exclaimed. "Them old folks are still singing—even in Chicago! . . . Funny how old folks like to sing that way, ain't it?"

"It's beautiful!" Sandy cried—for, vibrant and steady like a stream of living faith, their song filled the whole night:

An' we'll understand it better by an' by!

THE WAYS OF WHITE FOLKS

To Noël Sullivan

CONTENTS

The ways of white folks,
I mean some *white folks. . . .*

BERRY

1
CORA UNASHAMED

MELTON WAS ONE of those miserable in-between little places, not large enough to be a town, nor small enough to be a village—that is, a village in the rural, charming sense of the word. Melton had no charm about it. It was merely a nondescript collection of houses and buildings in a region of farms—one of those sad American places with side-walks, but no paved streets; electric lights, but no sewage; a station, but no trains that stopped, save a jerky local, morning and evening. And it was 150 miles from any city at all—even Sioux City.

Cora Jenkins was one of the least of the citizens of Melton. She was what the people referred to when they wanted to be polite, as a Negress, and when they wanted to be rude, as a nigger—sometimes adding the word "wench" for no good reason, for Cora was usually an inoffensive soul, except that she sometimes cussed.

She had been in Melton for forty years. Born there. Would die there probably. She worked for the Studevants, who treated her like a dog. She stood it. Had to stand it; or work for poorer white folks who would treat her worse; or go jobless. Cora was like a tree—once rooted, she stood, in spite of storms and strife, wind, and rocks, in the earth.

She was the Studevants' maid of all work—washing, ironing, cooking, scrubbing, taking care of kids, nursing old folks, making fires, carrying water.

Cora, bake three cakes for Mary's birthday tomorrow night. You Cora, give Rover a bath in that tar soap I bought. Cora, take Ma some jello, and don't let her have even a taste of that raisin pie. She'll keep us up all night if you do. Cora, iron my stockings. Cora, come here . . . Cora, put . . . Cora . . . Cora . . . Cora! Cora!

And Cora would answer, "Yes, m'am."

The Studevants thought they owned her, and they were perfectly right: they did. There was something about the teeth in the trap of economic circumstance that kept her in their power practically all her life—in the Studevant kitchen, cooking; in the Studevant parlor, sweeping; in the Studevant back yard, hanging clothes.

You want to know how that could be? How a trap could close so tightly? Here is the outline:

Cora was the oldest of a family of eight children—the Jenkins niggers. The only Negroes in Melton, thank God! Where they came from originally—that is, the old folks—God knows. The kids were born there. The old folks are still there now: Pa drives a junk wagon. The old woman ails around the house, ails and quarrels. Seven kids are gone. Only Cora remains. Cora simply couldn't go, with nobody else to help take care of Ma. And before that she couldn't go, with nobody to see that her brothers and sisters got through school (she the oldest, and Ma ailing). And before that—well, somebody had to help Ma look after one baby behind another that kept on coming.

As a child Cora had no playtime. She always had a little brother, or a little sister in her arms. Bad, crying, bratty babies, hungry and mean. In the eighth grade she quit school and went to work with the Studevants.

After that, she ate better. Half day's work at first, helping Ma at home the rest of the time. Then full days, bringing home her pay to feed her father's children. The old man was rather a drunkard. What little money he made from closet-cleaning, ash-hauling, and junk-dealing he spent mostly on the stuff that makes you forget you have eight kids.

He passed the evenings telling long, comical lies to the white riff-raff of the town, and drinking licker. When his horse died, Cora's money went for a new one to haul her Pa and his rickety wagon around. When the mortgage money came due, Cora's wages kept the man from taking the roof from over their heads. When Pa got in jail, Cora borrowed ten dollars from Mrs. Studevant and got him out.

Cora stinted, and Cora saved, and wore the Studevants' old

clothes, and ate the Studevants' left-over food, and brought her pay home. Brothers and sisters grew up. The boys, lonesome, went away, as far as they could from Melton. One by one, the girls left too, mostly in disgrace. "Ruinin' ma name," Pa Jenkins said, "ruinin' ma good name! They can't go out berryin' but what they come back in disgrace." There was something about the cream-and-tan Jenkins girls that attracted the white farm hands.

Even Cora, the humble, had a lover once. He came to town on a freight train (long ago now), and worked at the livery-stable. (That was before autos got to be so common.) Everybody said he was an I. W. W. Cora didn't care. He was the first man and the last she ever remembered wanting. She had never known a colored lover. There weren't any around. That was not her fault.

This white boy, Joe, he always smelt like the horses. He was some kind of foreigner. Had an accent, and yellow hair, big hands, and grey eyes.

It was summer. A few blocks beyond the Studevants' house, meadows and orchards and sweet fields stretched away to the far horizon. At night, stars in the velvet sky. Moon sometimes. Crickets and katydids and lightning bugs. The scent of grass. Cora waiting. That boy, Joe, a cigarette spark far off, whistling in the dark. Love didn't take long—Cora with the scent of the Studevants' supper about her, and a cheap perfume. Joe, big and strong and careless as the horses he took care of, smelling like the stable.

Ma would quarrel because Cora came home late, or because none of the kids had written for three or four weeks, or because Pa was drunk again. Thus the summer passed, a dream of big hands and grey eyes.

Cora didn't go anywhere to have her child. Nor tried to hide it. When the baby grew big within her, she didn't feel that it was a disgrace. The Studevants told her to go home and stay there. Joe left town. Pa cussed. Ma cried. One April morning the kid was born. She had grey eyes, and Cora called her Josephine, after Joe.

Cora was humble and shameless before the fact of the child. There were no Negroes in Melton to gossip, and she didn't care what the white people said. They were in another world. Of course, she hadn't expected to marry Joe, or keep him. He was of that other world, too. But the child was hers—a living bridge between two worlds. Let people talk.

Cora went back to work at the Studevants'—coming home at night to nurse her kid, and quarrel with Ma. About that time, Mrs. Art Studevant had a child, too, and Cora nursed it. The Studevants' little girl was named Jessie. As the two children began to walk and talk, Cora sometimes brought Josephine to play with Jessie—until the Studevants objected, saying she could get her work done better if she left her child at home.

"Yes, m'am," said Cora.

But in a little while they didn't need to tell Cora to leave her child at home, for Josephine died of whooping-cough. One rosy afternoon, Cora saw the little body go down into the ground in a white casket that cost four weeks' wages.

Since Ma was ailing, Pa, smelling of licker, stood with her at the grave. The two of them alone. Cora was not humble before the fact of death. As she turned away from the hole, tears came—but at the same time a stream of curses so violent that they made the grave-tenders look up in startled horror.

She cussed out God for taking away the life that she herself had given. She screamed, "My baby! God damn it! My baby! I bear her and you take her away!" She looked at the sky where the sun was setting and yelled in defiance. Pa was amazed and scared. He pulled her up on his rickety wagon and drove off, clattering down the road between green fields and sweet meadows that stretched away to the far horizon. All through the ugly town Cora wept and cursed, using all the bad words she had learned from Pa in his drunkenness.

The next week she went back to the Studevants. She was gentle and humble in the face of life—she loved their baby. In the afternoons on the back porch, she would pick little Jessie up and rock her to sleep, burying her dark face in the milky smell of the white child's hair.

II

THE YEARS PASSED. Pa and Ma Jenkins only dried up a little. Old Man Studevant died. The old lady had two strokes. Mrs. Art Studevant and her husband began to look their age, greying hair and sagging stomachs. The children were grown, or nearly so. Kenneth took over the management of the hardware store that Grandpa had left. Jack went off to college. Mary was a teacher. Only Jessie remained a child—her last year in high school. Jessie, nineteen now, and rather slow in her studies, graduating at last. In the Fall she would go to Normal.

Cora hated to think about her going away. In her heart she had adopted Jessie. In that big and careless household it was always Cora who stood like a calm and sheltering tree for Jessie to run to in her troubles. As a child, when Mrs. Art spanked her, as soon as she could, the tears still streaming, Jessie would find her way to the kitchen and Cora. At each school term's end, when Jessie had usually failed in some of her subjects (she quite often failed, being a dull child), it was Cora who saw the report-card first with the bad marks on it. Then Cora would devise some way of breaking the news gently to the old folks.

Her mother was always a little ashamed of stupid Jessie, for Mrs. Art was the civic and social leader of Melton, president of the Woman's Club three years straight, and one of the pillars of her church. Mary, the elder, the teacher, would follow with dignity in her footsteps, but Jessie! That child! Spankings in her youth, and scoldings now, did nothing to Jessie's inner being. She remained a plump, dull, freckled girl, placid and strange. Everybody found fault with her but Cora.

In the kitchen Jessie bloomed. She laughed. She talked. She was sometimes even witty. And she learned to cook wonderfully. With Cora, everything seemed so simple—not hard and involved like algebra, or Latin grammar, or the civic problems of Mama's club, or the sermons at church. Nowhere in Melton, nor with anyone, did Jessie feel so comfortable as with Cora in the kitchen. She knew her mother looked down on her as a stupid girl. And with her father there was no bond. He was always too busy buying and selling to bother with the kids. And often he was off in the city. Old doddering Grandma made Jessie sleepy and sick. Cousin Nora (Mother's cousin) was as stiff and prim as a minister's daughter. And Jessie's older brothers and sister went their ways, seeing Jessie hardly at all, except at the big table at mealtimes.

Like all the unpleasant things in the house, Jessie was left to Cora. And Cora was happy. To have a child to raise, a child the same age as her Josephine would have been, gave her a purpose in life, a warmth inside herself. It was Cora who nursed and mothered and petted and loved the dull little Jessie through the years. And now Jessie was a young woman, graduating (late) from high school.

But something had happened to Jessie. Cora knew it before Mrs. Art did. Jessie was not too stupid to have a boy friend. She told Cora about it like a mother. She was afraid to tell Mrs. Art. Afraid! Afraid! Afraid!

Cora said, "I'll tell her." So, humble and unashamed about life, one afternoon she marched into Mrs. Art's sun-porch and announced quite simply, "Jessie's going to have a baby."

Cora smiled, but Mrs. Art stiffened like a bolt. Her mouth went dry. She rose like a soldier. Sat down. Rose again. Walked straight toward the door, turned around, and whispered, "What?"

"Yes, m'am, a baby. She told me. A little child. Its father is Willie Matsoulos, whose folks runs the ice-cream stand on Main. She told me. They want to get married, but Willie ain't here now. He don't know yet about the child."

Cora would have gone on humbly and shamelessly talking about the little unborn had not Mrs. Art fallen into uncontrollable hysterics. Cousin Nora came running from the library, her glasses on a chain. Old Lady Studevant's wheel-chair rolled up, doddering and shaking with excitement. Jessie came, when called, red and sweating, but had to go out, for when her mother looked up from the couch and saw her she yelled louder than ever. There was a rush for camphor bottles and water and ice.

Crying and praying followed all over the house. Scandalization! Oh, my Lord! Jessie was in trouble.

"She ain't in trouble neither," Cora insisted. "No trouble having a baby you want. I had one."

"Shut up, Cora!"

"Yes, m'am. . . . But I had one."

"Hush, I tell you."

"Yes, m'am."

III

THEN IT WAS that Cora began to be shut out. Jessie was confined to her room. That afternoon, when Miss Mary came home from school, the four white women got together behind closed doors in Mrs. Art's bedroom. For once Cora cooked supper in the kitchen without being bothered by an interfering voice. Mr. Studevant was away in Des Moines. Somehow Cora wished he was home. Big and gruff as he was, he had more sense than the women. He'd probably make a shot-gun wedding out of it. But left to Mrs. Art, Jessie would never marry the Greek boy at all. This Cora knew. No man had been found yet good enough for sister Mary to mate with. Mrs. Art had ambitions which didn't include the likes of Greek ice-cream makers' sons.

Jessie was crying when Cora brought her supper up. The black woman sat down on the bed and lifted the white girl's head in her dark hands. "Don't you mind, honey," Cora said. "Just sit tight, and when the boy comes back I'll tell him how things are. If he loves you he'll want you. And there ain't no reason why you can't marry, neither—you both white. Even if he is a foreigner, he's a right nice boy."

"He loves me," Jessie said. "I know he does. He said so."

But before the boy came back (or Mr. Studevant either) Mrs. Art and Jessie went to Kansas City. "For an Easter shopping trip," the weekly paper said.

Then Spring came in full bloom, and the fields and orchards at the edge of Melton stretched green and beautiful to the far horizon. Cora remembered her own Spring, twenty years ago, and a great sympathy and pain welled up in her heart for Jessie, who was the same age that Josephine would have been, had she lived. Sitting on the kitchen porch shelling peas, Cora thought back over her own life—years and years of working for the Studevants; years and years of going home to nobody but Ma and Pa; little Josephine dead; only Jessie to keep her heart warm. And she knew that Jessie was the dearest thing she had in the world. All the time the girl was gone now, she worried.

After ten days, Mrs. Art and her daughter came back. But Jessie was thinner and paler than she'd ever been in her life. There was no light in her eyes at all. Mrs. Art looked a little scared as they got off the train.

"She had an awful attack of indigestion in Kansas City," she told the neighbors and club women. "That's why I stayed away so long, waiting for her to be able to travel. Poor Jessie! She looks healthy, but she's never been a strong child. She's one of the worries of my life." Mrs. Art talked a lot, explained a lot, about how Jessie had eaten the wrong things in Kansas City.

At home, Jessie went to bed. She wouldn't eat. When Cora brought her food up, she whispered, "The baby's gone."

Cora's face went dark. She bit her lips to keep from cursing. She put her arms about Jessie's neck. The girl cried. Her food went untouched.

A week passed. They tried to *make* Jessie eat then. But the food wouldn't stay on her stomach. Her eyes grew yellow, her tongue white, her heart acted crazy. They called in old Doctor Brown, but within a month (as quick as that) Jessie died.

She never saw the Greek boy any more. Indeed, his father had lost his license, "due to several complaints by the mothers of children, backed by the Woman's Club," that he was selling tainted ice-cream. Mrs. Art Studevant had started a campaign to rid the town of objectionable tradespeople and questionable characters. Greeks were bound to be one or the other. For a while they even closed up Pa Jenkins' favorite bootlegger. Mrs. Studevant thought this would please Cora, but Cora only said, "Pa's been drinkin' so long he just as well keep on." She refused further to remark on her employer's campaign of purity. In the midst of this clean-up Jessie died.

On the day of the funeral, the house was stacked with flowers. (They held the funeral, not at the church, but at home, on account of old Grandma Studevant's infirmities.) All the family dressed in deep mourning. Mrs. Art was prostrate. As the hour for the services approached, she revived, however, and ate an omelette, "to help me go through the afternoon."

"And Cora," she said, "cook me a little piece of ham with it. I feel so weak."

"Yes, m'am."

The senior class from the high school came in a body. The Woman's Club came with their badges. The Reverend Doctor McElroy had on his highest collar and longest coat. The choir sat behind the coffin, with a special soloist to sing "He Feedeth His Flocks Like a Shepherd." It was a beautiful Spring afternoon, and a beautiful funeral.

Except that Cora was there. Of course, her presence created no comment (she was the family servant), but it was what she did, and how she did it, that has remained the talk of Melton to this day—for Cora was not humble in the face of death.

When the Reverend Doctor McElroy had finished his eulogy, and the senior class had read their memorials, and the songs had been sung, and they were about to allow the relatives and friends to pass around for one last look at Jessie Studevant, Cora got up from her seat by the dining-room door. She said, "Honey, I want to say something." She spoke as if she were addressing Jessie. She approached the coffin and held out her brown hands over the white girl's body. Her face moved in agitation. People sat stone-still and there was a long pause. Suddenly she screamed. "They killed you! And for nothin'. . . . They killed your child. . . . They took you away from here in the Spring-time of your life, and now you'se gone, gone, gone!"

Folks were paralyzed in their seats.

Cora went on: "They preaches you a pretty sermon and they don't say nothin'. They sings you a song, and they don't say nothin'. But Cora's here, honey, and she's gone tell 'em what they done to you. She's gonna tell 'em why they took you to Kansas City."

A loud scream rent the air. Mrs. Art fell back in her chair, stiff as a board. Cousin Nora and sister Mary sat like stones. The men of the family rushed forward to grab Cora. They stumbled over wreaths and garlands. Before they could reach her, Cora pointed her long fingers at the women in black and said, "They killed you, honey. They killed you and your child. I told 'em you loved it, but they didn't care. They killed it before it was . . ."

A strong hand went around Cora's waist. Another grabbed her arm. The Studevant males half pulled, half pushed her through the aisles of folding chairs, through the crowded dining-room, out into the empty kitchen, through the screen-door into the back yard. She struggled against them all the way, accusing their women. At the door she sobbed, great tears coming for the love of Jessie.

She sat down on a wash-bench in the back yard, crying. In the parlor she could hear the choir singing weakly. In a few moments she gathered herself together, and went back into the house. Slowly, she picked up her few belongings from the kitchen and pantry, her aprons and her umbrella, and went off down the alley, home to Ma. Cora never came back to work for the Studevants.

Now she and Ma live from the little garden they raise, and from the junk Pa collects—when they can take by main force a part of his meager earnings before he buys his licker.

Anyhow, on the edge of Melton, the Jenkins niggers, Pa and Ma and Cora, somehow manage to get along.

2
SLAVE ON THE BLOCK

THEY WERE PEOPLE who went in for Negroes—Michael and Anne—the Carraways. But not in the social-service, philanthropic sort of way, no. They saw no use in helping a race that was already too charming and naive and lovely for words. Leave them unspoiled and just enjoy them, Michael and Anne felt. So they went in for the Art of Negroes—the dancing that had such jungle life about it, the songs that were so simple and fervent, the poetry that was so direct, so real. They never tried to influence that art, they only bought it and raved over it, and copied it. For they were artists, too.

In their collection they owned some Covarrubias originals. Of course Covarrubias wasn't a Negro, but how he caught the darky spirit! They owned all the Robeson records and all the Bessie Smith. And they had a manuscript of Countee Cullen's. They saw all the plays with or about Negroes, read all the books, and adored the Hall Johnson Singers. They had met Doctor DuBois, and longed to meet Carl Van Vechten. Of course they knew Harlem like their own back yard, that is, all the speakeasies and night clubs and dance-halls, from the Cotton Club and the ritzy joints where Negroes couldn't go themselves, down to places like the Hot Dime, where white folks couldn't get in—unless they knew the man. (And tipped heavily.)

They were acquainted with lots of Negroes, too—but somehow the Negroes didn't seem to like them very much. Maybe the Carraways gushed over them too soon. Or maybe they looked a little like poor white folks, although they were really quite well off. Or maybe they tried too hard to make friends, dark friends, and the dark friends suspected something. Or perhaps their house in the Village was too far from Harlem, or too hard to find, being back in one of those queer and expensive little side streets that had once been alleys before the art invasion came. Anyway, occasionally, a furtive Negro might accept their invitation for tea, or cocktails; and sometimes a lesser Harlem celebrity or two would decorate their rather slow parties; but one seldom came back for more. As much as they loved Negroes, Negroes didn't seem to love Michael and Anne.

But they were blessed with a wonderful colored cook and maid—until she took sick and died in her room in their basement. And then the most marvellous ebony boy walked into their life, a boy as black as all the Negroes they'd ever known put together.

"He *is* the jungle," said Anne when she saw him.

"He's 'I Couldn't Hear Nobody Pray,' " said Michael.

For Anne thought in terms of pictures: she was a painter. And Michael thought in terms of music: he was a composer for the piano. And they had a most wonderful idea of painting pictures and composing music that went together, and then having a joint "concert-exhibition" as they would call it. Her pictures and his music. The Carraways, a sonata and a picture, a fugue and a picture. It would be lovely, and such a novelty, people would have to like it. And many of their things would be Negro. Anne had painted their maid six times. And Michael had composed several themes based on the spirituals, and on Louis Armstrong's jazz. Now here was this ebony boy. The essence in the flesh.

They had nearly missed the boy. He had come, when they were out, to gather up the things the cook had left, and take them to her sister in Jersey. It seems that he was the late cook's nephew. The new colored maid had let him in and given him the two suit-cases of poor dear Emma's belongings, and he was on his way to the Subway. That is, he was in the hall, going out just as the Carraways, Michael and Anne, stepped in. They could hardly see the boy, it being dark in the hall, and he being dark, too.

"Hello," they said. "Is this Emma's nephew?"

"Yes'm," said the maid. "Yes'm."

"Well, come in," said Anne, "and let us see you. We loved your aunt so much. She was the best cook we ever had."

"You don't know where *I* could get a job, do you?" said the boy. This took Michael and Anne back a bit, but they rallied at once. So charming and naive to ask right away for what he wanted.

Anne burst out, "You know, I think I'd like to paint you."

Michael said, "Oh, I say now, that would be lovely! He's so utterly Negro."

The boy grinned.

Anne said, "Could you come back tomorrow?"

And the boy said, "Yes, indeed. I sure could."

The upshot of it was that they hired him. They hired him to look after the garden, which was just about as big as Michael's grand piano—only a little square behind the house. You know those Village gardens. Anne sometimes painted it. And occasionally they set the table there for four on a spring evening. Nothing grew in the garden really, practically nothing. But the boy said he could plant things. And they had to have some excuse to hire him.

The boy's name was Luther. He had come from the South to his relatives in Jersey, and had had only one job since he got there, shining shoes for a Greek in Elizabeth. But the Greek fired him because the boy wouldn't give half his tips over to the proprietor.

"I never heard of a job where I had to pay the boss, instead of the boss paying me," said Luther. "Not till I got here."

"And then what did you do?" said Anne.

"Nothing. Been looking for a job for the last four months."

"Poor boy," said Michael; "poor, dear boy."

"Yes," said Anne. "You must be hungry." And they called the cook to give him something to eat.

Luther dug around in the garden a little bit that first day, went out and bought some seeds, came back and ate some more. They made a place for him to sleep in the basement by the furnace. And the next day Anne started to paint him, after she'd bought the right colors.

"He'll be good company for Mattie," they said. "She claims she's afraid to stay alone at night when we're out, so she leaves."

They suspected, though, that Mattie just liked to get up to Harlem. And they thought right. Mattie was not as settled as she looked. Once out, with the Savoy open until three in the morning, why come home? That was the way Mattie felt.

In fact, what happened was that Mattie showed Luther where the best and cheapest hot spots in Harlem were located. Luther hadn't even set foot in Harlem before, living twenty-eight miles away, as he did, in Jersey, and being a kind of quiet boy. But the second night he was there Mattie said, "Come on, let's go. Working for white folks all day, I'm tired. They needn't think I was made to answer telephones all night." So out they went.

Anne noticed that most mornings Luther would doze almost as soon as she sat him down to pose, so she eventually decided to paint Luther asleep. "The Sleeping Negro," she would call it. Dear, natural childlike people, they would sleep anywhere they wanted to. Anyway, asleep, he kept still and held the pose.

And he *was* an adorable Negro. Not tall, but with a splendid body. And a slow and lively smile that lighted up his black, black face, for his teeth were very white, and his eyes, too. Most effective in oil and canvas. Better even than Emma had been. Anne could stare at him at leisure when he was asleep. One day she decided to paint him nude, or at least half nude. A slave picture, that's what she would do. The market at New Orleans for a background. And call it "The Boy on the Block."

So one morning when Luther settled down in his sleeping pose, Anne said, "No," she had finished that picture. She wanted to paint him now representing to the full the soul and sorrow of his people. She wanted to paint him as a slave about to be sold. And since slaves in warm climates had no clothes, would he please take off his shirt.

Luther smiled a sort of embarrassed smile and took off his shirt.

"Your undershirt, too," said Anne. But it turned out that he had on a union suit, so he had to go out and change altogether. He came back and mounted the box that Anne said would serve just then for a slave block, and she began to sketch. Before luncheon Michael came in, and went into rhapsodies over Luther on the box without a shirt, about to be sold into slavery. He said he must put him into music right now. And he went to the piano and began to play something that sounded like Deep River in the jaws of a dog, but Michael said it was a modern slave plaint, 1850 in terms of 1933. Vieux Carré remembered on 135th Street. Slavery in the Cotton Club.

Anne said, "It's too marvellous!" And they painted and played till dark, with rest periods in between for Luther. Then they all knocked off for dinner. Anne and Michael went out later to one of Lew Leslie's new shows. And Luther and Mattie said, "Thank God!" and got dressed up for Harlem.

Funny, they didn't like the Carraways. They treated them nice and paid them well. "But they're too strange," said Mattie, "they makes me nervous."

"They is mighty funny," Luther agreed.

They didn't understand the vagaries of white folks, neither Luther nor Mattie, and they didn't want to be bothered trying.

"I does my work," said Mattie. "After that I don't want to be painted, or asked to sing songs, nor nothing like that."

The Carraways often asked Luther to sing, and he sang. He knew a lot of southern worksongs and reels, and spirituals and ballads.

> *"Dear Ma, I'm in hard luck:*
> *Three days since I et,*
> *And the stamp on this letter's*
> *Gwine to put me in debt."*

The Carraways allowed him to neglect the garden altogether. About all Luther did was pose and sing. And he got tired of that.

Indeed, both Luther and Mattie became a bit difficult to handle as time went on. The Carraways blamed it on Mattie. She had got hold of Luther. She was just simply spoiling a nice simple young boy. She was old enough to know better. Mattie was in love with Luther.

At least, he slept with her. The Carraways discovered this one night about one o'clock when they went to wake Luther up (the first time they'd ever done such a thing) and ask him if he wouldn't sing his own marvellous version of John Henry for a man who had just come from St. Louis and was sailing for Paris tomorrow. But Luther wasn't in his own bed by the furnace. There was a light in Mattie's room, so Michael knocked softly. Mattie said, "Who's that?" And Michael poked his head in, and here were Luther and Mattie in bed together!

Of course, Anne condoned them. "It's so simple and natural for Negroes to make love." But Mattie, after all, was forty if she was a day. And Luther was only a kid. Besides Anne thought that Luther had been ever so much nicer when he first came than he was now. But from so many nights at the Savoy, he had become a marvellous dancer, and he was teaching Anne the Lindy Hop to Cab Calloway's records. Besides, her picture of "The Boy on the Block" wasn't anywhere near done. And he did take pretty good care of the furnace. So they kept him. At least, Anne kept him, although Michael said he was getting a little bored with the same Negro always in the way.

For Luther had grown a bit familiar lately. He smoked up all their cigarettes, drank their wine, told jokes on them to their friends, and sometimes even came upstairs singing and walking about the house when the Carraways had guests in who didn't share their enthusiasm for Negroes, natural or otherwise.

Luther and Mattie together were a pair. They quite frankly lived with one another now. Well, let that go. Anne and Michael prided themselves on being different; artists, you know, and liberal-minded people—maybe a little scatter-brained, but then (secretly, they felt) that came from genius. They were not ordinary people, bothering about the liberties of others. Certainly, the last thing they would do would be to interfere with the delightful simplicity of Negroes.

But Mattie must be giving Luther money and buying him clothes. He was really dressing awfully well. And on her Thursday afternoons off she would come back loaded down with packages. As far as the Carraways could tell, they were all for Luther.

And sometimes there were quarrels drifting up from the basement. And often, all too often, Mattie had moods. Then Luther would have moods. And it was pretty awful having two dark and glowering people around the house. Anne couldn't paint and Michael couldn't play.

One day, when she hadn't seen Luther for three days, Anne called downstairs and asked him if he wouldn't please come up and take off his shirt and get on the box. The picture was almost done. Luther came dragging his feet upstairs and humming:

> *"Before I'd be a slave*
> *I'd be buried in ma grave*
> *And go home to my Jesus*
> *And be free."*

And that afternoon he let the furnace go almost out.

That was the state of things when Michael's mother (whom Anne had never liked) arrived from Kansas City to pay them a visit. At once neither Mattie nor Luther liked her either. She was a mannish old lady, big and tall, and inclined to be bossy. Mattie, however, did spruce up her service, cooked delicious things, and treated Mrs. Carraway with a great deal more respect than she did Anne.

"I never play with servants," Mrs. Carraway had said to Michael, and Mattie must have heard her.

But Luther, he was worse than ever. Not that he did anything wrong, Anne thought, but the way he did things! For instance, he didn't need to sing now all the time, especially since Mrs. Carraway had said she didn't like singing. And certainly not songs like "You Rascal, You."

But all things end! With the Carraways and Luther it happened like this: One forenoon, quite without a shirt (for he expected to pose) Luther came sauntering through the library to change the flowers in the vase. He carried red roses. Mrs.

Carraway was reading her morning scripture from the Health and Life.

"Oh, good morning," said Luther. "How long are you gonna stay in this house?"

"I never liked familiar Negroes," said Mrs. Carraway, over her nose glasses.

"Huh!" said Luther. "That's too bad! I never liked poor white folks."

Mrs. Carraway screamed, a short loud, dignified scream. Michael came running in bathrobe and pyjamas. Mrs. Carraway grew tall. There was a scene. Luther talked. Michael talked. Anne appeared.

"Never, never, never," said Mrs. Carraway, "have I suffered such impudence from servants—and a nigger servant—in my own son's house."

"Mother, Mother, Mother," said Michael. "Be calm. I'll discharge him." He turned on the nonchalant Luther. "Go!" he said, pointing toward the door. "Go, go!"

"Michael," Anne cried, "I haven't finished 'The Slave on the Block.' " Her husband looked nonplussed. For a moment he breathed deeply.

"Either he goes or I go," said Mrs. Carraway, firm as a rock.

"He goes," said Michael with strength from his mother.

"Oh!" cried Anne. She looked at Luther. His black arms were full of roses he had brought to put in the vases. He had on no shirt. "Oh!" His body was ebony.

"Don't worry 'bout me!" said Luther. "I'll go."

"Yes, we'll go," boomed Mattie from the doorway, who had come up from below, fat and belligerent. "We've stood enough foolery from you white folks! Yes, we'll go. Come on, Luther."

What could she mean, "stood enough"? What had they done to them, Anne and Michael wondered. They had tried to be kind. "Oh!"

"Sneaking around knocking on our door at night," Mattie went on. "Yes, we'll go. Pay us! Pay us! Pay us!" So she remembered the time they had come for Luther at night. That was it.

"I'll pay you," said Michael. He followed Mattie out.

Anne looked at her black boy.

"Good-bye," Luther said. "You fix the vases."

He handed her his armful of roses, glanced impudently at old Mrs. Carraway and grinned—grinned that wide, beautiful, white-toothed grin that made Anne say when she first saw him, "He looks like the jungle." Grinned, and disappeared in the dark hall, with no shirt on his back.

"Oh," Anne moaned distressfully, "my 'Boy on the Block'!"

"Huh!" snorted Mrs. Carraway.

3
HOME

WHEN THE BOY came back, there were bright stickers and tags in strange languages the home folks couldn't read all over his bags, and on his violin case. They were the marks of customs stations at far-away borders, big hotels in European cities, and steamers that crossed the ocean a long way from Hopkinsville. They made the leather-colored bags and black violin case look very gay and circus-like. They made white people on the train wonder about the brown-skinned young man to whom the baggage belonged. And when he got off at a village station in Missouri, the loafers gathered around in a crowd, staring.

Roy Williams had come home from abroad to visit his folks, his mother and sister and brothers who still remained in the old home town. Roy had been away seven or eight years, wandering the world. He came back very well dressed, but awfully thin. He wasn't well.

It was this illness that had made Roy come home, really. He had a feeling that he was going to die, and he wanted to see his mother again. This feeling about death had been coming over him gradually for two or three years now. It seemed to him that it must have started in Vienna, that gay but dying city in Central Europe where so many people were hungry, and yet some still had money to buy champagne and caviar and women in the night clubs where Roy's orchestra played.

But the glittering curtains of Roy's jazz were lined with death. It made him sick to see people fainting in the streets of Vienna from hunger, while others stuffed themselves with wine and food. And it made him sad to refuse the young white women trailing behind him when he came home from work late at night, offering their bodies for a little money to buy something to eat.

In Vienna Roy had a room to himself because he wanted to study and keep up his music. He studied under one of the best violin teachers. But it was hard to keep beautiful and hungry women out of his place, who wanted to give themselves to a man who had a job because in turn the man might let them sleep in his room, or toss them a few bills to take home to their starving parents.

"Folks catch hell in Europe," Roy thought. "I never saw people as hungry as this, not even Negroes at home."

But it was even worse when the orchestra moved back to Berlin. Behind the apparent solidity of that great city, behind doors where tourists never passed, hunger and pain were beyond understanding. And the police were beating people who protested, or stole, or begged. Yet in the cabaret where Roy played, crowds of folks still spent good gold. They laughed and danced every night and didn't give a damn about the children sleeping in doorways outside, or the men who built houses of packing boxes, or the women who walked the streets to pick up trade.

It was in Berlin that the sadness weighed most heavily on Roy. And it was there that he began to cough. One night in Prague, he had a hemorrhage. When he got to Paris, his girl friend took care of him, and he got better. But he had all the time, from then on, that feeling that he was going to die. The cough stayed, and the sadness. So he came home to see his mother.

He landed in New York on the day that Hoover drove the veterans out of Washington. He stayed a couple of days in Harlem. Most of his old friends there, musicians and actors, were hungry and out of work. When they saw Roy dressed so well, they asked him for money. And at night women whispered in the streets, "Come here, baby! I want to see you, darlin'."

"Rotten everywhere," Roy thought. "I want to go home."

That last night in Harlem, he couldn't sleep. He thought of his mother. In the morning he sent her a telegram that he was on his way.

II

"AN UPPTY NIGGER," said the white loafers when they saw him standing, slim and elegant, on the station platform in the September sunlight, surrounded by his bags with the bright stickers. Roy had got off a Pullman—something unusual for a Negro in those parts.

"God damn!" said the white loafers.

Suddenly a nasal voice broke out, "Well, I'll be dogged if it ain't Roy Williams!"

Roy recognized an old playmate, Charlie Mumford, from across the alley—a tall red-necked white boy in overalls. He took off his glove and held out his hand. The white man took it, but he didn't shake it long. Roy had forgotten he wasn't in Europe, wearing gloves and shaking hands glibly with a white man! Damn!

"Where you been, boy?" the white fellow asked.

"Paris," said Roy.

"What'd yuh come back for?" a half-southern voice drawled from the edge of a baggage truck.

"I wanted to come home," said Roy, "to see my mother."

"I hope she's gladder to see yuh than we are," another white voice drawled.

Roy picked up his bags, since there were no porters, and carried them toward a rusty old Ford that seemed to be a taxi. He felt dizzy and weak. The smoke and dust of travel had made him cough a lot. The eyes of the white men about the station were not kind. He heard some one mutter, "Nigger." His skin burned. For the first time in half a dozen years he felt his color. He was home.

III

SING A SONG of Dixie, cotton bursting in the sun, shade of chinaberry trees, persimmons after frost has fallen. Hounds treeing possums October nights. O, sweet potatoes, hot, with butter in their yellow hearts.

"Son, I'm glad you's done come home. What can Ma cook for you? I know you's hungry for some real food. Corn bread and greens and salt pork. Lawd! . . . You's got some mighty nice clothes, honey, but you looks right thin. . . . Chile, I hope you's gonna stay home awhile. . . . These colored girls here'll go crazy about you. They fightin' over you already. . . . Honey, when you plays that violin o' your'n it makes me right weak, it's so purty. . . . Play yo' violin, boy! God's done give you a gift! Yes, indeedy! . . . It's funny how all these Hopkinsville white folks is heard about you already. De woman where yo' sister works say she read someplace 'bout that orchestry you was playin' with in Paris. She says fo' Sister to bring you up to de house to play fo' her sometime. I told Sister, no indeedy, you don't go around playin' at nobody's house. Told her to tell that white woman de Deacon's Board's arrangin' a concert at de church fo' you where everybody can come and pay twenty-five cents to de glory of God and hear you play. Ain't that right, son? You gwine play fo' de Lawd here in Hopkinsville. You been playin' fo' de devil every night all over Europy. . . . Jesus have mercy! Lemme go and get ma washin' out! And whiles you's practicin', I'm gonna make you a pumpkin pie this afternoon. I can see yo' mouth a-waterin' now. . . . Honey, Ma's sho glad you's done come home. . . . Play yo' violin, son!"

IV

CAPRICE VIENNOIS

AIR FOR G STRING

SONATA IN A

AVE MARIA

THE GYPSY DANCES

WHAT LITTLE HOUSE anywhere was ever big enough to hold Brahms and Beethoven, Bach and César Franck? Certainly not Sister Sarah Williams's house in Hopkinsville. When Roy played, ill as he was, the notes went bursting out the windows and the colored folks and white folks in the street heard them. The classic Mr. Brahms coming out of a nigger's house in the southern end of Missouri. O, my God! Play yo' violin, Roy! Tonight's your concert.

The Deacons and the Ladies' Aid sold a lot of tickets to the white folks they worked for. Roy's home-coming concert at Shiloh Church was a financial success. The front rows were fifty cents and filled with white folks. The rest of the seats were a quarter and filled with Negroes. Methodist and Baptist both came, forgetting churchly rivalry. And there were lots of colored girls with powdered bonbon faces—sweet black and brown and yellow girls with red mouths pointed at Roy. There was lots of bustle and perfume and smothered giggling and whispered talk as the drab little church filled. New shoes screeched up and down the aisles. People applauded because it was past the hour, but the concert started colored folks' time anyhow—late. The church was crowded.

V

HELLO, MR. BRAHMS on a violin from Vienna at a colored church in Hopkinsville, Missouri. The slender brown-skin hands of a sick young man making you sing for an audience of poor white folks and even poorer Negroes. Good-evenin', Mr. Brahms, a long ways from home, travellin' in answer to your dream, singin' across the world. I had a dream, too, Mr. Brahms, a big dream that can't come true, now. Dream of a great stage in a huge hall, like Carnegie Hall or the Salle Gaveau. And you, Mr. Brahms, singin' out into the darkness, singin' so strong and true that a thousand people look up at me like they do at Roland Hayes singing the Crucifixion. Jesus, I dreamed like that once before I got sick and had to come home.

And here I am giving my first concert in America for my

mother and the Deacons of Shiloh Church and the quarters and fifty cent pieces they've collected from Brahms and me for the glory of God. This ain't Carnegie Hall. I've only just come home. . . . But they're looking at me. They're all looking at me. The white folks in the front rows and the Negroes in the back. Like one pair of eyes looking at me.

This, my friends . . . I should say, *Ladies and Gentlemen.* (There are white folks in the audience who are not my friends.) . . . This is the *Meditation from Thaïs* by Massenet. . . . This is the broken heart of a dream come true not true. This is music, and me, sitting on the door-step of the world needing you. . . . O, body of life and love with black hands and brown limbs and white breasts and a golden face with lips like a violin bowed for singing. . . . Steady, Roy! It's hot in this crowded church, and you're sick as hell. . . . This, the dream and the dreamer, wandering in the desert from Hopkinsville to Vienna in love with a street-walker named Music. . . . Listen, you bitch, I want you to be beautiful as the moon in the night on the edge of the Missouri hills. I'll make you beautiful. . . . The *Meditation from Thaïs.* . . . You remember, Ma (even to hear me play, you've got your seat in the amen corner tonight like on Sunday mornings when you come to talk to God), you remember that Kreisler record we had on the phonograph with the big horn when I was a kid? Nobody liked it but me, but you didn't care how many times I played it, over and over. . . . Where'd you get my violin? Half the time you didn't have the money to pay old man Miller for my lesson every week. . . . God rest his unpaid soul, as the Catholics say. . . . Why did you cry, Ma, when I went away with the minstrel show, playing coon songs through the South instead of hymns? What did you cry for, Ma, when I wrote you I had a job with a night-club jazz band on State Street in Chicago? . . . Why did you pray all night when I told you we had a contract to go to Berlin and work in a cabaret there? I tried to explain to you that the best violin teachers in the world were in Berlin and that I'd come back playing like that Kreisler record on the old victrola. . . . And didn't I send you money home? . . . Spray like sand in the eyes. . . . O, dream on the door-step of the world! Thaïs! Thaïs! . . . You sure don't look like Thaïs, you scrawny white woman in a cheap coat and red hat staring up at me from the first row. You don't look a bit like Thaïs. What is it you want the music to give you? What do you want from me? . . . This is Hopkinsville, Missouri. . . . Look at all those brown girls back there in the crowd of Negroes, leaning toward me and the music. First time most of them ever saw a man in evening clothes, black or white. First time most of them ever heard the *Meditation from Thaïs*. First time they ever had one of their own race come home from abroad playing a violin. See them looking proud at me and music over the heads of the white folks in the first rows, over the head of the white woman in the cheap coat and red hat who knows what music's all about. . . . Who are you, lady?

When the concert was over, even some of the white folks shook Roy's hand and said it was wonderful. The colored folks said, "Boy, you sure can play!" Roy was shaking a little and his eyes burned and he wanted terribly to cough. Pain shot across his shoulders. But he smiled his concert-jazz-band smile that the gold spending ladies of the European night clubs had liked so much. And he held out a feverish hand to everybody. The white woman in the red hat waited at the edge of the crowd.

When people thinned out a little from the pulpit, she came to Roy and shook his hand. She spoke of symphony concerts in St. Louis, of the fact that she was a teacher of music, of piano and violin, but that she had no pupils like Roy, that never in the town of Hopkinsville had anyone else played so beautifully. Roy looked into her thin, freckled face and was glad she knew what it was all about. He was glad she liked music.

"That's Miss Reese," his mother told him after she had gone. "An old maid musicianer at the white high school."

"Yes'm," said Roy. "She understands music."

VI

THE NEXT TIME he saw Miss Reese was at the white high school shortly after it opened the fall session. One morning a note had come asking him if he would play for her Senior class in music appreciation some day. She would accompany him if he would bring his music. It seems that one of Miss Reese's duties was the raising of musical standards in Hopkinsville; she had been telling her students about Bach and Mozart, and she would so appreciate it if Roy would visit the school and play those two great masters for her young people. She wrote him a nice note on clean white paper.

Roy went. His mother thought it was a great honor for the white high school to send for her colored son to play for them. "That Miss Reese's a right nice woman," Sister Williams said to her boy. "Sendin' for you to play up there at de school. First time I ever knowed 'em to have a Negro in there for anything but cleanin' up, and I been in Hopkinsville a long time. Go and play for 'em, son, to de glory of God!"

Roy played. But it was one of those days when his throat was hot and dry, and his eyes burned. He had been coughing all morning and, as he played, his breath left him and he stood covered with a damp sweat. He played badly.

But Miss Reese was more than kind to him. She accompanied him at the piano. And when he had finished, she turned to the assembled class of white kids sprawled in their seats and said, "This is art, my dear young people, this is true art!"

The students went home that afternoon and told their parents that a dressed-up nigger had come to school with a violin and played a lot of funny pieces nobody but Miss Reese liked. They went on to say that Miss Reese had grinned all over herself and cried, "Wonderful!" And had even bowed to the nigger when he went out!

Roy went home to bed. He was up and down these days, thinner and thinner all the time, weaker and weaker. Sometimes not practicing any more. Often not eating the food his mother cooked for him, or that his sister brought from where she worked. Sometimes being restless and hot in the night and getting up and dressing, even to spats and yellow gloves, and walking the streets of the little town at ten and eleven o'clock after nearly every one else had gone to bed. Midnight was late in Hopkinsville. But for years Roy had worked at night. It was hard for him to sleep before morning now.

But one night he walked out of the house for the last time. The moon had risen and Roy scarcely needed to light the oil-lamp to dress by when he got up. The moon shone into his little room, across the white counterpane of his bed, down onto the bags with the bright stickers piled against the wall. It glistened on the array of medicine bottles on the side table. But Roy lighted the light, the better to see himself in the warped mirror of the dresser. Ashy pale his face was, that had once been brown. His cheeks were sunken. Trembling, he put on his suit and spats and his yellow gloves and soft felt hat. He got into an overcoat. He took a cane that he carried lately from weakness rather than from style. And he went out into the autumn moonlight.

Tip-toeing through the parlor, he heard his mother snoring on the couch there. (She had given up her room to him.) The front door was still unlocked. His brothers, Roy thought, were out with their girl friends. His sister had gone to bed.

In the streets it was very quiet. Misty with moonlight, the trees stood half clad in autumn leaves. Roy walked under the dry falling leaves toward the center of the town, breathing in the moonlight air and swinging his cane. Night and the streets always made him feel better. He remembered the boulevards of Paris and the Unter den Linden. He remembered Tauber singing *Wien, Du Stadt Meiner Traume*. His mind went back to the lights and the music of the cities of Europe. How like a dream that he had ever been in Europe at all, he thought. Ma never had any money. Her kids had barely managed to get through the grade school. There was no higher school for Negroes in Hopkinsville. For him there had been only a minstrel show to run away with for further education. Then that chance with a jazz band going to Berlin. And his violin for a mistress all the time—with the best teachers his earnings could pay for abroad. Jazz at night and the classics in the morning. Hard work and hard practice, until his violin sang like nobody's business. Music, real music! Then he began to cough in Berlin.

Roy was passing lots of people now in the brightness of the main street, but he saw none of them. He saw only dreams and memories, and heard music. Some of the people stopped to stare and grin at the flare of the European coat on his slender brown body. Spats and a cane on a young nigger in Hopkinsville, Missouri! What's the big idea, heh? A little white boy or two catcalled, "Hey, coon!" But everything might have been all right, folks might only have laughed or commented and cussed, had not a rather faded woman in a cheap coat and a red hat, a white woman, stepping out of the drugstore just as Roy passed, bowed pleasantly to him, "Good evening."

Roy started, bowed, nodded, "Good evening, Miss Reese," and was glad to see her. Forgetting he wasn't in Europe, he took off his hat and his gloves, and held out his hand to this lady who understood music. They smiled at each other, the sick young colored man and the aging music teacher in the light of the main street. Then she asked him if he was still working on the Sarasate.

"Yes," Roy said. "It's lovely."

"And have you heard that marvellous Heifetz record of it?" Miss Reese inquired.

Roy opened his mouth to reply when he saw the woman's face suddenly grow pale with horror. Before he could turn around to learn what her eyes had seen, he felt a fist like a ton of bricks strike his jaw. There was a flash of lightning in his brain as his head hit the edge of the plate glass window of the drugstore. Miss Reese screamed. The side-walk filled with white young ruffians with red-necks, open sweaters, and fists doubled up to strike. The movies had just let out and the crowd, passing by and seeing, objected to a Negro talking to a white woman—insulting a White Woman—attacking a WHITE woman—RAPING A WHITE WOMAN. They saw Roy remove his gloves and bow. When Miss Reese screamed after

Roy had been struck, they were sure he had been making love to her. And before the story got beyond the rim of the crowd, Roy had been trying to rape her, right there on the main street in front of the brightly-lighted windows of the drugstore. Yes, he did, too! Yes, sir!

So they knocked Roy down. They trampled on his hat and cane and gloves as a dozen men tried to get to him to pick him up—so some one else could have the pleasure of knocking him down again. They struggled over the privilege of knocking him down.

Roy looked up from the side-walk at the white mob around him. His mouth was full of blood and his eyes burned. His clothes were dirty. He wondered why Miss Reese had stopped to ask him about Sarasate. He knew he would never get home to his mother now.

Some one jerked him to his feet. Some one spat in his face. (It looked like his old playmate, Charlie Mumford.) Somebody cussed him for being a nigger, and another kicked him from behind. And all the men and boys in the lighted street began to yell and scream like mad people, and to snarl like dogs, and to pull at the little Negro in spats they were dragging through the town towards the woods.

The little Negro whose name was Roy Williams began to choke on the blood in his mouth. And the roar of their voices and the scuff of their feet were split by the moonlight into a thousand notes like a Beethoven sonata. And when the white folks left his brown body, stark naked, strung from a tree at the edge of town, it hung there all night, like a violin for the wind to play.

4
PASSING

Chicago,
Sunday, Oct. 10.

DEAR MA,

I felt like a dog, passing you downtown last night and not speaking to you. You were great, though. Didn't give a sign that you even knew me, let alone I was your son. If I hadn't had the girl with me, Ma, we might have talked. I'm not as scared as I used to be about somebody taking me for colored any more just because I'm seen talking on the street to a Negro. I guess in looks I'm sort of suspect-proof, anyway. You remember what a hard time I used to have in school trying to convince teachers I was really colored. Sometimes, even after they met you, my mother, they wouldn't believe it. They just thought I had a mulatto mammy, I guess. Since I've begun to pass for white, nobody has ever doubted that I am a white man. Where I work, the boss is a Southerner and is always cussing out Negroes in my presence, not dreaming I'm one. It is to laugh!

Funny thing, though, Ma, how some white people certainly don't like colored people, do they? (If they did, then I wouldn't have to be passing to keep my good job.) They go out of their way sometimes to say bad things about colored folks, putting it out that all of us are thieves and liars, or else diseased—consumption and syphilis, and the like. No wonder it's hard for a black man to get a good job with that kind of false propaganda going around. I never knew they made a practice of saying such terrible things about us until I started passing and heard their conversations and lived their life.

But I don't mind being "white", Ma, and it was mighty generous of you to urge me to go ahead and make use of my light skin and good hair. It got me this job, Ma, where I still get $65 a week in spite of the depression. And I'm in line for promotion to the chief office secretary, if Mr. Weeks goes to Washington. When I look at the colored boy porter who sweeps out the office, I think that that's what I might be doing if I wasn't light-skinned enough to get by. No matter how smart that boy'd get to be, they wouldn't hire him for a clerk in the office, not if they knew it. Only for a porter. That's why I sometimes get a kick out of putting something over on the boss, who never dreams he's got a colored secretary.

But, Ma, I felt mighty bad about last night. The first time we'd met in public that way. That's the kind of thing that makes passing hard, having to deny your own family when you see them. Of course, I know you and I both realize it is all for the best, but anyhow it's terrible. I love you, Ma, and hate to do it, even if you say you don't mind.

But what did you think of the girl with me, Ma? She's the kid I'm going to marry. Pretty good looking, isn't she? Nice disposition. The parents are well fixed. Her folks are German-Americans and don't have much prejudice about them, either. I took her to see a colored revue last week and she thought it was great. She said, "Darkies are so graceful and gay." I wonder what she would have said if I'd told her *I* was colored, or half-colored—that my old man was white, but you weren't? But I guess I won't go into that. Since I've made up my mind to live in the white world, and have found my place in it (a good place), why think about race any more? I'm glad I don't have to, I know that much.

I hope Charlie and Gladys don't feel bad about me. It's funny I was the only one of the kids light enough to pass. Charlie's darker than you, even, Ma. I know he sort of resented it in school when the teachers used to take me for white, before they knew we were brothers. I used to feel bad about it, too, then. But now I'm glad you backed me up, and told me to go ahead and get all I could out of life.

That's what I'm going to do, Ma. I'm going to marry white and live white, and if any of my kids are born dark I'll swear they aren't mine. I won't get caught in the mire of color again. Not me. I'm free, Ma, free!

I'd be glad, though, if I could get away from Chicago, transferred to the New York office, or the San Francisco branch of the firm—somewhere where what happened last night couldn't ever occur again. It was awful passing *you* and not speaking. And if Gladys or Charlie were to meet me in the street, they might not be as tactful as you were—because they don't seem to be very happy about my passing for white. I don't see why, though. I'm not hurting them any, and I send you money every week and help out just as much as they do, if not more. Tell them not to queer me, Ma, if they should ever run into me and the girl friend any place. Maybe it would have been better if you and they had stayed in Cincinnati and I'd come away alone when we decided to move after the old man died. Or at least, we should have gone to different towns, shouldn't we?

Gee, Ma, when I think of how papa left everything to his white family, and you couldn't legally do anything for us kids, my blood boils. You wouldn't have a chance in a Kentucky court, I know, but maybe if you'd tried anyway, his white children would have paid you something to shut up. Maybe they wouldn't want it known in the papers that they had colored brothers. But you was too proud, wasn't you, Ma? I wouldn't have been so proud.

Well, he did buy you a house and send all us kids through school. I'm glad I finished college in Pittsburgh before he died. It was too bad about Charlie and Glad having to drop out, but I hope Charlie gets something better to do than working in a garage. And from what you told me in your last letter about Gladys, I don't blame you for being worried about her—wanting to go in the chorus of one of those South Side cabarets. Lord! But I know it's really tough for girls to get any kind of a job during this depression, especially for colored girls, even if Gladys is high yellow, and smart. But I hope you can keep her home, and out of those South Side dumps. They're no place for a good girl.

Well, Ma, I will close because I promised to take my weakness to the movies this evening. Isn't she sweet to look at, all blonde and blue-eyed? We're making plans about our house when we get married. We're going to take a little apartment on the North Side, in a good neighborhood, out on one of those nice quiet side streets where there are trees. I will take a box at the Post Office for your mail. Anyhow, I'm glad there's nothing to stop letters from crossing the color-line. Even if we can't meet often, we can write, can't we, Ma?

With love from your son,

JACK.

5

A GOOD JOB GONE

IT WAS A good job. Best job I ever had. Got it my last year in high school and it took me damn near through college. I'm sure sorry it didn't last. I made good money, too. Made so much I changed from City College to Columbia my Sophomore year. Mr. Lloyd saw to it I got a good education. He had nothing against the Negro race, he said, and I don't believe he did. He certainly treated me swell from the time I met him till that high brown I'm gonna tell you about drove him crazy.

Now, Mr. Lloyd was a man like this: he had plenty of money, he liked his licker, and he liked his women. That was all. A damn nice guy—till he got hold of this jane from Harlem. Or till she got hold of him. My people—they won't do. They'd mess up the Lord if He got too intimate with 'em. Poor Negroes! I guess I was to blame. I should of told Mr. Lloyd she didn't mean him no good. But I was minding my own business, and I minded it too well.

That was one of the things Mr. Lloyd told me when I went to work there. He said, "Boy, you're working for me—nobody else. Keep your mouth shut about what goes on here, and I'll look out for you. You're in school, ain't you? Well, you won't have to worry about money to buy books and take your friends out—if you stay with me."

He paid me twenty-two dollars a week, and I ate and slept in. He had a four-room apartment, as cozy a place as you'd want to see, looking right over Riverside Drive. Swell view. In the summer when Mr. Lloyd was in Paris, I didn't have a damn thing to do but eat and sleep, and air the furniture. I got so tired that I went to summer school.

"What you gonna be, boy?" he said.

I said, "A dentist, I reckon."

He said, "Go to it. They make a hell of a lot of money—if they got enough sex appeal."

He was always talking about sex appeal and lovin'. He knew more dirty stories, Mr. Lloyd did! And he liked his women young and pretty. That's about all I'd do, spend my time cleaning up after some woman he'd have around, or makin' sandwiches and drinks in the evenings. When I did something extra, he'd throw me a fiver any time. I made oodles o' money. Hell of a fine guy, Mr. Lloyd, with his 40-11 pretty gals—right out of the Scandals or the back pages of Vanity Fair—sweet and willing.

His wife was paralyzed, so I guess he had to have a little outside fun. They lived together in White Plains. But he had a suite in the Hotel Roosevelt, and a office down on Broad. He says, when I got the job, "Boy, no matter what you find out about me, where I live, or where I work, don't *you* connect up with no place but here. No matter what happens on Riverside Drive, don't you take it no further."

"Yes, sir, Mr. Lloyd," I said, I knew where my bread was buttered. So I never went near the office or saw any of his other help but the chauffeur—and him a Jap.

Only thing I didn't like about the job, he used to bring some awfully cheap women there sometimes—big timers, but cheap inside. They didn't know how to treat a servant. One of 'em used to nigger and darkie me around, till I got her told right quietly one time, and Mr. Lloyd backed me up.

The boss said, "This is no ordinary boy, Lucille. True, he's my servant, but I've got him in Columbia studying to be a dentist, and he's just as white inside as he is black. Treat him right, or I'll see why." And it wasn't long before this Lucille dame was gone, and he had a little Irish girl with blue eyes he treated mean as hell.

Another thing I didn't like, though. Sometimes I used to have to drink a lot with him. When there was no women around, and Mr. Lloyd would get one of his blue spells and start talking about his wife, and how she hadn't walked for eighteen years, just laying flat on her back, after about an hour of this, he'd want me to start drinking with him. And when he felt good from licker he'd start talking about women in general, and he'd ask me what they were like in Harlem. Then he'd tell me what they were like in Montreal, and Havana, and Honolulu. He'd even had Gypsy women in Spain, Mr. Lloyd.

Then he would drink and drink, and make me drink with him. And we'd both be so drunk I couldn't go to classes the next morning, and he wouldn't go to the office all day. About four o'clock he'd send me for some clam broth and an American Mercury, so he could sober up on Mencken. I'd give him an alcohol rub, then he'd go off to the Roosevelt and have dinner with the society folks he knew. I might not see him again for days. But he'd slip me a greenback usually.

"Boy, you'll never lose anything through sticking with me! Here," and it would be a fiver.

Sometimes I wouldn't see Mr. Lloyd for weeks. Then he'd show up late at night with a chippie, and I'd start making drinks and sandwiches and smoothing down the bed. Then there'd be a round o' women, six or eight different ones in a row, for days. And me working my hips off keeping 'em fed and lickered up. This would go on till he got tired, and had the blues again. Then he'd beat the hell out of one of 'em and send her off. Then we'd get drunk. When he sobered up he'd telephone for his chauffeur and drive to White Plains to see his old lady, or down to the hotel where he lived with a secretary. And that would be that.

He had so damn much money, Mr. Lloyd. I don't see where folks get so much cash. But I don't care so long as they're giving some of it to me. And if it hadn't been for this colored woman, boy, I'd still be sitting pretty.

I don't know where he got her. Out of one of the Harlem night clubs, I guess. They came bustin' in about four o'clock one morning. I heard a woman laughing in the living-room, and I knew it was a colored laugh—one of ours. So deep and pretty, it couldn't have been nothing else. I got up, of course, like I always did when I heard Mr. Lloyd come in. I broke some ice, and took 'em out some drinks.

Yep, she was colored, all right. One of those golden browns, like an Alabama moon. Swell looking kid. She had the old man standing on his ears. I never saw him looking so happy before. She kept him laughing till daylight, hugging and kissing. She had a hot line, that kid did, without seemin' serious. He fell for it. She hadn't worked in Harlem speakeasies for nothing. Jesus! She was like gin and vermouth mixed. You know!

We got on swell, too, that girl and I. "Hy, Pal," she said when she saw me bringing out the drinks. "If it ain't old Harlem, on the Drive."

She wasn't a bit hinkty like so many folks when they're light-complexioned and up in the money. If she hadn't been the boss's girl, I'd have tried to make her myself. But she had a black boy friend—a number writer on 135th Street—so she didn't need me. She was in love with him. Used to call him up soon as the boss got in the elevator bound for the office.

"Can I use this phone?" she asked me that very morning.

"Sure, Madam," I answered.

"Call me Pauline," she said, "I ain't white." And we got on swell. I cooked her some bacon and eggs while she called up her sweetie. She told him she'd hooked a new butter and egg man with bucks.

Well, the days went on. Each time, the boss would show up with Pauline. It looked like blondes didn't have a break—a sugar-brown had crowded the white babies out. But it was good for Mr. Lloyd. He didn't have the blues. And he stopped asking me to drink with him, thank God!

He was crazy about this Pauline. Didn't want no other woman. She kept him laughing all the time. She used to sing him bad songs that didn't seem bad when she was singing them, only seemed funny and good natured. She was nice, that girl. A gorgeous thing to have around the house.

But she knew what it was all about. Don't think she didn't. "You've got to kid white folks along," she said to me. "When you're depending on 'em for a living, make 'em *think* you like it."

"You said it," I agreed.

And she really put the bee on Mr. Lloyd. He bought her everything she wanted, and was as faithful to her as a husband. Used to ask me when she wasn't there, what I thought she needed. I don't know what got into him, he loved her like a dog.

She used to spend two or three nights a week with him—and the others with her boy friend in Harlem. It was a hell of a long time before Mr. Lloyd found out about this colored fellow. When he did, it was pure accident. He saw Pauline going into the movies with him at the Capitol one night—a tall black good-looking guy with a diamond on his finger. And it made the old man sore.

That same night Mr. Lloyd got a ring-side table at the Cabin Club in Harlem. When Pauline came dancing out in the two o'clock revue, he called her, and told her to come there. He looked mad. Funny, boy, but that rich white man was jealous of the colored guy he had seen her with. Mr. Lloyd, jealous of a jig! Wouldn't that freeze you?

They had a hell of a quarrel that morning when they came to the apartment. First time I ever heard them quarrel. Pauline told him finally he could go to hell. She told him, yes, she loved that black boy, that he was the only boy she loved in the wide world, the only man she wanted.

They were all drunk, because between words they would drink licker. I'd left two bottles of Haig & Haig on the tray when I went to bed. I thought Pauline was stupid, talking like that, but I guess she was so drunk she didn't care.

"Yes, I love that colored boy," she hollered. "Yes, I love him. You don't think you're buying my heart, do you?"

And that hurt the boss. He'd always thought he was a great lover, and that women liked him for something else besides his money. (Because most of them wanted his money, nobody ever told him he wasn't so hot. His girls all swore they loved him, even when he beat them. They all let *him* put *them* out. They hung on till the last dollar.)

But that little yellow devil of a Pauline evidently didn't care what she said. She began cussing the boss. Then Mr. Lloyd slapped her. I could hear it way back in my bedroom where I was sleeping, with one eye open.

In a minute I heard a crash that brought me to my feet. I ran out, through the kitchen, through the living-room, and opened Mr. Lloyd's door. Pauline had thrown one of the whisky bottles at him. They were battling like hell in the middle of the floor.

"Get out of here, boy!" Mr. Lloyd panted. So I got. But I stood outside the door in case I was needed. A white man beating a Negro woman wasn't so good. If she wanted help, I was there. But Pauline was a pretty tough little scrapper herself. It sounded like the boss was getting the worst of it. Finally, the tussling stopped. It was so quiet in there I thought maybe one of them was knocked out, so I cracked the door to see. The boss was kneeling at Pauline's feet, his arms around her knees.

"My God, Pauline, I love you!" I heard him say. "I want you, child. Don't mind what I've done. Stay here with me. Stay, stay, stay."

"Lemme out of here!" said Pauline, kicking at Mr. Lloyd.

But the boss held her tighter. Then she grabbed the other whisky bottle and hit him on the head. Of course, he fell out. I got a basin of cold water and put him in bed with a cloth on his dome. Pauline took off all the rings and things he'd given her and threw them at him, lying there on the bed like a ghost.

"A white bastard!" she said. "Just because they pay you, they always think they own you. No white man's gonna own me. I laugh with 'em and they think I like 'em. Hell, I'm from Arkansas where the crackers lynch niggers in the streets. How could *I* like 'em?"

She put on her coat and hat and went away.

When the boss came to, he told me to call his chauffeur. I thought he was going to a doctor, because his head was bleeding. But the chauffeur told me later he spent the whole day driving around Harlem trying to find Pauline. He wanted to bring her back. But he never found her.

He had a lot of trouble with that head, too. Seems like a piece of glass or something stuck in it. I didn't see him again for eight weeks. When I did see him, he wasn't the same man.

No, sir, boy, something had happened to Mr. Lloyd. He didn't seem quite right in the head. I guess Pauline dazed him for life, made a fool of him.

He drank more than ever and had me so high I didn't know B from Bull's Foot. He had his white women around again, but he'd got the idea from somewhere that he was the world's greatest lover, and that he didn't have to give them anything but himself—which wasn't so forty for them little Broadway gold diggers who wanted diamonds and greenbacks.

Women started to clearing out early when they discovered Mr. Lloyd had gone romantic—and cheap. There were scandals and fights and terrible goings on when the girls didn't get their presents and checks. But Mr. Lloyd just said, "To hell with them," and drank more than ever, and let the pretty girls go. He picked up women off the streets and then wouldn't pay them, cheap as they are. Late in the night he would start drinking and crying about Pauline. The sun would be rising over the Hudson before he'd stop his crazy carryings on—making me drink with him and listen to the nights he'd spent with Pauline.

"I loved her, boy! She thought I was trying to buy her. Some black buck had to come along and cut me out. But I'm just as good a lover as that black boy any day."

And he would begin to boast about the women he could have—without money, too. (Wrong, of course.) But he sent me to Harlem to find Pauline.

I couldn't find her. She'd gone away with her boy friend. Some said they went to Memphis. Some said Chicago. Some said Los Angeles. Anyway, she was gone—that kid who looked like an Alabama moon.

I told Mr. Lloyd she was gone, so we got drunk again. For more'n a week, he made no move to go to the office. I began to be worried, cutting so many classes, staying up all night to drink with the old man, and hanging around most of the day. But if I left him alone, he acted like a fool. I was scared. He'd take out women's pictures and beat 'em and stamp on 'em and then make love to 'em and tear 'em up. Wouldn't eat. Didn't want to see anybody.

Then, one night, I knew he was crazy—so it was all up. He grabs the door like it was a woman, and starts to kiss it. I couldn't make him stop pawing at the door, so I telephoned his chauffeur. The chauffeur calls up one of Mr. Lloyd's broker friends. And they take him to the hospital.

That was last April. They've had him in the sanatorium ever since. The apartment's closed. His stuff's in storage, and I have no more job than a snake's got hips. Anyway, I went through college on it, but I don't know how the hell I'll get to dental school. I just wrote Ma down in Atlanta and told her times was hard. There ain't many Mr. Lloyd's, you can bet your life on that.

The chauffeur told me yesterday he's crazy as a loon now. Sometimes he thinks he's a stud-horse chasing a mare. Sometimes he's a lion. Poor man, in a padded cell! He was a swell guy when he had his right mind. But a yellow woman sure did drive him crazy. For me, well, it's just a good job gone!

Say, boy, gimme a smoke, will you? I hate to talk about it.

6
REJUVENATION THROUGH JOY

MR. EUGENE LESCHE in a morning coat, handsome beyond words, stood on the platform of the main ballroom of the big hotel facing Central Park at 59th Street, New York. He stood there speaking in a deep smooth voice, with a slight drawl, to a thousand well dressed women and some two or three hundred men who packed the place. His subject was "Motion and Joy," the last of his series of six Friday morning lectures, each of which had to do with something and Joy.

As the hour of his last lecture approached, expensive chauffeured motors turned off Fifth Avenue, circled around from the Park, drew up at the 59th Street entrance, discharged women. In the elevators leading to the level of the hotel ballroom, delicate foreign perfumes on the breasts of befurred ladies scented the bronze cars.

"I've just heard of it this week. Everybody's talking about him. Did you hear him before?"

"My dear, I shall have heard all six. . . . He sent me an announcement."

"Oh, why didn't I . . .?"

"He's marvellous!"

"I simply can't tell you . . ."

The great Lesche speaking.

As he spoke, a thousand pairs of feminine eyes gazed as one. The men gazed, too. Hundreds of ears heard, entranced: Relax and be happy. Let Lesche tell you how to live. Lesche knows. Look at Lesche in a morning coat, strong and handsome, right here before you. Listen!

At $2.50 a seat (How little for his message!) they listened.

"Joy," said the great Lesche, "what is life without joy? . . . And how can we find joy? Not through sitting still with our world of troubles on our minds; not through taking thought—too often only another phrase for brooding; not by the sedentary study of books or pamphlets, of philosophies and creeds, of ancient lore; not through listening to *me* lecture or listening to any other person lecture," this was the *last* talk of his series, "but only through motion, through joyous motion; through life in motion! Lift up your arms to the sun," said Lesche. "Lift them up now! Right now," appealing to his audience. "Up, up, up!"

A thousand pairs of female arms, and some few hundred men's, were lifted up with great rustle and movement, then and there, toward the sun. They were really lifted up toward Lesche, because nobody knew quite where the sun was in the crowded ballroom—besides all eyes were on Lesche.

"Splendid," the big black-haired young man on the platform said, "beautiful and splendid! That's what life is, a movement up!" He paused. "But not always up. The trees point toward the sun, but they also sway in the wind, joyous in the wind. . . . Keep your hands skyward," said Lesche, "sway! Everybody sway! To the left, to the right, like trees in the wind, sway!" And the huge audience began, at Lesche's command, to sway. "Feet on the floor," said Lesche, "sway!"

He stood, swaying, too.

"Now," said Lesche suddenly, "stop! Try to move your hips! . . . Ah, you cannot! Seated as you are in chairs, you cannot! The life-center, the balance-point, cannot move in a chair. That is one of the great crimes of modern life, one of the murders of ourselves, we sit too much in chairs. We need to stand up—no, not now my friends." Some were already standing. "Not *just* when you are listening to *me*. I am speaking now of a way of life. We need to *live* up, point ourselves at the sun, sway in the wind of our rhythms, walk to an inner and outer music, put our balance-points in motion. (Do you not remember my talk on 'Music and Joy'?) Primitive man never sits in chairs. Look at the Indians! Look at the Negroes! They know how to move from the feet up, from the head down. Their centers live. They walk, they stand, they dance to their drum-beats, their earth rhythms. They squat, they kneel, they lie—but they never, in their natural states, *never* sit in chairs. They do not mood and brood. No! They live through motion, through movement, through music, through joy! (Remember my lecture, 'Negroes and Joy'?) Ladies, and gentlemen, I offer you today—rejuvenation through joy."

Lesche bowed and bowed as he left the platform. With the greatest of grace he returned to bow again to applause that was thunderous. To a ballroom that was full of well-dressed women and cultured men, he bowed and bowed. Black-haired and handsome beyond words, he bowed. The people were loath to let him go.

Lesche had learned to bow that way in the circus. He used to drive the roan horses in the Great Roman Chariot Races—but nobody in the big ballroom of the hotel knew that. The women thought surely (to judge from their acclaim) that he had come fullblown right out of heaven to bring them joy.

Lesche knew what they thought, too, for within a month after the closing of his series of Friday Morning Lectures, they all received, at their town addresses, most beautifully written personal notes announcing the opening in Westchester of his Colony of Joy for the rebuilding of the mind, the body, and the soul.

Unfortunately, we did not hear Lesche's lecture on "Negroes and Joy" (the third in the series) but he said, in substance, that Negroes were the happiest people on earth. He said that they alone really knew the secret of rhythms and of movements. How futile, he said, to study Delsarte in this age! Go instead, he said, to Cab Calloway, Bricktop's, and Bill Robinson! Move to music, he said, to the gaily primitive rhythms of the first man. Be Adam again, be Eve. Be not afraid of life, which is a garden. Be all this not by turning back time, but merely by living to the true rhythm of our own age, to music as modern as today, yet old as life, music that the primitive Negroes brought with their drums from Africa to America—that music, my friends, known to the vulgar as jazz, but which is so much *more* than jazz that we know not how to appreciate it; that music which is the Joy of Life.

His letter explained that these rhythms would play a great part in leading those—who would come—along the path to joy. And at Lesche's initial Westchester colony, the leader of the music would be none other than the famous Happy Lane (*a primitif de luxe*), direct from the Moon Club in Harlem, with the finest Negro band in America. To be both smart and modern in approaching the body and soul, was Lesche's aim. And to bring gaiety to a lot of people who had known nothing more joyous than Gurdjieff was his avowed intention—for those who could pay for it.

For Lesche's proposed path to life was not any less costly than that of the now famous master's at Fontainebleau. Indeed, it was even slightly more expensive. A great many ladies (and gentlemen, too) who received Lesche's beautifully written letter gasped when they learned the size of the initial check they would have to draw in order to enter, as a resident member, his Colony of Joy.

Some gasped and did *not* pay (because they could not), and so their lives went on without Joy. Others gasped, and paid. And several (enough to insure entirely Lesche's first season) paid without even gasping. These last were mostly old residents of Park Avenue or the better section of Germantown, ladies who had already tried everything looking toward happiness—now they wanted to try Joy, especially since it involved so new and novel a course as Lesche proposed—including the gaiety of Harlem Negroes, of which most of them knew nothing except through the rather remote chatter of the younger set who had probably been to the Cotton Club.

So Lesche opened up his house on an old estate in Westchester with a mansion and several cottages thereon that the crash let him lease for a little or nothing. (Or rather, Sol, his manager, did the leasing.) Instead of chairs, they bought African stools, low, narrow, and backless.

"I got the best decorator in town, too," said Sol, "to do it over primitive—modernistic—on a percentage of the profits, if there are any."

"It's got to be comfortable," said Lesche, "so people can relax after they get through enjoying themselves."

"It'll be," said Sol.

"We're admitting nobody west of Fifth Avenue," said Lesche.

"No Broadwayites," said Sol.

"Certainly not," said Lesche. "Only people with souls to save—and enough Harlemites to save 'em."

"Ha! Ha!" said Sol.

All the attendants were French—maids, butlers, and pages. Lesche's two assistants were a healthy and hard young woman, to whom he had once been married, a Hollywood Swede with Jean Harlow hair; and a young Yale man who hadn't graduated, but who read Ronald Firbank seriously, adored Louis Armstrong, worshipped Dwight Fisk, and had written Lesche's five hundred personal letters in a seven-lively-arts Gilbert Seldes style.

Sol, of course, handled the money, with a staff of secretaries, bookkeepers, and managers. And Happy Lane's African band, two tap-dancers, and a real blues-singer were contracted to spread joy, and act as the primordial pulse beat of the house. In other words, they were to furnish the primitive.

Within a month after the Colony opened in mid-January, its resident guests numbered thirty-five. Applications were legion. The demand for places was very great. The price went up.

"It's unbelievable how many people with money are unhappy," said Sol.

"It's unbelievable how they need what we got," drawled Lesche.

The press agents wrote marvellous stories about Lesche; how he had long been in his youth at Del Monte a student of the occult, how he had turned from that to the primitive and, through Africa, had discovered the curative values of Negro jazz.

The truth was quite otherwise.

Lesche had first worked in a circus. He rode a Roman chariot in the finale. All the way across the U.S.A. he rode twice daily, from Indianapolis where he got the job to Los Angeles where he quit, because nobody knew him there, and he liked the swimming at Santa Monica—and because he soon found a softer job posing for the members of a modernistic art colony who were modeling and painting away under a most expensive teacher at a nearby resort, saving their souls through art.

Lesche ate oranges and posed and swam all that summer and met a lot of nice, rich, and slightly faded women. New kind of people for him. Cultured people. He met, among others, Mrs. Oscar Willis of New Haven, one of the members of this colony of art expression. Her husband owned a railroad. She was very unhappy. She was lonely in her soul—and her pictures expressed that loneliness. She invited Lesche to tea at her bungalow near the beach.

Lesche taught her to swim. After that she was less unhappy. She began a new study in the painting class. She painted a circle and called it her impression of Lesche. It was hard to get it just right, so she asked him to do some extra posing for her in the late afternoons. And she paid him very well.

But summers end. Seasonal art classes too, and Mrs. Willis went back East.

Lesche worked in the movies as an extra. He played football for football pictures. Played gigolos for society films. Played a sailor, a cave man, a cop. He studied tap-dancing. He did pretty well as far as earning money went, had lots of time for cocktails, parties, and books. Met lots of women.

He liked to read. He'd been a bright boy in high school back home in South Bend. And now at teas out Wilshire way he learned what one ought to read, and what one ought to have read. He spent money on books. Women spent money on him. He swam enough to keep a good body. Drank enough to be a good fellow, and acted well enough to have a job at the studios occasionally. He got married twice, but the other women were jealous, so divorces followed.

Then his friend Sol Blum had an idea. Sol ran a gym for the Hollywood elite. He had a newly opened swimming pool that wasn't doing so well. He asked Lesche if he would take charge of the lessons.

"Don't hurt yourself working, you know. Just swim around a little and show 'em that it looks easy. And be nice to the women," Sol said.

The swimming courses boomed. The fees went up. Sol and Lesche made money. (Lesche got a percentage cut.) He swam more and drank less. His body was swell, even if licker and women, parties and studio lights had made his face a little hard.

"But he's so damn nice," the women would say—who took swimming lessons for no good reason but to be held up by the black-haired Lesche.

Then one summer Lesche and Sol closed the gym and went to Paris. They drank an awful lot of licker at Harry's bar. And at Bricktop's they met an American woman who was giving a farewell party. She was Mrs. Oscar Willis, the artist—again—a long way from California.

"What's the idea?" said Lesche. "Are you committing suicide, Mrs. Willis, or going home, or what? Why a farewell party?"

"I am retiring from life," said Mrs. Willis, shouting above the frenzy of the Negro band. "I'm giving up art. I'm going to look for happiness. I'm going into the colony near Digne."

"Whose colony?" said Lesche. He remembered how much colonies cost, thinking of the art group.

"Mogador Bonatz's colony," said Mrs. Willis. "He's a very great Slav who can do so much for the soul. (Art does nothing.) Only one must agree to stay there six months when one goes."

"Is it expensive?" Lesche asked delicately. "I'm feeling awfully tired, too."

"Only $30 a day," said Mrs. Willis. "Have a drink?"

They drank a lot of champagne and said farewell to Mrs. Willis while the jazz band boomed and Bricktop shouted an occasional blues. Then Sol had an idea. After all, he was tired of gyms—why not start a colony? He mentioned it to Lesche when they got out into the open air.

"Hell, yes," said Lesche as they crossed Pigalle. "Let's start a colony."

From then on in Paris, Sol and Lesche studied soul cults. By night they went to Montmartre. By day they read occult books and thought how much people needed to retire and find beauty—and pay for it. By night they danced to the Negro jazz bands. And all the time they thought how greatly they needed a colony.

"You see how much people pay that guy Bonatz?" said Sol.

"Um-huh!" said Lesche, drinking from a tall glass at Josephine's. "And you see how much they'll spend on Harlem jazz, even in Paris?"

"Yeah," said Sol, "we're spending it ourselves. But what's that got to do with colonies?"

"Looks like to me," said Lesche, "a sure way to make money would be, combine a jazz band and a soul colony, and let it roll from there—black rhythm and happy souls."

"I see," said Sol. "That's not as silly as it sounds."

"Let 'em be mystic and have fun, too," said Lesche.

"What do you mean, mystic?" asked Sol.

"Highbrow fun," said Lesche. "Like they get from Bonatz. What do you suppose he's got we can't get?"

"Nothing," said Sol, who learned to sell ideas in Hollywood. "Now, you got the personality. With me for manager, a jazz band for background, and a little showmanship, it could be a riot."

"A riot is right," said Lesche.

When they returned to America, they stayed in New York. Sol got hold of a secretary who knew a lot of rich addresses and some rich people. Together they got hold of a smart young man from Yale who prepared a program of action for a highbrow cult of joy—featuring the primitive. Then they got ready to open a Colony.

They cabled Mrs. Willis at Digne for the names of some of her friends who might need their souls fixed up—in America. They sent out a little folder. And they had the young Yale man write a few articles on *Contentment and Aboriginal Rhythms* for Lesche to try on the highbrow magazines.

They really had a lot of nerve.

Lesche learned his lectures by heart that the college boy wrote. Then, he improvised, added variations of his own, made them personal, and bought a morning coat. Nightly he went to Harlem, brushing up on the newer rhythms. In November, they opened cold in the grand ballroom of the hotel facing the Park, without even a try-out elsewhere: Six lectures by Eugene Lesche on Joy in Relation to the Mind, Body, and Soul.

"Might as well take a big chance," said Sol. "Win or lose."

They won. In Sol's language, they wowed 'em. When the Friday Morning Series began, the ballroom was half full. When it ended, it was crowded and Sol had already signed the lease for the old Westchester estate.

So many people were in need of rejuvenating their souls and could seemingly still afford to pay for it that Sol gave up the idea for returning immediately to his gym in Hollywood. Souls seemed more important than bodies.

"How about it, Lesche?"

The intelligentsia dubbed their highly publicized efforts neo-paganism; others called it one more return to the primitive; others said out loud, it was a gyp game. Some said the world was turning passionate and spiritual; some said it was merely a sign of the decadence of the times. But everybody talked about it. The papers began to write about it. And the magazines that winter, from the *Junior League Bulletin* to the *Nation*, even the *New Masses*, remarked—usually snootily—but nevertheless remarked—about this Cult of Joy. (Harlem Hedonism, the *Forum* called it.) Lesche's publicity men who'd started it all, demanded higher wages, so Sol fired them. The thing went rolling of its own accord. The world was aware—of Joy! The Westchester Colony prospered.

Ten days before the January opening of the Colony, the huge mansion of the once aristocratic estate hummed with activity. It looked like a Broadway theatre before a première. Decorators were working for big effects. (They hoped *House and Garden*, *Vogue*, or *Vanity Fair* would picturize their super-modernistic results.) The house manager, a former hotel-head out of work, was busy getting his staff together—trying to keep them French—for the swank of it.

The bedrooms were receiving special attention. At Lesche's, sleep also was to be a joy. And each private bathroom was being fitted with those special apparatus at colonies necessary for the cleansing of the body—for Sol and Lesche had hired a doctor to tell them what the best cults used.

"Body and soul," said Sol. "Body and soul."

"Gimme the body," said Lesche, "and let the Yale man take care of the soul."

Occult assistants, chefs and waitresses, *masseurs* and hair-dressers, began to arrive—for the house was to be fully staffed. And there were plenty of first-class people out of work and willing to take a chance, too.

Upstairs in a third-floor room, Lesche, like an actor preparing for a role, studied his lectures word for word. His former wife listened to him daily, reciting them by heart, puzzling over their allusions.

In another room, the Yale man, surrounded by books on primitive art, spiritual guidance, Negro jazz, German eurythmics, psychoanalysis, Yogi philosophy, all of Krishnamurti, half of Havelock Ellis, and most of Freud, besides piles of spirituals, jazz records, Paul Robeson, and Ethel Waters, and in the midst of all this—a typewriter. There sat the Yale man creating lectures—preparing, for a month in advance, twenty-minute daily talks for the great Lesche.

On the day when the Negroes arrived for their rehearsals, just prior to the opening of the place, Sol gave them a lecture. "Fellows," he said, addressing the band, "and Miss Lucas," to the blues-singing little coal-black dancer, "listen! Now I want to tell you about this place. This will not be no night club. Nor will it be a dance-hall. This place is more like a church. It's for the rebuilding of souls—and bodies. It's for helping people.

People who are wore out and tired, sick and bored, *ennui-ed* in other words, will come here for treatments, the kind of treatments, that Mr. Lesche and I have devised, which includes music, the best music, jazz, real primitive jazz out of Africa (you know, Harlem) to help 'em learn to move, to walk, to live in harmony with their times and themselves. Now, I want you all to be ladies and gentlemen (I know you are), to play with abandon, to give 'em all you got, but don't treat this like a rough house, nor like the Moon Club either. We allow only champagne drinkers here, cultured ladies, nice gentlemen, the best, the very best. Park Avenue. You know what I mean. . . . Now this is the order of the day. In the morning at eleven, Mr. Lesche will lecture in the Palm Garden, glass-enclosed, on the Art of Motion and Rhythm. You, Miss Tulane Lucas, and you two tap-dancers there, will illustrate. You will show grace in modern movements, aliveness, the beat of Africa as expressed through the body. Mr. Lesche will illustrate, too. He's one of Bill Robinson's disciples, you know! You all know how tap-dancing has preserved Bill. A man of his age, past fifty! Well, we want to show our clients how it can preserve them. But don't do no stunts now, just easy rhythm stuff. We got to start 'em off slow. Some of 'em is old. And I expect some is Christian Scientists. . . . Then in the late afternoon, we will have tea-dancing, just for pleasure. We want to give 'em plenty of exercise, so they won't be bored. And so they will eat. We expect to make money on our table, and on massages, too. In the evening for one hour, put on the best show you got, singing and dancing—every week we gonna bring up new specialities—send 'em to bed feeling happy, before Mr. Lesche gives his goodnight and sweet dreams talk. . . . Now, you boys understand, you'll be off early here, by ten or eleven. Not like at the Club. You got your own cottage here on the estate to live in, you got your cars. Don't mind you driving to town, if you want to, but I want you back here for the eleven o'clock services in the morning. And I don't want you sleepy, either. This house is dedicated to Joy, and all who work here have got to be bright and snappy. That's what our people are paying for. . . . Lesche! Where is Lesche, Miss Boxall?"

The secretary looked startled. "He was in the halls talking to the new French maids."

"Well, get him in here. Tell him to explain to these boys how he wants to fix up his routine for his lectures. Let's get down to business now."

"What kind of clothes you want us to wear?" Happy Lane, the Negro leader, asked.

"Red," said Sol. "Red is the color of Joy."

"Lord!" said the blues-singer, "I'm too dark to wear red!"

"That's what we want," said Sol, "darkness and light! We want to show 'em how much light there is in darkness."

"Now, here!" said the blues-singer to herself, "I don't like no white folks talkin' 'bout me being dark."

"Lesche," Sol called to his partner strolling in through the door, "let's get going."

"O.K.," Lesche said. "Where's my boy?" meaning the Yale man.

"Right here, Gene."

"Now, how does that first lecture go?"

"My Gawd!" said Sol.

The Yale man referred to his notes. "*Joy*," he read, "*Joy, springing from the dark rhythm of the primitive. . . .*"

"Oh, yes," said Lesche, turning to the band. "Now for that, give me *Mood Indigo*, you know, soft and syncopated, moan it soft and low. Then you, Miss Lucas," to the dancer, "you come gliding on. Give it plenty hip movement. I want 'em to learn to use their life-center. Then I'm gonna say . . . what's that boy friend?" to the Yale man.

"*See how the . . .*"

"Oh, yes . . . *See how the Negroes live, dark as the earth, the primitive earth, swaying like trees, rooted in the deepest source of life. . . .* Then I'm gonna have 'em all rise and sway, like Miss Lucas here. . . . That ought to keep 'em from being bored until lunch-time."

"Lawd," said Miss Lucas, muttering to herself, "what is this, a dancing school or a Sunday-school?" And louder, "All right, Mr. Lesche, sounds like it might be a good act."

"Act, nothing," said Sol. "This is the art of life."

"Must be, if you say so," said Miss Lucas.

"Well, let's go," commanded the great Lesche. "Let's rehearse this first lecture now. Come on, boys."

The jazz band began to cry *Mood Indigo* in the best manner of the immortal Duke Ellington. Lesche began to speak in his great soft voice. Bushy-haired Tulane Lucas began to glide across the floor.

"Goddamn!" said Sol, "It's worth the money!"

"Hey! Hey!" said Miss Lucas.

"Sh-ss-ss-s!" said Lesche. "Be dignified . . . *rooted in the deepest source of life* . . . er-r-r?"

"*. . . O, early soul in motion* . . ." prompted the Yale man.

"*O, early soul* . . ." intoned Lesche.

The amazing collection of people gathered together in the Colony of Joy astounded even Lesche, whose very blasé-ness was what really made him appear so fresh. His thirty-seven clients in residence came almost all from families high in the Social Register, and equally high in the financial world. When Mrs. Carlos Gleed's check of entrance came in, Sol said, "Boy, we're made" . . . for of society there could be no higher—blue blood straight out of Back Bay.

The opening of the Colony created a furor among all the smart neurasthenics from Park Avenue right on up to New England. Dozens applied too late, and failed to get in. Others drove up daily for the lectures.

Of those who came, some had belonged formerly to the self-denial cults; others to Gurdjieff; others had been analyzed in Paris, Berlin, Vienna; had consulted Adler, Hirschfeld, Freud. Some had studied *under* famous Yogi. Others had been at Nyack. Now they had come to the Colony of Joy.

Up and down Park Avenue miraculous gossip flew.

Why, Mrs. Charles Duveen Althouse of Newport and Paris—feeling bad for years—is said to look like a cherub since she's gone into the Colony. . . . My dear, the famous Oriental fan-painter, Vankulmer Jones—he's *another* man these days. The rhythms, he says, the rhythms have worked wonders! And just the very presence of Lesche . . . Nothing America has ever known—rumor flew about the penthouses of the East River—nothing is equal to it. . . . The Baroness Langstrund gasped in a letter to a talkative friend, "My God, it's marvellous!"

Far better than Indian thought, Miss Joan Reeves, the heiress of Meadow Brook, was said to have said by her best friends. "The movement is amazing."

Almost all of them had belonged to cults before—cults that had never satisfied. Some had even been injured by them. To a cult that based the soul-search on self-denial—deny what you like best, have it around you all the time, but never touch it, *never*—then you will be strong—Mrs. Duveen Althouse had belonged. She denied chocolates for a whole year; kept fresh candy sitting in each corner of her boudoir—resisted with all her soul—and at the end of a year was a wreck.

Mr. Jones, the fan-painter, had belonged to a group on Cape Cod that believed in change through change: that is, whatever you want to be, you can. And all the members, after they had paid their fees, were told by the Mystic Master to change their names to whatever they most wished to be, or whoever, past or present, they admired. Some, without much depth, chose Napoleon or Cleopatra. But others, Daphne or Zeus or Merry del Val. Mr. Jones chose Horse. He'd always wanted to be an animal, to possess their strength and calm, their vigor, their ways. But after a whole summer at the Cape he was even less of a horse than before. And greatly mosquito bitten.

Mrs. Ken Prather, II, a member of Lesche's group, had once spent months entire kneeling holding her big toes behind her, deep in contemplation. A most handsome Indian came once a week to her home on East 64th, for an enormous consideration, and gave her lessons in silence, and in positions of thought. But finally she just couldn't stand it any more.

Others of the Colony of Joy had been Scientists in their youth. Others had wandered, disappointed, the ways of spiritualism, never finding soul-mates; still others had gazed solemnly into crystals, but had seen nothing but darkness; now, they had come to Joy!

How did it happen that nobody before had ever offered them Rejuvenation through Joy? Why, that was what they had been looking for all these years! And who would have thought it might come through the amusing and delightful rhythms of Negroes?

Nobody but Lesche.

In the warm glass-enclosed Palm Garden that winter, where the cupid fountain had been replaced by an enlargement of an African plastic and where a jazz band played soft and low behind the hedges, they felt (those who were there by virtue of their check books) all a-tremble in the depths of their souls after they had done their African exercises looking at Lesche—those slow, slightly grotesque, center-swaying exercises that he and Tulane Lucas from the Moon Club had devised. When they had finished, the movement, the music, and Lesche's voice, made them feel all warm and close to the earth, and as though they never wanted to leave the Colony of Joy or to be away from their great leader again.

Of course, there were a few who left, but their places were soon filled by others more truly mystic in the primitive sense than those whose arteries had already hardened, and who somehow couldn't follow a modern path to happiness, or sit on African stools. Clarence Lochard, for one, with *his* spine, had needed actual medical treatment not to be found at the Colony of Joy. And Mrs. J. Northcliff Hill, in the seventies, was a little too old for even the simple exercises that led to center-swaying. But for the two or three who went away, four or five came. And the house was full of life and soul. Every morning, *ensemble*, they lifted up their hands to the sun when the earth-drums rang out—and the sun was Lesche, standing right there.

Lesche was called the New Leader. The Negro band-master was known as Happy Man. The dancers were called the Primitives. The drummer was ritualized as Earth-Drummer. And the devotees were called New Men, New

Women—for the Yale man had written in one of the lectures, "*and the age-old rhythm of the earth as expressed by the drums is also the ever new rhythm of life. And all you who walk to it, dance to it, live to it, are New Men and New Women. You shall call one another, not by the old names but only New Man, New Woman, New One, forgetting the past.*"

They called Lesche, Dear New Leader.

"*For,*" continued the gist of that particular lecture, "*newness, eternal renewal, is the source of all growth, all life, and as we grow from day to day here in this colony, we shall be ever new, ever joyous and new.*"

"Gimme sweet jazz on that line," Lesche had instructed at rehearsals. So on the thrilling morning of that lecture, the saxophones and clarinets moaned so beautiful and low, the drumbeats called behind the palms with such wistful syncopation, that everybody felt impelled to move a new way as Lesche said, "Let us rise this morning and do a new dance, the dance of our new selves." And thirty-nine life-centers began to sway with the greatest of confidence in the palm court, for by now many inhibitions had fallen away, and the first exercise had been learned perfectly.

Who knows how long all might have gone on splendidly with Lesche and Sol and their Colony of Joy had not a most unhappy monster entered in to plague them. "The monster that's in every man," wrote the Yale man later in his diary, "the monster of jealousy—came to break down joy."

For the various New Ones became jealous of Lesche.

"It's your fault," stormed Sol. "Your fault. I told you to treat 'em all the same. I told you if you had to walk in the snow by moonlight, walk with your used-to-be wife, and leave the rest of these ladies alone. You know how women are. I told you not to start that Private Hour in the afternoon. I knew it would make trouble, create jealousy."

For out of the Private Hour devoted to the problems of each New One once a fortnight, where Lesche never advised (he couldn't) but merely received alone in confidence their troubles for contemplation, out of this private hour erelong, howls, screams, and recriminations were heard to issue almost daily. And in late March, New Woman Althouse was known to have thrown an African mask at New Leader Lesche because he kept her waiting a whole hour overtime while he devoted his attentions to the Meadow Brook heiress, New Woman Reeves.

"My Gawd!" said Sol, "the house is buzzing with scandal—I heard it all from Vankulmer Jones."

"These damn women," said Lesche, "I got to get rid of some of these women."

"You can't," said Sol. "They've all paid."

"Well, I will," said Lesche, "I'm tired! Why even my divorced wife's in love with me again. Fire her, will you?"

"Don't be foolish," said Sol, "she's a good secretary."

"Well, I'm gonna quit," said Lesche.

"You can't," said Sol. "I got you under contract."

"Oh, yeah?" said Lesche. "Too much is enough! And sometimes enough is too much! I'm tired, I tell you."

So they fell out. But Lesche didn't quit. It might have been better if he had, for Spring that year was all too sudden and full of implications. The very earth seemed to moan with excess of joy. Life was just too much to bear alone. It needed to be shared, its beauty given to others, taken in return. Its eternal newness united.

To the Colony, Lesche was their Leader, their life. And they wanted him, each one, alone. In desperation, he abolished the Private Hour. But that didn't help any. Mrs. Duveen Althouse was desperately in love with him now. (She called him Pan.) Miss Joan Reeves could not turn her eyes away. (He was her god.) Mrs. Carlos Gleed insisted that he summer at her island place in Maine. Baroness Langstrund announced quite definitely she intended to marry him—whereupon Mrs. Althouse, who had thrown the mask, threatened, without ceremony, to wring at once the Baroness' neck. Several other New Ones stopped speaking to each other over Lesche. Even the men members were taking sides for or against Lesche, or against each other.

That dear soul Vankulmer Jones said he simply couldn't stand it any more—and left.

In the city, the Broadway gossip columns got hold of it—this excitement over Joy—and began to wise-crack. Then suddenly a minister started a crusade against the doings of the rich at the Colony and the tabloids sent men up to get pictures. Blackmailers, scenting scandal, began to blackmail. The righteous and the racketeers both sprang into action. And violets bloomed in April.

Sol tore his hair. "We're ruined!"

"Who cares?" said Lesche, "let's go back to the Hollywood gym. We made plenty on this. And I've still got the Hispano Mrs. Hancock donated."

"But we could've made millions."

"We'll come back to it next year," said Lesche. "And get some fresh New Ones. I'm damn tired of these old ones." And so they bickered.

But the final fireworks were set off by Miss Tulane Lucas, the dusky female of the Primitives. They began over the Earth-Drummer, and really had nothing to do with the Colony. But fire, once started, often spreads beyond control.

The drummer belonged to Miss Lucas. But when Spring came, he got a bad habit of driving down to New York after work every night and not getting back till morning.

"Another woman," said Tulane to herself, "after all I've done." She warned him, but he paid her no mind.

One April morning, just in time to play for the eleven o'clock lecture, with Lesche already on the platform, the little colored drummer arrived late and, without even having gone by the cottage to greet Tulane—rushed into the palm court and took his place at the earth-drums.

"Oh, no!" said Tulane suddenly from among the palms while all the New Ones, contemplating on their African stools, started at the unwonted sound. "Oh, no, you don't," she said. "You have drummed for your last time." And she took a pistol from her bosom and shot.

Bang! . . . Bang! . . . Bang!

Screams rent the palm court. As the drummer fled, bang! a bullet hit somewhere near his life-center, but he kept on. Pandemonium broke out.

"My Gawd!" said Sol. "Somebody grab that gun." But Mrs. Duveen Althouse beat him to it. From Tulane, she snatched the weapon for herself and approached the great Lesche.

"How right to shoot the one you love!" she cried. "How primitive, how just!" And she pointed the gun directly at their dear Leader.

Again shots rang out. One struck the brass curve of the bass horn, glanced upward toward the ceiling, and crashed through the glass of the sun court, showering slivers on everybody.

But by that time, Baroness Langstrund had thrown herself on Duveen Althouse. "Aw-oo!" she screamed. "You wretch, shooting the man I love." Her fingers sought the other's hair, her nails tore at her eyes. Meanwhile, Mrs. Carlos Gleed threw an African stool.

Mrs. Althouse fired once more—but Lesche had gone. The final bullet hit only the marble floor, flew upward through the piano, and sounded a futile chord.

By this time, Sol had grabbed the gun. The screams died. Somebody separated the two women. Little French maids came running with water for the fainting. Happy Lane emerged from behind the bass-viol, pale as an African ghost—but nobody knew where the rest of the jazz band had disappeared, nor Lesche either. They were long gone.

There was no lecture that morning. Indeed, there were never any more lectures. That was the end of the Colony of Joy.

The newspapers laughed about it for weeks, published pictures and names of the wealthy inmates; the columnists wise-cracked. It was all very terrible! As a final touch, one of the tabloids claimed to have discovered that the great Lesche was a Negro—passing for white!

7

THE BLUES I'M PLAYING

OCEOLA JONES, PIANIST, studied under Philippe in Paris. Mrs. Dora Ellsworth paid her bills. The bills included a little apartment on the Left Bank and a grand piano. Twice a year Mrs. Ellsworth came over from New York and spent part of her time with Oceola in the little apartment. The rest of her time abroad she usually spent at Biarritz or Juan les Pins, where she would see the new canvases of Antonio Bas, a young Spanish painter who also enjoyed the patronage of Mrs. Ellsworth. Bas and Oceola, the woman thought, both had genius. And whether they had genius or not, she loved them, and took good care of them.

Poor dear lady, she had no children of her own. Her husband was dead. And she had no interest in life now save art, and the young people who created art. She was very rich, and it gave her pleasure to share her richness with beauty. Except that she was sometimes confused as to where beauty lay—in the youngsters or in what they made, in the creators or the creation. Mrs. Ellsworth had been known to help charming young people who wrote terrible poems, blue-eyed young men who painted awful pictures. And she once turned down a garlic-smelling soprano-singing girl who, a few years later, had all the critics in New York at her feet. The girl was so sallow. And she really needed a bath, or at least a mouth wash, on the day when Mrs. Ellsworth went to hear her sing at an East Side settlement house. Mrs. Ellsworth had sent a small check and let it go at that—since, however, living to regret bitterly her lack of musical acumen in the face of garlic.

About Oceola, though, there had been no doubt. The Negro girl had been highly recommended to her by Ormond Hunter, the music critic, who often went to Harlem to hear the church concerts there, and had thus listened twice to Oceola's playing.

"A most amazing tone," he had told Mrs. Ellsworth, knowing her interest in the young and unusual. "A flair for the piano such as I have seldom encountered. All she needs is training—finish, polish, a repertoire."

"Where is she?" asked Mrs. Ellsworth at once. "I will hear her play."

By the hardest, Oceola was found. By the hardest, an appointment was made for her to come to East 63rd Street and play for Mrs. Ellsworth. Oceola had said she was busy every day. It seemed that she had pupils, rehearsed a church choir, and played almost nightly for colored house parties or dances. She made quite a good deal of money. She wasn't tremendously interested, it seemed, in going way downtown to play for some elderly lady she had never heard of, even if the request did come from the white critic, Ormond Hunter, via the pastor of the church whose choir she rehearsed, and to which Mr. Hunter's maid belonged.

It was finally arranged, however. And one afternoon, promptly on time, black Miss Oceola Jones rang the door bell of white Mrs. Dora Ellsworth's grey stone house just off Madison. A butler who actually wore brass buttons opened the door, and she was shown upstairs to the music room. (The butler had been warned of her coming.) Ormond Hunter was already there, and they shook hands. In a moment, Mrs. Ellsworth came in, a tall stately grey-haired lady in black with a scarf that sort of floated behind her. She was tremendously intrigued at meeting Oceola, never having had before amongst all her artists a black one. And she was greatly impressed that Ormond Hunter should have recommended the girl. She began right away, treating her as a protegee; that is, she began asking her a great many questions she would not dare ask anyone else at first meeting, except a protegee. She asked her how old she was and where her mother and father were and how she made her living and whose music she liked best to play and was she married and would she take one lump or two in her tea, with lemon or cream?

After tea, Oceola played. She played the Rachmaninoff

Prelude in G Sharp Minor. She played from the Liszt *Études.* She played the *St. Louis Blues.* She played Ravel's *Pavane pour une Infante Défunte.* And then she said she had to go. She was playing that night for a dance in Brooklyn for the benefit of the Urban League.

Mrs. Ellsworth and Ormond Hunter breathed, "How lovely!"

Mrs. Ellsworth said, "I am quite overcome, my dear. You play so beautifully." She went on further to say, "You must let me help you. Who is your teacher?"

"I have none now," Oceola replied. "I teach pupils myself. Don't have time any more to study—nor money either."

"But you must have time," said Mrs. Ellsworth, "and money, also. Come back to see me on Tuesday. We will arrange it, my dear."

And when the girl had gone, she turned to Ormond Hunter for advice on piano-teachers to instruct those who already had genius, and need only to be developed.

II

THEN BEGAN ONE of the most interesting periods in Mrs. Ellsworth's whole experience in aiding the arts. The period of Oceola. For the Negro girl, as time went on, began to occupy a greater and greater place in Mrs. Ellsworth's interests, to take up more and more of her time, and to use up more and more of her money. Not that Oceola ever asked for money, but Mrs. Ellsworth herself seemed to keep thinking of so much more Oceola needed.

At first it was hard to get Oceola to need anything. Mrs. Ellsworth had the feeling that the girl mistrusted her generosity, and Oceola did—for she had never met anybody interested in pure art before. Just to be given things for *art's sake* seemed suspicious to Oceola.

That first Tuesday, when the colored girl came back at Mrs.

Ellsworth's request, she answered the white woman's questions with a why-look in her eyes.

"Don't think I'm being personal, dear," said Mrs. Ellsworth, "but I must know your background in order to help you. Now, tell me . . ."

Oceola wondered why on earth the woman wanted to help her. However, since Mrs. Ellsworth seemed interested in her life's history, she brought it forth so as not to hinder the progress of the afternoon, for she wanted to get back to Harlem by six o'clock.

Born in Mobile in 1903. Yes, m'am, she was older than she looked. Papa had a band, that is her step-father. Used to play for all the lodge turn-outs, picnics, dances, barbecues. You could get the best roast pig in the world in Mobile. Her mother used to play the organ in church, and when the deacons bought a piano after the big revival, her mama played that, too. Oceola played by ear for a long while until her mother taught her notes. Oceola played an organ, also, and a cornet.

"My, my," said Mrs. Ellsworth.

"Yes, m'am," said Oceola. She had played and practiced on lots of instruments in the South before her step-father died. She always went to band rehearsals with him.

"And where was your father, dear?" asked Mrs. Ellsworth.

"My step-father had the band," replied Oceola. Her mother left off playing in the church to go with him travelling in Billy Kersands' Minstrels. He had the biggest mouth in the world, Kersands did, and used to let Oceola put both her hands in it at a time and stretch it. Well, she and her mama and step-papa settled down in Houston. Sometimes her parents had jobs and sometimes they didn't. Often they were hungry, but Oceola went to school and had a regular piano-teacher, an old German woman, who gave her what technique she had today.

"A fine old teacher," said Oceola. "She used to teach me half the time for nothing. God bless her."

"Yes," said Mrs. Ellsworth. "She gave you an excellent foundation."

"Sure did. But my step-papa died, got cut, and after that

Mama didn't have no more use for Houston so we moved to St. Louis. Mama got a job playing for the movies in a Market Street theater, and I played for a church choir, and saved some money and went to Wilberforce. Studied piano there, too. Played for all the college dances. Graduated. Came to New York and heard Rachmaninoff and was crazy about him. Then Mama died, so I'm keeping the little flat myself. One room is rented out."

"Is she nice," asked Mrs. Ellsworth, "your roomer?"

"It's not a she," said Oceola. "He's a man. I hate women roomers."

"Oh!" said Mrs. Ellsworth. "I should think all roomers would be terrible."

"He's right nice," said Oceola. "Name's Pete Williams."

"What does he do?" asked Mrs. Ellsworth.

"A Pullman porter," replied Oceola, "but he's saving money to go to Med school. He's a smart fellow."

But it turned out later that he wasn't paying Oceola any rent.

That afternoon, when Mrs. Ellsworth announced that she had made her an appointment with one of the best piano-teachers in New York, the black girl seemed pleased. She recognized the name. But how, she wondered, would she find time for study, with her pupils and her choir, and all. When Mrs. Ellsworth said that she would cover her *entire* living expenses, Oceola's eyes were full of that why-look, as though she didn't believe it.

"I have faith in your art, dear," said Mrs. Ellsworth, at parting. But to prove it quickly, she sat down that very evening and sent Oceola the first monthly check so that she would no longer have to take in pupils or drill choirs or play at house parties. And so Oceola would have faith in art, too.

That night Mrs. Ellsworth called up Ormond Hunter and told him what she had done. And she asked if Mr. Hunter's maid knew Oceola, and if she supposed that that man rooming with her were anything to her. Ormond Hunter said he would inquire.

Before going to bed, Mrs. Ellsworth told her housekeeper to order a book called "Nigger Heaven" on the morrow, and also anything else Brentano's had about Harlem. She made a mental note that she must go up there sometime, for she had never yet seen that dark section of New York; and now that she had a Negro protegee, she really ought to know something about it. Mrs. Ellsworth couldn't recall ever having known a single Negro before in her whole life, so she found Oceola fascinating. And just as black as she herself was white.

Mrs. Ellsworth began to think in bed about what gowns would look best on Oceola. Her protegee would have to be well-dressed. She wondered, too, what sort of a place the girl lived in. And who that man was who lived with her. She began to think that really Oceola ought to have a place to herself. It didn't seem quite respectable. . . .

When she woke up in the morning, she called her car and went by her dressmaker's. She asked the good woman what kind of colors looked well with black; not black fabrics, but a black skin.

"I have a little friend to fit out," she said.

"A *black* friend?" said the dressmaker.

"A black friend," said Mrs. Ellsworth.

III

SOME DAYS LATER Ormond Hunter reported on what his maid knew about Oceola. It seemed that the two belonged to the same church, and although the maid did not know Oceola very well, she knew what everybody said about her in the church. Yes, indeedy! Oceola were a right nice girl, for sure, but it certainly were a shame she were giving all her money to that man what stayed with her and what she was practically putting through college so he could be a doctor.

"Why," gasped Mrs. Ellsworth, "the poor child is being preyed upon."

"It seems to me so," said Ormond Hunter.

"I must get her out of Harlem," said Mrs. Ellsworth, "at once. I believe it's worse than Chinatown."

"She might be in a more artistic atmosphere," agreed Ormond Hunter. "And with her career launched, she probably won't want that man anyhow."

"She won't need him," said Mrs. Ellsworth. "She will have her art."

But Mrs. Ellsworth decided that in order to increase the rapprochement between art and Oceola, something should be done now, at once. She asked the girl to come down to see her the next day, and when it was time to go home, the white woman said, "I have a half-hour before dinner. I'll drive you up. You know I've never been to Harlem."

"All right," said Oceola. "That's nice of you."

But she didn't suggest the white lady's coming in, when they drew up before a rather sad-looking apartment house in 134th Street. Mrs. Ellsworth had to ask could she come in.

"I live on the fifth floor," said Oceola, "and there isn't any elevator."

"It doesn't matter, dear," said the white woman, for she meant to see the inside of this girl's life, elevator or no elevator.

The apartment was just as she thought it would be. After all, she had read Thomas Burke on Limehouse. And here was just one more of those holes in the wall, even if it was five stories high. The windows looked down on slums. There were only four rooms, small as maids' rooms, all of them. An upright piano almost filled the parlor. Oceola slept in the dining-room. The roomer slept in the bed-chamber beyond the kitchen.

"Where is he, darling?"

"He runs on the road all summer," said the girl. "He's in and out."

"But how do you breathe in here?" asked Mrs. Ellsworth. "It's so small. You must have more space for your soul, dear. And for a grand piano. Now, in the Village . . ."

"I do right well here," said Oceola.

"But in the Village where so many nice artists live we can get . . ."

"But I don't want to move yet. I promised my roomer he could stay till fall."

"Why till fall?"

"He's going to Meharry then."

"To marry?"

"Meharry, yes m'am. That's a colored Medicine school in Nashville."

"Colored? Is it good?"

"Well, it's cheap," said Oceola. "After he goes, I don't mind moving."

"But I wanted to see you settled before I go away for the summer."

"When you come back is all right. I can do till then."

"Art is long," reminded Mrs. Ellsworth, "and time is fleeting, my dear."

"Yes, m'am," said Oceola, "but I gets nervous if I start worrying about time."

So Mrs. Ellsworth went off to Bar Harbor for the season, and left the man with Oceola.

IV

THAT WAS SOME years ago. Eventually art and Mrs. Ellsworth triumphed. Oceola moved out of Harlem. She lived in Gay Street west of Washington Square where she met Genevieve Taggard, and Ernestine Evans, and two or three sculptors, and a cat-painter who was also a protegee of Mrs. Ellsworth. She spent her days practicing, playing for friends of her patron, going to concerts, and reading books about music. She no longer had pupils or rehearsed the choir, but she still loved to play for Harlem house parties—for nothing—now that she no longer needed the money, out of sheer love of jazz. This rather disturbed Mrs. Ellsworth, who still believed in art of the old school, portraits that really and truly looked like people, poems about nature, music that had soul in it, not syncopation. And she felt the dignity of art. Was it in keeping with genius, she wondered, for Oceola to have a studio full of white and colored people every Saturday night (some of them actually drinking gin *from bottles*) and dancing to the most tomtom-like music she had ever heard coming out of a grand piano? She wished she could lift Oceola up bodily and take her away from all that, for art's sake.

So in the spring, Mrs. Ellsworth organized week-ends in the up-state mountains where she had a little lodge and where Oceola could look from the high places at the stars, and fill her soul with the vastness of the eternal, and forget about jazz. Mrs. Ellsworth really began to hate jazz—especially on a grand piano.

If there were a lot of guests at the lodge, as there sometimes were, Mrs. Ellsworth might share the bed with Oceola. Then she would read aloud Tennyson or Browning before turning out the light, aware all the time of the electric strength of that brown-black body beside her, and of the deep drowsy voice asking what the poems were about. And then Mrs. Ellsworth would feel very motherly toward this dark girl whom she had taken under her wing on the wonderful road of art, to nurture and love until she became a great interpreter of the piano. At such times the elderly white woman was glad her late husband's money, so well invested, furnished her with a large surplus to devote to the needs of her protegees, especially to Oceola, the blackest—and most interesting of all.

Why the most interesting?

Mrs. Ellsworth didn't know, unless it was that Oceola really was talented, terribly alive, and that she looked like nothing Mrs. Ellsworth had ever been near before. Such a rich velvet black, and such a hard young body! The teacher of the piano raved about her strength.

"She can stand a great career," the teacher said. "She has everything for it."

"Yes," agreed Mrs. Ellsworth, thinking, however, of the Pullman porter at Meharry, "but she must learn to sublimate her soul."

So for two years then, Oceola lived abroad at Mrs. Ellsworth's expense. She studied with Philippe, had the little apartment on the Left Bank, and learned about Debussy's

African background. She met many black Algerian and French West Indian students, too, and listened to their interminable arguments ranging from Garvey to Picasso to Spengler to Jean Cocteau, and thought they all must be crazy. Why did they or anybody argue so much about life or art? Oceola merely lived—and loved it. Only the Marxian students seemed sound to her for they, at least, wanted people to have enough to eat. That was important, Oceola thought, remembering, as she did, her own sometimes hungry years. But the rest of the controversies, as far as she could fathom, were based on air.

Oceola hated most artists, too, and the word *art* in French or English. If you wanted to play the piano or paint pictures or write books, go ahead! But why talk so much about it? Montparnasse was worse in that respect than the Village. And as for the cultured Negroes who were always saying art would break down color lines, art could save the race and prevent lynchings! "Bunk!" said Oceola. "My ma and pa were both artists when it came to making music, and the white folks ran them out of town for being dressed up in Alabama. And look at the Jews! Every other artist in the world's a Jew, and still folks hate them."

She thought of Mrs. Ellsworth (dear soul in New York), who never made uncomplimentary remarks about Negroes, but frequently did about Jews. Of little Menuhin she would say, for instance, "He's a *genius*—not a Jew," hating to admit his ancestry.

In Paris, Oceola especially loved the West Indian ball rooms where the black colonials danced the beguine. And she liked the entertainers at Bricktop's. Sometimes late at night there, Oceola would take the piano and beat out a blues for Brick and the assembled guests. In her playing of Negro folk music, Oceola never doctored it up, or filled it full of classical runs, or fancy falsities. In the blues she made the bass notes throb like tomtoms, the trebles cry like little flutes, so deep in the earth and so high in the sky that they understood everything. And when the night club crowd would get up and dance to her blues, and Bricktop would yell, "Hey! Hey!" Oceola felt as happy as if she were performing a Chopin étude for the nicely gloved Oh's and Ah-ers in a Crillon salon.

Music, to Oceola, demanded movement and expression, dancing and living to go with it. She liked to teach, when she had the choir, the singing of those rhythmical Negro spirituals that possessed the power to pull colored folks out of their seats in the amen corner and make them prance and shout in the aisles for Jesus. She never liked those fashionable colored churches where shouting and movement were discouraged and looked down upon, and where New England hymns instead of spirituals were sung. Oceola's background was too well-grounded in Mobile, and Billy Kersands' Minstrels, and the Sanctified churches where religion was a joy, to stare mystically over the top of a grand piano like white folks and imagine that Beethoven had nothing to do with life, or that Schubert's love songs were only sublimations.

Whenever Mrs. Ellsworth came to Paris, she and Oceola spent hours listening to symphonies and string quartettes and pianists. Oceola enjoyed concerts, but seldom felt, like her patron, that she was floating on clouds of bliss. Mrs. Ellsworth insisted, however, that Oceola's spirit was too moved for words at such times—therefore she understood why the dear child kept quiet. Mrs. Ellsworth herself was often too moved for words, but never by pieces like Ravel's *Bolero* (which Oceola played on the phonograph as a dance record) or any of the compositions of *les Six*.

What Oceola really enjoyed most with Mrs. Ellsworth was not going to concerts, but going for trips on the little river boats in the Seine; or riding out to old chateaux in her patron's hired Renault; or to Versailles, and listening to the aging white lady talk about the romantic history of France, the wars and uprising, the loves and intrigues of princes and kings and queens, about guillotines and lace handkerchiefs, snuff boxes and daggers. For Mrs. Ellsworth had loved France as a girl, and had made a study of its life and lore. Once she used to sing simple little French songs rather well, too. And she always regretted that her husband never understood the lovely words—or even tried to understand them.

Oceola learned the accompaniments for all the songs Mrs. Ellsworth knew and sometimes they tried them over together. The middle-aged white woman loved to sing when the colored girl played, and she even tried spirituals. Often, when she stayed at the little Paris apartment, Oceola would go into the kitchen and cook something good for late supper, maybe an oyster soup, or fried apples and bacon. And sometimes Oceola had pigs' feet.

"There's nothing quite so good as a pig's foot," said Oceola, "after playing all day."

"Then you must have pigs' feet," agreed Mrs. Ellsworth.

And all this while Oceola's development at the piano blossomed into perfection. Her tone became a singing wonder and her interpretations warm and individual. She gave a concert in Paris, one in Brussels, and another in Berlin. She got the press notices all pianists crave. She had her picture in lots of European papers. And she came home to New York a year after the stock market crashed and nobody had any money—except folks like Mrs. Ellsworth who had so much it would be hard to ever lose it all.

Oceola's one time Pullman porter, now a coming doctor, was graduating from Meharry that spring. Mrs. Ellsworth saw her dark protegee go South to attend his graduation with tears in her eyes. She thought that by now music would be enough, after all those years under the best teachers, but alas, Oceola was not yet sublimated, even by Philippe. She wanted to see Pete.

Oceola returned North to prepare for her New York concert in the fall. She wrote Mrs. Ellsworth at Bar Harbor that her doctor boy friend was putting in one more summer on the railroad, then in the autumn he would intern at Atlanta. And Oceola said that he had asked her to marry him. Lord, she was happy!

It was a long time before she heard from Mrs. Ellsworth. When the letter came, it was full of long paragraphs about the beautiful music Oceola had within her power to give the world.

Instead, she wanted to marry and be burdened with children! Oh, my dear, my dear!

Oceola, when she read it, thought she had done pretty well knowing Pete this long and not having children. But she wrote back that she didn't see why children and music couldn't go together. Anyway, during the present depression, it was pretty hard for a beginning artist like herself to book a concert tour—so she might just as well be married awhile. Pete, on his last run in from St. Louis, had suggested that they have the wedding at Christmas in the South. "And he's impatient, at that. He needs me."

This time Mrs. Ellsworth didn't answer by letter at all. She was back in town in late September. In November, Oceola played at Town Hall. The critics were kind, but they didn't go wild. Mrs. Ellsworth swore it was because of Pete's influence on her protegee.

"But he was in Atlanta," Oceola said.

"His spirit was here," Mrs. Ellsworth insisted. "All the time you were playing on that stage, he was here, the monster! Taking you out of yourself, taking you away from the piano."

"Why, he wasn't," said Oceola. "He was watching an operation in Atlanta."

But from then on, things didn't go well between her and her patron. The white lady grew distinctly cold when she received Oceola in her beautiful drawing-room among the jade vases and amber cups worth thousands of dollars. When Oceola would have to wait there for Mrs. Ellsworth, she was afraid to move for fear she might knock something over—that would take ten years of a Harlemite's wages to replace, if broken.

Over the tea cups, the aging Mrs. Ellsworth did not talk any longer about the concert tour she had once thought she might finance for Oceola, if no recognized bureau took it up. Instead, she spoke of that something she believed Oceola's fingers had lost since her return from Europe. And she wondered why any one insisted on living in Harlem.

"I've been away from my own people so long," said the girl, "I want to live right in the middle of them again."

Why, Mrs. Ellsworth wondered further, did Oceola, at her last concert in a Harlem church, not stick to the classical items listed on the program. Why did she insert one of her own variations on the spirituals, a syncopated variation from the Sanctified Church, that made an old colored lady rise up and cry out from her pew, "Glory to God this evenin'! Yes! Hallelujah! Whooo-oo!" right at the concert? Which seemed most undignified to Mrs. Ellsworth, and unworthy of the teachings of Philippe. And furthermore, why was Pete coming up to New York for Thanksgiving? And who had sent him the money to come?

"Me," said Oceola. "He doesn't make anything interning."

"Well," said Mrs. Ellsworth, "I don't think much of him." But Oceola didn't seem to care what Mrs. Ellsworth thought, for she made no defense.

Thanksgiving evening, in bed, together in a Harlem apartment, Pete and Oceola talked about their wedding to come. They would have a big one in a church with lots of music. And Pete would give her a ring. And she would have on a white dress, light and fluffy, not silk. "I hate silk," she said. "I hate expensive things." (She thought of her mother being buried in a cotton dress, for they were all broke when she died. Mother would have been glad about her marriage.) "Pete," Oceola said, hugging him in the dark, "let's live in Atlanta, where there are lots of colored people, like us."

"What about Mrs. Ellsworth?" Pete asked. "She coming down to Atlanta for our wedding?"

"I don't know," said Oceola.

"I hope not, 'cause if she stops at one of them big hotels, I won't have you going to the back door to see her. That's one thing I hate about the South—where there're white people, you have to go to the back door."

"Maybe she can stay with us," said Oceola. "I wouldn't mind."

"I'll be damned," said Pete. "You want to get lynched?"

But it happened that Mrs. Ellsworth didn't care to attend the wedding, anyway. When she saw how love had triumphed over art, she decided she could no longer influence Oceola's life. The period of Oceola was over. She would send checks, occasionally, if the girl needed them, besides, of course, something beautiful for the wedding, but that would be all. These things she told her the week after Thanksgiving.

"And Oceola, my dear, I've decided to spend the whole winter in Europe. I sail on December eighteenth. Christmas—while you are marrying—I shall be in Paris with my precious Antonio Bas. In January, he has an exhibition of oils in Madrid. And in the spring, a new young poet is coming over whom I want to visit Florence, to really know Florence. A charming white-haired boy from Omaha whose soul has been crushed in the West. I want to try to help him. He, my dear, is one of the few people who live for their art—and nothing else. . . . Ah, such a beautiful life! . . . You will come and play for me once before I sail?"

"Yes, Mrs. Ellsworth," said Oceola, genuinely sorry that the end had come. Why did white folks think you could live on nothing but art? Strange! Too strange! Too strange!

V

THE PERSIAN VASES in the music room were filled with long-stemmed lilies that night when Oceola Jones came down from Harlem for the last time to play for Mrs. Dora Ellsworth. Mrs. Ellsworth had on a gown of black velvet, and a collar of pearls about her neck. She was very kind and gentle to Oceola, as one would be to a child who has done a great wrong but doesn't know any better. But to the black girl from Harlem, she looked very cold and white, and her grand piano seemed like the biggest and heaviest in the world—as Oceola sat down to play it with the technique for which Mrs. Ellsworth had paid.

As the rich and aging white woman listened to the great roll of Beethoven sonatas and to the sea and moonlight of the Chopin nocturnes, as she watched the swaying dark strong shoulders of Oceola Jones, she began to reproach the girl aloud for running away from art and music, for burying herself in Atlanta and love—love for a man unworthy of lacing up her boot straps, as Mrs. Ellsworth put it.

"You could shake the stars with your music, Oceola. Depression or no depression, I could make you great. And yet you propose to dig a grave for yourself. Art is bigger than love."

"I believe you, Mrs. Ellsworth," said Oceola, not turning away from the piano. "But being married won't keep me from making tours, or being an artist."

"Yes, it will," said Mrs. Ellsworth. "He'll take all the music out of you."

"No, he won't," said Oceola.

"You don't know, child," said Mrs. Ellsworth, "what men are like."

"Yes, I do," said Oceola simply. And her fingers began to wander slowly up and down the keyboard, flowing into the soft and lazy syncopation of a Negro blues, a blues that deepened and grew into rollicking jazz, then into an earth-throbbing rhythm that shook the lilies in the Persian vases of Mrs. Ellsworth's music room. Louder than the voice of the white woman who cried that Oceola was deserting beauty, deserting her real self, deserting her hope in life, the flood of wild syncopation filled the house, then sank into the slow and singing blues with which it had begun.

The girl at the piano heard the white woman saying, "Is this what I spent thousands of dollars to teach you?"

"No," said Oceola simply. "This is mine. . . . Listen! . . . How sad and gay it is. Blue and happy—laughing and crying. . . . How white like you and black like me. . . . How much like a man. . . . And how like a woman. . . . Warm as Pete's mouth. . . . These are the blues. . . . I'm playing."

Mrs. Ellsworth sat very still in her chair looking at the lilies trembling delicately in the priceless Persian vases, while Oceola made the bass notes throb like tomtoms deep in the earth.

O, if I could holler

sang the blues,

Like a mountain jack,
I'd go up on de mountain

sang the blues,

And call my baby back.

"And I," said Mrs. Ellsworth rising from her chair, "would stand looking at the stars."

8
RED-HEADED BABY

"DEAD, DEAD AS HELL, these little burgs on the Florida coast. Lot of half-built skeleton houses left over from the boom. Never finished. Never will be finished. Mosquitoes, sand, niggers. Christ, I ought to break away from it. Stuck five years on same boat and still nothin' but a third mate puttin' in at dumps like this on a damned coast-wise tramp. Not even a good time to be had. Norfolk, Savannah, Jacksonville, ain't bad. Ain't bad. But what the hell kind of port's this? What the hell is there to do except get drunk and go out and sleep with niggers? Hell!"

Feet in the sand. Head under palms, magnolias, stars. Lights and the kid-cries of a sleepy town. Mosquitoes to slap at with hairy freckled hands and a dead hot breeze, when there is any breeze.

"What the hell am I walkin' way out here for? She wasn't nothin' to get excited over—last time I saw her. And that must a been a full three years ago. She acted like she was a virgin then. Name was Betsy. Sure ain't a virgin now, I know that. Not after we'd been anchored here damn near a month, the old man mixed up in some kind of law suit over some rich guy's yacht we rammed in a midnight squall off the bar. Damn good thing I wasn't on the bridge then. And this damn yellow gal, said she never had nothing to do with a seaman before. Lyin' I guess. Three years ago. She's probably on the crib-line now. Hell, how far was that house?"

Crossing the railroad track at the edge of town. Green lights. Sand in the road, seeping into oxfords and the cuffs of dungarees. Surf sounds, mosquito sounds, nigger-cries in the night. No street-lights out here. There never is where niggers live. Rickety run-down huts, under palm-trees. Flowers and vines all over. Always growing, always climbing. Never finished.

Never will be finished climbing, growing. Hell of a lot of stars these Florida nights.

"Say, this ought to be the house. No light in it. Well, I remember this half-fallin'-down gate. Still fallin' down. Hell, why don't it go on and fall? Two or three years, and ain't fell yet. Guess *she's* fell a hell of a lot, though. It don't take them yellow janes long to get old and ugly. Said she was seventeen then. A wonder her old woman let me come in the house that night. They acted like it was the first time a white man had ever come in the house. They acted scared. But she was worth the money that time all right. She played like a kid. Said she liked my red hair. Said she'd never had a white man before. . . . Holy Jesus, the yellow wenches I've had, though. . . . Well, it's the same old gate. Be funny if she had another mule in my stall, now wouldn't it? . . . Say, anybody home there?"

"Yes, suh! Yes, suh! Come right in!"

"Hell, I know they can't recognize my voice. . . . It's the old woman, sure as a yard arm's long. . . . Hello! Where's Betsy?"

"Yes, suh, right here, suh. In de kitchen. Wait till I lights de light. Come in. Come in, young gentleman."

"Hell, I can't see to come in."

Little flare of oil light.

"Howdy! Howdy do, suh! Howdy, if 'tain't Mister Clarence, now, 'pon my word! Howdy, Mister Clarence, howdy! Howdy! After sich a long time."

"You must-a knowed my voice."

"No, suh, ain't recollected, suh. No, suh, but I knowed you was some white man comin' up de walk. Yes, indeedy! Set down, set down. Betsy be here directly. Set *right* down. Lemme call her. She's in de kitchen. . . . You Betsy!"

"Same old woman, wrinkled as hell, and still don't care where the money comes from. Still talkin' loud. . . . She knew it was some white man comin' up the walk, heh? There must be plenty of 'em, then, comin' here now. She knew it was some white man, heh! . . . What yuh sayin', Betsy, old gal? Damn if yuh ain't just as plump as ever. Them same damn moles on your cheek! Com'ere, lemme feel 'em."

Young yellow girl in a white house dress. Oiled hair. Skin like an autumn moon. Gold-ripe young yellow girl with a white house dress to her knees. Soft plump bare legs, color of the moon. Barefooted.

"Say, Betsy, here is Mister Clarence come back."

"Sure is! Claren—Mister Clarence! Ma, give him a drink."

"Keepin' licker in the house, now, heh? Yes? I thought you was church members last time I saw yuh? You always had to send out and get licker then."

"Well, we's expectin' company some of the times these days," smiling teeth like bright-white rays of moon, Betsy, nearly twenty, and still pretty.

"You usin' rouge, too, ain't yuh?"

"Sweet rouge."

"Yal?"

"Yeah, man, sweet and red like your hair."

"Yal?"

No such wise-cracking three years ago. Too young and dumb for flirtation then: Betsy. Never like the old woman, talkative, "This here rum come right off de boats from Bermudy. Taste it, Mister Clarence. Strong enough to knock a mule down. Have a glass."

"Here's to you, Mister Clarence."

"Drinkin' licker, too, heh? Hell of a baby, ain't yuh? Yuh wouldn't even do that last time I saw yuh."

"Sure wouldn't, Mister Clarence, but three years a long time."

"Don't Mister Clarence *me* so much. Yuh know I christened yuh. . . . Auntie, yuh right about this bein' good licker."

"Yes, suh, I knowed you'd like it. It's strong."

"Sit on my lap, kid."

"Sure. . . ."

Soft heavy hips. Hot and browner than the moon—good licker. Drinking it down in little nigger house Florida coast palm fronds scratching roof hum mosquitoes night bugs flies ain't loud enough to keep a man named Clarence girl named Betsy old woman named Auntie from talking and drinking in a little nigger house on Florida coast dead warm night with the licker browner and more fiery than the moon. Yeah, man! A blanket of stars in the Florida sky—outside. In oil-lamp house you don't see no stars. Only a white man with red hair—third mate on a lousy tramp, a nigger girl, and Auntie wrinkled as an alligator bringing the fourth bottle of licker and everybody drinking—when the door . . . slowly . . . opens.

"Say, what the hell? Who's openin' that room door, peepin' in here? It can't be openin' itself?"

The white man stares intently, looking across the table, past the lamp, the licker-bottles, the glasses and the old woman, way past the girl. Standing in the door from the kitchen—Look! a damn red-headed baby. Standing not saying a damn word, a damn runt of a red-headed baby.

"What the hell?"

"You Clar—— . . . Mister Clarence, 'cuse me! . . . You hatian, you, get back to you' bed this minute—fo' I tan you in a inch o' yo' life!"

"Ma, let him stay."

Betsy's red-headed child stands in the door looking like one of those goggly-eyed dolls you hit with a ball at the County Fair. The child's face got no change in it. Never changes. Looks like never will change. Just staring—blue-eyed. Hell! God damn! A red-headed blue-eyed yellow-skinned baby!

"You Clarence! . . . 'Cuse me, Mister Clarence. I ain't talkin' to you suh. . . . You, Clarence, go to bed. . . . That chile near 'bout worries de soul-case out o' me. Betsy spiles him, that's why. De po' little thing can't hear, nohow. Just deaf as a post. And over two years old and can't even say, 'Da!' No, suh, can't say, 'Da!' "

"Anyhow, Ma, my child ain't blind."

"Might just as well be blind fo' all de good his eyesight do him. I show him a switch and he don't pay it no mind—'less'n I hit him."

"He's mighty damn white for a nigger child."

"Yes, suh, Mister Clarence. He really ain't got much colored blood in him, a-tall. Betsy's papa, Mister Clarence, now he were a white man, too. . . . Here, lemme pour you some licker. Drink, Mister Clarence, drink."

Damn little red-headed stupid-faced runt of a child, named Clarence. Bow-legged as hell, too. Three shots for a quarter like a loaded doll in a County Fair. Anybody take a chance. For Christ's sake, stop him from walking across the floor! Will yuh?

"Hey! Take your hands off my legs, you lousy little bastard!"

"He can't hear you, Mister Clarence."

"Tell him to stop crawlin' around then under the table before I knock his block off."

"You varmint. . . ."

"Hey! Take him up from there, will you?"

"Yes, suh, Mister Clarence."

"Hey!"

"You little . . ."

"Hurry! Go on! Get him out then! What's he doin' crawlin' round dumb as hell lookin' at me up at me. I said, *me*. Get him the hell out of here! Hey, Betsy, get him out!"

A red-headed baby. Moonlight-gone baby. No kind of yellow-white bow-legged goggled-eyed County Fair baseball baby. Get him the hell out of here pulling at my legs looking like me at me like me at myself like me red-headed as me.

"Christ!"

"Christ!"

Knocking over glasses by the oil-lamp on the table where the night flies flutter Florida where skeleton houses left over from boom sand in the road and no lights in the nigger section across the railroad's knocking over glasses at edge of town where a moon-colored girl's got a red-headed baby deaf as a post like the dolls you wham at three shots for a quarter in the County Fair half full of licker and can't hit nothing.

"Lemme pay for those drinks, will yuh? How much is it?"

"Ain't you gonna stay, Mister Clarence?"

"Lemme pay for my licker, I said."

"Ain't you gonna stay all night?"

"Lemme pay for that licker."

"Why, Mister Clarence? You stayed before."

"How much is the licker?"
"Two dollars, Mister Clarence."
"Here."
"Thank you, Mister Clarence."
"Go'bye!"
"Go'bye."

9
POOR LITTLE BLACK FELLOW

AMANDA LEE HAD been a perfect servant. And her husband Arnold likewise. That the Lord had taken them both so soon was a little beyond understanding. But then, of course, the Lord was just. And He had left the Pembertons poor little black Arnie as their Christian duty. There was no other way to consider the little colored boy whom they were raising as their own, *their very own*, except as a Christian duty. After all, they were white. It was no easy thing to raise a white child, even when it belonged to one, whereas this child was black, and had belonged to their servants, Amanda and Arnold.

But the Pembertons were never known to shirk a duty. They were one of New England's oldest families, one of the finest. They were wealthy. They had a family tree. They had a house in a charming maple-shaded town a few hours from Boston, a cottage at the beach, and four servants. On Tuesdays and Fridays Mr. Pemberton went to town. He had an office of some sort there. But the ladies, Grace Pemberton and her sister, sat on the wide porch at home and crocheted. Or maybe they let James take them for a drive in the car. One of them sang in the choir.

Sometimes they spoke about the two beautiful Negro servants they once had, Amanda and Arnold. They liked to tell poor little Arnie how faithful and lovely his parents had been in life. It would encourage the boy. At present, of course, all their servants were white. Negroes were getting so unsteady. You couldn't keep them in the villages any more. In fact, there were none in Mapleton now. They all went running off to Boston or New York, sporting their money away in the towns. Well, Amanda and Arnold were never like that. They had been simple, true, honest, hard-working. Their qualities had caused the Pembertons to give, over a space of time, more than ten thousand dollars to a school for Negroes at Hampton, Va. Because they thought they saw in Amanda and Arnold the real qualities of an humble and gentle race. That, too, was why they had decided to keep Arnie, poor little black fellow.

The Pembertons had lost nobody in the war except Arnold, their black stable man, but it had been almost like a personal loss. Indeed, after his death, they had kept horses no longer. And the stable had been turned into a garage.

Amanda, his wife, had grieved terribly, too. She had been all wrapped up in Arnold, and in her work with the Pembertons (she was their housekeeper) and in her little dark baby, Arnold, Junior. The child was five when his father went to war; and six when Amanda died of pneumonia a few weeks after they learned Arnold had been killed in the Argonne. The Pembertons were proud of him. A Negro who died for his country. But when that awful Winter of 1919 ended (the Pembertons judged it must have been awful from what they read), when that Winter ended the family was minus two perfect servants who could never come back. And they had on their hands an orphan.

"Poor little black fellow," said Grace Pemberton to her husband and her sister. "In memory of Arnold and Amanda, I think it is our Christian duty to keep it, and raise it up in the way it should go." Somehow, for a long time she called Arnie "it".

"We can raise it, without keeping it," said her husband. "Why not send it to Hampton?"

"Too young for that," said Emily, Mrs. Pemberton's sister. "I have been to Hampton, and they don't take them under twelve there."

So it was decided to keep the little black boy right in Mapleton, to send him to the village school, and to raise him up a good Christian and a good worker. And, it must be admitted, things went pretty well for some years. The white servants were kind to Arnie. The new housekeeper, a big-bosomed Irish woman who came after Amanda's death, treated him as though he were her very own, washed him and fed him. Indeed, they all treated him as if he were their very own.

II

MR. PEMBERTON TOOK Arnie to Boston once a season and bought him clothes. On his birthday, they gave him a party—on the lawn—because, after all, his birthday came in the Spring, and there was no need of filling the living-room with children. There was much more room on the lawn. In Summer Arnie went to the sea-shore with the rest of the family.

And Arnie, dark as he was, thrived. He grew up. He did well in his classes. He did well at home, helped with the chores about the house, raked the yard in the Fall, and shovelled snow when the long Winters set in. On Sundays he went to church with the family, listened to a dry and intelligent sermon, chanted the long hymns, and loved the anthems in which Miss Emily sang the solo parts.

Arnie, in church, a little black spot in a forest of white heads above stiff pews. Arnie, out of church, a symbol of how Christian charity should really be administered in the true spirit of the human brotherhood.

The church and the Pembertons were really a little proud of Arnie. Did they not all accept him as their own? And did they not go out of their way to be nice to him—a poor little black fellow whom they, through Christ, had taken in? Throughout the years the whole of Mapleton began to preen itself on its charity and kindness to Arnie. One would think that nobody in the town need ever again do a good deed: that this acceptance of a black boy was quite enough.

Arnie realized how they felt, but he didn't know what to do about it. He kept himself quiet and inconspicuous, and studied hard. He was very grateful, and very lonely. There were no other colored children in the town. But all the grown-up white people made their children be very nice to him, always very nice. "Poor little black boy," they said. "An orphan, and colored. And the Pembertons are so good to him. You be nice to him, too, do you hear? Share your lunch with him. And don't fight him. Or hurt his feelings. He's only a poor little Negro who has no parents." So even the children were over-kind to Arnie.

Everything might have been all right for ever had not Arnie begun to grow up. The other children began to grow up, too. Adolescence. The boys had girls. They played kissing games, and learned to dance. There were parties to which Arnie was not invited—really couldn't be invited—with the girls and all. And after generations of peace the village of Mapleton, and the Pembertons, found themselves beset with a Negro problem. Everyone was a little baffled and a little ashamed.

To tell the truth, everybody had got so used to Arnie that nobody really thought of him as a Negro—until he put on long trousers and went to high school. Now they noticed that he was truly very black. And his voice suddenly became deep and mannish, even before the white boys in Arnie's class talked in the cracks and squeaks of coming manhood.

Then there had arisen that problem of the Boy Scouts. When Arnie was sixteen the Pembertons applied for him to be admitted to a Summer camp for the Scouts at Barrow Beach, and the camp had refused. In a personal letter to Mr. Pemberton, they said they simply could not admit Negroes. Too many parents would object. So several of Arnie's friends and classmates went off to camp in June, and Arnie could not go. The village of Mapleton and the Pembertons felt awfully apologetic for American democracy's attitude to Arnie, whose father had died in the War. But, after all, they couldn't control the Boy Scout Camp. It was a semi-private institution. They were extra nice to Arnie, though—everybody.

That Summer, the Pembertons bought him a bicycle. And toward the end of the Summer (because they thought it was dull for him at the bungalow) they sent him to a Negro charity camp near Boston. It would be nice for him to come to know some of his own people. But Arnie hated it. He stayed a week and came home. The charity camp was full of black kids from the slums of Boston who cussed and fought and made fun of him because he didn't know how to play the dozens. So Arnie, to whom Negroes were a new nation, even if he was black, was amazed and bewildered, and came home. The Pembertons were embarrassed to find him alone in his attic room in the big empty house when they and the servants returned from the beach.

But they wanted so to be nice to him. They asked him if he'd met any friends he'd like to ask down for a week-end. They thought they would give him the whole top floor of the garage that year for a little apartment of his own and he could have his colored friends there. But Arnie hadn't met anyone he wanted to have. He had no colored friends.

The Pembertons knew that he couldn't move in the social world of Mapleton much longer. He was too big. But, really, what could they do? Grace Pemberton prayed. Emily talked it over with the mission board at church, and Mr. Pemberton spoke to the Urban League in Boston. Why not send him to Hampton now?

Arnie had only one more year in the high school. Then, of course, he would go to college. But to one of the nicer Negro colleges like Fisk, they decided, where those dear Jubilee singers sang so beautifully, and where he would be with his own people, and wouldn't be embarrassed. No, Fisk wasn't as good as Harvard, they knew, but then Arnie had to find his own world after all. They'd have to let him go, poor black fellow! Certainly, he was their very own! But in Mapleton, what could he do, how could he live, whom could he marry? The Pembertons were a bit worried, even, about this one more year. So they decided to be extra nice to him. Indeed, everybody in Mapleton decided to be extra nice to him.

The two rooms over the garage made a fine apartment for a growing boy. His pennants and books and skis were there. Sometimes the white boys came in the evenings and played checkers and smoked forbidden cigarettes. Sometimes they walked out and met the girls at the soda-fountain in Dr. Jourdain's drugstore, and Arnie had a soda with the group. But he always came away alone, while the others went off in pairs. When the Christmas parties were being given, many of the girls were lovely in dresses that looked almost like real evening gowns, but Arnie wasn't invited anywhere but to the Allens'. (And they really didn't count in Mapleton—they were very poor white folks.)

The Pembertons were awfully sorry, of course. They were one of New England's oldest families, and they were raising Arnie as their son. But he was an African, a nice Christian African, and he ought to move among his own people. There he could be a good influence and have a place. The Pembertons couldn't help it that there were no Negroes in Mapleton. Once there had been some, but now they had all moved away. It was more fashionable to have white help. And even as a servant in Mapleton, Arnie would have been a little out of place. But he was smart in school, and a good clean boy. He sang well. (All Negroes were musical.) He skated and swam and played ball. He loved and obeyed the Pembertons. They wanted him to find his place in the world, poor fine little black fellow. Poor dear Arnie.

So it was decided that he would go to Fisk next year. When Arnie agreed, the Pembertons breathed a sort of sigh of joy. They thought he might remember the camp at Boston, and not want to go to a Negro college.

III

AND NOW THE Summer presented itself, the last Summer before they let Arnie go away—the boy whom they'd raised as their own. They didn't want that last Summer spoiled for him. Or for them. They wanted no such incidents as the Boy Scout business. The Pembertons were kind people. They wanted Arnie to remember with pleasure his life with them.

Maybe it would be nice to take him to Europe. They themselves had not been abroad for a long time. Arnie could see Paris and his father's grave and the Tower of London. The

Pembertons would enjoy the trip, too. And on their return, Arnie could go directly to Fisk, where his life at college, and in the grown-up world, would begin. Maybe he'd marry one of those lovely brown girls who sang spirituals so beautifully, and live a good Christian man—occasionally visiting the Pembertons, and telling them about his influence on the poor black people of the South.

Graduation came. Arnie took high honors in the class, and spoke on the program. He went to the senior prom, but he didn't dance with any of the girls. He just sort of stood around the punch-bowl, and joked with the fellows. So nobody was embarrassed, and everyone was glad to see him there. The one dark spot in a world of whiteness. It was too bad he didn't have a partner to stand with him when they sang the Alma Mater after the final dance. But he was a lucky chap to be going to Europe. Not many youngsters from Mapleton had been. The Pembertons were doing well by him, everybody said aloud, and the church board had got him into Fisk.

But with all their careful planning, things weren't going so well about the European trip. When the steamship company saw the passports, they cancelled the cabin that had been engaged for Arnie. Servants always went second class, they wrote. That Arnie wasn't a servant, it was revealed ultimately, made no difference. He was a Negro, wasn't he?

So it ended with the Pembertons going first, and Arnie second class on the same boat. They would have all gone second, out of sympathy for Arnie, except that accommodations in that class had been completely booked for months ahead. Only as a great favor to first-class passengers had the steamship company managed to find a place for Arnie at all. The Pembertons and their boy had a cross to bear, but they bore it like Christians. At Cherbourg they met the little black fellow again on an equal footing. The evening found them in Paris.

Paris, loveliest of cities, where at dusk the lights are a great necklace among the trees of the Champs Elysées. Paris, song-city of the world. Paris, with the lips of a lovely woman kissing without fear. June, in Paris.

The Pembertons stopped at one of the best hotels. They had a suite which included a room for Arnie. Everything was very nice. The Louvre and the Eiffel Tower and the Café de la Paix were very nice. All with Arnie. Very nice. Everything would have gone on perfectly, surely; and there would have been no story, and Arnie and the Pembertons would have continued in Christian love for ever—Arnie at Fisk, of course, and the Pembertons at Mapleton, then Arnie married and the Pembertons growing old, and so on and on—had not Claudina Lawrence moved into the very hotel where the Pembertons were staying. Claudina Lawrence! My God!

True, they had all seen dark faces on the boulevards, and a Negro quartet at the Olympia, but only very good Americans and very high English people were staying at this hotel with the Pembertons. Then Claudina Lawrence moved in—the Claudina who had come from Atlanta, Georgia, to startle the Old World with the new beauty of brown flesh behind footlights. That Claudina who sang divinely and danced like a dryad and had amassed a terrible amount of fame and money in five years. Even the Pembertons had heard of Claudina Lawrence in the quiet and sedate village of Mapleton. Even Arnie had heard of her. And Arnie had been a little bit proud. She was a Negro.

But why did she have to move next door to the Pembertons in this hotel? "Why, Lord, oh, why?" said Grace Pemberton. "For the sake of Arnie, why?" But here the tale begins.

IV

A LOT OF YOUNG Negroes, men and women, shiny and well-dressed, with good and sophisticated manners, came at all hours to see Claudina. Arnie and the Pembertons would meet them in the hall. They were a little too well dressed to suit the Pembertons. They came with white people among them, too—very pretty French girls. And they were terribly lively and gay and didn't seem dependent on anybody. Their music floated out of the windows on the Summer night. The Pembertons hoped they wouldn't get hold of Arnie. They would be a bad influence.

But they did get hold of Arnie.

One morning, as he came out to descend to the lobby to buy post-cards, Claudina herself stepped into the hall at the same time. They met at the elevator. She was the loveliest creature Arnie had ever seen. In pink, all tan and glowing. And she was colored.

"Hello," she said to the young black boy who looked old enough to be less shy. "You look like a home-towner."

"I'm from Mapleton," Arnie stuttered.

"You sound like you're from London," said Claudina, noting his New England accent and confusing it with Mayfair. "But your face says Alabama."

"Oh, I'm colored all right," said Arnie, happy to be recognized by one of his own. "And I'm glad to know you."

"Having a good time?" asked Claudina, as the elevator came.

"No," Arnie said, suddenly truthful. "I don't know anybody."

"Jesus!" said Claudina, sincerely. "That's a shame. A lot of boys and girls are always gathering in my place. Knock on the door some time. I can't see one of my down-home boys getting the blues in Paris. Some of the fellows in my band'll take you around a bit, maybe. They know all the holes and corners. Come in later."

"Thanks awfully," said Arnie.

Claudina left him half-dazed in the lobby. He saw her get into her car at the curb, saw the chauffeur tip his hat, and then drive away. For the first time in his life Arnie was really happy. Somebody had offered him something without charity, without condescension, without prayer, without distance, and without being nice.

All the pictures in the Luxembourg blurred before his eyes that afternoon, and Miss Emily's explanations went in one ear and out the other. He was thinking about Claudina and the friends he might meet in her rooms, the gay and well-dressed Negroes he had seen in the hall, the Paris they could show him, the girls they would be sure to know.

That night he went to see Claudina. He told the Pembertons he didn't care about going to the Odéon, so they went without him, a little reluctantly—because they didn't care about going either, really. They had been sticking rather strenuously to their program of cultural Paris. They were tired. Still, the Pembertons went to the Odéon—it was a play they really should see—and Arnie went next door to Claudina's. But only after he was sure the Pembertons were sitting in the theatre.

Claudina was playing whist. A young Englishman was her partner. Two sleek young colored men were their opponents. "Sit down, honey," Claudina said as if he had known Arnie for years. "You can take a hand in a minute, if you'd like to play. Meet Mr. So and so and so. . . ." She introduced him to the group. "It's kinda early yet. Most of our gang are at work. The theatres aren't out. . . . Marie, bring him a drink." And the French maid poured a cocktail.

A knock, and a rather portly brown-skinned woman, beautifully dressed, entered. "Hello! Who's holding all the trump cards? Glad to meet you, Mr. Arnie. From Boston, you say? My old stamping-ground. Do you know the Roundtrees there?"

"No'm," Arnie said.

"Well, I used to study at the Conservatory and knew all the big shots," the brown-skin woman went on. "Did you just come over? Tourist, heh? Well, what's new in the States now? I haven't been home for three years. Don't intend to go soon. The color line's a little too much for me. What are they dancing now-a-days? You must've brought a few of the latest steps with you. Can you do the Lindy Hop?"

"No'm," said Arnie.

"Well, I'm gonna see," said the brown-skin lady. She put a record on the victrola, and took Arnie in her arms. Even if he couldn't do the Lindy Hop, he enjoyed dancing with her and they got along famously. Several more people came in, a swell-looking yellow girl, some rather elderly musicians, in spats, and a young colored art student named Harry Jones. Cocktails went around.

"I'm from Chicago," Harry said eventually. "Been over here about a year and like it a hell of a lot. You will, too, soon as you get to know a few folks."

Gradually the room took on the life and gaiety of a party. Somebody sat down at a piano in the alcove, and started a liquid ripple of jazz. Three or four couples began to dance. Arnie and the lovely yellow girl got together. They danced a long time, and then they drank cocktails. Arnie forgot about the clock. It was long after midnight.

Somebody suggested that they all go to the opening of a new Martinique ball room where a native orchestra would play rattles and drums.

"Come on, Arnie," Harry Jones said. "You might as well make a night of it. Tomorrow's Sunday."

"I start rehearsals tomorrow," Claudina said, "so I can't go. But listen here," she warned. "Don't you-all take Arnie out of here and lose him. Some of these little French girls are liable to put him in their pockets, crazy as they are about chocolate."

Arnie hoped he wouldn't meet the Pembertons in the hall. He didn't. They were long since in bed. And when Arnie came in at dawn, his head was swimming with the grandest night he'd ever known.

At the Martinique ball he'd met dozens of nice girls: white girls and brown girls, and yellow girls, artists and students and dancers and models and tourists. Harry knew everybody. And everybody was gay and friendly. Paris and music and cocktails made you forget what color people were—and what color you were yourself. Here it didn't matter—color.

Arnie went to sleep dreaming about a little Rumanian girl named Vivi. Harry said she was a music student. But Arnie didn't care what she was, she had such soft black hair and bright grey eyes. How she could dance! And she knew quite a little English. He'd taken her address. Tomorrow he would go to see her. Aw, hell, tomorrow the Pembertons wanted to go to Versailles!

V

WHEN ARNIE WOKE up it was three o'clock. This time Grace Pemberton had actually banged on the door. Arnie was frightened. He'd never slept so late before. What would the Pembertons think?

"What ever is the matter, Arnold?" Mrs. Pemberton called. Only when she was put out did she call him Arnold.

"Up late reading," Arnie muttered through the closed door. "I was up late reading." And then was promptly ashamed of himself for having lied.

"Well, hurry up," Mrs. Pemberton said. "We're about to start for Versailles."

"I don't want to go," said Arnie.

"What ever is the matter with you, boy?" gasped Grace Pemberton.

Arnie had slipped on a bathrobe, so he opened the door.

"Good morning," he said. "I've met some friends. I want to go out with them."

The contrariness of late adolescence was asserting itself. He felt stubborn and mean.

"Friends?" said Grace Pemberton. "What friends, may I ask?"

"A colored student and some others."

"Where did you meet them?"

"Next door, at Miss Lawrence's."

Grace Pemberton stiffened like a bolt. "Get ready, young man," she said, "and come with us to Versailles." She left the room. The young man got ready.

Arnie pouted, but he went with the Pembertons. The sun gave him a headache, and he didn't give a damn about Versailles. That evening, after a private lecture by Mr. Pemberton on the evils of Paris (Grace and Emily had spoken about the beauty of the city), he went to bed feeling very black and sick.

For several days, he wasn't himself at all, what with constant excursions to museums and villages and chateaux, when he wanted to be with Vivi and Harry and Claudina. (Once he did sneak away with Harry to meet Vivi.) Meanwhile, the Pembertons lectured him on his surliness. They were inclined to be dignified and distant to the poor little black fellow now. After all, it had cost them quite a lot to bring him to Paris. Didn't he appreciate what they were doing for him? They had raised him. Had they then no right to forbid him going about with a crowd of Negroes from the theatres?

"He's a black devil," said Mr. Pemberton.

"Poor little fellow," said Grace. She was a little sorry for him.

"After all, he doesn't know. He's young. Let us just try loving him, and being very nice to him."

So once again the Pembertons turned loose on Arnie their niceness. They took him to the races, and they bought him half a dozen French ties from a good shop, and they treated him better than if he were their own.

But Arnie was worse than ever. He stayed out all night one night. Grace knew, because she knocked on his door at two o'clock. And the Negroes next door, how they laughed! How they danced! How the music drifted through the windows. It seemed as if the actual Devil had got into Arnie. Was he going to the dogs before their very eyes? Grace Pemberton was worried. After all, he *was* the nearest thing she'd ever had to a son. She was really fond of him.

As for Arnie, it wasn't the Devil at all that had got him. It wasn't even Claudina. It was Vivi, the little girl he'd met through Harry at the Martinique ball. The girl who played Chopin on the piano, and had grey eyes and black hair and came from Rumania. By himself, Arnie had managed to find, from the address she had given him, the tall house near the Parc Monceau where she lived in an attic room. Up six flights of stairs he walked. He found her with big books on theory in front of her and blank music pages, working out some sort of exercise in harmony. Her little face was very white, her grey eyes very big, and her black hair all fluffy around her head.

Arnie didn't know why he had come to see her except that he liked her very much.

They talked all afternoon and Arnie told her about his life at home, how white people had raised him, and how hard it was to be black in America. Vivi said it didn't make any difference in Rumania, or in Paris either, about being black.

"Here it's only hard to be poor," Vivi said.

But Arnie thought he wouldn't mind being poor in a land where it didn't matter what color you were.

"Yes, you would mind," Vivi said. "Being poor's not easy anywhere. But then," and her eyes grew bigger, "by and by the Revolution will come. In Rumania the Revolution will come. In France, too. Everywhere poor people are tired of being poor."

"What Revolution?" Arnie asked, for he hadn't heard about it in Mapleton.

Vivi told him.

"Where we live, it's quiet," he said. "My folks come from Massachusetts."

VI

AND THEN THE devil whispered to Arnie. Maybe Vivi would like to meet some real Americans. Anyway, he would like the Pembertons to meet her. He'd like to show them that there actually was a young white girl in the world who didn't care about color. They were always educating him. He would educate them a bit. So Arnie invited Vivi to dinner at the hotel that very night.

The Pembertons had finished their soup when he entered the sparkling dining-room of the hotel. He made straight for their table. The orchestra was playing Strauss. Gentlemen in evening clothes and ladies in diamonds scanned a long and expensive menu. The Pembertons looked up and saw Arnie coming, guiding Vivi by the hand. Grace Pemberton gasped and put her spoon back in the soup. Emily went pale. Mr. Pemberton's mouth opened. All the Americans stared. Such a white, white girl and such a black, black boy coming across the dining-room floor! The girl had a red mouth and grey eyes.

The Pembertons had been waiting for Arnie since four o'clock. Today a charming Indian mystic, Nadjuti, had come to tea with them, especially to see the young Negro student they had raised in America. The Pembertons were not pleased that Arnie had not been there.

"This is my friend," Arnie said. "I've brought her to dinner."

Vivi smiled and held out her hand, but the Pembertons bowed in their stiffest fashion. Nobody noticed her hand.

"I'm sorry," said Grace Pemberton, "but there's room for only four at our table."

"Oh," said Arnie. He hadn't thought they'd be rude. Polite and formal, maybe, but not rude. "Oh! Don't mind us then. Come on, Vivi." His eyes were red as he led her away to a vacant table by the fountain. A waiter came and took their orders with the same deference he showed everyone else. The Pembertons looked and could not eat.

"Where ever did he get her?" whispered Emily in her thin New England voice, as her cheeks burned. "Is she a woman from the streets?" The Pembertons couldn't imagine that so lovely a white girl would go out with a strange Negro unless she were a prostitute. They were terribly mortified. What would he do next?

"But maybe he doesn't know. Did you warn him, John?" Grace Pemberton addressed her husband.

"I did," replied Mr. Pemberton shortly.

"A scarlet woman," said Emily faintly. "A scarlet . . . I think I shall go to my room. All the Americans in the dining-room must have seen." She was white as she rose. "We've been talked about enough as it is—travelling with a colored boy. For our sakes, he might have been careful."

The Pembertons left the dining-room. But Grace Pemberton was afraid for Arnie. Near the door, she turned and came over to the table by the fountain. "Please, Arnold, come to my room before you go."

"Yes, Miss Grace, I'll come," he said.

"You mustn't mind." Vivi patted his arm. The orchestra was playing "The Song of India." "All old people are the same."

As they ate, Vivi and Arnie talked about parents. Vivi told him how her folks hadn't allowed her to come away to study music, how they'd even tried to stop her at the station. "Most elderly people are terrible," she said, "especially parents."

"But they're not my parents," Arnie said. "They are white people."

When he took Vivi home, he kissed her. Then he came back and knocked on the living-room door.

VII

"COME IN," Grace Pemberton said. "Come in, Arnie, I want to talk to you." She was sitting there alone, very straight with her iron-grey hair low on her neck. "Poor little black fellow," she said, as through Arnie had done a great and careless wrong. "Come here."

When Arnie saw her pale white face from the door, he was a little sad and ashamed that he might have done something to hurt her. But when she began to pity him, "poor little black fellow," a sudden anger shook him from head to foot. His eyes grew sultry and red, his spirit stubborn.

"Arnold," she said, "I think we'd better go home, back to America."

"I don't want to go," he replied.

"But you don't seem to appreciate what we are doing for you here," she said, "at all."

"I don't," Arnie answered.

"You don't!" Grace Pemberton's throat went dry. "You don't? We're showing you the best of Paris, and you don't? Why, we've done all we could for you always, Arnie boy. We've raised you as our own. And we want to do more. We're going to send you to college, of course, to Fisk this Fall."

"I don't want to go to Fisk," Arnie said.

"What?"

"No," said Arnie. "I don't want to go. It'll be like that camp in Boston. Everything in America's like that camp in Boston." His eyes grew redder. "Separate, segregated, shut-off! Black people kept away from everybody else. I go to Fisk; my classmates, Harvard and Amherst and Yale . . . I sleep in the garage, you sleep in the house."

"Oh," Grace Pemberton said. "We didn't mean it like that!"

Arnie was being cruel, just cruel. She began, in spite of herself, to cry.

"I don't want to go back home," Arnie went on. "I hate America."

"But your father *died* for America," Grace Pemberton cried.

"I guess he was a fool," said Arnie.

The hall door opened. Mr. Pemberton and his sister-in-law came in from a walk through the park. They saw Mrs. Pemberton's eyes wet, and Arnie's sultry face. Mrs. Pemberton told them what he'd said.

"So you want to stay here," said Mr. Pemberton, trying to hold his temper. "Well, stay. Take your things and stay. Stay now. Get out! Go!"

Anger possessed him, fury against this ungrateful black boy who made his wife cry. Grace Pemberton never cried over anything Mr. Pemberton did. And now, she was crying over this . . . this . . . In the back of his mind was the word *nigger.* Arnold felt it.

"I want to go," said Arnie. "I've always wanted to go."

"You little black fool!" said Emily.

"Where will you go?" Grace Pemberton asked. Why, oh why, didn't Arnie say he was sorry, beg their pardon, and stay? He knew he could if he wanted to.

"I'll go to Vivi," Arnie said.

"Vivi?" a weak voice gasped.

"Yes, marry Vivi!"

"Marry white, eh?" said Mr. Pemberton. Emily laughed drily. But Grace Pemberton fainted.

Next door, just then, the piano was louder than ever.

Somebody was doing a tap-dance. The dancing and the music floated through the windows on the soft Paris air. Outside, the lights were a necklace of gold over the Champs Elysées. Autos honked. Trees rustled. People passed.

Arnie went out.

10
LITTLE DOG

MISS BRIGGS HAD a little apartment all alone in a four-story block just where Oakwood Drive curved past the park and the lake. Across the street, beneath her window, kids skated in winter, and in the spring the grass grew green. In summer, lovers walked and necked by the lake in the moonlight. In fall brown and red-gold leaves went skithering into the water when the wind blew.

Miss Briggs came home from work every night at eight, unless she went to the movies or the Women's Civics Club. On Sunday evenings she sometimes went to a lecture on Theosophy. But she was never one to gad about, Miss Briggs. Besides she worked too hard. She was the head bookkeeper for the firm of Wilkins and Bryant, Wood, Coal And Coke. And since 1930, when they had cut down the staff, she had only one assistant. Just two of them now to take care of the books, bills, and everything. But Miss Briggs was very efficient. She had been head bookkeeper for twenty-one years. Wilkins and Bryant didn't know what they would do without her.

Miss Briggs was proud of her record as a bookkeeper. Once the City Hall had tried to get her, but Wilkins and Bryant said, "No, indeed. We can pay as much as the city, if not more. You stay right here with us." Miss Briggs stayed. She was never a person to move about much or change jobs.

As a young girl she had studied very hard in business school. She never had much time to go out. A widowed mother, more or less dependent on her then, later became completely dependent—paralyzed. Her mother had been dead for six years now.

Perhaps it was the old woman's long illness that had got Miss Briggs in the habit of staying home every night in her youth, instead of going out to the theatre or to parties. They had never been able to afford a maid even after Miss Briggs became so well paid—for doctors' bills were such a drain, and in those last months a trained nurse was needed for her mother—God rest her soul.

Now, alone, Miss Briggs usually ate her dinner in the Rose Bud Tea Shoppe. A number of genteel business women ate there, and the colored waiters were so nice. She had been served by Joe or Perry, flat-footed old Negro gentlemen, for three or four years now. They knew her tastes, and would get the cook to make little special dishes for her if she wasn't feeling very well.

After dinner, with a walk of five or six blocks from the Rose Bud, the park would come into view with its trees and lights. The Lyle Apartments loomed up. A pretty place to live, facing the park. Miss Briggs had moved there after her mother died. Trying to keep house alone was just a little too much. And there was no man in view to marry. Most of them would want her only for her money now, at her age, anyway. To move with another woman, Miss Briggs thought, would be a sort of sacrilege so soon after her mother's death. Besides, she really didn't know any other woman who, like herself, was without connections. Almost everybody had somebody, Miss Briggs reflected. Every woman she knew had either a husband, or sisters, or a friend of long standing with whom she resided. But Miss Briggs had nobody at all. Nobody.

Not that she thought about it very much. Miss Briggs was too used to facing the world alone, minding her own business, and going her own way. But one summer, while returning from Michigan where she had taken her two weeks' rest, as she came through Cleveland, on her way from the boat to the station there, she happened to pass a dog shop with a window full of fuzzy little white dogs. Miss Briggs called to the taxi man to stop. She got out and went in. When she came back to the taxi, she carried a little white dog named Flips. At least, the dealer said he had been calling it Flips because its ears were so floppy.

"They just flip and flop," the man said, smiling at the tall middle-aged woman.

"How much is he?" Miss Briggs asked, holding the puppy up.

"I'll let you have him for twenty-five dollars," the man said.

Miss Briggs put the puppy down. She thought that was a pretty steep price. But there was something about Flips that she liked, so she picked him up again and took him with her. After all, she allowed herself very few indulgences. And somehow, this summer, Miss Briggs sort of hated going back to an empty flat—even if it did overlook the park.

Or maybe it was because it overlooked the park that had made it so terrible a place to live lately. Miss Briggs had never felt lonely, not *very* lonely, in the old house after her mother died. Only when she moved to the flat, did her loneliness really come down on her. There were some nights there, especially summer nights, when she thought she couldn't stand it, to sit in her window and see so many people going by, couple by couple, arms locked; or else in groups, laughing and talking. Miss Briggs wondered why she knew no one, male or female, to walk out with, laughing and talking. She knew only the employees where she worked, and with whom she associated but little (for she hated to have people know her business). She knew, of course, the members of the Women's Civics Club, but in a cultural sort of way. The warmth of friendship seldom mellowed her contacts there. Only one or two of the club women had ever called on her. Miss Briggs always believed in keeping her distance, too. Her mother used to say she'd been born poor but proud, and would stay that way.

"Folks have to amount to something before Clara takes up with them," old Mrs. Briggs always said. "Men'll have a hard time getting Clara."

Men did. Now, with no especial attractions to make them keep trying, Miss Briggs, tall and rail-like, found herself left husbandless at an age when youth had gone.

So, in her forty-fifth year, coming back from a summer boarding house in Michigan, Miss Briggs bought herself a little white dog. When she got home, she called on the janitor and asked him to bring her up a small box for Flips. The janitor, a tow-headed young Swede, brought her a grapefruit crate from the A. & P. Miss Briggs put it in the kitchen for Flips.

She told the janitor to bring her, too, three times a week, a dime's worth of dog meat or bones, and leave it on the back porch where she could find it when she came home. On other nights, Flips ate dog biscuits.

Flips and Miss Briggs soon settled on a routine. Each evening when she got home she would feed him. Then she would take him for a walk. This gave Miss Briggs an excuse for getting out, too. In warm weather she would walk around the little lake fronting her apartment with Flips on a string. Sometimes she would even smile at other people walking around the lake with dogs at night. It was nice the way dogs made things friendly. It was nice the way people with dogs smiled at her occasionally because she had a dog, too. But whenever (as seldom happened) someone in the park, dog or no dog, tried to draw her into conversation, Miss Briggs would move on as quickly as she could without being rude. You could never tell just who people were, Miss Briggs thought, or what they might have in their minds. No, you shouldn't think of taking up with strange people in parks. Besides, she was head bookkeeper for Wilkins and Bryant, and in these days of robberies and kidnappings maybe they just wanted to find out when she went for the pay roll, and how much cash the firm kept on hand. Miss Briggs didn't trust people.

Always, by ten o'clock, she was back with Flips in her flat. A cup of hot milk then maybe, with a little in a saucer for Flips, and to bed. In the morning she would let Flips run down the back steps for a few minutes, then she gave him more milk, left a pan of water, and went to work. A regular routine, for Miss Briggs took care of Flips with great seriousness. At night when she got back from the Rose Bud Tea Shoppe, she fed him biscuits; or if it were dog meat night, she looked out on the back porch for the package the janitor was paid to leave. (That is, Miss Briggs allowed the Swede fifty cents a week to buy bones. He could keep the change.)

But one night, the meat was not there. Miss Briggs thought perhaps he had forgotten. Still he had been bringing it regularly for nearly two years. Maybe the warm spring this year made the young janitor listless, Miss Briggs mused. She fed Flips biscuits.

But two days later, another dog meat night, the package was not there either. "This is too much!" thought Miss Briggs. "Come on, Flipsy, let's go downstairs and see. I'm sure I gave him fifty cents this week to buy your bones."

Miss Briggs and the little white beast went downstairs to ask why there was no meat for her dog to eat. When they got to the janitor's quarters in the basement, they heard a mighty lot of happy laughter and kids squalling, and people moving. They didn't sound like Swedes, either. Miss Briggs was a bit timid about knocking, but she finally mustered up courage with Flips there beside her. A sudden silence fell inside.

"You Leroy," a voice said. "Go to de door."

A child's feet came running. The door opened like a flash and a small colored boy stood there grinning.

"Where—where is the janitor?" Miss Briggs said, taken aback.

"You mean my papa?" asked the child, looking at the gaunt white lady. "He's here." And off he went to call his father.

Surrounded by children, a tall broad-shouldered Negro of perhaps forty, gentle of face and a little stooped, came to the door.

"Good evenin'," he said pleasantly.

"Why, are you the janitor?" stammered Miss Briggs. Flips had already begun to jump up on him with friendly mien.

"Yes'm, I'm the new janitor," said the Negro in a softly beautiful voice, kids all around him. "Is there something I can help you to do?"

"Well," said Miss Briggs, "I'd like some bones for my little dog. He's missed his meat two times now. Can you get him some?"

"Yes'm, sure can," said the new janitor, "if all the stores ain't closed." He was so much taller than Miss Briggs that she had to look up at him.

"I'd appreciate it," said Miss Briggs, "please."

As she went back upstairs she heard the new janitor calling in his rich voice, "Lora, you reckon that meat store's still open?"

And a woman's voice and a lot of children answered him.

It turned out that the store was closed. So Miss Briggs gave the Negro janitor ten cents and told him to have the meat there the next night when she came home.

"Flips, you shan't starve," she said to the little white dog, "new janitor or no new janitor."

"Wruff!" said Flips.

But the next day when she came home there was no meat on the back porch either. Miss Briggs was puzzled, and a little hurt. Had the Negro forgotten?

Scarcely had she left the kitchen, however, when someone knocked on the back door and there stood the colored man with the meat. He was almost as old as Miss Briggs, she was certain of it, looking at him. Not a young man at all, but he was awfully big and brown and kind looking. So sort of sure about life as he handed her the package.

"I thought some other dog might get it if I left it on the porch," said the colored man. "So I kept it downstairs till you come."

Miss Briggs was touched. "Well, thank you very much," she said.

When the man had gone, she remembered that she had not told him how often to get meat for the dog.

The next night he came again with bones, and every night from then on. Miss Briggs did not stop him, or limit him to three nights a week. Just after eight, whenever she got home, up the back porch steps the Negro would come with the dog meat. Sometimes there would be two or three kids with him. Pretty little brown-black rather dirty kids, Miss Briggs thought, who were shy in front of her, but nice.

Once or twice during the spring, the janitor's wife, instead, brought the dog meat up on Saturday nights. Flips barked rudely at her. Miss Briggs didn't take to the creature, either. She was fat and yellow, and certainly too old to just keep on having children as she evidently did. The janitor himself was so solid and big and strong! Miss Briggs felt better when he brought her the bones for her dog. She didn't like his wife.

That June, on warm nights, as soon as she got home, Miss Briggs would open the back door and let the draft blow through. She could hear the janitor better coming up the rear stairs when he brought the bones. And, of course, she never said more than good-evening to him and thank you. Or here's a dollar for the week. Keep the change.

Flips ate an awful lot of meat that spring. "Your little dog's a regular meat-hound," the janitor said one night as he handed her the bones; and Miss Briggs blushed, for no good reason.

"He does eat a lot," she said. "Goodnight."

As she spread the bones out on paper for the dog, she felt that her hands were trembling. She left Flips eating and went into the parlor, but found that she could not keep her mind on the book she was reading. She kept looking at the big kind face of the janitor in her mind, perturbed that it was a Negro face, and that it stayed with her so.

The next night, she found herself waiting for the dog meat to arrive with more anxiety than Flips himself. When the colored man handed it to her, she quickly closed the door, before her face got red again.

"Funny old white lady," thought the janitor as he went back downstairs to his basement full of kids. "Just crazy about that dog," he added to his wife. "I ought to tell her it ain't good to feed a dog so much meat."

"What do you care, long as she wants to?" asked his wife.

The next day in the office Miss Briggs found herself making errors over the books. That night she hurried home to be sure and be there on time when he brought the dog meat up, in case he came early.

"What's the matter with me," she said sharply to herself, "rushing this way just to feed Flips? Whatever is the matter with me?" But all the way through the warm dusky streets, she seemed to hear the janitor's deep voice saying, "Good evenin'," to her.

Then, when the Negro really knocked on the door with the meat, she was trembling so that she could not go to the kitchen to get it. "Leave it right there by the sink," she managed to call out. "Thank you, Joe."

She heard the man going back downstairs sort of humming to himself, a kid or so following him. Miss Briggs felt as if she were going to faint, but Flips kept jumping up on her, barking for his meat.

"Oh, Flips," she said, "I'm so hungry." She meant to say, "*You're* so hungry." So she repeated it. "You're so hungry! Heh, Flipsy, dog?"

And from the way the little dog barked, he must have been hungry. He loved meat.

The next evening, Miss Briggs was standing in the kitchen when the colored man came with the bones.

"Lay them down," she said, "thank you," trying not to look at him. But as he went downstairs, she watched through the window his beautifully heavy body finding the rhythm of the steps, his big brown neck moving just a little.

"Get down!" she said sharply to Flips barking for his dinner.

To herself she said earnestly, "I've got to move. I can't be worried being so far from a meat shop, or from where I eat my dinner. I think I'll move downtown where the shops are open at night. I can't stand this. Most of my friends live downtown anyway."

But even as she said it, she wondered what friends she meant. She had a little white dog named Flips, that was all. And she was acquainted with other people who worked at Wilkins and Bryant, but she had nothing to do with them. She was the head bookkeeper. She knew a few women in the Civics Club fairly well. And the Negro waiters at the Rose Bud Shoppe.

And this janitor!

Miss Briggs decided that she could not bear to have this janitor come upstairs with a package of bones for Flips again. She was sure he was happy down there with his portly yellow wife and his house full of children. Let him stay in the basement, then, where he belonged. She never wanted to see him again, never.

The next night, Miss Briggs made herself go to a movie

before coming home. And when she got home, she fed Flips dog biscuits. That week she began looking for a new apartment, a small one for two, her and the dog. Fortunately there were plenty to be had, what with people turned out for not being able to pay their rent—which would never happen to her, thank God! She had saved her money. When she found an apartment, she deposited the first month's rent at once. On her coming Saturday afternoon off, she planned to move.

Friday night, when the janitor came up with the bones, she decided to be just a little pleasant to him. Probably she would never see him again. Perhaps she would give him a dollar for a tip, then. Something to remember her by.

When he came upstairs, she was aware a long time of his feet approaching. Coming up, up, up, bringing bones for her dog. Flips began to bark. Miss Briggs went to the door. She took the package in one hand. With the other she offered the bill.

"Thank you so much for buying bones for my little dog," she said. "Here, here is a dollar for your trouble. You keep it all."

"Much obliged, m'am," said the astonished janitor. He had never seen Miss Briggs so generous before. "Thank you, m'am! He sure do eat a heap o' bones, your little dog."

"He almost keeps me broke buying bones," Miss Briggs said, holding the door.

"True," said the janitor. "But I reckon you don't have much other expenses on hand, do you? No family and all like me?"

"You're right," answered Miss Briggs. "But a little dog is so much company, too."

"Guess they are, m'am," said the janitor, turning to go. "Well, goodnight, Miss Briggs. I'm much obliged."

"Goodnight, Joe."

As his broad shoulders and tall brown body disappeared down the stairs, Miss Briggs slowly turned her back, shut the door, and put the bones on the floor for Flipsy. Then suddenly she began to cry.

The next day she moved away as she had planned to do. The janitor never saw her any more. For a few days, the walkers in the park beside the lake wondered where a rather gaunt middle-aged woman who used to come out at night with a little white dog had gone. But in a very short while the neighborhood had completely forgotten her.

11
BERRY

WHEN THE BOY arrived on the four o'clock train, lo and behold, he turned out to be colored! Mrs. Osborn saw him the minute he got out of the station wagon, but certainly there was nothing to be done about it that night—with no trains back to the city before morning—so she set him to washing dishes. Lord knows there were a plenty. The Scandinavian kitchen boy had left right after breakfast, giving no notice, leaving her and the cook to do everything. Her wire to the employment office in Jersey City brought results—but dark ones. The card said his name was Milberry Jones.

Well, where was he to sleep? Heretofore, the kitchen boy and the handy-man gardener-chauffeur shared the same quarters. But Mrs. Osborn had no idea how the handy-man might like Negroes. Help were so touchy, and it was hard keeping good servants in the country. So right after dinner, leaving Milberry with his arms in the dish water, Mrs. Osborn made a bee line across the side lawn for Dr. Renfield's cottage.

She heard the kids laughing and playing on the big screened-in front porch of the sanatorium. She heard one of the nurses say to a child, "Behave, Billy!" as she went across the yard under the pine and maple-trees. Mrs. Osborn hoped Dr. Renfield would be on his porch. She hated to knock at the door and perhaps be faced with his wife. The gossip among the nurses and help at Dr. Renfield's Summer Home for Crippled Children had it that Mrs. Osborn was in love with Dr. Renfield, that she just worshipped him, that she followed him with her eyes every chance she got—and not only with her eyes.

Of course, there wasn't a word of truth in it, Mrs. Osborn said to herself, admitting at the same time that that Martha Renfield, his wife, was certainly not good enough for the doctor. Anyway tonight, she was not bound on any frivolous errand toward the Doctor's cottage. She had to see him about this Negro in their midst. At least, they'd have to keep him there overnight, or until they got somebody else to help in the kitchen. However, he looked like a decent boy.

Dr. Renfield was not at home. His wife came to the door, spoke most coldly, and said that she presumed, as usual, the Doctor would make his rounds of the Home at eight. She hoped Mrs. Osborn could wait until then to see him.

"Good evening!"

Mrs. Osborn went back across the dusk-dark yard. She heard the surf rushing at the beach below, and saw the new young moon rising. She thought maybe the Doctor was walking along the sea in the twilight alone. Ah, Dr. Renfield, Dr. Ren. . . .

When he made the usual rounds at eight he came, for a moment, by Mrs. Osborn's little office where the housekeeper held forth over her linens and her accounts. He turned his young but bearded face toward Mrs. Osborn, cast his great dark eyes upon her, and said, "I hear you've asked to see me?"

"Yes, indeed, Dr. Renfield," Mrs. Osborn bubbled and gurgled. "We have a problem on our hands. You know the kitchen man left this morning so I sent a wire to the High Class Help Agency in the city for somebody right away by the four o'clock train—and they sent us a Negro! He seems to be a nice boy, and all that, but I just don't know how he would fit in our Home. Now what do you think?"

The doctor looked at her with great seriousness. He thought. Then he answered with a question, "Do the other servants mind?"

"Well, I can't say they do. They got along all right tonight during dinner. But the problem is, where would he sleep?"

"Oh, yes," said Dr. Renfield, pursing his lips.

"And whether we should plan to keep him all summer, or just till we get someone else?"

"I see," said Dr. Renfield.

And again he thought. "You say he can do the work? . . . How about the attic in this building? It's not in use. . . . And by the way, how much did we pay the other fellow?"

"Ten dollars a week," said Mrs. Osborn raising her eyes.

"Well, pay the darkie eight," said Dr. Renfield, "and keep him." And for a moment he gazed deep into Mrs. Osborn's eyes. "Goodnight." Then turned and left her. Left her. Left her.

So it was that Milberry entered into service at Dr. Renfield's Summer Home for Crippled Children.

Milberry was a nice black boy, big, good natured and strong—like what Paul Robeson must have been at twenty. Except that he wasn't educated. He was from Georgia, where they don't have many schools for Negroes. And he hadn't been North long. He was glad to have a job, even if it was at a home for Crippled Children way out in the country on a beach five miles from the nearest railroad. Milberry had been hungry for weeks in Newark and Jersey City. He needed work and food.

And even if he wasn't educated, he had plenty of mother wit and lots of intuition about people and places. It didn't take him long to realize that he was doing far too much work for the Home's eight dollars a week, and that everybody was imposing on him in that taken-for-granted way white folks do with Negro help.

Milberry got up at 5:30 in the mornings, made the fire for the cook, set the water to boiling for the head nurse's coffee, started peeling potatoes, onions, and apples. After breakfast he washed up all the dishes, scoured the pots and pans, scrubbed the floors, and carried in wood for the fireplace in the front room (which really wasn't his job at all, but the handy-man's who had put it off on Milberry). The waitresses, too, got in the habit of asking him to polish their silver, and ice their water. And Mrs. Osborn always had something extra that needed to be done (not kitchen-boy work), a cellar to be cleaned out, or the linen in her closet reshelved, or the dining-room windows washed. Milberry knew they took him for a work horse, a fool—and a nigger. Still he did everything, and didn't look mad—jobs were too hard to get, and he had been hungry too long in town.

"Besides," Milberry said to himself, "the ways of white folks,

I mean some white folks, is too much for me. I reckon they must be a few good ones, but most of 'em ain't good—leastwise they don't treat me good. And Lawd knows, I ain't never done nothin' to 'em, nothin' a-tall."

But at the Home it wasn't the work that really troubled him, or the fact that nobody ever said anything about a day off or a little extra pay. No, he'd had many jobs like this one before, where they worked you to death. But what really worried Milberry at this place was that he seemed to sense something wrong—something phoney about the whole house—except the little crippled kids there like himself because they couldn't help it. Maybe it was the lonesomeness of that part of the Jersey coast with its pines and scrubs and sand. But, more nearly, Milberry thought it was that there doctor with the movie beard and the woman's eyes at the head of the home. And it was the cranky nurses always complaining about food and the little brats under them. And the constant talk of who was having an affair with Dr. Renfield. And Mrs. Osborn's grand manner to everybody but the doctor. And all the white help kicking about their pay, and how far it was from town, and how no-good the doctor was, or the head nurse, or the cook, or Mrs. Osborn.

"It's sho a phoney, this here place," Milberry said to himself. "Funny how the food ain't nearly so good 'cept when some ma or pa or some chile is visitin' here—then when they gone, it drops right back down again. This here hang-out is jest Doc Renfield's own private gyp game. Po' little children."

The Negro was right. The Summer Home was run for profits from the care of permanently deformed children of middle-class parents who couldn't afford to pay too much, but who still paid well—too well for what their children got in return. Milberry worked in the kitchen and saw the good cans opened for company, and the cheap cans opened for the kids. Somehow he didn't like such dishonesty. Somehow, he thought he wouldn't even stay there and work if it wasn't for the kids.

For the children grew terribly to like Milberry.

One afternoon, during his short period of rest between meals, he had walked down to the beach where those youngsters who could drag themselves about were playing, and others were sitting in their wheel-chairs watching. The sky was only a little cloudy, and the sand was grey. But quite all of a sudden it began to rain. The nurses saw Milberry and called him to help them get the young ones quickly back to the house. Some of the children were too heavy for a nurse to lift easily into a wheel-chair. Some couldn't run at all. The handy-man helper wasn't around. So Milberry picked up child after child, sometimes two at once, and carried them up to the broad screened-in porch of the Home like a big gentle horse. The children loved it, riding on his broad back, or riding in his arms in the soft gentle rain.

"Come and play with us sometimes," one of them called as Milberry left them all on the safe dry porch with their nurses.

"Sure, come back and play," another said.

So Milberry, the next day, went down to the beach again in the afternoon and played with the crippled children. At first the nurses, Miss Baxter and Mrs. Hill, didn't know whether to let him stay or not, but their charges seemed to enjoy it. Then when the time came to go in for rest before dinner, Milberry helped push the wheel-chairs, a task which the nurses hated. And he held the hands of those kids with braces and twisted limbs as they hobbled along. He told them stories, and he made up jokes in the sun on the beach. And one rainy afternoon on the porch he sang songs, old southern Negro songs, funny ones that the children loved.

Almost every afternoon then, Milberry came to the beach after the luncheon dishes were done, and he had washed himself—except those afternoons when Mrs. Osborn found something else for him to do—vases to be emptied or bath-tubs scoured. The children became Milberry's friends. They adored him and he them. They called him Berry. They put their arms about him.

The grown-up white folks only spoke to him when they had some job for him to do, or when they were kidding him about being dark, and talking flat and Southern, and mispronouncing words. But the kids didn't care how he talked. They loved his songs and his stories.

And he made up stories out of his own head just for them—po' little crippled-up things that they were—for Berry loved them, too.

So the summer wore on. August came. In September the Home would close. But disaster overtook Milberry before then.

At the end of August a week of rain fell, and the children could not leave the porch. Then, one afternoon, the sun suddenly came out bright and warm. The sea water was blue again and the sand on the beach glistened. Miss Baxter (who by now had got the idea it was part of Milberry's job to help her with the children) went to the kitchen and called him while he was still washing luncheon dishes.

"Berry, we're going to take the children down to the beach. Come on and help us with the chairs as soon as you get through."

"Yes, m'am," said Berry.

When he came out on the porch, the kids were all excited about playing in the sun once more. Little hunchbacks jumped and cried and clapped their hands, and little paralytics laughed in their wheel-chairs. And some with braces on had already hobbled out the screen-door and were gathered on the walk.

"Hello, Berry," the children called.

"Hey, Berry," they cried to the black boy.

Berry grinned.

It was a few hundred yards to the beach. On the cement walk, you could push a couple of wheel-chairs at a time to the sand's edge. Some of the children propelled their own. Besides the nurses, today the handy-man was helping for the sun might not last long.

"Take me," a little boy called from his wheel-chair, "Berry, take me."

"Sho, I will," the young Negro said gently.

But when Berry started to push the chair down from the porch to the walk, the child, through excess of joy, suddenly leaned forward laughing, and suddenly lost his balance. Berry saw that he was going to fall. To try to catch the boy, the young Negro let the chair go. But quick as a wink, the child had fallen one way onto the lawn, the chair the other onto the cement walk. The back of the chair was broken, snapped off, except for the wicker. The little boy lay squalling on the ground in the grass.

Lord have mercy!

All the nurses came running, the handy-man, and Mrs. Osborn, too. Berry picked up the boy, who clung to his neck sobbing, more frightened, it seemed, than hurt.

"Po' little chile," Berry kept saying. "Is you hurt much? I's so sorry."

But the nurses were very angry, for they were responsible. And Mrs. Osborn—well, she lit out for Dr. Renfield.

The little boy still clung to Berry, and wouldn't let the nurses take him at all. He had stopped crying when Dr. Renfield arrived, but was still sniffling. He had his arms tight around the black boy's neck.

"Give that child to me," Dr. Renfield said, his brown beard pointing straight at Berry, his mind visualizing irate parents and a big damage suit, and bad publicity for the Home.

But when the doctor tried to take the child, the little boy wriggled and cried and wouldn't let go of Berry. With what strength he had in his crooked braced limbs, he kicked at the doctor.

"Give me that child!" Dr. Renfield shouted at Berry. "Bring him into my office and lay him down." He put on his nose glasses. "You careless black rascal! And you, Miss Baxter—" the doctor shrivelled her with a look. "I want to see you."

In the clinic, it turned out that the child wasn't really hurt, though. His legs had been, from birth, twisted and deformed. Nothing could injure them much further. And fortunately his spine wasn't weak.

But the doctor kept saying, "Criminal carelessness! Criminal carelessness!" Mrs. Osborn kept agreeing with him, "Yes, it is! Indeed, it is!" Milberry was to blame.

The black boy felt terrible. But nobody else among the grown-ups seemed to care how he felt. They all said: What dumbness! he had let that child fall!

"Get rid of him," Dr. Renfield said to the housekeeper, "today. The fool nigger! And deduct ten dollars for that broken chair."

"We don't pay him but eight," Mrs. Osborn said.

"Well, deduct that," said the doctor.

So, without his last week's wages, Milberry went to Jersey City.

12
MOTHER AND CHILD

"AIN'T NOBODY SEEN IT," said old lady Lucy Doves. "Ain't nobody seen it, but the midwife and the doctor, and her husband, I reckon. They say she won't let a soul come in the room. But it's still living, 'cause Mollie Ransom heard it crying. And the woman from Downsville what attended the delivery says it's as healthy a child as she ever seed, indeed she did."

"Well, it's a shame," said Sister Wiggins, "it's here. I been living in Boyd's Center for twenty-two years, at peace with these white folks, ain't had no trouble yet, till this child was born—now look at 'em. Just look what's goin' on! People acting like a pack o' wolves."

"Poor little brat! He ain't been in the world a week yet," said Mrs. Sam Jones, taking off her hat, "and done caused more trouble than all the rest of us in a life time. I was born here, and I ain't never seen the white folks up in arms like they are today. But they don't need to think they can walk over Sam and me—for we owns our land, it's bought and paid for, and we sends our children to school. Thank God, this is Ohio. It ain't Mississippi."

"White folks is white folks, honey, South or North, North or South," said Lucy Doves. "I's lived both places and I know."

"Yes, but in Mississippi they'd lynched Douglass by now."

"Where is Douglass?" asked Mattis Crane. "You all know I don't know much about this mess. Way back yonder on that farm where I lives, you don't get nothing straight. Where is Douglass?"

"Douglass is here! Saw him just now out in de field doin' his spring plowin' when I drive down de road, as stubborn and bold-faced as he can be. We told him he ought to leave here."

"Well, I wish he'd go on and get out," said Sister Wiggins.

"If that would help any. His brother's got more sense than he has, even if he is a seventeen-year-old child. Clarence left here yesterday and went to Cleveland. But their ma, poor Sister Carter, she's still trying to battle it out. She told me last night, though, she thinks she have to leave. They won't let her have no more provisions at de general store. And they ain't got their spring seed yet. And they can't pay cash for 'em."

"Don't need to tell me! Old man Hartman's got evil as de rest of de white folks. Didn't he tell ma husband Saturday night he'd have to pay up every cent of his back bill, or he couldn't take nothing out of that store. And we been trading there for years."

"That's their way o' striking back at us niggers."

"Yes, but Lord knows my husband ain't de father o' that child."

"Nor mine."

"Jim's got too much pride to go foolin' round any old loose white woman."

"Child, you can't tell about men."

"I knowed a case once in Detroit where a nigger lived ten years with a white woman, and her husband didn't know it. He was their chauffeur."

"That's all right in the city, but please don't come bringing it out here to Boyd's Center where they ain't but a handful o' us colored—and we has a hard enough time as it is."

"You right! This sure has brought de hammer down on our heads."

"Lawd knows we's law-biding people, ain't harmed a soul, yet some o' these white folks talking 'bout trying to run all de colored folks out o' de country on account o' Douglass."

"They'll never run me," said Mrs. Sam Jones.

"Don't say what they *won't* do," said Lucy Doves, "cause they might."

"Howdy, Sister Jenkins."

"Howdy!"

"Good evenin'."

"Yes, de meetin' due to start directly."

"Soon as Madam President arrives. Reckon she's having trouble gettin' over that road from High Creek."

"Sit down and tell us what you's heard, Sister Jenkins."

"About Douglass?"

"Course 'bout Douglass. What else is anybody talkin' 'bout nowadays?"

"Well, my daughter told me Douglass' sister say they was in love."

"Him and that white woman?"

"Yes. Douglass' sister say it's been going on 'fore de woman got married."

"Un-huh! Then why didn't he stop foolin' with her after she got married? Bad enough, colored boy foolin' 'round a unmarried white woman, let alone a married one."

"Douglass' sister say they was in love."

"Well, why did she marry the *white* man, then?"

"She's white, ain't she? And who wouldn't marry a rich white man? Got his own farm, money and all, even if he were a widower with grown children gone to town. He give her everything she wanted, didn't he?"

"Everything but the right thing."

"Well, she must not o' loved him, sneaking 'round meeting Douglass in de woods."

"True."

"But what you reckon she went on and had that colored baby for?"

"She must a thought it was the old man's baby."

"She don't think so now! Mattie say when the doctor left and they brought the child in to show her, she like to went blind. It were near black as me."

"Do tell!"

"And what did her husband say?"

"Don't know. Don't know."

"He must a fainted."

"That old white woman lives across the crick from us said he's gonna put her out soon's she's able to walk."

"Ought to put her out!"

"Maybe that's what Douglass waitin' for."

"I heard he wants to take her away."

"He better take his fool self away, 'fore these white folks get madder. Ain't nobody heard it was a black baby till day before yesterday. Then it leaked out. And now de white folks are rarin' to kill Douglass!"

"I sure am scared!"

"And how come they all said right away it were Douglass?"

"Honey, don't you know? Colored folks knowed Douglass been eyeing that woman since God knows when, and she been eyeing back at him. You ought to seed 'em when they meet in de store. Course they didn't speak no more 'n Howdy, but their eyes followed one another 'round just like dogs."

"They was in love, I tell you. Been in love."

"Mighty funny kind o' love. Everybody knows can't no good come out o' white and colored love. Everybody knows that. And Douglass ain't no child. He's twenty-six years old, ain't he? And Sister Carter sure did try to raise her three chillun right. You can't blame her."

"Blame that fool boy, that's who, and that woman. Plenty colored girls in Camden he could of courted ten miles up de road. One or two right here. I got a daughter myself."

"No, he had to go foolin' round with a white woman."

"Yes, a white woman."

"They say he loved her."

"What do Douglass say, since it happened?"

"He don't say nothing."

"What could he say?"

"Well, he needn't think he's gonna keep his young mouth shut and let de white folks take it out on us. Down yonder at de school today, my Dorabella says they talkin' 'bout separatin' de colored from de white and makin' all de colored children go in a nigger room next term."

"Ain't nothing like that ever happened in Boyd's Center long as I been here—these twenty-two years."

"White folks is mad now, child, mad clean through."

"Wonder they ain't grabbed Douglass and lynched him."

"It's a wonder!"

"And him calmly out yonder plowin' de field this afternoon."

"He sure is brave."

"Woman's husband's liable to kill him."

"Her brother's done said he's gunning for him."

"They liable to burn Negroes' houses down."

"Anything's liable to happen. Lawd, I'm nervous as I can be."

"You can't tell about white folks."

"I ain't nervous. I'm *scared*."

"Don't say a word!"

"Why don't Sister Carter make him leave here?"

"I wish I knew."

"She told me she were nearly crazy."

"And she can't get Douglass to say nothin', one way or another—if he go, or if he stay. . . . Howdy, Madam President."

"Good evenin', Madam President."

"I done told you Douglass loves her."

"He wants to see that white woman, once more again, that's what he wants."

"A white hussy!"

"He's foolin' with fire."

"Poor Mis' Carter. I'm sorry for his mother."

"Poor Mis' Carter."

"Why don't you all say poor Douglass? Poor white woman? Poor child?"

"Madam President's startin' de meetin'."

"Is it boy or girl?"

"Sh-s-s-s! There's de bell."

"I hear it's a boy."

"Thank God, ain't a girl then."

"I hope it looks like Douglass, cause Douglass a fine-looking nigger."

"He's too bold, too bold."

"Shame he's got us all in this mess."

"Shame, shame, shame!"

"Sh-sss-sss!"

"Yes, indeedy!"

"Sisters, can't you hear this bell?"

"Shame!"

"Sh-sss!"

"Madam Secretary, take your chair."

"Shame!"

"The March meeting of the Salvation Rock Ladies' Missionary Society for the Rescue o' the African Heathen is hereby called to order. . . . Sister Burns, raise a hymn. . . . Will you-all ladies *please* be quiet? What are you talking 'bout back there anyhow?"

Ring a golden bell,

"Heathens, daughter, heathens."

Aw, ring a golden bell,

"They ain't in Africa neither!"

Ring a golden bell for me.
Ring a golden bell,
Aw, ring a golden bell,
My Lawd's done set me free!

I was a sinner
Lost and lone,
Till Jesus claimed me
For His own.
Ring a golden bell,
Ring a golden bell,
Aw, ring a golden bell for me. . . .

13

ONE CHRISTMAS EVE

STANDING OVER THE hot stove cooking supper, the colored maid, Arcie, was very tired. Between meals today, she had cleaned the whole house for the white family she worked for, getting ready for Christmas tomorrow. Now her back ached and her head felt faint from sheer fatigue. Well, she would be off in a little while, if only the Missus and her children would come on home to dinner. They were out shopping for more things for the tree which stood all ready, tinsel-hung and lovely in the living-room, waiting for its candles to be lighted.

Arcie wished she could afford a tree for Joe. He'd never had one yet, and it's nice to have such things when you're little. Joe was five, going on six. Arcie, looking at the roast in the white folks' oven, wondered how much she could afford to spend tonight on toys. She only got seven dollars a week, and four of that went for her room and the landlady's daily looking after Joe while Arcie was at work.

"Lord, it's more'n a notion raisin' a child," she thought.

She looked at the clock on the kitchen-table. After seven. What made white folks so darned inconsiderate? Why didn't they come on home here to supper? They knew she wanted to get off before all the stores closed. She wouldn't have time to buy Joe nothin' if they didn't hurry. And her landlady probably wanting to go out and shop, too, and not be bothered with little Joe.

"Dog-gone it!" Arcie said to herself. "If I just had my money, I might leave the supper on the stove for 'em. I just got to get to the stores fo' they close." But she hadn't been paid for the week yet. The Missus had promised to pay her Christmas Eve, a day or so ahead of time.

Arcie heard a door slam and talking and laughter in the front of the house. She went in and saw the Missus and her kids shaking snow off their coats.

"Umm-mm! It's swell for Christmas Eve," one of the kids said to Arcie. "It's snowin' like the deuce, and mother came near driving through a stop light. Can't hardly see for the snow. It's swell!"

"Supper's ready," Arcie said. She was thinking how her shoes weren't very good for walking in snow.

It seemed like the white folks took as long as they could to eat that evening. While Arcie was washing dishes, the Missus came out with her money.

"Arcie," the Missus said, "I'm so sorry, but would you mind if I just gave you five dollars tonight? The children have made me run short of change, buying presents and all."

"I'd like to have seven," Arcie said. "I needs it."

"Well, I just haven't got seven," the Missus said. "I didn't know you'd want all your money before the end of the week, anyhow. I just haven't got it to spare."

Arcie took five. Coming out of the hot kitchen, she wrapped up as well as she could and hurried by the house where she roomed to get little Joe. At least he could look at the Christmas trees in the windows downtown.

The landlady, a big light yellow woman, was in a bad humor. She said to Arcie, "I thought you was comin' home early and get this child. I guess you know I want to go out, too, once in awhile."

Arcie didn't say anything for, if she had, she knew the landlady would probably throw it up to her that she wasn't getting paid to look after a child both night and day.

"Come on, Joe," Arcie said to her son, "let's us go in the street."

"I hears they got a Santa Claus downtown," Joe said, wriggling into his worn little coat. "I wants to see him."

"Don't know 'bout that," his mother said, "but hurry up and get your rubbers on. Stores'll all be closed directly."

It was six or eight blocks downtown. They trudged along

through the falling snow, both of them a little cold. But the snow was pretty!

The main street was hung with bright red and blue lights. In front of the City Hall there was a Christmas tree—but it didn't have no presents on it, only lights. In the store windows there were lots of toys—for sale.

Joe kept on saying, "Mama, I want . . ."

But mama kept walking ahead. It was nearly ten, when the stores were due to close, and Arcie wanted to get Joe some cheap gloves and something to keep him warm, as well as a toy or two. She thought she might come across a rummage sale where they had children's clothes. And in the ten-cent store, she could get some toys.

"O-oo! Lookee . . .," little Joe kept saying, and pointing at things in the windows. How warm and pretty the lights were, and the shops, and the electric signs through the snow.

It took Arcie more than a dollar to get Joe's mittens and things he needed. In the A. & P. Arcie bought a big box of hard candies for 49c. And then she guided Joe through the crowd on the street until they came to the dime store. Near the ten-cent store they passed a moving picture theatre. Joe said he wanted to go in and see the movies.

Arcie said, "Ump-un! No, child! This ain't Baltimore where they have shows for colored, too. In these here small towns, they don't let colored folks in. We can't go in there."

"Oh," said little Joe.

In the ten-cent store, there was an awful crowd. Arcie told Joe to stand outside and wait for her. Keeping hold of him in the crowded store would be a job. Besides she didn't want him to see what toys she was buying. They were to be a surprise from Santa Claus tomorrow.

Little Joe stood outside the ten-cent store in the light, and the snow, and people passing. Gee, Christmas was pretty. All tinsel and stars and cotton. And Santa Claus a-coming from somewhere, dropping things in stockings. And all the people in the streets were carrying things, and the kids looked happy.

But Joe soon got tired of just standing and thinking and waiting in front of the ten-cent store. There were so many things to look at in the other windows. He moved along up the block a little, and then a little more, walking and looking. In fact, he moved until he came to the white folks' picture show.

In the lobby of the moving picture show, behind the plate glass doors, it was all warm and glowing and awful pretty. Joe stood looking in, and as he looked his eyes began to make out, in there blazing beneath holly and colored streamers and the electric stars of the lobby, a marvellous Christmas tree. A group of children and grown-ups, white, of course, were standing around a big jovial man in red beside the tree. Or was it a man? Little Joe's eyes opened wide. No, it was not a man at all. It was Santa Claus!

Little Joe pushed open one of the glass doors and ran into the lobby of the white moving picture show. Little Joe went right through the crowd and up to where he could get a good look at Santa Claus. And Santa Claus was giving away gifts, little presents for children, little boxes of animal crackers and stick-candy canes. And behind him on the tree was a big sign (which little Joe didn't know how to read). It said, to those who understood, MERRY XMAS FROM SANTA CLAUS TO OUR YOUNG PATRONS.

Around the lobby, other signs said, WHEN YOU COME OUT OF THE SHOW STOP WITH YOUR CHILDREN AND SEE OUR SANTA CLAUS. And another announced, GEM THEATRE MAKES ITS CUSTOMERS HAPPY—SEE OUR SANTA.

And there was Santa Claus in a red suit and a white beard all sprinkled with tinsel snow. Around him were rattles and drums and rocking horses which he was not giving away. But the signs on them said (could little Joe have read) that they would be presented from the stage on Christmas Day to the holders of the lucky numbers. Tonight, Santa Claus was only giving away candy, and stick-candy canes, and animal crackers to the kids.

Joe would have liked terribly to have a stick-candy cane.

He came a little closer to Santa Claus, until he was right in the front of the crowd. And then Santa Claus saw Joe.

Why is it that lots of white people always grin when they see a Negro child? Santa Claus grinned. Everybody else grinned, too, looking at little black Joe—who had no business in the lobby of a white theatre. Then Santa Claus stooped down and slyly picked up one of his lucky number rattles, a great big loud tin-pan rattle such as they use in cabarets. And he shook it fiercely right at Joe. That was funny. The white people laughed, kids and all. But little Joe didn't laugh. He was scared. To the shaking of the big rattle, he turned and fled out of the warm lobby of the theatre, out into the street where the snow was and the people. Frightened by laughter, he had begun to cry. He went looking for his mama. In his heart he never thought Santa Claus shook great rattles at children like that—and then laughed.

In the crowd on the street he went the wrong way. He couldn't find the ten-cent store or his mother. There were too many people, all white people, moving like white shadows in the snow, a world of white people.

It seemed to Joe an awfully long time till he suddenly saw Arcie, dark and worried-looking, cut across the side-walk through the passing crowd and grab him. Although her arms were full of packages, she still managed with one free hand to shake him until his teeth rattled.

"Why didn't you stand where I left you?" Arcie demanded loudly. "Tired as I am, I got to run all over the streets in the night lookin' for you. I'm a great mind to wear you out."

When little Joe got his breath back, on the way home, he told his mama he had been in the moving picture show.

"But Santa Claus didn't give me nothin'," Joe said tearfully. "He made a big noise at me and I runned out."

"Serves you right," said Arcie, trudging through the snow. "You had no business in there. I told you to stay where I left you."

"But I seed Santa Claus in there," little Joe said, "so I went in."

"Huh! That wasn't no Santa Claus," Arcie explained. "If it was, he wouldn't a-treated you like that. That's a theatre for white folks—I told you once—and he's just a old white man."

"Oh . . .," said little Joe.

14

FATHER AND SON

COLONEL THOMAS NORWOOD stood in his doorway at the Big House looking down the dusty plantation road. Today his youngest son was coming home. A heavy Georgia spring filled the morning air with sunshine and earth-perfumes. It made the old man feel strangely young again. Bert was coming home.

Twenty years ago he had begotten him.

This boy, however, was not his real son, for Colonel Thomas Norwood had no real son, no white and legal heir to carry on the Norwood name; this boy was a son by his Negro mistress, Coralee Lewis, who kept his house and had borne him all his children.

Colonel Norwood never would have admitted, even to himself, that he was standing in his doorway waiting for this half-Negro son to come home. But in truth that is what he was doing. He was curious about this boy. How would he look after all these years away at school? Six or seven surely, for not once in that long time had he been allowed to come back to Big House Plantation. The Colonel had said then that never did he want to see the boy. But in truth he did—for this boy had been, after all, the most beautiful of the lot, the brightest and the badest of the Colonel's five children, lording it over the other children, and sassing not only his colored mother, but his white father, as well. Handsome and mischievous, favoring too much the Colonel in looks and ways, this boy Bert, at fourteen, had got himself sent off to school to stay. Now a student in college (or what they call a college in Negro terms in Georgia) he was coming home for the summer vacation.

Today his brother, Willie, had been sent to the station to meet him in the new Ford. The ten o'clock train must have reached the Junction by now, thought the Colonel, standing in the door. Soon the Ford would be shooting back down the road in a cloud of dust, curving past the tall white pillars of the front porch, and around to the kitchen stoop where Cora would greet her child.

Thinking thus, Colonel Norwood came inside the house, closed the screen, and pulled at a bellcord hanging from the wall of the great dark living-room with its dignified but shabby horse-hair furniture of the nineties. By and by, an old Negro servant, whose name was Sam and who wore a kind of old-fashioned butler's coat, came and brought the Colonel a drink.

"I'm going in my library where I don't want to be disturbed."

"Yes, suh," said the Negro servant.

"You hear me?"

"Yes, suh," said the servant, knowing that when Colonel Norwood said "library," he meant he did not want to be disturbed.

The Colonel entered the small room where he kept his books and papers of both a literary and a business nature. He closed the door. He did this deliberately, intending to let all the Negroes in the house know that he had no interest whatsoever in the homecoming about to take place. He intended to remain in the library several hours after Bert's arrival. Yet, as he bent over his desk peering at accounts his store-keeper had brought him, his head kept turning toward the window that gave on the yard and the road, kept looking to see if a car were coming in a cloud of dust.

An hour or so later, when shouts of welcome, loud warm Negro-cries, laughter, and the blowing of an auto horn filled the Georgia sunlight outside, the Colonel bent more closely over his ledgers—but he did turn his eyes a little to catch the dust sifting in the sunny air above the road where the car had passed. And his mind went back to that little olive-colored kid he had beaten one day in the stables years ago—the kid grown up now, and just come home.

He had always been a little ashamed of that particular beating he had given the boy. But his temper had got the best of him. That child, Bert, looking almost like a white child (a hell of a lot favoring the Colonel), had come running out to the stables one afternoon when he was showing his horses to some guests from in town. The boy had come up to him crying, "Papa!" (He knew better, right in front of company.) "Papa, Ma says she's got dinner ready."

The Colonel had knocked him down under the feet of the horses right there in front of the guests. And afterwards he had locked him in the stable and beaten him severely. The boy had to learn not to call him papa, and certainly not in front of white people from the town.

But it had been hard to teach Bert anything, the Colonel ruminated. Trouble was, the boy was too smart. There were other unpleasant memories of that same saucy ivory-skinned youngster playing about the front yard, even running through the Big House, in spite of orders that Coralee's children and all other pickaninnies keep to the back of the house, or down in the Quarters. But as a child, Bert had never learned his place.

"He's too damn much like me," the Colonel thought. "Quick as hell. Cora's been telling me he's leading his class at the Institute, and a football captain. . . . H-m-m-m, so they waste their time playing football at these darkie colleges. . . . Well, anyway, he must be a smart darkie. Got my blood in him."

The Colonel had Sam bring some food into the library. He pretended to be extremely busy, and did not give the old Negro, bursting with news, a chance to speak. The Colonel acted as though he were unaware of the presence of the newly arrived boy on the plantation; or if he were aware, completely uninterested, and completely occupied.

But in the late afternoon, the Colonel got up from his desk, went out into the parlor, picked up an old straw hat, and strolled through the front door, across the wide-porticoed porch with its white pillars, and down the road toward the South Field. The Colonel saw the brown backs of his Negroes in the green cotton. He smelt the earth-scent of a day that had been long and hot. He turned off by the edge of a field, went down to the creek, and back toward the house along a path that took him through a grove of pecan-trees skirting the old slave quarters, to the back door of the Big House.

Long before he approached the Big House, he could hear Negroes' voices, musical and laughing. Then he could see a small group of dark bare arms and faces about the kitchen stoop. Cora was sitting on a stool in the yard, probably washing fruit for jelly. Livonia, the fat old cook, was on the porch shelling peas for dinner. Seated on the stoop, and on the ground, and standing around, were colored persons the Colonel knew had no good reason to be there at that time of day. Some of them, when they saw the Colonel coming, began to move away, back toward the barns, or whatever work they were doing.

He was aware, too, standing in the midst of this group, of a tall young man in sporty white trousers, black-and-white oxfords, and a blue shirt. He looked very clean and well-dressed, like a white man. The Colonel took this to be his son, and a certain vibration shook him from head to foot. Across the wide dusty yard, their eyes met. The Colonel's brows came together, his shoulders lifted and went back as though faced by an indignity just suffered. His chin went up. And he began to think, on the way toward them, how he would walk through this group like a white man. The Negroes, of course, would be respectful and afraid, as usual. He would say merely, "Good evening, Bert," to this boy, his son, then wait a moment, perhaps, and see what the boy said before passing on into the house.

Laughter died and dripped and trickled away, and talk quieted, and silence fell degree by degree, each step the white man approached. A strange sort of stiffness like steel nearing steel grew and straightened between the colored boy in the black-and-white shoes and the old Colonel who had just come from looking at his fields and his Negroes working.

"Good evening, Bert," the Colonel said.

"Good evening, Colonel Tom," the boy replied quickly, politely, almost eagerly. And then, like a puppet pulled by some perverse string, the boy offered his hand.

The Colonel looked at the strong young near-white hand held out toward him, and made no effort to take it. His eyes lifted to the eyes of the boy, his son, in front of him. The boy's eyes did not fall. But a slow flush reddened the olive of his skin as the old man turned without a word toward the stoop and into the house. The boy's hand went to his side again. A hum of dark voices broke the silence.

This happened between father and son. The mother, sitting there washing plums in a pail, did not understand what had happened. But the water from which she took the plums felt cool to her hands that were suddenly burning hot.

II

CORALEE LEWIS, SITTING washing plums, had been Colonel Norwood's mistress for thirty years. She had lived in the Big House, supervised his life, given him children, and loved him. In his turn, he felt something very like love for her. Now, in his sixties, without Cora he would have been lost, but of course he did not realize that—consciously.

The history of their liaison, like that of so many between Negro women and white men in the South, began without love, at least on his part. For a long while its motif was lust—whose sweeter name, perhaps, is passion.

The Colonel had really known Cora all her life. As a half-grown boy, he had teased her as a baby, pulling her kinky braids and laughing at the way she rolled in the dust with the other pickaninnies born to the black servants and share-croppers on his father's plantation. He had seen her as a girl, bare-footed and shy, brown face shining, bringing milk to the Big House night and morning, for her father took care of the cows. Her mother worked sometimes in the house but mostly in the fields. And Cora knew early how to pick cotton, too.

Then there came years when young Norwood had no contact with Cora: years when he had been away at Military School; those first few years when he had come back from Macon with his new bride; those years of love and worry with the delicate and lovely woman he had wedded. During his early married life the Colonel could not truthfully remember ever having laid eyes on Cora, although she was about the place surely.

But Cora remembered often seeing the Colonel. Young and handsome, tall and straight, he drove over the plantation roads with the wisp of a pretty little lady he had married. She remembered him particularly well the day of his father's funeral, when he came back from the burial—he and his wife, master and mistress of the Big House now. How sad and worried young Colonel Norwood looked that day descending from the carriage.

And as the months went by, he began to look more and more worried and weary. Servants' gossip from the Big House, drifting down to the humbler Negroes in the cabins, said that a wall had grown up between the young Colonel and his little wife, who seemed to be wasting away day by day. A wall like a mist. And the Negroes began to laugh that there were never no children born to Mister and Missus. Then gossip began to say that the young Colonel had taken up with the cook's daughter, black but comely Livonia, who worked in the pantry. Then the Quarters laughed all the more—for Livonia had four or five Negro lovers, too. And she wasn't faithful to anybody—just liked to love.

Cora heard all this and in her mind a certain envy sprang up. Livonia! Huh! Cora began to look more carefully into the cracked mirror in her mother's cabin. She combed her hair and oiled it better than before. She was seventeen then.

"Time you was takin' some pride about yo'self," said her mother, noting the change.

"Yes'm," said Cora. And when she took milk to the Big House now, she tried to look her best.

One night, there was a party there. A great many people came from the Junction, and even seventy miles off from in town, by horse and by carriage, by train, and even some by that new-fangled auto-buggy that most of the plantation hands had never seen before. The Negroes were all excited at having so many white folks around. It was the Missus' birthday. There were great doings at Big House Plantation.

The first evening, the party went on until late in the night. Some people left at dawn. Others slept awhile and left in the afternoon. Some were house guests, and on the second night there was a party again. But that night everybody was pretty tired. And got pretty drunk, too, mostly. The Colonel was very gay and very drunk; but his little wife cried, and went to bed. She was mighty touchy, all the Negroes knew. Always poutin' and spattin' and actin' funny with the Colonel.

Wonder why? Wonder why?

There was a party in the Quarters among the Negroes, too, that second night. Livonia was there, dancing fit to kill. And the music was wild. In the heat of the night, Cora went out of the barn where the party was, out into the moonlight, and looked up at the lights of the Big House on the rise. She stretched, and breathed in the warm night air, and walked through the trees toward the road that ran to town. She made a big circle about the Big House, wondering a little what was going on there. When she got to the road, she sat down under a huge live oak-tree. She could hear the laughter and clapping of the Negroes down on the edge of the cotton fields. But in the Big House, where it should have been gay, too, it was mighty quiet. Sometimes a loud and quarrelsome voice could be heard. Probably the men were gambling, and the ladies gone to bed.

The trees cast great shadows across the road in the warm light of the moon. Cora stretched, breathed deeply again, and got up to go, when she saw very near her a figure walking in the silvery dusk, a tall thin young white man walking in the cotton. Suddenly he called her.

"Who're you?" It was young Norwood speaking.

"I's Coralee Lewis, Aunt Tobie Lewis' daughter."

The white man came up to her, took her brown face in his hands and lifted it at the moon. "You're out mighty late," he said.

Cora's body trembled. Her mouth opened. In the shadow of the live oak-tree there by the road, thirty years ago, in a night of moon. . . .

III

WHEN THE FIRST child, Willie, was in her, she told her mother all about it. The old woman was glad. "It's better'n slavin' in the cotton fields," she said. "I's known colored women what's wore silk dresses and lived like queens on plantations right here in Georgy. . . ."

Even before the young Mrs. Norwood died (she did die—and childless) Cora was working in the Big House. And after Mrs. Norwood's death, Cora came there to sleep.

Now the water where the plums were felt cool to her hands this spring afternoon many years later as the Colonel went into the house leaving their youngest boy dazed in front of her; and the nigger-voices all around her humming and chattering into loudness and laughter.

IV

"LISTEN HYAR," BROTHER Willie said to Bert on the way from the Junction to the plantation that morning his brother arrived. "Listen hyar, I hopes you don't expect to go around all dressed up like you is now after you gets out to de place, 'cause de Colonel won't 'low it. He made Sis put away all them fine clothes she brought hyar last year—till she left."

"Tell him to kiss my behind," Bert said.

Willie bucked his eyes, stuttered, then kept quiet. His brother was the same Bert as he had been as a child. Crazy! Trouble coming. William made up his mind not to be in it, himself, one way or another. Though he was eight years older, he had always been afraid of Bert with a fear worse than physical, afraid of the things that happened around Bert.

From the new Ford, Bert looked out at the straggling streets of the village of the Junction, at the Negroes lounging in front of stores, at the red-necked crackers, at the unkempt women. He heard the departing train whistle as it went deeper into

Georgia, into Alabama. As they rode, he looked at the wide fields of young cotton stretching on either side, at the cabins of the share-croppers, at the occasional house of a white owner or overseer. Then he saw the gradual rise of the Norwood plantation, the famous Big House, surrounded by its live oaks and magnolias and maples, and its many acres of cotton. And he knew he was nearing home.

Six years away. Kid of fourteen when he left, wearing his first long trousers bought in the commissary store, feeling funny out of overalls, feeling very proud going away to school. Only the Lewis niggers (old man Norwood's kids by Cora) went away to school in these parts. And with the going of Sallie, the youngest, the little county school at Norwood's Crossroads closed up, and didn't open any more. Sallie was the *Colonel's* last child—no other niggers needed a school.

Old Aunt Tobie, the grandma, before she died, used to keep on saying that the Lewis young 'uns ought to appreciate what the Colonel was doing for 'em. No white man she ever heard of cared anything 'bout educatin' his tar-brush chillun. But the Colonel did. Somehow 'nother Cora was able to put it in the Colonel's mind and keep it there until the last child, Sallie, got sent off to Atlanta.

In Atlanta, Bert had entered the same run-down Negro boarding school, the Institute, that brother Willie and his oldest sister, Bertha, had attended. But Willie, several years before, hadn't stayed there long, being a dumb boy who liked the plantation better. Bertha had gone up North once with the Spiritual Jubilee Singers, and liked it so well that she remained to work in Chicago. Now, little sister Sallie, seventeen, went to the Institute also, but had come home this spring ahead of Bert, who fooled around Atlanta a week or so before leaving, not wanting to come home really.

"Home, hell!"

Bert didn't want to come home. He felt he had no home. A brown mother, and a white father; bed for him in a nigger cabin down on the edge of the cotton fields. Soon as Cora's kids stopped nursing they went to live outside the Big House. Aunt

Tobie, the grandmother, had really raised them, until she died. Then a cousin of Cora's brought up Sallie.

"Hell of a way to live," Bert thought, the night before his arrival, sitting in the Jim Crow car bound for south Georgia. During the long ride, he had turned over in his mind incidents of his childhood on the Big House Plantation. Sitting in the smoky half-coach allotted to Negroes (the other half being a baggage car) he thought of what it meant growing up as one of Colonel Norwood's yard-niggers (a term used by field-hands for the mulatto children of a white planter).

"It's hell," Bert thought.

Not that Cora's other kids had found it hell. Only he had found it so, strangely enough. "The rest of 'em are too dumb, except little Sallie, and she don't say nothing—but it's hell to her, too, I reckon," the boy thought to himself as the train rocked and rumbled over the road. "Willie don't give a damn so long as his belly's full. And Bertha's got up North away from it all. I don't know what she really thought. . . . But I wish it hadn't happened to me."

With the self-pity of bewildered youth, he began to think about himself. Always, he had known the Colonel was his father, from the earliest he could remember. For one thing, Bert had been lighter than any of the other colored children on the plantation—a sort of ivory white. And as a small child, his hair had been straight and brown, his eyes grey, like Norwood's. His grandma, old Aunt Tobie, used to refer to them all, Willie and Bertha and Bert and Sallie, not without pride, as Colonel Tom's children. (There had been another brother who died.) Bert noticed early in life that all the other kids in the Quarters were named after their fathers, whereas he and his brother and sisters bore the mother's name, Lewis. He was Bert Lewis—not Bert Norwood. His mother slept in the Big House—but the children lived outside with Aunt Tobie or Cousin Betty. Those things puzzled little Bert.

As he grew up, he used to hear folks remarking on how much he looked like Colonel Tom, and how little like Cora. Nearly light enough to pass for white, folks said, spittin' image of his father, too. Bert had a temper and ways like white folks, too. Indeed, "You needn't act so much like quality with me," was one of Aunt Tobie's favorite ways of reprimanding him when she wanted to take him down a peg or two.

He was always getting into mischief, playing pranks and worrying his mother at the back door of the Big House. There was a time once when the Colonel seemed to get pleasure out of letting little Bert trail around at his heels, but that period didn't last very long, for young Bert sassed the Colonel too, just as though he were colored. And somehow, he had acquired that way of referring to Norwood as papa. The Colonel told him, sternly and seriously, "Boy, don't *you* use that word to me." But still, forgetful little devil that he was, he had come running up to the Colonel that day in the stables yelling, "Papa, dinner's ready."

The slap that he received made him see stars and darkness, Bert remembered. As though he were brushing a fly out of the way, the Colonel had knocked him down under the feet of the horses, and went on talking to his guests. After the guests had gone, he switched Bert mercilessly.

"Can't nobody teach you nothin' but a switch, nohow," said old Aunt Tobie afterwards. "I tole you 'bout gittin' familiar wid that white man."

"But he didn't need to scar him all up," Bert remembered Cora's saying when she saw the black and blue marks on his back. "I ain't bearin' him children for to beat 'em to death. . . . You stay way from him, son, you hear?"

From that time on, between Bert and the Colonel, there had been a barrier of fear—a fear that held a certain mysterious fascination for Bert's sense of defiance, a fear that Bert from afar was continually taunting and baiting. For instance, the Colonel had a complex, Bert recalled, that all the Negroes knew, about the front door of the Big House. His orders were that no Negroes go in and out of that door, or cross his front porch. When the old house-man, Sam, wanted to sweep off the porch, he would have to go out the back and come all the way around. It was as absurd as that. Yet Bert, as a child, in the Big House visiting or helping Cora, would often dart out the front way when he thought the Colonel was in town or down in the South Field, or asleep in his library. Cora used to spank him for it, but it was a habit he kept up until he went away, a big boy, to Atlanta.

Bert, home-bound now, smiled to himself in the stuffy Jim Crow car, and wondered if the Colonel were still as tall and stern and stiff-fronted as he used to be. No wonder his young white wife had died years ago—having to live with him—although, according to Aunt Tobie's version, the Colonel had humored her in every way. He really loved her, folks said, and had sworn after her death that he would never marry again. He hadn't—he had taken Cora.

And here Bert's mind balked and veered away from speculating about the intimate life of this old man and his mother. Bert knew that in a sense the white man had been kind to her. He remembered as a child the extra little delicacies that came down to Aunt Tobie and Cousin Betty and Cora's other relatives in the Quarters, especially at Christmas. He remembered how he had always known that the little colored school had not been there before Cora's children were born, and that it was no longer at the Cross Roads now. (For the Colonel and Mr. Higgins, being political powers in the county, were in charge of education, and their policy was to let Negroes remain unlettered. They worked better.) Bert knew, too, that it was his mother's influence that had got her children sent off to the Institute in Atlanta. But it was the *Colonel's* dislike of Bert that had kept him there, summer and winter, until now. Not that Bert minded. Summer school was fun, too. And tennis. And the pleasures of the town. And he was never homesick for the plantation—but he did wish sometimes that he had a home, and that the Colonel would treat him like a son.

Tall and light and good-looking, as Bert was now at twenty, he could have a very good time in Atlanta. Colored society had taken him up. He went around with the sons and daughters of Negro doctors and dentists and insurance brokers and professors. He had his hands full of pretty girls. Lots of cream-colored girls, chocolate brown girls, velvet-soft night-shade girls all liked Bert. And already he had been involved in a scandal with a doctor's wife.

To add to his good looks, Bert was an excellent athlete. He had been as far north as Washington with Institute teams, and had seen colored people at the Capitol riding in street-cars where there had been no Jim Crow signs, and getting on trains that had no coaches especially for Negroes. Bert made up his mind to come North to live, as soon as he finished school. He had one more year. And this last summer, Cora wanted him to spend with her—because she sensed he might never come back to the plantation again.

Sallie, his sister, three classes behind him at the Institute, was frankly worried about his going home. She was afraid. "Colonel Tom's getting old. He ain't nice a-tall like he kinder used to be. He's getting more and more touchy," Sallie said to her brother. "And I know he ain't gonna like the looks of you. You don't look a bit like a Georgia boy any more."

"To hell with him," said Bert.

"I wouldn't even know you and Willie were brothers," Sallie said. For Sallie went home every summer and worked in the Big House with her mother, and saw Willie, and knew how things were on the plantation. Willie and the Colonel got along fine, because Willie was docile and good-natured and nigger-like, bowing and scraping and treating white folks like they expected to be treated. "But Bert, you ain't a bit like that."

"Why should I be?" Bert asked. "I'm the old man's son, ain't I? Got white blood in me, too."

"Yes, but . . ."

"But what?" Bert said. "Let old knotty-headed Willie go on being a white folks' nigger if he wants to, I won't!"

And that's the way it was when he came home.

V

THERE ARE PEOPLE (you've probably noted it also) who have the unconscious faculty of making the world spin around themselves, throb and expand, contract and go dizzy. Then, when they are gone away, you feel sick and lonesome and meaningless.

In the chemistry lab at school, did you ever hold a test tube, pouring in liquids and powders and seeing nothing happen until a *certain* liquid or a *certain* powder is poured in and then everything begins to smoke and fume, bubble and boil, hiss to foam, and sometimes even explode? The tube is suddenly full of action and movement and life. Well, there are people like those certain liquids or powders; at a given moment they come into a room, or into a town, even into a country—and the place is never the same again. Things bubble, boil, change. Sometimes the whole world is changed. Alexander came. Christ. Marconi. A Russian named Lenin.

Not that there is any comparing Bert to Christ or Lenin. But after he returned to the Big House Plantation that summer, life was never the same. From Bert's very first day on the place something was broken, something went dizzy. The world began to spin, to ferment, and move into a new action.

Not to be a *white folks' nigger*—Bert had come home with that idea in his head.

The Colonel sensed it in his out-stretched hand and his tall young body—and had turned his back and walked into the house. Cora with her hands in the cool water where the plums were, suddenly knew in her innermost soul a period of time had closed for her. That first night she prayed, cried in her room, asked the Lord why she had ever let her son come home. In his cabin Willie prayed, too, humble, Lord, humble. The Colonel rocked alone on his front porch sucking a black cigar and cussing bitterly at he knew not what. The hum and laughter of the Negro voices went on as usual on the vast plantation down to the last share-cropper's cabin, but not quite, not *quite* the same as they had been in the morning. And never to be the same again.

"Is you heard about Bert?"

Not to be a *white folks' nigger!*

Bow down and pray in fear and trembling, go way back in the dark afraid; or work harder and harder; or stumble and learn; or raise up your fist and strike—but once the idea comes into your head you'll never be the same again. Oh, test tube of life! Crucible of the South, find the right powder and you'll never be the same again—the cotton will blaze and the cabins will burn and the chains will be broken and men, all of a sudden, will shake hands, black men and white men, like steel meeting steel!

"The bastard," Bert said. "Why couldn't he shake hands with me? I'm a Norwood, too."

"Hush, son," said Cora with the cool water from the plums on her hands.

And the hum of the black voices that afternoon spread to the cabins, to the cotton fields, to the dark streets of the Junction, what Bert had said—Bert with the ivory-yellow skin and the tall proud young body, Bert come home not to be a white folks' nigger.

"Lawd, chile, Bert's come home. . . ."

"Lawd, chile, and he said . . ."

"Lawd, chile, he said . . ."

"Lawd, chile . . ."

"Lawd . . ."

VI

JULY PASSED, AND AUGUST. The hot summer sun marched across the skies. The Colonel ordered Bert to work in the fields. Bert had not done so. Talbot, the white foreman, washed his hands of it, saying that if he had his way, "that nigger would be run off the place."

For the Colonel, the summer was hectic enough, what with

cotton prices dropping on the market; share-croppers restless and moving; one black field-hand beaten half to death by Talbot and the store-keeper because he "talked high" to a neighboring white planter; news of the Scottsboro trials and the Camp Hill shootings exciting black labor.

Colonel Norwood ordered the colored rural Baptist minister to start a revival and keep it going until he said stop. Let the Negroes sing and shout their troubles away, as in the past. White folks had always found revivals a useful outlet for sullen over-worked darkies. As long as they were singing and praying, they forgot about the troubles of this world. In a frenzy of rhythm and religion, they laid their cross at the feet of Jesus.

Poor over-worked Jesus! Somehow since the War, he hadn't borne that cross so well. Too heavy, it's too heavy! Lately, Negroes seem to sense that it's not Jesus' cross, anyhow, it's their own. Only old people praise King Jesus any more. On the Norwood plantation, Bert's done told the young people to stop being white folks' niggers. More and more, the Colonel felt it was Bert who brought trouble into the Georgia summer. The revival was a failure.

One day he met the boy coming back from the river where he had been swimming. The Colonel lit into him with all the cuss words at his command. He told him in no uncertain language to get down in the South Field to work. He told him there would be no more school at Atlanta for him; that he would show him that just because Cora happened to be his mother, he was no more than any other nigger on the place. God damn him!

Bert stood silent and red in front of his father, looking as the Colonel must have looked forty years ago—except that he was a shade darker. He did not go down to the South Field to work. And all Cora's pleadings could not make him go. Yet nothing happened. That was the strange thing about it. The Colonel did nothing—to Bert. But he lit into Cora, nagged and scolded her for days, told her she'd better get some sense into her boy's head if she wanted any skin left on his body.

So the summer passed. Sallie, having worked faithfully in

the house throughout the hottest months, went away to school again. Bert remained sullenly behind.

The day that ends our story began like this:

The sun rose burning and blazing, flooding the earth with the heat of early autumn, making even the morning oppressive. Folks got out of bed feeling like over-ripe fruit. The air of the morning shimmered with heat and ill-humor. The night before, Colonel Norwood had been drinking. He got up trembling and shaky, yelling for Cora to bring him something clean to put on. He went downstairs cussing.

The Colonel did not want to eat. He drank black coffee, and walked out on the tall-pillared porch to get a breath of air. He was standing there looking through the trees at his cotton, when the Ford swept by in a cloud of dust, past the front of the house and down the highway to town. Bert was driving.

The Colonel cussed out loud, bit his cigar, turned and went into the house, slamming the door, storming to Cora, calling up the stairs where she was working, "What the hell does he think he is, driving off to town in the middle of the morning? Didn't I tell Bert not to touch that Ford, to stay down yonder in the fields and work?"

"Yes, suh, Colonel Tom," Cora said. "You sure did."

"Tell him I want to see him soon as he comes back here. Send him in here. And tell him I'll skin his yellow hide for him." The Colonel spoke of Bert as though he were still a child.

"Yes, suh, Colonel Tom."

VII

THE DAY GREW hotter and hotter. Heat waves rose from the fields. Sweat dampened the Colonel's body. Sweat dampened the black bodies of the Negroes in the cotton fields, too, the hard black bodies that had built the Colonel's fortune out of earth and sun and barehanded labor. Yet the Colonel, in spite of the fact that he lived on this labor, sat in his shaded house fanning that morning and wondering what made niggers so contrary—he was thinking of Bert—as the telephone rang. The fat and testy voice of his old friend, Mr. Higgins, trembled at the other end of the wire. He was calling from the Junction.

Accustomed as he was to his friend's voice on the phone, at first the Colonel could not make out what he was saying. When he did understand, his neck bulged and the palms of the hands that held the phone were wet with sweat. Anger and shame made his tall body stoop and bend like an animal about to spring. Mr. Higgins was talking about Bert.

"That yellow nigger . . ." Mr. Higgins said. "One of your yard-niggers sassed . . ." Mr. Higgins said. "I thought I'd better tell you . . ." Mr. Higgins said. "Everybody . . ." Mr. Higgins said.

The whole town was excited about Bert. In the heat of this over-warm autumn day, the hot heads of the white citizens of the town had suddenly become inflamed about Bert. Mr. Higgins, county politician and Postmaster at the Junction, was well qualified to know. His Office had been the center of the news.

It seemed that Bert had insulted the young white woman who sold stamps and made out money-orders at the Post Office. And Mr. Higgins was telling the Colonel about it on the phone, warning him to get rid of Bert, that people around the Junction were getting sick and tired of seeing him.

At the Post Office this is what happened: a simple argument over change. But the young woman who sold the stamps was not used to arguing with Negroes, or being corrected by them when she made a mistake. Bert said, "I gave you a dollar," holding out the incorrect change. "You gave me back only sixty-four cents."

The young woman said, counting the change, "Yes, but you have eight three-cent stamps. Move on now, there're others waiting." Several white people were in line.

Bert said, "Yes, but eight times three is not thirty-six. You owe me twelve cents more."

The girl looked at the change and realized she was wrong. She looked at Bert—light near-white nigger with grey-blue eyes. You gotta be harder on those kind than you have on the black ones. An educated nigger, too! Besides it was hot and she wasn't feeling well. A light near-white nigger with grey eyes! Instead of correcting the change, she screamed, and let her head fall forward in front of the window.

Two or three white men waiting to buy stamps seized Bert and attempted to throw him out of the Post Office. Bert remembered he'd been a football player—and Colonel Norwood's son—so he fought back. One of the white men got a bloody mouth. Women screamed. Bert walked out of the Post Office, got in the Ford and drove away. By that time, the girl who sold stamps had recovered. She was telling everyone how Bert had insulted her.

"Oh, my God! It was terrible," she said.

"That's one nigger don't know his place, Tom," Mr. Higgins roared over the phone. "And it's your fault he don't—sendin' 'em off to school to be educated." The Colonel listened to his friend at the other end of the wire. "Why that yellow buck comes to my store and if he ain't waited on quick as the white folks are, he walks out. He said last week standin' out on my corner, he wasn't *all* nigger no how; said his name was Norwood—not Lewis, like the rest of Cora's family; said your plantation would be his when you passed out—and all that kind o' stuff, boasting to the niggers listening about you being his father." The Colonel almost dropped the phone. "Now, Tom, you know that stuff don't go 'round these parts o' Georgia. Ruinous to other niggers hearing that sort of talk, too. There ain't been no race trouble in our county for three years—since the Deekins lynching—but I'm telling you, Norwood, folks ain't gonna stand for this. I'm speaking on the quiet, but I see ahead. What happened this morning in the Post Office ain't none too good."

"When I get through with him," said the Colonel hoarsely, "you won't need to worry. Goodbye."

The white man came out of the library, yelled for Sam, shouted for Cora, ordered whisky. Drank and screamed.

"God damn that son of yours! I'm gonna kill him," he said

to Cora. "Get out of here," he shouted at Sam, who came back with cigars.

Cora wept. The Colonel raved. A car shot down the road. The Colonel rushed out, brandishing a cane to stop it. It was Bert. He paid no attention to the old man standing on the steps of the pillared porch waving his stick. Ashen with fury, the Colonel came back into the house and fumbled with his keys at an old chest. Finally, a drawer opened and he took out a pistol. He went toward the door as Cora began to howl, but on the porch he became suddenly strengthless and limp. Shaking, the old man sank into a chair holding the gun. He would not speak to Cora.

VIII

LATE IN THE AFTERNOON, Colonel Norwood sent Cora for their son. The gun had been put away. At least Cora did not see it.

"I want to talk to that boy," the Colonel said. "Fetch him here." Damned young fool . . . bastard . . . of a nigger. . . .

"What's he gonna do to my boy?" Cora thought. "Son, be careful," as she went across the yard and down toward Willie's cabin to find Bert. "Son, you be careful. I didn't bear you for no white man to kill. Son, you be careful. You ain't white, don't you know that? You be careful. O, Lord God Jesus in heaven! Son, be careful!" Cora was crying when she reached Willie's door, crying all the way back to the Big House with her son.

"To hell with the old man," Bert said. "He ain't no trouble! Old as he is, what can he do to me?"

"Lord have mercy, son, is you crazy? Why don't you be like Willie? He ain't never had no fusses with de Colonel."

"White folks' nigger," Bert said.

"Why don't you talk sense?" Cora begged.

"Why didn't he keep his promise then and let me go back to school in Atlanta, like my sister? You said if I came home this summer he'd lemme go back to the Institute, didn't you? Then why didn't he?"

"Why didn't you act right, son? Oh-o-o!" Cora moaned. "You can't get nothin' from white folks if you don't act right."

"Act like Willie, you mean, and the rest of these cotton pickers? Then I don't want anything."

They had reached the back door now. It was nearly dark in the kitchen where Livonia was making biscuits.

"Don't rile him, Bert, child," Cora said as she took him through the house. "I don't know what he might do to you. He's got a gun."

"Don't worry 'bout me," Bert answered.

The setting sun made long paths of golden light across the parlor floor through the tall windows opening on the West. The air was thick and sultry with autumn heat. The Colonel sat, bent and old, near a table where there were whisky and cigars and a half-open drawer. When Bert entered he suddenly straightened up and the old commanding look came into his eyes. He told Cora to go upstairs to her room.

Of course, he never asked Bert to sit down.

The tall mulatto boy stood before his father, the Colonel. The old white man felt the steel of him standing there, like the steel of himself forty years ago. Steel of the Norwoods darkened now by Africa. The old man got up, straight and tall, too, and suddenly shook his fist in the face of the boy.

"You listen to me," he said, trembling with quiet. "I don't want to have to whip you again like I did when you were a child." He was almost hissing. "The next time I might kill you. I been running this plantation thirty-five years and never had to beat a nigger old as you are. Never had any trouble out of none of Cora's children before either, but you." The old man sat down. "I don't have trouble with my colored folks. They do what I say or what Talbot says, and that's all there is to it. If they turn in crops, they get a living. If they work for wages, they get paid. If they spend their money on licker, or old cars, or fixing up their cabins—they can do what they choose, long as they know their places and it don't hinder their work. To Cora's young ones—you hear me, boy?—I gave all the chances any nigger ever had in these parts. More'n many a white child's had, too. I sent you off to school. I gave your brother, Willie, that house he's living in when he got married, pay him for his work, help him out if he needs it. None of my darkies suffer. You went off to school. Could have kept on, would have sent you back this fall, but I don't intend to pay for no nigger, or white boy either if I had one, that acts the way you been acting." Colonel Norwood got up again, angrily. "And certainly not for no black fool! I'm talking to *you* like this only because you're Cora's child—but you know damn well it's my habit to *tell* people what to do, not discuss it with them. I just want to know what's the matter with you, though—whether you're crazy or not? And if you're not, you'd better change your ways a damn sight or it won't be safe for you here, and you know it—venting your impudence on white women, ruining my niggers, driving like mad through the Junction, carrying on just as you please. I'm warning you, boy, God damn it! . . . Now I want you to answer me, and talk right." The old man sat down in his chair again by the whisky bottle and the partly opened drawer. He took a drink.

"What do you mean, talk right?" Bert said.

"I mean talk like a nigger should to a white man," the Colonel snapped.

"Oh, but I'm not a nigger, Colonel Norwood," Bert said, "I'm your son."

The old man frowned at the boy in front of him. "Cora's son," he said.

"Fatherless?" Bert asked.

"Bastard," the old man said.

Bert's hands closed into fists, so the Colonel opened the drawer where the pistol was. He took it out and laid it on the table.

"You black bastard," he said.

"I've heard that before." Bert just stood there. "You're talking about my mother."

"Well," the Colonel answered, his fingers playing over the surface of the gun, "what can you do about it?"

The boy felt his whole body suddenly tighten and pull. The muscles of his forearms rippled.

"Niggers like you are hung to trees," the old man went on.

"I'm not a nigger," Bert said. "Ain't you my father? And a hell of a father you are, too, holding a gun on me."

"I'll break your black neck for you," the Colonel shouted. "Don't talk to me like that!" He jumped up.

"You'll break my neck?" The boy stood his ground as the father came toward him.

"Get out of here!" The Colonel shook with rage. "Get out! Or I'll do more than that if I ever lay eyes on you again." The old man picked up the pistol from the table, yet the boy did not move. "I'll fill you full of bullets if you come back here. Get off this place! Get to hell out of this county! Now, tonight. Go on!" The Colonel motioned with his pistol toward the door that led to the kitchen and the back of the house.

"Not that way," Bert said. "I'm not your servant. You must think I'm scared. Well, you can't drive me out the back way like a dog. You're not going to run me off, like a field-hand you can't use any more. I'll go," the boy said, starting toward the front door, "but not out the back—from my own father's house."

"You nigger bastard!" Norwood screamed, springing between his son and the door, but the boy kept calmly on. The steel of the gun was between them, but that didn't matter. Rather, it seemed to pull them together like a magnet.

"Don't you . . .," Norwood began, for suddenly Bert's hand grasped the Colonel's arm, "dare put your . . .," and his old bones began to crack, "black hands on . . ."

"Why don't you shoot?" Bert interrupted him, slowly turning his wrist.

". . . me!"

"Why don't you shoot, then?"

The old man twisted and bent in fury and pain, but the gun fell to the floor.

"Why don't you shoot?" Bert said again as his hands sought his father's throat. With furious sureness they took the old white neck in their strong young fingers. "Why don't you shoot then, papa?"

Colonel Norwood clawed the air, breathing hoarsely and loud, his tongue growing stiff and dry, his eyes beginning to burn.

"Shoot—why don't you, then? Huh? Why?"

The chemicals of their two lives exploded. Everything was very black around them. The white man's hands stopped clawing the air. His heart stood still. His blood no longer flowed. He wasn't breathing.

"Why don't you shoot?" Bert said, but there was no answer.

When the boy's eyes cleared, he saw his mother standing at the foot of the stairs, so he let the body drop. It fell with a thud, old and white in a path of red from the setting sun.

"Why didn't he shoot, mama? He didn't want me to live. He was white. Why didn't he shoot then?"

"Tom!" Cora cried, falling across his body. "Colonel Tom! Tom! Tom!"

"He's dead," Bert said. "I'm living though."

"Tom!" Cora screamed, pulling at the dead man. "Colonel Tom!"

Bert bent down and picked up the pistol. "This is what my father wanted to use on me," he said. "He's dead. But I can use it on all the white men in Georgia—they'll be coming to get me now. They never wanted me before, but I know they'll want me now." He stuffed the pistol in his shirt. Cora saw what her son had done.

"Run," she said, rising and going to him. "Run, chile! Out the front way quick, so's they won't see you in the kitchen. Make fo' de swamp, honey. Cross de fields fo' de swamp. Go de crick way. In runnin' water, dogs can't smell no tracks. Hurry, son!"

"Yes, mama," Bert said slowly. "But if I see they gonna get me before I reach the swamp, then I'm coming back here. Let them take me out of my father's house—if they can." He patted the gun inside his shirt, and smiled. "They'll never string me up to some roadside tree for the crackers to laugh at. Not me!"

"Hurry, chile," Cora opened the door and the sunset streamed in like a river of blood. "Hurry, chile."

Bert went out across the wide pillared porch and down the road. He saw Talbot and the store-keeper coming, so he turned off through the trees. And then, because he wanted to live, he began to run. The whole sky was a blaze of color as he ran. Then it began to get dark, and the glow went away.

In the house, Cora started to talk to the dead man on the floor, just as though he were not dead. She pushed and pulled at the body, trying to get him to get up himself. Then she heard the footsteps of Talbot and the store-keeper on the porch. She rose and stood as if petrified in the middle of the floor. A knock, and two men were peering through the screen-door into the dusk-dark room. Then Talbot opened the door.

"Hello, Cora," he said. "What's the matter with you, why didn't you let us in? Where's that damn fool boy o' your'n goin', comin' out the front way liked he owned the place? What's the matter with you, woman? Can't you talk? Where's Colonel Norwood?"

"Let's have some light in here," said the store-keeper, turning a button beside the door.

"Great God!" Talbot cried. "Jim, look at this!" The Colonel's body lay huddled on the floor, old and purple-white, at Cora's feet.

"Why, he's blue in the face," the store-keeper said bending over the body. "Oh! Get that nigger we saw walking out the door! That nigger bastard of Cora's. Get that nigger! . . . Why, the Colonel's dead!"

Talbot rushed toward the door. "That nigger," he cried. "He must be running toward the swamps now. . . . We'll get him. Telephone town, Jim, there in the library. Telephone the sheriff. Telephone the Beale family down by the swamp. Get men, white men, after that nigger."

The store-keeper ran into the library and began to call on the phone. Talbot looked at Cora standing in the center of the room. "Where's Norwood's car? In the barn? Talk, you black wench, talk!"

But Cora didn't say a word. She watched the two white men rush out of the house into the yard. In a few minutes, she heard the roar of a motor hurtling down the road. It was dark outside. Night had come.

Cora turned toward the body on the floor. "My boy," she said, "he can't get to de swamp now. They telephoned the white folks down that way to head him off. He'll come back home." She called aloud, "Colonel Tom, why don't you get up from there and help me? You know they're after our boy. You know they got him out there runnin' from de white folks in de night. Runnin' from de hounds and de guns and de ropes and all what they uses to kill poor niggers with. . . . Ma boy's out there runnin'. Why don't you help him?" Cora bent over the body. "Colonel Tom, you hear me? You said he was ma boy, ma bastard boy. I heard you. But he's your'n, too—out yonder in de dark runnin'—from your people. Why don't you get up and stop 'em? You know you could. You's a power in Polk County. You's a big man, and yet our son's out there runnin'—runnin' from po' white trash what ain't worth de little finger o' nobody's got your blood in 'em, Tom." Cora shook the dead body fiercely. "Get up from there and stop 'em, Colonel Tom." But the white man did not move.

Gradually Cora stopped shaking him. Then she rose and backed away from this man she had known so long. "You's cruel, Tom," she whispered. "I might a-knowed it—you'd be like that, sendin' ma boy out to die. I might a-knowed it ever since you beat him that time under de feet of de horses. Well, you won't mistreat him no more now. That's finished." She went toward the steps. "I'm gonna make a place for him. Upstairs under ma bed. He's ma chile, and I'll look out for him. And don't you come in ma bedroom while he's up there. Don't you come to my bed either no more a-tall. I calls for you to help me now, Tom, and you just lays there. I calls you to get up now, and you don't move. Whenever you called *me* in de night, I woke up. Whenever you wanted me to love you, I reached out ma arms to you. I bored you five children and now," her voice rose hysterically, "one of 'em's out yonder runnin' from your people. Our youngest boy's out yonder in de dark, runnin'! I 'spects you's out there, too, with de rest of de white folks. Uh-um! Bert's runnin' from *you*, too. You said he warn't your'n—Cora's po' little yellow bastard. But he is your'n, Colonel Tom, and he's runnin' from you. Yes, out yonder in de dark, you, *you* runnin' our chile with a gun in yo' hand, and Talbot followin' behind you with a rope to hang Bert with." She leaned against the wall near the staircase, sobbing violently. Then she went back toward the man on the floor. Her sobs gradually ceased as she looked down at his crumpled body. Then she said slowly, "Listen, I been sleepin' with you too long not to know that this ain't you, Tom, layin' down here with yo' eyes shut on de floor. You can't fool me—you ain't never been so still like this before—you's out yonder runnin' ma boy! Colonel Thomas Norwood runnin' ma boy through de fields in de dark, runnin' ma po' little helpless Bert through de fields in de dark for to lynch him and to kill him. . . . God damn you, Tom Norwood!" Cora cried, "God damn you!"

She went upstairs. For a long time the body lay alone on the floor in the parlor. Later Cora heard Sam and Livonia weeping and shouting in the kitchen, and Negro voices outside in the dark, and feet going down the road. She thought she heard the baying of hounds afar off, too, as she prepared a hiding place for Bert in the attic. Then she came down to her room and put the most beautiful quilts she had on her bed. "Maybe he'll just want to rest here first," she thought. "Maybe he'll be awful tired and just want to rest."

Then she heard a loud knock at the door, and white voices talking, and Sam's frightened answers. The doctor and the undertakers had come to take the body away. In a little while she heard them lifting it up and putting it in the dead wagon. And all the time, they kept talking, talking.

". . . 'll be havin' his funeral in town . . . ain't nothin' but niggers left out here . . . didn't have no relatives, did he, Sam? . . . Too bad. . . . Nobody to look after his stuff tonight. Every white man's able to walk's out with the posse . . . that young nigger'll swing before midnight . . . what a neck-tie party! . . . Say, Sam!"

"Yes, sah! Yes, sah!"

". . . that black housekeeper, Cora? . . . murderin' bastard's mother?"

"She's upstairs, I reckon, sah."

". . . like to see how she looks. Get her down here."

"Yes, sah!" Sam's teeth were chattering.

"And how about a little drink before we start back to town?"

"Yes, sah! Cora's got de keys fo' de licker, sah."

"Well, get her down, double quick, then!"

"Yes, sah!" Cora heard Sam coming up for her.

Downstairs, the voices went on. They were talking about her. ". . . lived together . . . ain't been a white woman here overnight since the wife died when I was a kid . . . bad business, though, livin' with a," in drawling cracker tones, "nigger."

As Cora came down the steps, the undertakers looked at her half-grinning. "So you're the black wench that's got these educated darkie children? Hum-m! Well I guess you'll see one of 'em swinging full o' bullet holes before you get up in the morning. . . . Or maybe they'll burn him. How'd you like a roasted darkie for breakfast, girlie?"

Cora stood quite still on the stairs. "Is that all you wanted to say to me?" she asked.

"Now, don't get smart," the doctor said. "Maybe you think there's nobody to boss you now. We're goin' to have a little drink before we go. Get out a bottle."

"I take ma orders from Colonel Norwood, suh," Cora said.

"Well, you'll take no more orders from him," the undertaker declared. "He's outside in the dead wagon. Get along now and get out a bottle."

"He's out yonder with de mob," Cora said.

"I tell you he's in my wagon, dead as a door nail."

"I tell you he's runnin' with de mob," Cora said.

"I believe this black woman's done gone nuts," the doctor cried. "Sam, you get the licker."

"Yes, sah!" Sam sputtered with fright. "Co-r-r-ra, gimme . . ."

But Cora did not move.

"Ah-a-a-a, Lawd hab mercy!" Sam cried.

"To hell with the licker, Charlie," the undertaker said nervously. "Let's start back to town. We want to get in on some of that excitement, too. They should've found that nigger by now—and I want to see 'em drag him out here."

"All right, Jim," the other agreed. Then, to Cora, "But don't you darkies go to bed until you see the bonfire. You all are gettin' beside yourselves around Polk County. We'll burn a few more of you if you don't watch out."

The men left and the wheels of the wagon turned on the drive. Sam began to cry.

"Hab mercy! Lawd Jesus, hab mercy! Cora, is you a fool? *Is* you? Then why didn't you give de mens de licker, riled as these white folks is? In ma old age, is I gonna be burnt by de crackers? Lawd, is I sinned? Lawd, what has I done?" He looked at Cora. "I sho ain't gonna stay heah tonight. I's gwine."

"Go on," she said. "The Colonel can get his own drinks when he comes back."

"Lawd God Jesus!" Sam, his eyes bucking from their sockets, bolted from the room fast as his old legs could carry him. Cora heard him running blindly through the house, moaning.

She went to the kitchen where pots were still boiling on the stove, but Livonia had fled, the biscuits burnt in the oven. She looked out the back door, but no lights were visible anywhere. The cabins were quiet.

"I reckon they all gone," she said to herself. "Even ma boy, Willie. I reckon he gone, too. You see, Colonel Tom, everybody's scared o' you. They know you done gone with de mob again, like you did that time they hung Luke Jordan and you went to help 'em. Now you's out chasin' ma boy, too. I hears you hollerin'."

And sure enough, all around the Big House in the dark, in a

wide far-off circle, men and dog-cries and auto-horns sounded in the night. Nearer they came even as Cora stood at the back door, listening. She closed the door, bolted it, put out the light, and went back to the parlor. "He'll come in by de front," she said. "Back from de swamp way. He won't let 'em stop him from gettin' home to me agin, just once. Po' little boy, he ain't got no place to go, no how. Po' boy, what growed up with such pride in his heart. Just like you, Colonel Tom. Spittin' image o' you. . . . Proud! . . . And got no place to go."

Nearer and nearer the man-hunt came, the cries and the horns and the dogs. Headlights began to flash in the dark down the road. Off through the trees, Cora heard men screaming. And suddenly feet running, running, running. Nearer, nearer. She knew it was him. She knew they had seen him, too.

Then there were voices shouting very near the house.

"Don't shoot, men. We want to get him alive."

"Close in on him!"

"He must be in them bushes there by the porch."

"Look!"

And suddenly shots rang out. The door opened. Cora saw flashes of fire spitting into the blackness, and Bert's tall body in the doorway. He was shooting at the voices outside in the dark. The door closed.

"Hello, Ma," he said. "One or two of 'em won't follow me no further."

Cora locked the door as bullets splintered through the wood, shattered the window-panes. Then a great volley of shots struck the house, blinding headlights focused on the porch. Shouts and cries of, "Nigger! Nigger! Get the nigger!" filled the night.

"I was waitin' for you, honey," Cora said. "Quick! Your hidin' place's ready for you, upstairs in de attic. I sawed out a place under de floor. Maybe they won't find you, chile. Hurry, 'fore your father comes."

"No time to hide, Ma," Bert panted. "They're at the door now. They'll be coming in the back way, too. They'll be coming in the windows. They'll be coming in everywhere. I got one bullet left, Ma. It's mine."

"Yes, son, it's your'n. Go upstairs in mama's room and lay down on ma bed and rest. I won't let 'em come up till you're gone. God bless you, chile."

Quickly, they embraced. A moment his head rested on her shoulder.

"I'm awful tired running, Ma. I couldn't get to the swamp. Seems like they been chasing me for hours. Crawling through the cotton a long time, I got to rest now."

Cora pushed him toward the stairs. "Go on, son," she said gently.

At the top, Bert turned and looked back at this little brown woman standing there waiting for the mob. Outside the noise was terrific. Men shouted and screamed, massing for action. All at once they seemed to rush in a great wave for the house. They broke the doors and windows in, and poured into the room—a savage crowd of white men, red and wild-eyed, with guns and knives, sticks and ropes, lanterns and flashlights. They paused at the foot of the stairs where Cora stood looking down at them silently.

"Keep still, men," one of the leaders said. "He's armed. . . . Say where's that yellow bastard of yours, Cora—upstairs?"

"Yes," Cora said. "Wait."

"Wait, hell!" the men cried. "Come on, boys, let's go!"

A shot rang out upstairs, then Cora knew it was all right.

"Go on," she said, stepping aside for the mob.

IX

THE NEXT MORNING when people saw a bloody and unrecognizable body hanging in the public square at the Junction, some said with a certain pleasure, "That's what we do to niggers down here," not realizing Bert had been taken dead, and that all the fun for the mob had been sort of stale at the end.

But others, aware of what had happened, thought, "It'd be a hell of a lot better lynching a live nigger. Say, ain't there nobody else mixed up in this here Norwood murder? Where's that boy's brother, Willie? Heh?"

So the evening papers carried this item in the late editions:

DOUBLE LYNCHING IN GEORGIA

A large mob late this afternoon wreaked vengeance on the second of two Negro field hands, the murderers of Colonel Thomas Norwood, wealthy planter found dead at Big House Plantation. Bert Lewis was lynched last night, and his brother, Willie Lewis, today. The sheriff of the county is unable to identify any members of the mob. Colonel Norwood's funeral has not yet been held. The dead man left no heirs.

E L